PRAISE FOR JENN[illegible]

“For a sexy, fun-filled, warmhearted rea[illegible]
Probst!”

—Jill Shalvis, *New York Times* bestselling author

“Jennifer Probst is an absolute auto-buy author for me.”

—J. Kenner, *New York Times* bestselling author

“Jennifer Probst knows how to bring the swoons and the sexy.”

—Amy E. Reichert, author of *The Coincidence of Coconut Cake*

“As always, Jennifer Probst never fails to deliver romance that sizzles and has a way of tugging those emotional heartstrings.”

—*Four Chicks Flipping Pages*

“Jennifer Probst’s books remind me of delicious chocolate cake. Bursting with flavor, decadently rich . . . very satisfying.”

—*Love Affair with an e-Reader*

“There’s a reason Probst is the gold standard in contemporary romance.”

—Lauren Layne, *New York Times* bestselling author

PRAISE FOR *MEANT TO BE*

“*Meant to Be* was a great start to this new romance series. Sparky, fun, sexy, heartbreaking . . .”

—*BJ’s Book Blog*

"*Meant to Be* is a story of grief, betrayal, and loneliness; guilt and acceptance, second chances and love. The premise is engaging; the characters are spirited; the romance is fated . . ."

—*The Reading Cafe*

PRAISE FOR *FOREVER IN CAPE MAY*

"Probst's entertaining take on the friends-to-lovers trope hits all the right beats, enhanced by well-shaded characters readers will immediately love. This irresistible finale does not disappoint."

—*Publishers Weekly*

PRAISE FOR *TEMPTATION ON OCEAN DRIVE*

"*Temptation on Ocean Drive* was an adorable and sad and sparky and emotional and wedding-y New Jersey Beach Town love story! I loved it! Run to your nearest Amazon for your own Gabe—this one is mine!"

—*BJ's Book Blog*

PRAISE FOR *LOVE ON BEACH AVENUE*

"Probst (*All Roads Lead to You*) opens her Sunshine Sisters series with an effervescent rom-com. The characters leap off the page, the love story is perfectly paced, and an adorable dog named Lucy adds charm. Readers will eagerly await the next in the series."

—*Publishers Weekly*

"The perfect enemies-to-lovers, best-friend's-brother romance! I laughed, smiled, cheered, cried a few tears, and loved Carter and Avery!"

—*Two Book Pushers*

"*Love on Beach Avenue* is a three-layer wedding cake of best-friend's-brother, enemies-to-lovers, and just plain fun. Another yummy confection by Jennifer Probst!"

—Laurelin Paige, *New York Times* bestselling author

"I could feel the ocean breeze on my face as I turned the pages. *Love on Beach Avenue* is chock-full with magic ingredients: a dreamy seaside, a starchy hero with a tiny dog, sparkling wit, and fabulous female friendship—a must-read romance!"

—Evie Dunmore, author of *Bringing Down the Duke*

"*Love on Beach Avenue* is the perfect enemies-to-lovers romance with well-developed characters, sexy banter, and so many swoon-worthy moments! Jennifer Probst knocked it out of the park with this book! Looking forward to the rest of the series!"

—Monica Murphy, *New York Times* bestselling author

"Fantastic start to a brand-new series from Jennifer Probst! *Love on Beach Avenue* is beautifully heartfelt and epically romantic!"

—Emma Chase, *New York Times* bestselling author

PRAISE FOR *ALL ROADS LEAD TO YOU*

"Funny, sexy, emotional, and full of scenes that make your heart swell and the tears drop, *All Roads Lead to You* is a beautiful story set in hometown America and one you will want to read again and again."

—*A Midlife Wife*

"Harper's story was everything I wanted it to be and so much more."

—*Becca the Bibliophile*

"Ms. Probst has a way of writing that I can't help but be 100 percent invested from the first page!"

—*Franci's Fabulous Reads*

"Jennifer Probst shines when she talks about her animal rescues in real life, and the saying is true: write what you know, and it will always be the best story. The same goes for this one; it's one of her best stories to date."

—*AJ's Book re-Marks*

"JP writes beautiful words, and I just loved this story. There was enough action, adventure, passion, and swoon factor, not to mention romance."

—*The Guide to Romance Novels*

"A read that will not only fill your emotional romance need but will fill your heart with the fulfilling need to care for a goat that needed to be hugged and be besties with a horse to feel safe."

—*The Book Fairy Reviews*

PRAISE FOR *A BRAND NEW ENDING*

"Don't miss another winner from Jennifer Probst."

—Mary from *USA TODAY*'s *Happy Ever After*

PRAISE FOR *THE START OF SOMETHING GOOD*

"The must-have summer romance read of 2018!"

—*Gina's Bookshelf*

"Achingly romantic, touching, realistic, and just plain beautiful, *The Start of Something Good* lingers with you long after you turn the last page."

—Katy Evans, *New York Times* bestselling author

Save the Best for Last

OTHER BOOKS BY JENNIFER PROBST

Twist of Fate Series

Meant to Be

So It Goes

The Sunshine Sisters Series

Love on Beach Avenue

Temptation on Ocean Drive

Forever in Cape May

The Stay Series

The Start of Something Good

A Brand New Ending

All Roads Lead to You

Something Just Like This

Begin Again

Nonfiction

Write Naked: A Bestseller's Secrets to Writing Romance & Navigating the Path to Success

Write True: A Bestseller's Guide to Writing Craft & Achieving Success in the Romance Industry

Women's Fiction

Our Italian Summer

The Secret Love Letters of Olivia Moretti

The Billionaire Builders Series

Everywhere and Every Way

Any Time, Any Place

Somehow, Some Way

All or Nothing at All

The Searching For . . . Series

Searching for Someday

Searching for Perfect

Searching for Beautiful

Searching for Always

Searching for You

Searching for Mine

Searching for Disaster

The Marriage to a Billionaire Series

The Marriage Bargain

The Marriage Trap

The Marriage Mistake

The Marriage Merger

The Book of Spells

The Marriage Arrangement

The Steele Brothers Series

Catch Me

Play Me

Dare Me

Beg Me

Reveal Me

The Sex on the Beach Series

Beyond Me

Chasing Me

The Hot in the Hamptons Series

Summer Sins

Stand-Alone Novels

Dante's Fire

Executive Seduction

All the Way

The Grinch of Starlight Bend

The Charm of You

Save the Best for Last

JENNIFER PROBST

This is a work of fiction. Names, characters, organizations, places, events, and incidents are either products of the author's imagination or are used fictitiously. Otherwise, any resemblance to actual persons, living or dead, is purely coincidental.

Published by Montlake, Seattle

www.apub.com

ISBN-13: 9781542038539 (paperback)
ISBN-13: 9781542038522 (digital)

Cover design by Caroline Teagle Johnson
Cover photography by Regina Wamba of ReginaWamba.com
Cover images: © Guy Banville / Shutterstock; © Nature Peaceful / Shutterstock; © Asia Images / Getty

Printed in the United States of America

To Marlaine, Lisa, and Nancy . . .
My own female posse, who have been by my side throughout the years—from drunken poker nights, road trips, weddings, babies, and houses to endless dinners with inappropriate conversations and hysterical laughter—you are my family. Mad love to each of you.

Whatever is in any way beautiful hath its source of beauty in itself, and is complete in itself; praise forms no part of it. So it is none the worse nor the better for being praised.

—*Marcus Aurelius Antoninus*

Everything has beauty; but not everyone sees it.

—*Confucius*

Chapter One

Tessa Harper knew exactly what it took to hook a man. Or a woman.

Unfortunately, most of her hopeful readers didn't realize the focus of their ardent affections was almost never worth it. Not that they ever listened. She'd learned over the years of makeovers and helping women become their best selves that this rarely aligned with who they insisted on loving.

Tessa tamped down a sigh as she gazed at the woman before her, who was currently frowning as she turned around in the mirror. The dress had a high neckline in a drapey midnight-blue fabric that accented all her curves and swept low to the ground. The deep cut in the back gave a touch of sensuality without being in-your-face sexy.

"I don't know, Tessa. I don't think it's enough. He likes boobs and ass. Don't you think I should go with the short sequined dress?"

Tessa kept her voice crisp. "Absolutely not. The whole point of this shopping expedition is to find a dress that is innately you, yet a bit out of your comfort zone. You've been hiding your body in baggy pants and blazers for a long time. A little skin goes a long way."

Autumn bit her lip. It had taken weeks to get her comfortable stepping out of her shy exterior. Ramping up her confidence in the body God gave her. Helping her realize her quirky humor and sharp intellect were a gift rather than a nerdy embarrassment she needed to hide. Tessa had agreed to feature her in the successful column Dear Tessa because Autumn deserved to shine.

Not to catch the eye of some marketing director who liked boobs and ass.

But she swallowed her admonishments and concentrated on helping Autumn pick out a dress for her upcoming holiday party at work. "Will it be enough to catch his attention? This is my opportunity. I want to reveal my new self and watch his jaw drop." Autumn swiveled around with worry. "You think he'll notice, right?"

Yes. Many men had a fantasy of the butterfly story—the plain, shy coworker who transforms into a sexy siren. Was it wrong Tessa suddenly wanted to encourage Autumn to forget about her crush and go live her best life? Seeking self-worth through some man's approval of her appearance was taking critical steps backward from all the work they'd done together. Yet, here Tessa was again, finding herself responsible for a woman who wanted to chase the wrong guy.

The emotion welled up and spilled out without her consent. "It shouldn't matter," Tessa snapped.

Autumn's lovely green eyes widened. "What do you mean?"

"Autumn, I've worked with a lot of women who finally got their so-called dream man only to find out it was a nightmare. You don't know him." She blew out a breath in frustration. "I just want you to pick out a dress that makes *you* feel good. We did this so you'd be able to speak up in meetings and enjoy happy hour without worrying you're not enough. Remember?"

For a moment, Tessa believed she'd gotten through. Autumn's sharp features, now softened with some natural makeup, seemed to lose their foggy shadow. Her blunt bob swung sharply under her chin as she nodded in agreement. It had once reached her waist and covered her face like her favorite oversize gray sweater. Hope sprang inside as Autumn seemed to come alive and realize this journey belonged to her. Tessa waited while she stepped into her power.

"You're right. I'm going with the sequined dress. It makes me feel hot, and confident I can walk right up to Mark and dazzle him." Her smile reached megawatt status. "Thank you, Tessa. My life is going to change because I had the guts to reach out to you, and you picked me. I'll finally find the love I always dreamed of."

Disappointment crashed over her as a sense of déjà vu hit. Tessa strengthened her voice in conviction. "The real love is of yourself. Remember that."

But it was too late. Autumn nodded but was obviously dreaming of her *moment*—the exact time Mark noticed her. Would all the work they had done together hold up the foundation if Mark broke her heart? Or would Autumn fall apart and judge her worth against his approval? Tessa wouldn't know. The readers she picked to work with for her column sometimes kept in touch, but others disappeared into their lives without a look back.

Tessa helped Autumn grab the *wrong* dress, gave her a hug, and headed back to the office.

Her four-inch nude Louboutins clicked against the frosty sidewalk as she made her way to the car. She shivered and tightened the sash of her camel-colored wool coat and gave in to her gloomy thoughts. God, she was so tired of her work ending up being about some guy. Or girl. As she had been the past few months, she began to question the value of what she was doing for Quench, the multimillion-dollar media empire that focused on self-care for women. She'd built the company with her three best friends, and it had been her main passion for a decade. But lately, her role as director of beauty and fashion, along with her viral advice column, was becoming less satisfying.

She needed to figure out what to do about it.

Tessa climbed in the car, glanced at the dashboard clock, and hit the accelerator. The shopping expedition had taken a bit more time than she'd anticipated, and she didn't like being the last one at the weekly founders' meeting. She hated being late.

Deftly pulling into an open spot on Main Street, she cut the engine and patted the hood of her baby, a bright yellow Alfa Romeo 4C Spider that got her more attention than if she'd walked naked down the block. It was her best asset for meeting men. So much better than online dating.

By the time she walked into Mike's Place, the lady gang was already assembled. Tessa slid into the booth and smiled at her besties, who both regarded her with affectionate amusement. "What?" she asked.

"Nothing. We already ordered for you since I've got to leave early to meet Palmer," Malia said.

"You live together. Can't you wait till he comes home?" Tessa teased.

Her friend rolled her eyes. "We're looking at a reception place," she said. Her voice was calm, but excitement slithered underneath.

Chiara didn't bother to hide her reaction. She clapped her hands with glee. "Where is it? I swear, this is going to be the event of the year! With you as the bride and Palmer running a wedding company, I bet it'll be picked up by all the press."

Malia groaned. "Exactly what I didn't want, but at the same time, I'm not gonna lie. I've dreamed of a big, romantic wedding, and now that I found the man for me, I don't want to have regrets."

"Agreed. Be obnoxious," Tessa said. "I can give you lessons if you need them."

They laughed. "We're looking at the Mohonk Mountain House in New Paltz. It's so beautiful there in the late fall when the leaves change and the air gets crisp. But we still have a few more places to check off our list."

"Then I apologize for my lateness."

"Forgiven." Malia sighed. "It's so strange the way things happen. Last year, I couldn't find a date, let alone a husband. I was so terrified I'd never be a mom, freezing my eggs was my main focus. But now, I'm just happy to enjoy exactly where we are."

"Palmer does want kids, though, right?" Chiara asked gently.

Her billionaire client, who Malia once hated, stole her heart, but they'd had a tough journey since marriage and parenthood hadn't been in his plans, and motherhood was always the ultimate goal for her. Eventually, love did end up conquering all, and Palmer was now fully committed to being a husband and father.

"Yes. We know the road to pregnancy may be difficult with my ovarian cysts, but we're trying not to worry about it. The main thing is I found the man I love and want to build a life with. Whatever that life looks like."

Tessa enjoyed the giddy look on Malia's face and her heart squeezed. With her elegantly braided dark hair and red power suit, Malia was the perfect person to head the new Quench Foundation, a not-for-profit that matched wealthy donors with local charities to offer unique funding opportunities. She'd been wildly successful in the past year and already doubled their initial number of matches. Now, she finally had it all—a successful career and a man who adored her. Emotion choked her throat. "I'm so happy for you, Malia."

Tessa glanced over at Chiara, the current editor in chief of Quench. With her fiery red hair, hot-pink blouse, and sleek black pants, she was a powerhouse who'd once lived for her career but was now a wife and new mom. She'd also gone through a difficult journey, unexpectedly getting pregnant and falling for their late friend's widower. The loss of Rory in a car accident had shattered their group for a long time. Rory had been the one to spearhead Quench and her dream of working side by side with all her best friends. Now, it was a successful multimillion-dollar business, and Rory was forever gone. The wound of her loss still ached for all of them, but they were proud of what they'd accomplished and had stayed true to her vision. It seemed like in the last two years fate had made some cruel choices but also stepped in to create opportunities that had changed Chiara and Malia forever.

But not her. Tessa knew she was a different breed. She was a serial dater with no desire to compromise to build a life with a man. Though lately, she'd felt complacent and unsatisfied. She needed a challenge to shake things up, or a new hot guy to give her butterflies in her tummy. Something new and exciting and . . . different.

Maybe fate would decide it was her turn. After all, wasn't the cliché "Save the best for last"?

"What are you smiling about?" Chiara asked.

Tessa shook her head. "Nothing. Just thinking of how you two came to meet your soul mates. Speaking of which, how's Veronica?" They'd named their baby after Sebastian Ryder's wife, a way to honor Rory's legacy and importance in both their lives.

Chiara beamed. "Wonderful! I can't thank you enough for letting us use your house for her first birthday party. Everyone's still talking about how much fun it was."

"I loved planning it."

"My sister wants the name of the hostess you used," Malia said. "She was so good with the kids, I think it was the first time no one cried at a birthday party."

Tessa laughed. "I'll send over the website link. She's very popular with the toddler crowd. Knows exactly how to keep their attention while moving from activity to activity. I saw Palmer fascinated with the magic tricks she did. Maybe you should hire her for your wedding."

Malia rolled her eyes but couldn't help grinning.

"We got so many toys we decided to donate most to the children's hospital. I think Veronica's party rivaled a Kardashian's," Chiara said.

"Nothing is too good for my goddaughter."

"She's mine, too," Malia reminded her. "We're co-godmothers, remember?"

Tessa snorted. "Sure. But I'm cooler."

Malia threw a balled-up napkin, which bounced off her friend's shoulder.

"Now, girls, I don't want any food fights in my place," a booming voice echoed out. They looked up and Tessa grinned as Mike laid their plates down with his usual economical motions. The owner of Mike's Place and Rory's father, he was an important part of all their lives as their mentor, friend, and second dad. They made sure to dine regularly at the restaurant they'd all grown up in and to carve out time for the occasional Sunday night Scrabble game.

The restaurant was a cornerstone of Main Street, a cross between a fancy café and a diner, with roomy red booths, an old-fashioned countertop that served ice cream sodas and sundaes, and the familiar black-and-white checkered floor. An antique jukebox belted out classics, and the scents of grease, meat, and coffee drifted in the air, swarming with comfort. Besides daily specials, craft beer and wine were offered, and Mike always seemed to know when they needed to indulge.

"We'll be good," Tessa said, hungrily digging into her chicken Caesar salad and side of sweet potato fries. "How have you been?"

"Busy. Holidays bring in a lot more business."

She shared a concerned look with her friends. "I mean your personal life. Have you done anything interesting lately?" Mike had been a longtime widower after losing his wife to cancer, and after Rory died, he'd retreated to his house and the diner, rarely venturing anywhere else.

Mike shrugged, but his cheeks grew red. "Not really."

"Have you seen Emma?" Emma was a retired high school English teacher who they'd all taken under their wing and become close friends with after seeing her regularly dine alone at Mike's Place. She'd had a crush on Mike for a long time, but her being socially awkward and shy had ended up in a miscommunication, and Mike had been cold and distant to her. It had been heartbreaking to watch.

Tessa had helped tweak her appearance—no more baggy, dull clothes, elaborate hats and clunky glasses that hid her face, or garish orange lipstick—and with some pep talks, the woman's confidence had shot up. Now, Emma had flourished and seemed to be enjoying her life. She'd finally given up on Mike, announcing she was moving on and would no longer chase after him.

Which is when Mike realized he really liked her and admitted he'd acted like a total asshole. He'd been trying to make it up to her with apologies, but after being alone for so long, he was just as socially awkward at dating as Emma. They were in a holding pattern, where Emma now remained cool and polite while Mike tried to scramble up the courage to ask her on a proper date.

Mike's face turned redder. "Sure. She comes in for pancakes. Sometimes with that guy. Her friend. Art." He spit out the name like a curse.

Chiara cleared her throat. "Have you tried to ask her out yet, Mike?"

He shifted his weight and fussed with his apron tie. "No. I will, though. I'm waiting for the right time."

Tessa let out a sigh. "There won't be a perfect time. Just ask her out to coffee."

"And then what? Make her some here?"

Malia seemed to swallow a laugh before speaking. "No! There's an adorable tea shop in Piermont. They do little cakes and tea and it's sweet. Kind of romantic. She'd love that."

He scratched his head and began to back up. "Yeah, I will. Sounds good. Better get to work!"

Mike disappeared into the kitchen, where he was most comfortable, leaving them all frustrated. "It's been four months," Tessa muttered, stabbing her grilled chicken. "He gave her those apology flowers and now she's coming back to the diner, but he can't seem to close the deal. I need to help."

"Oh no you don't!" Malia said, taking a sip of her iced tea. "You've done enough interfering. Mike needs to figure this out himself. In the meantime, we need to mind our own business."

Chiara began to laugh. "As if Tessa could ever do that. She's a helper through and through. Even if you don't want it."

"What is this, pick-on-Tessa day? I still sense there could be something special between them. Mike is just scared. He needs to step up if he wants to set things right with Emma."

"We've done all we can and it's now up to them. Hey, how did your makeover with Autumn go?" Malia asked.

Tessa caught her obvious effort to change the subject but reluctantly followed. "Great, I guess. She's got the confidence to go after the guy she wants, and I have no doubt he'll fall for her. She's revealing her new appearance at the office holiday party."

Chiara tilted her head. "Then why don't you sound happy? Autumn's story has had a ton of hits on the site. She has quite the following now, and whatever happens, she's learned her self-worth."

Unease itched beneath her skin. Since it was a new feeling, Tessa wasn't sure what to do with it but tried to explain. "*Has* she discovered her true worth? Or has she only used her physical appearance to win someone who was never meant for her in the first place?"

Malia gasped. "You've never doubted the process before. She asked for a promotion and got it, right? That's so much more than appearance. You made her realize she has power."

Tessa stared moodily at her salad. "Maybe. Maybe not. Why does change always seem to revolve around a guy?"

Chiara shrugged. "Readers love watching a *My Fair Lady* moment. Anything that reminds them there are possibilities within themselves."

"I don't know, I'm just wondering if I need to reset my focus. I know the makeovers are successful and a big part of Quench, but I feel like I'm missing out on a key element."

"What?" Malia asked.

"I'm not sure yet. When I figure it out, I'll let you know."

Chiara nodded. "You will. How are the internships going? You have five now, right?"

The launch of the new internship program at Quench had given Tessa a new direction she loved more with each day. The program matched interested high school and college students with jobs within the company that would help them learn new skills and find their passion. Tessa had volunteered to oversee the program. "Yes, and so far they're all doing well. Maria is excited about photography, and Magda has been surprisingly good with her." Magda was Quench's main photographer and was known to be temperamental, moody, and a bit standoffish with people she didn't understand or like. Thankfully, teenagers seemed to escape her wrath—unlike cute, cuddly animals—and Maria's snark was a perfect match. "Willa has been learning a lot with me for the beauty and fashion column, and Kelsey has been great with Scott."

"It's nice to have another male around," Malia said, stealing a fry and munching happily. "I love that he wants to learn about administration and is eager to start at the ground floor."

"Kelsey knows everything about the business because she's learned all the areas," Chiara added, deciding to copy Malia and grab a fry from Tessa's plate. "Admins are the most powerful people in the room, and Kelsey is like my right hand. Which leads me to a topic I wanted to bring up with both of you. I've been doing some research, and you know that last survey we got in from readers?"

"Yeah, you said there was nothing to worry about," Tessa said, pausing to stare at her friend. "Are there gaps we're missing?"

"Actually, yes. Quite a large one."

"What is it?" Malia asked.

"Sports."

Tessa couldn't help the groan that ripped from her lips. "Ugh, who cares? Sure, sports are important in society and the world. I watch the Olympics. I know how passionate people can be, but it's another reason we don't have a political column—Quench is a place to come for self-care, not to fight about which team is better."

Malia tapped her lip thoughtfully. "I used to feel the same, but times have changed. The sports world is a big draw for women, and female athletes have become the new celebrities so many look up to. It may be time we delve into the market."

Chiara gave her a look of sympathy, but her voice was firm. "Agreed. I know you hate the idea, Tessa, but we can't cut out an entire segment of readership because we personally don't like it."

Personally, she wanted to throw an old-fashioned tantrum to keep her beloved site free from sports maniacs, but the businesswoman in her refused to buckle. "Have you considered the expense and time it'd take to build an entire division from the ground up? We'd need to hire writers with experience and create a specific slant for the types of stories to feature. Do we really need to take this on right now when the foundation and internship program are still new and growing?"

Her friends shared a glance. "Maybe," Chiara finally said. "I'd like to create a comparison model and get Yvonne to crunch some numbers. But my gut is saying to take the leap. Better now than later, when we've identified a hole in our audience that's too big to fix. We still have time to get on board and make it what we want."

"I'm with Chiara. We need to have a serious discussion and bring it to the team," Malia said.

Tessa let out a breath. "Fine. Majority rules. But I'll be checking my own stats on this."

"Wouldn't have it any other way," Chiara said with a grin. She rested back in the booth and groaned. "I just wish I could get more sleep! I took Veronica to the doctor again and asked when she would finally begin a decent sleeping pattern."

"What was the answer?" Malia asked with sympathy.

"To be determined. Sebastian and I have been trying different things, but I'm beginning to think she's a vampire. Never wants to go to sleep in case she misses something good."

Tessa laughed. "My kind of girl."

"Sebastian has a big retirement party this Friday night, and I wish we could go together. I miss dressing up and having date night."

"I thought you were doing that regularly?" Malia asked.

"We did for a while, but it's easy to fall away from it. Pj's and an early night seems easier." Chiara made a face. "I miss my husband, though. We rarely go out anymore, and I love date nights. Is that bad to say?"

Empathy flared. Chiara was passionate about all the roles in her life, but as many women did, she judged herself a bit too harshly at times. "Absolutely not. Why can't you go with him?"

She shot them a guilty look. "I don't want to ask Mike to close the restaurant again, and you both are so busy. It's okay—I'll make sure to get something on the calendar soon."

Malia frowned. "I can try to reschedule the family dinner."

Tessa shook her head hard. "No way—I can watch Veronica. Didn't I tell you my date canceled?"

Chiara stared at her with suspicion. "No. Are you lying?"

"No, and I'm kind of relieved. I wasn't feeling him, and spending time with my girl is more fun. Hey, I have a great idea—why don't you surprise your hubby? Pretend you're staying home and then show up at the party looking like your sexy self. He'll freak."

Her friend's face lit up. "Really? Oh, that would be fun. I have the perfect dress in mind."

"Good. What time do you need me there?"

"Six thirty. Are you sure it's okay?"

Tessa gave her a look. "Yes. I wouldn't offer if I didn't want to."

"Thanks, Tessa. You're the best."

She preened. "I know. Best godmother ever."

A fry hit her mouth and made her gasp in astonishment. Malia burst into giggles.

"You threw food at me! I'm telling Mike!"

"Remember when you told me to let you know when you were being too egotistical?" Malia asked, her lips twitching.

"No!"

"Oh, well, I decided it would be a good lesson for you."

Chiara joined in on the laughter, and Tessa shook her head.

Worst friends ever.

It was a good thing she loved them.

Chapter Two

Ford Maddox stripped off his headphones and settled back in his battered leather chair. Raising a hand to Isaac, his production manager, he grinned as the replay of his morning show flickered in his mind.

With baseball tucked away until spring, he was focused on the wheeling and dealing within MLB and who the Yankees and Mets would be able to recruit. And keep. And get rid of. It was always an exciting time full of gambles, big talk, and lies, and Ford embraced the hit of adrenaline from spending the past few hours talking about his favorite thing in the world.

Sports.

Hell, ever since he'd held a ball in his hands, he'd realized it pulsed with a magical force. The way a person pitched, hit, caught, and handled a ball could be life-changing. Thank God his parents hadn't questioned his obsession—just bought him basketballs, soccer balls, footballs, and baseballs, and he played every sport that was in season.

It was a good thing he had a good voice, because Ford learned early on he wasn't going to be a professional player in any sport. He was a bit too awkward, his gait slightly imbalanced as if his center of gravity was off. Mom would tell him when he carried a plate, it was always tilted to the side, though he swore it was dead center.

None of it mattered. He'd discovered his niche and passion and never regretted he was the one watching and analyzing the plays rather than executing them. Being a well-known, respected sportscaster on one of the hottest XM stations gave him a jolt more intense than drugs, candy, or women.

Well, most women. Unfortunately, he hadn't met a woman he'd drop a game for, and he'd been looking a damn long time. Hell, he was open to all of it if she were the one.

On cue, his head swiveled around, and he caught sight of her walking past his booth. Long legs. Shiny, straight honey-brown hair that begged for a man's fingers. A body so hot his sweat glands acted like he'd eaten a habanero pepper. Those sexy black-rimmed glasses she wore when her contacts bothered her only added to her appeal.

As if she sensed his intense stare, Patricia Mann met Ford's gaze and gave him a warm smile.

He smiled back, waving, and leaned too far back in his chair. It made a groaning sound, then wobbled, and he crashed to the floor.

Fuck.

Ford prayed she missed the scene and would keep walking, but it was too much to ask. The door flung open, and she was standing over him, shock reflected in those gorgeous gray-violet eyes that reminded him of America the Beautiful and purple mountain majesties.

"Oh my God, are you okay?" she asked, reaching out to help him.

He sprang up as fast as possible and forced a boisterous laugh. "I'm fine! Sorry to scare you, but I had to do something drastic to get a new chair. Gage said there wasn't enough money in the budget."

Patricia studied him as if to be sure he wasn't hurt, then relaxed. Humor laced her words. "If he gives you a hard time, let me know. I'll make sure supply approves it ASAP."

His heart twinged. She was beyond cool. She was *nice*. "Thanks. Off to a meeting?"

She shook her hair and the glossy strands lifted, then settled over her trim shoulders. Today, she wore a soft-pinkish jacket that made her complexion look all pretty and blush-like. A silky T-shirt was tucked into slim black pants that skimmed her body like a gift. What he wouldn't give to be able to open such a package. To have her look at him with heat and want. To have her lips open under his. To—

"Yeah, I'm slammed. Better get going. Glad you're not hurt—we wouldn't last around here without you, Ford. You're the funniest guy I know." She walked out, hips swinging, leaving the scent of earthy florals that smelled of all the good things in the world.

Mostly sex.

His words fell flat in the silence of the room. "Sure. Bye. I love you." Feeling pathetic, he righted the damn chair and slumped back in it.

Patricia was a rising star in the sales department for booking advertisements and helped out with promotions at KTUZ. Men, women, it didn't matter—everyone loved her.

He tried asking her out once, but she'd smoothly sidestepped the invite and told him how important his friendship was. He'd been too embarrassed to try again, so for two years, he'd lusted and dreamed of Patricia finally realizing he was more than a funny work buddy. She'd dated a few coworkers, but the short-term relationships all ended quickly and amicably. It was a testament to her personality and work ethic that there'd never been any messy breakups or bad words exchanged.

For the past few months, she'd been hooked up with a fancy CEO type who was her client, but the gossip mill said there was trouble in paradise. Ford would have loved to step in and fill the void, but with every encounter, he got no closer to breaking the friend barrier.

It was time to give up. Someone of her caliber just wasn't meant for him. Since grade school, he'd been zapped with a gift that most men never received . . . or would want: he never did the right thing with women. Whether he uttered the wrong statement or made the wrong move, it was in his DNA to screw up his love life. Somewhere along the way, fate had cursed him, and he was still desperately trying to reverse it.

Scratching his head, he tried to regain his focus and go back to work. He had a packed day and needed to work on building some of his new contacts with minor league players who might get called up to the big show. The better he knew them, the better his analysis could get, since a personal relationship trumped all others. He'd learned from watching and listening to the very best—Ron Darling, Keith Hernandez, Scott Braun, Joe Buck, and of course, Len Kasper. Success was much more than knowing the game. Listeners and sports fans needed to hear the passion; needed to know there was a respect for the game and the players no matter who he was praising or tearing up. It was the heart of his success, and Ford never let himself forget it.

If only Patricia could see it. He'd have no trouble turning all that heat burning inside him from the game straight to her. Frustration flicked at his nerve endings. When was the last time a woman he'd been interested in had given him a decent chance? It was like he wore a T-shirt that said TRANSITIONAL MAN, because women flocked to him to get over broken hearts or get revenge on their exes. He was never chosen as the *forever* guy.

Crap. Enough of the pity party. Maybe he'd try that new dating app he'd seen in the news. Or the new bar that just opened in the financial district. He needed to rally.

The phone buzzed and he picked it up. "Hey, Ryder. What's up?"

His best friend let out a hard breath, and the sound of chatter rose from the background. "Sorry, heading to my office. Great show this morning."

"Thanks. You going to be at the youth center later?" Ford and Sebastian Ryder had been volunteering at the Dream On Youth Center for a few years and loved being with the kids. The center served underprivileged teens but had been run-down and financially challenged. Gaining a large check from the Quench Foundation where Ryder's wife, Chiara, worked had been a game changer. The facilities were being expanded, with better sports equipment and a full kitchen. With more staff, they'd been able to offer more variety to kids and were finally going on an actual field trip.

"Definitely. I'm calling to ask for a favor, though."

"Shoot."

"I've got this retirement party on Friday, and I was wondering if you'd be able to watch the baby so Chiara can come with me."

Ryder rarely asked him to babysit, and he could tell from his friend's voice he was a bit strained. Probably just craved an evening out with his wife. They both had demanding jobs and were completely devoted to Veronica. He bet it was a struggle to consistently maintain balance. "Of course. About time you asked me to spend time with my goddaughter. When do you need me?"

"Friday at seven? I want it to be a surprise, though. I'm picturing Chiara's face when you show up and tell her to get dressed and meet me. I'll make sure she has a new outfit hidden in the closet so she doesn't have to worry about what to wear."

"Hmm, very *Pretty Woman* of you."

"Except Chiara's not a prostitute."

"Right. She kind of looks like Julia Roberts, though, with that red hair."

Ryder paused. "Not really, dude."

"Fine, I'm not here to fight about it. I'll save the day, as usual, and send your woman to meet you. Maybe you should buy her something pretty to go with the dress. Like shoes."

"Got it covered."

"Flowers are nice, too. Grab some of those. Or lingerie."

"Now things are getting weird." A clamor of teenage voices rose to Ford's ear. His friend was a high school guidance counselor and rarely had a quiet day. "Gotta go—the troops are restless. Thanks again, I appreciate it."

"No problem." Ford hung up.

At least his best friend was happy. Ryder's relationship with Chiara had had many bumps in the road, but now they had a beautiful family. Ford loved watching the couple gaze at each other with sheer adoration.

If only he wasn't a tiny bit jealous. It was an ugly look for him, but something inside reared up and craved that same type of connection with a woman who looked at him like that. He'd always been the one to love more—if *love* was even the word. The closest he felt to that type of emotion was with Patricia, and he hadn't even taken her out on a date. Was it wrong to sense they were meant to be together even though she didn't know it? And if so, how could he convince her to give him a chance?

Ford pushed the nagging thoughts to the side and got back to work.

Chapter Three

Tessa rapped on Chiara's front door and walked right in, throwing her purse on the sofa. "I'm here!" she yelled, heading toward the kitchen.

"Be right out!"

Dex came to greet her with his usual canine enthusiasm. She stroked his massive head and laughed when the black Lab dropped to the ground to expose his belly for rubs. "Some watchdog you are," Tessa murmured, hitting the spot he loved. His leg began to thump steadily. When she finally stopped, he rolled over and gave her a goofy look of adoration that made her consider getting her own dog.

She quickly dismissed the idea. She adored animals, but she also enjoyed her freedom and pristine house. Still, down the line, she could totally see herself having a dog like Dex. Especially if she ever took up running.

Tessa grabbed a glass of water, taking in the casual messiness of the rooms, mostly stuffed with baby equipment. Chiara had always liked a more modest home even though she had the money to get whatever she wanted. But with her husband and Veronica, she had definitely outgrown the space. Her friend was finally ready to invest in a larger property with room to flourish, and Tessa couldn't wait to help her house hunt. She already had a place picked out down her own street so they could be neighbors and she could cement her godmother status over Malia.

The click of heels echoed along with a waft of perfume. "Wow, you look amazing," Tessa said, taking in the sleek black dress and the artful updo of Chiara's gorgeous red hair. Diamond earrings and a matching heart pendant gave the necessary sparkle. "Ryder's going to freak when he sees you."

"I hope so. I just put Veronica in her crib with some toys and told her you were coming." Chiara grabbed her coat and sequined clutch. "Okay, so she already ate and should be ready to sleep by eight p.m. There's a stack of new books if you want to read to her before bed. She's teething, but I gave her some Tylenol. If she fusses, there's a teething ring in the freezer. You can also rub some organic oil on her gums or put her in the high chair and give her a snack. Oh, and don't lose the binky—it's become my saving grace." She paused, frowning. "If you have any trouble, text me and I'll come right home."

Tessa snickered. "Don't insult me."

Chiara laughed and gave her a quick hug. "You're the best."

"I heard car sex is hot when you're married!" she called out.

Her friend laughed and shut the door behind her.

Time for some fun.

Tessa walked into the nursery, Dex trotting behind. Veronica was sitting down, surrounded by stuffed animals and a few learning toys that had buttons and ropes and squeakers to manipulate. Tiptoeing over, she peeked in the crib and the baby looked up, her blue eyes startled. Her red hair was a few tufts springing wildly around her head. Chubby cheeks were puffed out like a chipmunk. She wore a duck-printed pink onesie with feet.

Their gazes met and Veronica let out a shriek, her hands reaching out, drool sliding down her chin from her gummy smile.

Tessa's heart melted into a pile of goo. "Hey, gorgeous, it's Aunt Tessa!" She picked the baby up, cradling her close, while Veronica went straight for her favorite thing.

Her curls.

Chunky hands grabbed a fistful of hair and tugged, probably fascinated by the springiness and texture.

Tessa laughed, bouncing Veronica on her hip. "Now that Mommy's gone, we're gonna have some real fun. I brought a new makeup bag with me, and you can dump out the whole thing. Then we'll cuddle up and do some reading to get you ready for bed."

Veronica must have thought that was the best thing she'd ever heard, because those baby blues widened and she gurgled in excitement. Tessa's heart scrunched tight, then expanded in her chest. She'd never been a grinch, but being around her godchild did all sorts of things to her emotions. *Who would've thought?*

Tessa put her down next to the toy basket. Veronica removed each item to display it proudly, spending a few minutes playing before quickly losing interest. The doorbell surprised her. She frowned, hitching the baby onto her hip. "Hmm, who could that be?" Tessa headed to the door and peered out the side window. Then froze.

What was *he* doing here?

Unlocking the door, she eased it open. "Hey. What's up?"

Ford blinked. "Where's Chiara?"

Irritation hit. They'd never gotten along since the first time they were introduced. Being around Ford Maddox was like mixing expensive, rare extra-virgin olive oil with cheap-ass water. They just didn't blend. "Out with Ryder. I'm babysitting."

Dex ran out with enthusiasm, giving him a greeting reserved for his favorite people. "Hey, buddy! Miss me?" Tessa noticed he also knew the perfect places to scratch, his ease with the dog showing him as a regular visitor.

When Ford looked back up, annoyance skittered across his craggy face, as if she was the one who'd ruined his plans. "This doesn't make sense," he muttered under his breath. He crashed into the house like he owned the place, ignoring her protests and shutting the door behind him. "Ryder wanted to surprise Chiara so she could go to this retirement party. I'm here to watch Ronnie."

She clutched the cooing baby to her chest as if he were a kidnapper. "Chiara decided to surprise him, so she made arrangements for me to babysit."

His face cleared at the explanation and his shoulders relaxed. "Oh, okay. For a moment I thought I'd screwed up. That's kind of cute they had the same idea. Well, feel free to head out—I got this covered."

Tessa regarded him like an insect who'd managed to slip under the door. "Excuse me?"

"You can leave now. Me and my girl here are going to spend some quality time together."

Her eyebrows climbed to her forehead and she took a step back. "Sorry, I think you misunderstood. *I* have this covered and *you* can leave. Veronica and I already have our evening well planned, and it's girls only. I'm sure you have plenty of other things you can do."

Unbelievably, the man scowled at her like she'd done something wrong. "I told Ryder I'd be here tonight to babysit. I'm staying."

"I told Chiara I'd be here! Don't you have a sports thing to watch or some other important task?"

"No. Don't you have some type of makeover to do?" he asked.

Oh, she despised his slight sneer and judgmental tone. Her hot temper flared. She raised her chin and glowered. "There's nothing more important than spending time with my goddaughter."

Ford's gaze narrowed. "Same."

They stared at one another in an old-fashioned high noon showdown.

Veronica burst into tears, and Dex let out a concerned whine.

Startled, Tessa began rocking and cooing, and Ford closed the distance to chuck her under the chin, his giant thumb gentle as he sang Veronica's name, getting her to calm down. "Ronnie doesn't like when we fight," he said, stretching his face into a fake grin. "Neither does Dex. If you insist on staying, you need to be nice."

Veronica chewed on her fist in worry, forcing Tessa to give him a strained smile back. She practically choked on her words. "Her name is Veronica, not Ronnie. We're not living in an Archie comic book. And I'm staying. I'll allow you to visit because I am nice and don't want to bother Chiara or Ryder."

"Good, then it's settled. You can stay." With a quick movement, he scooped up Veronica and headed toward the kitchen. "How about some Cheerios, kiddo? A little nighttime snack?"

Tessa trotted after him, almost catching her heel on the battered rug. "Snacks are if she gets cranky—she's teething."

"I know. She likes the yellow teething ring in the freezer. It's her favorite."

Oh, how she despised his haughty response, as if he knew Veronica's habits better than her. She refused to validate him. "There are also natural drops to rub on her gums, which reduce some of the swelling. She's going down by eight, so I planned to let her go through my makeup bag, then read to her. Here, why don't you give her back to me and—what are you doing?"

Her jaw dropped as Ford cranked up the Echo Dot and ordered Alexa to play Def Leppard. "Reading is boring. So is makeup. She needs to burn off some energy before she's ready to sleep. Right, darling? Let's boogie."

"Pour Some Sugar on Me" belted out in all its old-school sexual glory. Holding Veronica against his broad chest, Ford grasped her tiny hand and began dancing around the kitchen, his gravelly voice booming through the room.

Tessa watched in horror as her quiet babysitting night with her goddaughter exploded into shreds of chaos. Veronica giggled madly at his antics, and even Dex got in the act, barking and leaping around the two, as if dancing with them. Ford waltzed around the kitchen, ignoring her obvious disapproval, while she wondered how she'd gotten stuck with the only man who pushed all her buttons. In the wrong way.

She took a moment to study him. Average height at just under six foot. Long, shaggy, brown hair that didn't seem to hold a style. She always had a weakness for a goatee, but Ford's was a bit unruly, as if he couldn't seem to find the time to properly trim and sculpt it to fit his face. His clothes were always casual—ranging from humorous T-shirts with zany sayings or classic concert ones, as if he were stuck in the eighties. He preferred worn jeans and generic sneakers. He was the male equivalent of a plain Jane.

His best features were his eyes and voice. Hazel eyes, the most beautiful color of brown and green, could be mesmerizing, but Ford's got lost in all the facial hair and his hooded eyelids. His voice was legendary, but it didn't surprise her—it was the core asset of his job. Deep and hypnotic, like sand and gravel wrapped in satin. Alone, Tessa admitted a woman would practically swoon, imagining that sexy voice whispering commands in her ear. Until she saw him and realized he probably wouldn't know what to say.

Ford had never struck her as a smooth operator. The few times he showed up at a gathering of their friends with a date, he seemed to be the one more invested. At the last party, he'd actually lost his companion to another guy. Tessa felt bad when he discovered his date had gone home with someone else without telling him.

The music ended and she shook off her thoughts. It didn't matter what type of dating or social life Ford dealt with. She only needed to get along with him enough for Veronica's sake, and to please Chiara and Ryder. Being a co-godparent was a job she took seriously, so she reminded herself to be patient and just get through the evening the best she could.

Ford laughed, staring down at Veronica's joyous face. Tessa grudgingly admitted the two were adorable together even if she didn't approve of his babysitting methods.

She snapped her voice to crisp attention. "Okay, concert's over. If you get her all revved up, she's going to crash too early, then wake up in the middle of the night." She plucked the baby out of Ford's arms and tapped Veronica's nose. "You need to chill, girlfriend. Let's get you a small snack." She used her chin to motion toward the cabinet. "Can you grab some Cheerios and her sippy cup?"

"Thought you said snacks were for later."

She shot him a glare. "She won't be able to concentrate on reading after that stunt. Might as well let her eat."

He grinned. "Sure. Wonder if they have chips for me. All that dancing made me hungry."

Tessa rolled her eyes and set the baby in her high chair, buckling her in. Anticipating food, Veronica kicked with excitement, babbling nonsense in a long stream.

Ford set the cup and Cheerios on the tray, then headed to the refrigerator. "Want wine?" he asked.

"Yes, please."

He poured a glass of chardonnay, snapped the tab off an Allagash White beer, and grabbed a bag of Sour Cream & Onion Lay's. Settling onto the kitchen barstool, he began to munch on chips and sip his beer, his gaze on the baby. "Shouldn't she be talking by now?"

Tessa tossed him a glare. "She just turned one. Chiara said she's right on the edge. Says 'Da-Da.'"

He threw up his hands. "Okay, I was just asking. Why are you so defensive all the time?"

"Why do you ask rude questions?"

"It wasn't—I just don't know about benchmarks and stuff." He studied her through a squinted gaze. "Hey, can we cease fire for tonight? I won't comment on your babysitting clothes or your tendency to jump down everyone's throat if you don't insult me every time I open my mouth."

Tessa took a sip of her wine and regarded him icily. "What's wrong with my clothes?"

He snickered. "Really? That's how you dress to crawl around the floor with a toddler—in leather pants? Plus, you're wearing spiked heels. You can hurt her with those."

Tessa glanced down at her sleek Spanx faux-leather leggings and gold-heeled Stuart Weitzman boots, seeing nothing wrong. "I can move around fine in this outfit. I'm wearing a T-shirt."

"It's got sparkles. Who do you think you're gonna see? Derek Jeter?"

She blinked. "Who?"

Horror flashed on his face. "The hot Hall of Famer for the Yankees. Dear God, you know him, right? All women know him!"

She waved a hand in the air with dismissal. "Sure, he dated J.Lo."

"That's A-Rod!" His face got a bit red, and he muttered something under his breath, sipping more beer. "Didn't you ever go on a date to a baseball game?"

"No. One idiot took me to a basketball game on a first date. That ended quick."

"Why—did he not pay enough attention to you when the game started?" he joked.

"Exactly. A first date is to get to know someone. I don't consider screaming at every play, drinking too much beer, and spilling popcorn because of a goal a good intro to a relationship."

"A basket. Not a goal."

"Right. Like it matters."

Ford shuddered. Pleasure spiked. She always did love sparring with him even when he pissed her off. It was like drinking a bottle of jolt juice, trying to up each barb to perfection.

She pushed harder. "Seems you judge me just as harshly as you accuse me of."

"Hard not to. You're everything in a woman that terrifies a man."

She practically snarled back. "What—successful? With financial freedom and confidence? Knowing what I want?"

"I was thinking more like judgmental, snobby, and an elitist."

Oh, that one hurt enough to rip a gasp from her lips. "Are you kidding? Because I like designer clothes? I work my ass off for every dollar I earn and deserve to spend it the way I want. That's messed up, dude."

"Nah, didn't mean it like that. You seem to think when a guy doesn't look a certain way, he's beneath you."

Her laugh held no humor. "You have never met one man I dated."

One brow shot up. "Do any stick around after the first or second date?"

Her smile was smug. "If I want them to. I'm discerning, and that has nothing to do with a guy's job or appearance. It's who he is on the inside."

He snorted. "Yeah. Riiight."

"You don't believe me?"

"Nope. You do makeovers for a living. You like a shiny surface but don't want to admit it."

"Now who's judging?"

Ford jerked back, obviously surprised. A halfhearted grin curved his lips, which she couldn't really see past his generous mustache. "Got me."

Tessa shook her head and turned her back on him, scolding Dex lightly for eating all the dropped Cheerios Veronica happily threw to him. The well-behaved dog sat down and looked at her with sad puppy eyes. She patted his head, accepting his apology. "Look, let's backtrack. I accept your proposal to cease fire. It's obvious I don't understand your world and you don't understand mine. We'll deal with each other for the next few hours, enjoy Veronica, and head our separate ways. Deal?"

"Deal."

He drank his beer. She sipped her wine. And Veronica clapped as if she realized there would finally be some peace.

Chapter Four

Ford lounged on the floor with Ronnie settled in his lap. She was wriggly for a bit, but eventually Tessa lured her with a low, breathy voice, reading the story of a little girl on a magical hippo hunt in *Katie and the Hippo Egg*. Using expressive gestures and faces, she kept the baby's attention.

And Ford's.

Damn, why couldn't she be nicer? Why did she have to be Ronnie's godmother and Chiara's best friend so they were always in each other's orbit? And why did she affect him in such a way?

He was a laid-back guy. He flowed like a river. Not much bothered him, and he avoided conflict with women easily. Hell, his main flaw was becoming a friend instead of a hot hookup, but from the moment he'd locked gazes with this petite, stubborn, dynamic fireball, his only goal had been to poke and prod to see if he could get under her skin.

She was too . . . perfect. On the outside. Like a china doll, but if you peered underneath, she was more like Annabelle—the horror doll that haunts people. With her impeccable designer clothes, stilettos, and fierce glare, the woman didn't walk into a room, she stormed. Toffee-colored corkscrew curls bounced madly around her shoulders and framed a heart-shaped face with a wide mouth and gently curving chin. Her features were soft, but the moment she snapped you with those periwinkle blue eyes, eyebrows slashed together in her trademark frown, a guy knew she was trouble. She was opinionated, bossy, and thought she knew everything. He respected the hell out of her work ethic and what she'd built with her friends at Quench, but he wasn't a fan of her role. Making over women just so they could look better in the mirror seemed like a shallow career, especially since she seemed to mock his love for sports.

Even now, her ridiculous boots were crossed at the ankles, and those tight pants molded to every curve. She had a slamming body, with generous breasts and hips, but dealing with her nonsparkling personality for more than an evening would be a hellish prison.

Still, he was curious. Always had been. He wondered what her real story was since Ryder and the girls never spoke about it. Tessa was private. People said she had a generous heart and was always trying to help others, but Ford hadn't glimpsed that part of her, other than seeing her try to score a discount on another designer bag for her readers.

She finished the story, and he bounced Ronnie up and down, trying not to grin at Tessa's frown. The last time he'd bounced her hard, Ronnie threw up all over Tessa's white outfit.

"Stop bouncing her," she snapped, closing the book. "I don't want to clean up any vomit tonight."

"You're a good reader."

She stared at him in surprise. Her tone was grudging. "Thanks."

"Ever want to be an actress?"

That got her to laugh. "Why would you ask me that?"

"You're good at voices and expressions. Figured you'd love the spotlight, too."

"Hell no. I despise being the center of attention." She scooped the baby up and gracefully got to her feet. Ronnie grabbed at those curls and tugged. "Let's get you changed and see if you'll go down with your binky."

Her response confused him. Tessa never shrank from boldly declaring what she wanted and deserved. He figured she'd been a show-off most of her life, but the flash of distaste in her gaze at his assumption was clear.

Interesting.

He got up and followed her into the nursery. Ford liked the pale yellow walls and brightly colored art. The rug was soft under his feet, and a sense of joy and comfort seemed to permeate the air. A few seconds later, he began to gag, because a different smell hit him. "Uh, that's awful. Did she have a burrito for lunch or something?"

Tessa grinned, capably cleaning Ronnie's squirmy butt without a wince. "Chiara said once they begin solid foods, it keeps getting worse. Here, catch." She made a motion to throw the toxic diaper at him, and he fumbled in a panic. Her hearty laughter made him shake his head in both exasperation and appreciation at the joke. "Can you get her night mobile set up?" she asked.

A contraption by the crib had a few buttons and switches, but he figured it out, and soon, stars and moons began to softly flicker on the ceiling. Gentle, soothing sounds of waves washed through the air. Ford bet he'd be asleep in seconds if he had such a cushy setup at home.

He couldn't help but be impressed by the easy way Tessa handled Ronnie, as if she was born to be a mother. Weird, because he always thought of her as the least maternal of her friend group.

The baby went happily into her crib, hands locked in a death grip around the pacifier, and after kissing her night night, they headed into the living room.

"Well, that was easy," Tessa said, grabbing her wineglass again.

"It was definitely the dancing." He got her to laugh, which he admitted was a nice sound. If only she were able to relax a bit more, maybe she wouldn't be too bad to hang out with.

"You can take off now if you want. She'll probably sleep the whole time."

Ford grabbed his beer and settled into the comfy leather sectional. "Nope, I'm staying. I promised Ryder."

Tessa didn't look too thrilled, but it only amused him. "Fine. But I don't know what we're both supposed to do for the next few hours."

"Watch the football game? Giants may be playing."

"I have a better idea. How about we watch some Christmas Hallmark movies?"

He couldn't help the actual shudder that shook his body. "Fine, I get your point." A strange impulse struck him. "Let's get to know each other better. We'll play a game."

Suspicion laced her tone. "Why?"

"Don't you think it's time? I mean, we've known each other for years, yet I have no clue about who you are, T."

"Tessa. I'm a full person, not an initial."

He gave a suffering sigh. "You're not gonna give me a fair shot here, are you."

She gave a humph, crossing her arms in front of her chest. "You never cared before. What changed?"

"Ronnie."

"Veronica."

He grinned. "We'll be seeing each other a lot more. Wouldn't it be nice not to snap at each other during family functions? It would make Chiara and Ryder happy."

She seemed to consider it, her head tilting to the side, a tiny clucking of her tongue. Her glittery T-shirt pulled tight over her ripe breasts, so he quickly lifted his gaze, not wanting to get in trouble for his appreciation. Hell, with Tessa, she'd just coldcock him first, ask questions later.

"Good point. How do we start?"

"We'll need more alcohol." He retrieved another beer and the rest of the wine, setting them on the coffee table. "I propose we ask each other questions and agree to tell the truth."

She plopped into the easy chair, rocking a bit back and forth, as if her body just couldn't contain too much stillness for long. "What if we don't like the question?"

"We get one veto where we don't have to answer."

Tessa nodded. Her nails gleamed with pearl polish as she tapped her faux-leather-clad knee. "No asking about sex stuff."

He rolled his eyes. "As if I'd want to know."

Another husky laugh. "Oh, you would."

Heat punched his gut, taking him off guard. He'd never been attracted to Tessa, not because she wasn't gorgeous but more that she wasn't his type and was a pain in the ass. But the casual, flirty retort stirred something inside. He doused the flicker immediately.

That was the last thing he needed.

"Ladies first," he said, propping his feet up on the coffee table.

"How'd you get into sports radio?"

Ford liked that she was going slow and easy. "Loved sports my whole life. I happen to also have a photographic memory. Served me well in school, especially because I was a piss-poor student and hated studying. My main goal was to play professionally, but I wasn't good enough at baseball or basketball. So I decided instead of chasing something I couldn't get, I'd use my memory for stats and figures to get into broadcasting." He thought back on his journey, a familiar comfort to discover he was able to work in the world he loved. "I had a distinctive voice that got me in the door at a sports station and I slowly learned the business. Now, I have a well-known morning show where I interview guests and talk with callers." A touch of embarrassment swept through him. "Sorry—you probably wanted a one-sentence answer."

She shook her head. All those toffee curls bounced, then settled. He wondered briefly what the strands would feel like. "Not at all. I didn't know that. I'd assumed you were just born a beer-drinking, ranting, obsessive sports fan. Was it hard finding a niche in radio?"

"Yeah, but I got lucky because the people were good to me. Genuinely liked me. To be honest, it's been rough to see how hard women have fought for their place in sports. Rachel Nichols was told consistently she only got her gig because her husband was famous, which is ridiculous. The woman has extreme talent. And look at Michele Tafoya getting moved because she talked about Kaepernick and gave an honest opinion."

Tessa wrinkled her nose. "Now you lost me. Don't know who those people are."

"You should. Their stories are important."

"I know Simone Biles and Maria Sharapova."

"That's because they're superstars at the biggest competition in the world. Their stories are everywhere. What about the other lesser-known athletes? There are so many stories out there to tell and ways to feature women in sports that Quench is ignoring. I'm surprised you haven't gotten blowback from your readership about it yet."

"Quench readers don't care about endless scores and stats on random players, especially when competitors cover the main market with that stuff."

"But there's a story behind each athlete. Think of what it takes to compete at that level. The dedication and daily practice. The sacrifices and regrets about what had to be given up to get better, usually with no guarantees. What if you studied your whole life and gave up everything else, just to have to perform perfectly for a few minutes or hours? What if you lost it all? Could you live with yourself?"

Her blue eyes widened. Ford waited for a teasing comment or for her to shrug off his passionate speech, but instead she narrowed her gaze more intently. "I don't think I ever have," she said slowly. "I mean, intellectually, yes. But not the way you described it."

"That's what your readers would love, T. The real guts of what a person gives to pursue perfection. It's never about the stats or scores."

There was a spark that flared from her gaze, a lightning bolt of awareness. Like she was seriously listening to him on a soul level. "That was beautifully said, Ford."

He backed off, already doubting his instinct to trust her and this game; to trust she wouldn't use the information in the future to tease him. "Sorry. Got carried away. My turn."

She seemed to want to say something else but leaned back instead, sipping her wine. She showed no outward concern about any question he might ask.

"Why do you focus on makeovers as your main job at Quench? What do you get out of it?"

Ah, there it was. A flare of heat warmed her eyes, along with irritation. "I'm glad you asked. Because I was getting a bit tired of you mocking my career choice when you know nothing about it."

He held up his hands. "Sorry. You're right. I know nothing about what you do."

"Makeovers are more than you think, and it's not my primary job. My column went viral and became a backbone of Quench when I began choosing readers who reached out to me asking how they can change their lives and build their confidence. Most revolved around getting a job or proving they can do things others said they couldn't, et cetera. I worked with a young girl who was really smart but completely unsure of herself. I treated her to a fun makeover—hair, makeup, and new outfits based on the fit of her body. Then I had her chat with a dating coach and a therapist for a few sessions, to dig into her main issues. I documented every step, and when it was done, she was a changed person. It only took a few people to believe in her, but you know what else it really was?"

"What?"

She shook her head. "It's a placebo effect."

He frowned. "But you really do change their appearance."

"Yes, but especially with women, it may not take much to give us that needed kick to get to the next level. To spur a bit more confidence in our abilities just because we suddenly feel good about ourselves. No matter how bad we think it is, no matter how many articles are written about it, no matter how much women hate to admit it, how we feel when we look in a mirror is a big-ass deal. My goal was to try and tweak that, then build the rest of it." A soft sigh escaped her lips. "Unfortunately, it's begun to backfire."

"What do you mean?"

A wall slammed down between them. Normally, it wouldn't bother him, but Tessa had been open and now he was damn curious to know more.

"Never mind," she said. "Let's move on."

"No, tell me. It's just us, and what do I matter?"

She laughed then, collapsing deeper into the chair. "Ah, hell, why not? Basically, I'm getting tired of putting in the effort to watch a woman chase after a guy who's never going to love her like she deserves. I expanded the column to help more women and was riding high on success for a while. I really thought I'd hit on something, until I began to realize most of the men they were going after weren't worth the effort. My dream was to keep it pure, but like lots of things, I think the column got tainted along the way. All the readers really want to see is confirmation that if they change their looks, they'll get the man. And it's exactly the opposite of what Quench stands for."

Ford scratched his head and pondered her words. "Intentions are good. But you're probably giving yourself too much credit. Some makeup and a bit of confidence doesn't mean the guy they want is gonna fall for them. The women figure that out eventually, right?"

A tiny frown furrowed her brow. "You don't get it. I have a perfect rate of success with my reader column."

"For what?"

Tessa gave a deep sigh, as if she didn't want to explain, but finally relented. "Here's the thing. At first, I took on a few readers who wanted to live a bigger life. It seemed authentic. Then, it seemed to slowly switch, and it became all about guys my readers loved from afar but didn't have the confidence to approach. I took on a few of these cases, curious if I could make a difference. After only a few weeks, they made a connection and entered a relationship. I printed the results in the column, and suddenly, everyone wanted more. I was approached by thousands of readers asking me to help them. I swore to report on every woman I chose, even with unsuccessful results."

"A reasonable plan. What are your percentages?"

"I told you. One hundred percent. I haven't failed once."

Fascinated, he leaned in. "You're saying you did your magic stuff and the guy fell in love with the woman you helped?"

Tessa shrugged. "Love, lust, whatever it was, my reader always got the man they wanted and fell into some type of committed relationship."

"Just from looking better?"

She gave an impatient sigh. "More than that, though you should never underestimate the power of a woman on a good hair day. Something inside changed, too, and gave them the confidence in themselves to believe they were worthy. That's what the main attraction was. I may not approve of my reader's choices, but each got what they wanted. I was able to give them that."

He thought briefly to Patricia and knew he'd do anything to get her to notice him as a man, not a friend. If a makeover would help? Hell, he'd snatch up that opportunity immediately. But that wasn't possible. He was positive Tessa was overstating her skills in creating a connection under her tutelage.

Ford tried not to sound patronizing. "Do you really believe you have that much power?"

He waited for her to laugh, but she shot him a dead-serious look. "Yes."

He tried but couldn't smother his laugh. "That's ridiculous. I don't believe it. Maybe these women felt bad for all you did for them, so they lied. Pretended they got the guy and it ended."

Unbelievably, sympathy lit powder-blue eyes. "No, they didn't. My current reader has been focused on this marketing director, who seems pretty superficial. She's revealing her new look and revamped attitude at an office holiday party this weekend. I guarantee in about two weeks, he'll be smitten and they'll be dating."

Ford snorted. "Yeah, right."

She cocked her head and glared. "You don't believe me?"

"Nope."

The old rivalry between them seemed to catch and reignite. Annoyance swarmed from her in waves. "Wanna bet?"

He blinked. "On what?"

"Your wrongness. If my reader succeeds with getting the director to fall for her, I win."

He stretched out his legs and considered. "How would I know? You could spin your results to win the bet."

She stabbed her finger in the air, outrage bristling from her snapping gaze. "I don't lie. I report the truth in my column and wouldn't compromise my integrity on a silly bet with a man who means nothing to me."

Ford winced. "Ouch."

She slowly relaxed, but the dislike was clearly etched on her face. He almost chuckled. It was nice to have the freedom to be exactly who he was with Tessa. They didn't care about impressing each other and seemed to bring out their worst behavior. Yet, she entertained him and was more interesting to talk to than he originally believed. "I'll share the results with you as she reports to me."

"What are the parameters of success?" he asked.

A grin curved her lips. "Bringing out the big words today, huh?"

He shook his head. "Smart-ass."

"I usually judge success by the couple dating and deciding to enter into a relationship of their mutual choosing."

"Do you ever ask if they have sex?"

"Yes, I do. But my reader has a right not to tell me, of course. Most know raw honesty is what I'm looking for in my column and share more than you'd expect. But I don't think having sex equals a relationship."

"Me, either. I'm good with your standards. What do I get when I win?"

She rolled her eyes and sipped more wine. "When *I* win, it will just be nice to prove you wrong. But I'm good with raising the stakes a bit to make things interesting. How about whoever wins owes the other one a favor?"

Ford gave a slow nod. "Yeah, I like that. Favors are good."

She grunted. "Nonsexual."

"Don't flatter yourself, T."

Her face drew in a scowl. "Then we have a bet."

She surprised him by reaching over to shake his hand. When he did, Ford noticed her grip was firm and warm, her fingers curling around his in a sensual caress. A strange heat prickled up his arm, and when he pulled away, he fought the need to shake his hand to cool off.

Weird shit. Then again, she'd been the one to bring sex into the conversation, not him.

His thought was interrupted by the sharp cry of Ronnie. They both flew off the couch at the same time, but Dex beat them there. The dog was already at the crib, sniffing furiously and looking back as if he was frustrated by their slowness. The baby was standing up, rocking back and forth as she screamed, mouth open, face red, and definitely pissed off.

Tessa scooped her up first. "What's the matter, sweetie? Your teeth?"

Ronnie mashed her fist in her mouth, face twisted up. She uttered a long stream of babbles amid drools.

Ford looked concerned. "What should we do now?"

"Chiara gave her Tylenol before. Grab the teething ring."

When he got back, Tessa walked her back and forth, trying to soothe her. At first, the baby chewed frantically on the icy rubber, but soon she'd managed to chuck it a good distance so it hit the wall.

Ford grinned. "Hey, she's got a great pitching arm."

Tessa shot him a look. "Really? You're thinking about sports even now?"

"I'm always thinking about sports. Never too early to train. She can be in the WPF softball league."

"Or baseball."

"Nah, women still don't play baseball. Only softball."

Ronnie began to wail louder. Tessa rocked faster. "That's ridiculous. Even in this day and age we have to use the term *soft*? I'm so sick of the patriarchy."

"Yeah, me too. Female sports are getting huge but still lagging on equal pay and rights. The US women's soccer team really pushed hard on those issues and made progress. Hopefully it'll continue. Hey, maybe you can sing to her?"

She shot him a dirty look. "That will make her cry harder. I've been told I'm tone deaf."

"Okay, scrap that plan. I only know heavy metal, and there's too many bad words."

The howling was getting worse. His ears began to pound as the baby reached new soprano heights. Tessa walked through the house while Ford trailed behind. He rinsed off the teething ring, and Tessa grabbed it, pressing the object to the baby's lips.

Ronnie chucked it again, even farther this time. "No, TT! No!"

Ford's mouth dropped open.

Tessa gasped, staring at the baby's scrunched-up red face. "You said my name! You're talking!" An expression of joy and wonder flickered over her features, and Ford had the impulse to snap her picture, just so he could study the way she lit up from within.

He shook off the feeling and made a grab for the baby. "She called you an initial. I thought you were worth a full name."

The light faded and Tessa went back to her usual annoyed expression. "She's one. It's acceptable from her."

He focused on the baby's miserable face. "Good job, sweetheart. Now say *Ford*. F-O-R-D. Uncle F-O-R-D."

"She can't say that yet. It's too hard."

"Sure she can, Ronnie's a genius." He tried to take her again, but Tessa swiveled on her heel and began to walk faster, cooing and praising while Ronnie kept crying.

"Give her to me," Ford said. "You're not getting anywhere, and my ears are killing me."

He finally managed to scoop up the baby after following Tessa a few rounds around the house. Propping her on his hip, he made funny faces and noises, trying to distract her from the obvious pain of swollen gums.

Tessa crossed her arms in front of her chest and glared. "See? You're not doing much better. Let me rub some of that stuff on her gums Chiara recommended."

"My grandma said she used to rub whiskey on mine to put me to sleep."

She returned with a small jar, dipped her finger in, and stuck it into the baby's drooling mouth. Ronnie gummed at her frantically like a mini vampire. "I'm not getting my goddaughter drunk on babysitting duty."

"We need to distract her," Ford said, his heart twinging at the baby's obvious pain. "Can you dance?"

"I don't think my twerking will help at this point."

He raised a brow. "You twerk?"

Tessa rolled her eyes and headed to the play corner of the living room. She grabbed a few things from an overflowing basket and motioned him over. He noticed she needed to practically shout in order to be heard over the crying. "She's angry at the pain. I think allowing her to express emotion will help. Put her on the floor."

She lined up some maracas, a drum, and cymbals in front of Ronnie. The baby pitifully grabbed a shaker thing and began banging it on the carpet. Dex backed up a few steps before sitting, obviously a bit nervous about getting in Ronnie's way during her tantrum.

Smart, Ford thought. Any man learned early on to back away slowly from an angry female.

Tessa began pounding her hands against the toy drums and letting out some weird-ass chant. Ronnie grabbed the other shaker in her tiny hands and started slamming them both while she screamed. Ford watched the scene unfold with a fascinated horror as the two of them did some type of tribal bonding that he didn't understand but prayed worked for teething pain.

Tessa beamed at their goddaughter as she began throwing the shakers and hitting the cymbals. The clanging and crying rose in the air in waves, giving him an instant headache.

Mercifully, Tessa stopped the awful music and Ronnie grew quiet. Her breath came in tiny huffs. Drool trickled down her chin. He waited for the second act, but miraculously the baby remained quiet, staring at her aunt.

Pride emitted from Tessa's face. "See? Poor thing needed to tire herself out. I always knew I was a bit of a baby whisperer."

Ford snorted. "Doubt it. More like she needed time for the oil to work."

Ignoring him, Tessa picked up the baby, marched into the bedroom, and laid her back in the crib. She cranked up the mobile again and dimmed the lights.

Ford peeked around the corner and shared a surprised glance with Dex. Had that really worked? If so, he'd never hear the end of it. Allowing Tessa to hold something over him was the biggest form of torture he could think of.

On cue, Tessa came out, grinning smugly. "No need to thank me."

"Oh, you must be the worst loser ever," he muttered, shaking his head.

She just preened. "I am. Thank goodness I rarely lose." Patting his arm with a patronizing air, she grabbed her wine, took a seat, and settled back.

He grudgingly followed her. "Are you hooked up right now?"

She considered him with coolness. "Why do you want to know?"

"Just because."

Tessa hesitated. "Not now. I'm dating. Keeping my options open."

He nodded. "Exactly what I thought."

Her eyes simmered with irritation. "What is that supposed to mean?"

"It means I can't imagine any guy seeking out your company voluntarily. At least, not in an intimate relationship."

She gasped. "That's a rotten thing to say! Who are you to talk? You lost your date before the end of the evening at the last party!"

He leaned in, hating she was right. "Because I didn't care."

"Oh yes you did. Especially at your birthday party. What was that girl's name? You had moony eyes for her."

She remembered Patricia? Ford tried to keep calm. "I don't remember."

"Yes you do. She works with you. She friend-zoned you big-time." He gave her a cool stare back, but her eyes suddenly widened. A small laugh escaped her lips. "Oh my God, you still like her! I can tell!"

And just like that, their fragile truce shattered. "I bet you haven't had a relationship that lasted more than a month. That's how long you can fool a guy pretending you're nice."

Her face tightened. "And I bet you can't keep a woman because she eventually finds out you're like a frat boy and not a grown man."

"You don't know anything about me!" he yelled.

"You don't know anything about *me*!" she yelled back.

A sharp cry splintered the room. Ford smiled real slow. "Baby whisperer, huh?"

She stood up and jabbed her finger at him. "You woke her up on purpose! What type of godfather are you?"

"Better than you, godmother. I'll take care of this myself."

He went in to get Ronnie and swore to do anything it took to calm her down, then show off his skills to her arrogant, stuck-up, mean godmother.

Two hours later, Ford was practically staggering across the room, desperate for silence and jiggling Veronica in his arms. "What does Google say?" he asked. "Can we give her more Tylenol?"

"No, I'm afraid to overdose her. I don't know what else to do! I went through everything on the list."

"Why are they so late? It's like one a.m.!"

"Stop whining; I can't take the both of you," Tessa snapped, grabbing yet another teething object and offering it to Ronnie.

"Maybe you should text Chiara," he suggested. "What if she's sick?"

"She has no fever, and her gums are swollen. It's classic teething. Suck it up, buttercup. Our friends are getting some intimate alone time they desperately need."

"They can make it a quickie." Ford fumbled for his phone with one hand.

The sound of the front door opening made him want to weep with relief. Chiara and Ryder came inside, saying hello to Dex and giving each other adoring looks like they were teens who'd just gotten lucky on a date.

Ryder grinned. "Hey, guys, how's it going? Sorry for the confusion, it looks like we got two babysitters for the price of one."

Chiara's own smile faded as she took in the scene. "Oh no, how long has she been up? Is it the teething again?"

Chiara walked over, taking the weeping, gurgling baby from Ford's shaky arms.

Ronnie immediately stopped crying.

With a deep sigh, the baby patted Chiara's cheek. "Ma-Ma." Then she closed her eyes.

Ford gaped. "Did she just go to sleep?"

Ryder shot him a sympathetic look. “Sorry, buddy, she’s been having a hard time lately. You probably tired her out by walking around. How bad was it?”

Ford got ready to tell him how hard the evening had been, with Ronnie’s endless crying and obvious discomfort, along with Tessa’s bad attitude and sharp comments, but Tessa cut him off immediately. “It was great. She wasn’t crying for long. In fact, she was an angel, wasn’t she, Ford?”

He went to shake his head no and call her a liar, but her warning look scared the shit out of him. “Yeah. Sure. It was . . . great.”

“Thanks so much for staying. Sorry we’re so late,” Chiara whispered, pressing a kiss to the baby’s head. “You’re the best friends ever.”

“Anytime,” Tessa said coolly, giving her friend a quick hug. “We’re going to get out of here and let you settle in. Did you have a good time?”

“The best.” Chiara shot another intimate look at Ryder. *Oh, yeah, they’d definitely done it.* He supposed sex as new parents wasn’t too easy, but it was obvious tonight they’d re-bonded. At least Ford was still a great wingman.

“We’re glad. You deserve it,” Ford said. “Talk to you later this week.”

They put on their coats and walked out the door. He stopped by Tessa’s car, the air cold and crisp on his overheated skin. Hesitating, he stared at her, his words mingled in a knot in his head like his emotions. “Well, it was an interesting night.”

She gave a small huff. “That it was.”

They stared at each other in silence for a few seconds. The temporary truce had officially dissolved. He peered into her shuttered face. Ford shrugged. “See ya.”

“I’ll let you know about that favor you owe me,” she said, opening her car door.

He stopped from pivoting on his heel and shot her a look. "When your results come in, I'll be ready to collect my favor. Bye-bye, Baby Whisperer."

This time, he didn't wait to see her expression. He walked to his car, drove home, and got ready for bed. His head still throbbed from the noise, like he'd been at a Foo Fighters concert.

He grinned as a last thought popped into his head, imagining Tessa's face when she found out he'd won the bet.

Chapter Five

Tessa gave a long sigh and closed out her inbox.

It took a bit longer than average, but after a month she received the news from Autumn: she was officially in a relationship with her hot marketing director. After New Year's, the guy had begun to make excuses to bump into her, suddenly joining after-work happy hour and texting her to get her opinion on random issues. Those run-ins led to long dinners, sleepovers, and the "talk" about becoming exclusive. Autumn was in love and gushed with endless gratitude to Tessa about her remarkable ability.

Tessa was happy for her but still felt a bit uneasy about the relationship. Once again, it seemed playing games and looking hot led to love. But was it love? Or just lust?

Not that she ever promised in her column that things would last forever. Tessa wanted her readers to be served by a core confidence in their abilities, looks, and talents, no matter who they were. But were they? Or was her famous ability only forming false and shallow relationships that were bound to collapse?

Dammit, what was wrong with her? Autumn was in love with the man of her dreams. Tessa had won her bet with Ford Maddox. She would have another successful column ready for print that she knew would go viral. Everything was perfect.

She tapped a nude nail against her desk and tried to get excited. What could she ask from Ford that would make her happy and piss him off? She hadn't seen much of him since that fateful babysitting night, but pieces of their conversation would randomly drift through her mind. Then she'd get irritated and try not to think about him. He seemed to know exactly what buttons to push to get the worst reaction possible out of her. The man had quite a talent.

"Uh-oh. Who made you mad?"

She looked up. Malia was framed in the doorway, looking sharp as usual in a gorgeous apple-green suit, her long braids twisted up on top of her head. Tessa relaxed and grinned. "Nobody yet, but the day's young. You're slaying today. Got a big appointment?"

Her friend's face lit up with excitement. "I have a meeting with the CEO of Nyack Banking. If it works out and she sponsors a local charity, I'll have a better chance of securing more financial companies for the foundation."

Tessa clapped her hands. "That's amazing! You've really grown in this position, babe. I'm proud of you."

Malia smiled, flashing her gorgeous white teeth. "Thanks. How's the internship stuff going?"

"It's great but definitely challenging with all the different school schedules. I'm having a hard time with the new semester, trying to match up the right people in our departments, but I'm getting there. Some of the kids are intense and take it seriously, but others seem a bit reserved."

Malia nodded. "Makes sense. Some of them come from rough backgrounds, and they don't know what to expect. Maria seems to be thriving with Magda. Who knew she'd love photography so much?"

"Who knew Magda could actually be nice to teenagers? She scares most adults."

Maria had applied for an internship on the recommendation of Ryder. She was a regular attendee at the Dream On Youth Center, where he volunteered, and she had been having trouble figuring out what line of work to pursue or colleges to apply to. Matching her up with Magda had been a risk, but once Tessa saw the girl blossom with a camera in hand, everything clicked.

Tessa was more passionate lately about the new internship program at Quench, but the column and some features still demanded most of her attention. She pushed the annoying thought away. "Hey, Autumn emailed me today. We have another success story to report for the column."

"That's great! I swear, Tessa, you have a gift. You must feel amazing."

"Yep. I do. Feel amazing."

Malia frowned but shook her head. "Gotta go. Chiara wants to have a quick meeting around three. Does that work for you? The results from the comparison models came back after Yvonne crunched the numbers from the reader surveys. We need to create a sports division at Quench. Yvonne's report is in your inbox. Start brainstorming if you have ideas, and we'll talk about who we want to recruit to help out."

Tessa had seen it coming, even though she worried Quench was taking on too much. "Sure, I'm free."

"Perfect. See you later." Malia threw her an air-kiss and disappeared.

Tessa stretched in her chair. She needed to start writing her column. The feature with Autumn would hit big, so it had to be perfect. Restlessness nipped at her nerves, driving her up toward the window. Why was she so unmotivated? Where was her usual burst of pride and energy after realizing she'd been key to helping one more woman become confident and happy?

Tessa realized something awful: she was stuck in a rut. Nothing seemed to excite her anymore. The last few dates she'd been on were lackluster. Even worse, she'd been ghosted this weekend while waiting for her latest date at a popular wine bar. Humiliating. That hadn't happened since . . . well, never.

Watching her friends blossom with their partners was usually fulfilling, but lately she was beginning to wonder if she wasn't missing out on something. Something she never craved before. Something . . . more.

But what? Love? Did she even want to open her heart to some guy who'd make her change her life? Maybe she needed some great sex, but there hadn't been anyone she wanted to sleep with in a long time. Work was the driving force that usually satisfied her, but since the end of summer, she'd felt as if something was lacking.

Maybe she needed to do something completely different. Push past her comfort zone. Think big. Challenge the perfect little world she'd built and reigned over these past few years.

She just needed to find what it was, then jump.

~

"How do we want to approach this?" Chiara asked, steepling her fingers in front of her.

They were in the conference room, armed with laptops and scribbled notes and coconut lattes from the local Coffee Bean Café. The old purple Victorian house where they had begun their initial dreams of Quench once had drafty rooms, a leaky roof, and dusty antiques. Mike had helped them buy the place and convert it into fifteen offices with a kick-ass conference room and ladies' bathroom to rival a celebrity's. Tessa sipped her coffee, reminding herself how far they'd all come.

Now, the place held gorgeous Oriental rugs, crystal chandeliers, and polished mahogany floors. Their war room boasted a shiny cherrywood table with purple velvet chairs, and fresh flowers in elaborate vases were scattered about, filling the room with natural fragrance. It was a place they'd created together with the goal to be a company founded by women to serve women.

They'd grown as a company with a team of people they trusted, but whenever they decided to implement anything brand new, they began alone—just the three of them. Tessa knew their vision for Quench was truly personal and liked how they never believed they were too big to meet together on the smallest of details rather than delegate.

It wasn't just about self-care for women. It was about care for themselves as best friends and business partners.

As usual, she automatically looked toward the empty seat where Rory used to sit and felt her friend's presence humming in the air. Tessa breathed her in and settled in the purple chair. "I think it's important to decide how in depth we want Quench to be on the sports stuff," she said. "Do we want a weekly column? A daily blog? Podcasts? Feature articles?"

Malia nodded and sipped her latte. "Good starting point. I think we should start light so we can feel out what's working for our readers. I don't think investing significant time and money too early is smart."

"Agreed," Chiara said. "What did you think of the initial proposal I wrote based on Yvonne's report? Hire a heavy hitter to come in on a regular basis and create some exciting content?"

"A sports personality? Or a writer looking to cover sports?" Tessa asked. "Those are two different perspectives. Do we want entertainment or hard-hitting stats?"

Malia shuddered. "No to the stats. We can't do boring, and Quench isn't here to compete with serious sports news. What if we got some talent to do a weekly podcast to talk about lighter content? They could spotlight each sport and go over highlights or focus on specific athletes. Even a talk show type of thing could work, where various opinions are spouted to get discussion moving."

Chiara began typing furiously. "Love it. Our host needs a big personality, but I think they should be neutral on specific sports teams since our readers are global."

Tessa jumped in as ideas began to bubble. "It can't be male-centric or we'll get called out immediately. What if we focused on hot topics in female sports and book various guests on the podcast to keep it engaging?"

"Love," Malia snapped out. "So definitely yes to a podcast. Then we balance it with a regular column that dives into issues in sports and related to self-care?"

"Or feature certain players who are making a difference?" Chiara suggested. "In-depth interviews?"

They dug into the discussion, and after an hour, they had the plan solidly formed. Even though Tessa had resisted bringing sports into Quench, she recognized it was a good idea for their growing audience. Especially after the way Ford had presented its importance that night.

"The real challenge is picking the who," Chiara said, leaning back and tapping her pen against the table. "I don't think any one of us wants to head this new department, right?"

Tessa and Malia both shook their heads. Besides being overloaded, the true passion was lacking. Better to put someone in charge who clearly saw the value in the content and knew how to present it with uniqueness.

"I think we need a hit list," Malia said. "Let's bring it to the team. Put feelers out to sources at newspapers and media outlets for suggestions. We want someone savvy in the industry."

"Too bad we couldn't get a mentor," Chiara joked. Suddenly, her head snapped up. "Hey, what about Ford? He's famous in the sports world! I'm sure he'll help us out."

"That's a great idea," Malia said. "He could throw us some names. Maybe point us in the right direction."

Tessa arched a brow. "I see where you guys are going with this, but would he really know how to target our audience the way we need? He's a bit . . . rough."

Chiara laughed. "True, but he's smart, and I'm sure he'll at least give us a consult. Couldn't hurt."

"Have you ever listened to his show?" Malia asked.

Chiara winced. "Not really. Sebastian does, of course."

"Well, we should at least go check the man out," Tessa said. "See him in his studio and how he works. It could help to see what we do and don't like."

Then it happened. She regretted the moment the words popped out of her mouth.

"Great idea. I vote you do it," Malia said immediately.

"I second," Chiara quickly added.

Her mouth dropped open. "Are you kidding me? I have no interest in hanging out with Ford! One night babysitting was plenty. We don't get along."

Chiara's face turned pleading. "Tessa, please. You're the perfect person because you know exactly what will excite our readers."

"Plus, you told us once your new column is written, you may pull back from the makeover portion, so you'll have some time available," Malia said.

"What? I'm taking a step back to reevaluate. I still have the internship program, the beauty and fashion departments, and a bunch of other stuff. Don't you dare pull workload on me!"

"No, I know we're all busy, but all you have to do is shadow Ford for one day," Chiara cajoled. "Get an idea of how he works, what we should do when we're setting up our podcast, and get a list of names for prospective hires. I'll take care of all future communications."

"That puppy dog face may work on Ryder, but it doesn't move me," Tessa muttered, shaking her head. "I can't believe you picked me. I was the one against the whole thing."

"Exactly," Malia said. "That's why you should do it. You'll know what spin to bring to interest our readers."

Tessa knew she was in a losing battle. For some strange reason, her friends didn't see how wrong she was for the job, but they could be just as stubborn as her. She might as well surrender and get it over with. "Fine. But I think this sucks. Don't blame me if I come back with nada."

Malia grinned. "Just try to be nice to Ford on his own turf."

"I'll call him and see when we can set it up," Chiara said.

Tessa raised a brow. "And if he says no?"

"He won't. He's Veronica's godfather. I have an in."

Tessa did, too. She hadn't told her friends about the ridiculous bet and how Ford owed her a favor. She could've easily used it to get invited to the station, but since she wasn't interested in hanging out with the man anyway, she kept her mouth shut.

Besides, a favor was a precious thing. She'd use it for something better.

Chiara snapped her laptop shut. "I'll get Kelsey to clean this proposal up, and we'll bring it to the team. If we commit, I think we can get this in place for spring training."

Tessa snorted. "See, you're already using the lingo."

The others laughed. If she was going to do this, Tessa swore she'd go one hundred percent. If they were going to cover sports, it'd be done the right way. Her friends tasked her with this project because they knew she wouldn't half-ass it and counted on her to launch the next smashing success at Quench.

She'd have to see to it, even if it meant spending time with Ford.

Chapter Six

Ford walked into the studio with his coffee and stopped to check in with his producer, who regaled him with details about the night before, which included a bar hookup that he believed was love at first sight. Ford was patient with his friend and coworker as Isaac waxed poetic on his new woman, vowing this was the one.

Too bad Ford knew the truth. Isaac had been collecting one-night stands like pebbles in his pocket, always believing it would turn into a boulder.

Ford felt bad for the guy and, unfortunately, saw too many similarities. Ryder was always telling him to stop falling for women who weren't worth his attention, but Ford still believed in that elusive soul connection and swore he could feel it from a mile away. So far he'd been wrong, but one of his best traits was perseverance. Eventually, he'd be right, and it only took one win at the right time to succeed, just like in sports.

He patted Isaac on the shoulder and darted to the break room to check on the donut supply. A healthy breakfast may have been the meal of champions, but for him, a pastry put him in a good mood and set up his day. He scooped up a plain glazed, brushing the crumbs halfheartedly from his black AC/DC T-shirt, then froze as a sound hit his ears.

Crying. Definitely female.

Frowning, he took a few tentative steps down the hall. He stopped in front of the unisex bathroom, listening to the quiet, heartfelt sobs from behind the door.

Patricia.

He recognized the tones in her voice. Raking a hand through his hair, he rocked back on his heels and considered. Looked around. Then gently knocked. "Um, Patricia? Are you okay?"

Silence. He waited a bit, wondering if he should just disappear and pretend nothing happened, but the door suddenly cracked open. "Sorry. I'm okay."

Oh God, he should've known she was a perfect crier. Her gorgeous violet eyes glistened with unshed tears. Her lush, pink mouth trembled just a bit. Her bangs brushed over her brow like a model's, playing a game of sexy peekaboo.

Ford cleared his throat. "It doesn't look like you're okay. Can I help?"

Her lower lip shook. Then a small smile broke over her face, and it was like the rain clouds parted and sunshine burned over him. "You're so sweet," she murmured, giving a pretty little sniff. "But you need to get into the booth for your show. I'll be fine."

At that moment, the booth could explode and he wouldn't move an inch. "I have plenty of time. Come here. Talk to me."

Unbelievably, Patricia stepped out of the bathroom and followed him into the small conference area where they took guests before taping the show. The normal chaos of early-morning prep seemed eerily quiet, which Ford took as a sign. Any time alone with this woman was a gift, and he intended to use it well.

He quietly shut the door and turned to her.

She flipped her hair over her shoulder and let out a self-conscious laugh. "This is embarrassing. I've never done this at work before. Thank goodness no one else caught me."

"Your secret's safe with me. Did the microwave break down again? No, wait—I bet Paul told that same awful joke about the guy who walks into a bar, and you couldn't take it anymore."

Her laugh was more natural. He caught the floral scent drifting from her skin and tried not to take a big whiff to carry him through the day. She smelled absolutely edible. "I wish. It's so stupid, but I just got dumped. It was a surprise, so I'm still processing."

His heart thumped against his chest. "He must be officially the biggest idiot in the world."

Her face softened in gratitude. "Says my friend and champion."

Ford tried not to wince at the terms. "I mean it, Patricia. I've watched you this past year, and you're picking the wrong guys. You need a man to appreciate you."

She blinked. Thick, dark lashes framed a gentle gaze that turned him temporarily mute. "You are the nicest man, Ford Maddox. Next time, I'm just going to date you."

His head buzzed pleasantly. Okay, this was his shot. He couldn't blow it. "You should," he said. "Hey, why don't you meet me after work today? We'll grab a drink. Talk."

Mischief danced in her eyes, making them sparkle. "Your shift ends at noon. Are we having a martini lunch?"

He grinned and pressed a bit. "Actually, I have to work till four today. We can go to the Pier Room. You can tell me all the gory details, I'll put a hit out on him, and we'll eat fries and do shots."

Her laugh was all the sounds he loved rolled into one. She leaned over and kissed his cheek. "Why not? Thanks, Ford, for caring. I better get going—good luck on your show today."

Not able to utter a word, he watched her walk away. The black pencil skirt emphasized her swinging hips and accentuated her ass. Her silky hair swished back and forth. The click of her high heels echoed on the floor, then disappeared.

She'd called him sweet. Acted happy to talk to him. Maybe there was something he could finally build on now that she was in between boyfriends. It was so hard to get out of the friend zone she'd locked him up in, but this could be his time.

She'd agreed to a date! Sure, it was just a drink, but there was always potential for more. She'd share her story; he'd sympathize and charm her. Make her laugh but show how much more he could be to her other than a friend. He'd be sexy. She'd finally see him in a different light and realize he'd never hurt or dump her.

They'd get married and have babies. He'd be happy.

Patricia was the one.

Pumped up from the encounter, he whistled as employees started filling up the empty rooms. Isaac was frantically waving him over with only a few precious minutes before he went live, but Ford knew he'd dazzle on the segment today. He was feeling too damn good.

~

Tessa watched outside the booth as Ford wrapped up his show. She'd been a bit late this morning due to a nasty traffic jam, a broken nail, and the coffee shop getting her order wrong. Who wants to drink vanilla anything in the morning? She needed her Americano hot, strong, and energetic. Flavored drinks were for the 3:00 p.m. afternoon break, when pleasure was more important.

She sipped the hot beverage, tapped her heel, and listened to the end of the segment. Ford seemed to light up from within as he got into a lively debate about someone in right field who couldn't bat well enough to warrant his sticker price.

Tessa studied him with a critical eye, taking in his slightly disheveled appearance. Maybe he didn't care because no one really saw him. He was locked in a booth for hours. But he still met with guests. Didn't he ever dress up or act serious? Even now, he was waving his hands and guffawing in a faded concert T-shirt. The headphones smooshed his unruly hair until it exploded around his head. But his guest was animated, and they were engrossed in a passionate argument about who was going to do better in spring training. She noticed the lights flashing for the phone lines, so obviously listeners cared about what he was saying.

Hmm. Impressive. It took a lot to get people to really engage in media formats lately, because there were too many things tugging at their attention. Radio was kind of a dying industry, replaced now with podcasts. Yet Ford had created a name for himself in a narrow niche with his show.

She'd give him that. Not that she'd tell him.

Finally, he wrapped up, took care of a few things with the guy in the other booth—Tessa assumed it was a producer—and strolled toward her. Sweat clung to his brow. A grin tugged at his lips and didn't even disappear as his focus shifted to her. *Interesting.* Something had made him happy today. There was a lightness in his step she hadn't seen before.

"Hey, I saw you were late. Is that how you run all your meetings?"

And just like that, they were off and running.

"Technically, we were going to have our meeting after the show, so I was perfectly on time."

One brow shot up. "That's how you're gonna play it, huh? I thought the whole point was for you to listen to the segment and take some notes. Get an idea of what you wanted to bring to the Quench audience. Was coffee more important?"

Her cheeks burned with outrage. Oh, she disliked this man and suddenly wanted to break his happy bubble. Her voice dropped to an icy pitch. "Trust me, I got enough. I knew exactly what you were saying."

Ford rocked back on his heels with a delighted expression. "Oh, this I gotta hear. What did you learn?"

Irritation prickled her skin. "You don't think the right fielder is worth his contract amount. The guest disagreed. I'm familiar with this exact problem."

Surprise flickered in those glowing hazel eyes. "How did you relate professional baseball contracts to your own issues?"

Tessa gave a delicate shrug. "Are you kidding? Do you know how frustrated I get when I pay an exorbitant amount for a brand name, then discover it wears out, or tears, or breaks? I trusted that company and invested in a designer brand with expectations. I want what I paid for. Goodness, I could buy a knockoff if I was looking for average."

He blinked several times, as if trying to gather his thoughts. "That is the most screwed-up analogy I've ever heard in my life."

"Whatevs. All I know is if the Mets want to get to the World Series this year, they better make sure to sign players who aren't cheap imitations of the Yankees' players."

His jaw dropped. "You did not just say that. You're a Yankees fan?"

She could tell it bothered him a bit, so she leaned into it, even though she'd only learned that line after getting a crash course in baseball from Mike. "The Yankees have won more championships, right? I like winners."

A noise came from the back of his throat. Delight poured through her. Ford's happy bubble had popped.

Served him right.

"Why did I get stuck with you on this?" he asked aloud. "Why couldn't I deal with Chiara or Malia?"

She blew him a fake air-kiss. "I was elected, so I'm here. Now, shall we get started so we can move on with our day, away from each other?"

"God, yes. Follow me."

He took her into a small room with a fake leather couch, two chairs, and a worn gray industrial rug. The table had multiple scratches and tilted toward the left. The place smelled faintly of ocean air freshener, which made her nose crinkle. The overhead lights glared with a touch of blue light that made her blink. "Is this radio station broke?" she murmured, sliding into a cracked black chair, her butt rebelling.

"No, this is where we take people we want to leave quickly."

"Ha ha."

He shot her a suffering look and sat across from her. Tessa grabbed her mini laptop, opened up a fresh page of notes, then regarded him through a squinted gaze. "Okay, tell me what I need to know."

He rolled his eyes. "Only you would think sports can be condensed into a blurb for your readers. It doesn't work like that. What does Quench want to focus on?"

"Interesting stories of competition and inspiration. We don't need a place to relay scores or breakdowns of games. We have you for that."

"Why does that sound like I just rattle off stats and call it a day?"

She waved a manicured hand in the air. "No, I heard that segment, and it was good. You have a real feel for your guest and audience. You're an entertainer."

This time, he was the one who squinted. "You're a real flatterer."

"Not even close. Listen, I do appreciate you helping us out. I'm looking for tips on how I can hire a good writer for Quench who can bring something fresh from the sports world."

"Do you want Olympic champions to share their stories? Do you want to dive into the world of college basketball? Professional baseball? Do you want to focus on just women or all genders? Are you looking for plays of the week? Underdog stories? You need to narrow it down before I can truly help."

She liked his straightforwardness and how he didn't try to talk down to her. Too many men in business didn't realize they mansplained nonstop. At least Ford's disrespect wasn't wrapped up in phoniness when he poked fun at her makeovers. "We want to start with female athlete inspirations for a regular column. Then we'd like to do a roundup of sport spotlights."

"What angles?"

"We were thinking about an opinion column where certain players are picked and analyzed. That may be of interest."

He gave a skeptical look. "I'm not sure that would be interesting enough for folks who aren't hard-core sports lovers. I like the inspiration idea since that's broad enough for your readership, but what about forgetting another written piece and going with a podcast? You can do interviews, connect with people in the industry, spotlight certain sports depending on the season. I think it'll be more widely tapped into."

She blinked. "That's exactly what we discussed and planned to do. Podcasts are definitely a high audience for us now."

"Could've told me straightaway and saved us a good ten minutes of together time, T."

Oh, she despised his sultry voice as he insulted her. She pretended his words were shots deflected by Wonder Woman's gorgeous bracelets. "Needed to test you out first. Make sure your advice would help rather than hinder." She pursed her lips. "What type of segments would you suggest?"

Ford gave a cocky grin. "I'm not giving away my own secrets for my show, sweetheart. Nice try."

She shook her head. "Don't piss me off. We were doing so well, and I don't want to go back to Chiara and tell her you were an ass."

His grin disappeared. "Didn't know you were a tattletale. Fine. Take notes."

She did. He rattled off a long list of topics that seemed perfect for Quench, and as the time ticked by and they fell into a deeper discussion, Tessa became a tiny bit excited. Even though she disliked sports, the possibilities of new things always gave her a charge.

"I have some contacts you may want to check out," Ford said. "Some kick-ass women who may love an opportunity to work for Quench. I'll shoot them a quick email and let you know."

"Appreciate it. We're starting to reach out on our side, but I'm sure you know some of the best."

"No problem." He glanced down at his watch, and Tessa caught a gleam of fire in his eyes, like he couldn't wait to do something. "I think we covered it all."

"Who is she?"

He stared at her. "Huh?"

Satisfaction curled through her. "The woman you're seeing later. Who is she?"

He tried to look cool, but she'd been around lovesick men before, and Ford was exuding male pride. "Why do you care?"

She shrugged. "Don't really. Just curious why you look like Cupid shot you with his arrow."

His words came reluctantly. "Just a coworker. We're getting drinks later."

The light bulb went off. "The one you've been hot for forever? Polly?"

His face pulled like he'd tasted a lemon. "Patricia. And it hasn't been forever. Forget it, I'm not talking about this with you."

Tessa remembered he'd been practically salivating over her, but the woman hadn't given him the time of day. From what she remembered, Patricia carried a certain aura about her. She bet the woman liked brash, hot CEO types who'd dazzle her, then break her heart. Ford was too rough for her. And way too nice.

Tessa laughed. "Oh, come on, I'm just teasing. I'm glad she's giving you a shot. Did you finally get out of the friend zone?"

He seemed like he might not answer, but then spoke grudgingly. "She just broke up with someone. I'm meeting her so she can talk."

"Oh. Well, have fun." Too bad he'd be disappointed again, but it wasn't her business.

"What's that supposed to mean?"

"Nothing." She flipped her laptop closed and tucked it in her Michael Kors bag.

He crossed his arms in front of his chest like a grumpy bear. "Yes, it does. I saw your face. Why don't you just say it?"

She sighed. Sympathy leaked into her voice. "Look, Ford, she's not seeing you as her potential next date. You'll have a few beers, a few laughs, her ego will heal, and she'll take off again, blowing you air-kisses full of gratitude."

Irritation bristled from his figure. "Not this time. She said she should date me. I'm telling you, I can close this tonight."

"And I'm telling you, I've seen women like her before and know what type of men they want. She's not worth your time."

"She is. She's perfect."

Ah, crap, the man really has it bad. Tessa wished she could convince him this woman would never make him happy because she didn't value his true self, but she'd seen this stubbornness before. He'd have to go down the path on his own and follow it to the messy end. "Okay, forget I said anything."

"Did you hear back from your last makeover client yet?"

Damn. She'd wanted to brag about her win, but not now. Not before his heart was broken again by Patricia. "Yeah, I did."

"And? What happened?"

Tessa looked him dead in the eye. She wasn't going to lie. "They're officially in love and in a relationship. Guess I won the bet."

Ford looked so surprised, she began to get a bit annoyed.

"I can't believe it. How long did it take?" he asked.

"A month."

"Amazing. You just made her over and she got the guy she's been wanting."

"Yep, I told you I have some weird magic touch. Well, thanks again for all of your help. Good luck on your date."

She was surprised when he didn't try to challenge or convince her it would work out. He just nodded and watched her walk out with a thoughtful expression on his face, like he'd just discovered something he needed to analyze.

Tessa headed back to Quench, eager to get to work. At least she wouldn't have to see Ford again anytime soon.

Chapter Seven

Ford waited at the Pier Room bar and tried not to fidget. He'd changed three times, going for a casual yet nice look. He finally decided on jeans, a simple black T-shirt with the KTUZ logo, and an old denim blazer-type jacket he'd scored a few months ago. It was vintage yet had a chill vibe. He'd tried gelling his hair to tame it back and used the new, expensive cologne he'd gotten for Christmas.

He'd already ordered two glasses of merlot—Patricia's favorite wine. He wasn't big into red but figured she'd like that he drank the same thing. Ford had gotten here before happy hour so he could grab one of the high tables set back in the corner, tucked away from the streaming after-work crowds.

He was ready. Tonight was his chance to get Patricia to notice him as more than a friend.

She strolled in and even caught the bartender's eye. Sleek, shiny hair swinging past her shoulders, her face no longer filled with sadness. No, it was as if she was excited to see him. Those violet eyes held a familiar sparkle as her gaze snagged on him, and a smile curved her pink lips. She'd also changed, into dark-wash jeans, a fluffy blue sweater, and thigh-high black boots.

Ford smiled back, standing and pulling her chair out. "You look better. Did you have a good day?"

She thanked him and took a seat, setting her tiny glittery purse on the table. "Thanks to you, I managed to salvage the afternoon. Oh, is this merlot?"

"Yeah, is that okay? I can get you something else."

"No, it's perfect." She took a sip, and he tried not to stare as the red liquid clung to her lower lip before she slowly licked it away. "I think I owe you an apology. I was such a mess because the breakup took me by surprise. I hope I didn't embarrass myself."

"Don't say that. I'm glad you were able to talk to me. I want you to feel you can tell me anything."

Her gaze softened. "I really do, Ford. You're my favorite person at the station."

His heart beat madly. "Ditto."

"You know, I really thought about what you said to me before. Why do I keep running after these guys I'm attracted to but know only want a short fling? I'm looking for something deeper. Somebody I can grow with."

"I know exactly what you mean," Ford replied. "I've been looking for the same but kept going down too many side roads."

She laughed. "Exactly! Side roads! When I think of the crap I went through with Dean, I can't believe I was crying so hard this morning. I'm ready to move on to a healthy relationship. Maybe with a guy I never really looked at before."

He nodded, feeling the energy spark between them. "Yeah. You know, I read somewhere your true match is usually right under your nose. You just never noticed him before."

Her hand reached out and squeezed his arm. "Oh my God, exactly. It's like you're in my head right now and know my thoughts."

Ford tried not to think of the other places he'd like to be with her and focused on the delicate hand on his arm. Did she feel the connection, too? She had to, because she wasn't pulling back. "Great minds."

"Your girlfriend is lucky to have you."

Huh? He tried not to speak in a rush. "Oh, I don't have a girlfriend. I've been dating but can't seem to find anyone who fits for me long term."

Sympathy flashed over her face. "Oh, I'm sorry. It's hard to find the right person. I mean, it was only a few months for me and Dean, but I thought our relationship was special. I opened up and told him how I really felt, and he dumped me."

"I've had the same trouble," Ford admitted. "The moment I want to move to the next step, I seem to get cut. It'd be nice to find someone who's not afraid of commitment."

She leaned in, her gaze fastened to his. "Yes. Why is it so hard for a man to open up? I love how you're in touch with your feelings and not afraid to say what you want. It's brave."

"Just like you."

A delicate blush darkened her cheeks. She pulled back slowly, as if reluctant to break the touch. "Thanks, Ford. You make me feel like that." She cleared her throat. "So did you hear Charlie hired that new production assistant straight from NYU? Did you meet her yet? She has a fabulous voice and is looking for a mentor. He mentioned your name."

He sipped his beer, slightly disappointed she'd turned the topic to work. He'd hoped they could keep the personal vibe going a bit longer. But maybe she was a bit shy? A breather wasn't a bad idea. He wanted her to be comfortable sharing her feelings, and she'd just gotten hurt. He'd move slow. "No, not yet, but I'm always happy to help someone new in the industry. I was just meeting with Quench today to begin bringing sports into their regular lineup."

"Oh, I love Quench—it's my go-to place for all things. That's cool you know them personally. I have a bit of a girl crush on Chiara."

"She's married to my best friend."

Patricia gasped. "No way! Hey, do you think they'd be interested in advertising on the show?" she asked excitedly. "If they're launching a sports segment, some ads with us may go far. Can I use your name if I contact them? Ease my way through the cogs over there?"

"Sure. I'll make sure I set it up with someone and get you a direct number."

She beamed. "Simply the best," she sang. "I swear, I'm in such a better mood."

"Me, too."

They fell into work chatter, easy gossip, and Ford felt ridiculously happy as he basked in her presence. She had such good energy and was sweet and deserved a guy in her life who would treat her like a queen. He was the guy, and he was finally going to get his chance.

She drank the last of her wine and sighed. "I better get going. I can't thank you enough for the drink and the chat, Ford. You are an incredible man."

He ducked his head, hoping he looked humble. "Not a problem. Hey, would you like to go to dinner tomorrow night? We can grab some sushi, sake, and kick back after a long week."

She shot him a regretful look. "I'd love to, but I'm busy. Heading up to my sister's house in Syracuse and won't be back until Monday."

"Oh. Sounds like fun. Maybe the next weekend."

"Maybe—I'll let you know." She grabbed her purse and threw him an air-kiss. "You are wonderful! Have a great weekend!"

Ford watched her sashay out the door as the crowd seemed to magically part for her.

He sat there for a long time. Ordered a beer. Thought over what Tessa had told him before, and how Patricia had acted exactly like she'd described. What had happened? Why wasn't he able to get Patricia to see they'd be perfect together? Was it the ex-boyfriend and she just needed time?

Or was it him?

His mind churned over the possibilities, and his conclusion wasn't pretty. In fact, it was probably ridiculous, but he was ready to take the biggest risk of his life for the woman he loved.

He was going to win Patricia's heart, even if he had to change to do it.

And there was one person he needed to call who could help him.

~

Tessa gave a contented sigh and stretched out on the silver velvet lounger. A cut-crystal glass sat atop the side table with a mojito ready to sip. The television flickered with reruns of *Yellowstone*. A bowl of SkinnyPop was propped in her lap.

It was a perfect evening. She'd taken a hot bubble bath, then slathered on her seaweed mask, donned her long terry spa robe, and settled in. Her phone was in the other room on silent. She'd learned a while ago that periods of imposed social media detox were critical when running a successful company. Problems truly didn't need to be solved at all hours.

Plus, she had Malia and Chiara for backup. She wasn't that much of a control freak.

Kevin Costner strolled onto the screen, glaring under the brim of his cowboy hat. Luke Grimes met him halfway, his sexy mussed hair blowing in the wind. Her body shivered in bliss. What was it about a cowboy that was so timeless? Maybe she needed to start dating men from Montana.

The doorbell rang.

She tried to frown, but her brows were frozen by the mask. Letting out a pained groan, she cursed her friends under her breath, knowing they were the only ones it could be. Even Uncle Bart would never drive all the way to her house for any type of emergency.

Tessa peeked out the side window and froze.

No. Way.

What the hell was Ford doing here?

She decided to keep quiet and hoped he'd go away. She'd pretend she was still in the tub and couldn't hear him.

He began to pound on the door. "Tessa, please open the door! I kept trying to text and call, but you wouldn't answer. It's an emergency!"

Oh my God, what if someone is hurt? She fumbled for the lock and threw open the door. "What's the matter? What happened?"

His eyes widened as he took in her getup. "Wow, you really weren't expecting company, were you? Why didn't you answer your phone?"

Tessa almost stamped her foot in frustration. "I'm social detoxing! Why are you here?"

"I need to talk." He barreled in and closed the door behind him. "I need help."

"Damn right you need help. Someone needs to teach you the rules of polite society and how you don't go banging on people's doors late at night!"

"You can yell at me all you want as long as you listen." He cocked his head and studied her face. "Does that hurt? Why is it green?"

Oh. My. God.

She was still wearing the seaweed mask. If it had been anyone but Ford, she would've been mortified, but she refused to feel embarrassed when he was the one crashing into her safe space. Tessa pulled herself up to her full height and threw her shoulders back. Her voice dripped icicles. "None of your business. Talk fast."

"You don't happen to have any beer, do you?" Unbelievably, he was already moving into her kitchen and opening the refrigerator like he lived there. He pulled out a lone Heineken and beamed with pleasure.

"Sure. Help yourself," she said sarcastically. Tessa yanked her sash tighter and resettled on her couch. "What's this about?"

Ford took a slug of beer, wiped his mouth with the back of his hand, and burst out with his request. "I want you to give me a makeover. I want you to make Patricia fall in love with me."

Her jaw unhinged. In her wildest imagination, Tessa would've never come up with this scenario. Ford Maddox was asking her for a makeover. Something he'd been making fun of her about for years. The man she preferred to avoid. The man who didn't like her.

She couldn't help it. She collapsed into laughter. "This is a joke, right?"

Irritation crossed his craggy features. "No. I mean it. I know it's a bit unconventional, but I've thought long and hard about this, and you could be the solution to my problem."

Tessa grabbed her mojito and took a healthy sip. Her head still spun from his announcement. "Ford, this doesn't make any sense. I thought you had a date with her tonight."

His eyes filled with a touch of pain that struck her hard. "You were right," he said quietly. "She looks at me only as a friend. She even air-kissed me. Just like you said."

A tiny bit of regret leaked through. Tessa hadn't wanted the guy hurt. Wow, he really had deeper feelings for this woman than she'd believed. She nibbled on her lower lip, deep in thought. "Okay, tell me about the whole encounter. What happened?"

He did. She tried not to wince as he detailed his enthusiasm to see her, his sweet support of her heartbreak, and the obvious begging as he asked her out. He'd done everything wrong for a woman like Patricia. She'd be back in her ex's bed within the week, especially if the guy offered her excitement and the unknown.

"Ford, can I be truthful with you?"

"Absolutely."

"Patricia is not the woman meant for you. I've known the type, and I'm telling you, she doesn't have the heart you need for a long-term relationship. All that crap about her wanting to settle down? It's lies."

"She doesn't lie."

His emphatic defense caught Tessa off guard. She studied him for a bit, noting the absolute intensity of his gaze. *Hmm.* The man had passion. She'd underestimated his capacity for blind loyalty to the person he loved. A twinge in her chest startled her, but Tessa pushed it aside. "Not on purpose. She's lying to herself because she thinks she *should* want to settle down at this point. She's addicted to the game—the chase. She's not ready for a nice guy."

His jaw clenched. "If I can get a chance with her, I swear I can make her love me."

Tessa blinked. Pondered his words. Then told the truth. "I don't think so, Ford."

"I do. All I need is help to get there. To catch her attention and date her."

"Why her? There are a million other women out there! You don't even know her that well. You have no idea what lies beneath the surface."

Ford rubbed his head, tousling the mussed strands of hair. He began to pace, gripping his beer in one hand. "Have you ever wanted something so bad it fills up your entire being? I've been into this woman for over two years. I've watched her get screwed over by a number of guys. I've seen her heart—she's deserving of so much more, and I can give it to her. But I need help catching her interest. Become who she thinks she wants so I can then change her mind once we get to know one another. Do you follow?"

Tessa dropped her face in her palms, then remembered she still had goop coating her skin. "Dammit, why do you have to be so stubborn? I can't take this on for you. It's too much. I don't have the time or the heart. Plus, we don't get along. We'd fight. You'd never do anything I tell you."

"Yes, I would. I swear, you'd be the boss and I won't question you. And you'll get something out of it, too."

She snorted. "Like what? What could I possibly get out of turning you into Frankenstein's monster?"

"A column. A special column."

Tessa narrowed her gaze. "What are you talking about?"

"You've done makeover magic with women for Quench, right? What about a guy? What if I let you use me for a feature? As long as we can change the names and make it anonymous, I can give you all the info you need to do a different type of column. I bet the readers would love it."

She opened her mouth to tell him she'd decided to take a break from makeovers, then stopped. *Interesting,* she thought. She'd never offered an opposite view on the reader makeover. What would it be like to present a man in love with a woman, willing to do whatever to win her over? The angle was new and fresh, and it'd give the column a different perspective. Maybe it would reinvigorate her interest.

But doubt crept in her voice. "Would you really subject yourself to all of this, allowing me to document every step of the makeover and training? Opening up to readers in an intimate way? Listening to everything I say?"

"Not everything. Just how it applies to this," he corrected.

She tried to smile, but her lips were firmly frozen. "Close enough. But seriously, it's an intense process, Ford. And you have to know, if I take this on, you still may not get Patricia. You need to be realistic."

"I know there aren't guarantees." Determination radiated from his figure. "I just want a fair shot, and I'm willing to do anything to get it. She's worth it."

Tessa wondered what it would be like to have a man who loved her like that. But was it love? Ford had an image in his head of who Patricia was, just like so many of her past readers. Even if her makeover worked, he might be surprised at who he truly wins in the end.

But that wasn't her business.

As she stared at him, Tessa realized he wanted this badly. So badly, she might be able to up the stakes. "I'd need to have one more thing from you."

"The favor you won?"

She managed a small laugh between her stiff lips. "No, that favor is for later. For me. In addition, if I agree to take you on, I'd like you to do the first few podcasts for Quench. To get things set up in the right direction."

Ford shook his head. "You play dirty. Isn't exposing my inner life to the world enough for you? Now you want me to work for Quench?"

"We've got a lot to set up to get the new division going, but having you on a sports podcast with material geared toward our readers would make a splash. You're well known enough for it to be interesting."

"Your respect for my work is tear-worthy."

"Now, let's not get all emotional."

He threw back his head, but he was laughing. "You're such a pain in the ass."

"Hey, you came to me, remember? Interrupting my spa evening with your proposals. You should be thrilled I'm considering it."

"I stink of desperation. I'm embarrassed."

"Do we have a deal?"

"Yes, Black Lagoon Girl. We have a deal."

Tessa tried to laugh, but now her face was mummified. She put up a hand. "I have to wash this off. Be right back."

She headed to the bathroom and spent some time scrubbing off the seaweed. Her skin was fresh and dewy after she patted it dry. When she reentered the living room, Ford gave a long whistle. "You look like a completely different person. What a knockout."

She flopped back down on her lounger and shot him a look. "There's no need to kiss my ass. We've bargained and made our deal. I'm not a cheater."

Ford sat on the sofa next to her, wincing when his butt hit the hard cushion. "Ugh, how can you enjoy watching a show on this stuff? It's not soft and cushy."

"I prefer hard. Hard cushions, mattresses, and chairs. It keeps the posture straight and the back prepped."

He squirmed around. "Only you would create work for hanging around. Now, how do we start?"

"Ready to dive in, huh, Romeo? Why don't you take this last night off? You'll have a busy road ahead."

"I don't think this is going to be brain surgery. We change my wardrobe, give me some cool lines, and a bit of training. I'm a fast learner."

His comment made her laugh long and hard. "You have no clue, do you? My magic doesn't come easy. But since you're so eager to get started, I'll give you some homework that's important."

"Awesome. Shoot."

"Gather up everything you know about Patricia and write it down for me."

He gave her a disappointed look. "That's it? Are you going to hire a private investigator?"

"Nope. I don't need to. For now, think of everything you know about her. Her past, her present, her job, her dates—there's no detail too small. We'll start from there."

"Sounds easy."

Tessa practically purred and rubbed her hands together. Finally, she'd be able to show him what her work could really do. A makeover was an art form, not the bunch of fluff he believed. She'd break Ford down and transform him. By the time she was done, he'd have Patricia, but it wouldn't be easy. Nothing worthwhile ever was.

"Good. That's all I need for now."

He nodded and stared at her. Slowly, she raised a brow. "Oh, do you want me to go now?" he asked.

"Yes, please. And don't think just because we're working together I'm going to take nightly meetings. We'll adhere to a strict schedule."

Amusement gleamed in his eyes. "Sure. Wouldn't want to mess up your daily itinerary. Do you have breakdowns over surprises?"

Her voice clipped out in irritation. "Do you want me to change my mind about helping you?"

He waved his hands in the air. "I'm not being a jerk—I'm simply curious. You seem to need a lot of order. Doesn't leave much room for surprises or too much emotion."

"I have plenty of emotion in my life. And I enjoy surprises on my terms."

He grinned and got up from the couch. "Bet you do. Hey, I really do appreciate this, T—I mean, Tessa. I'll email you my notes ASAP."

Ford let himself out, leaving her in silence.

She sipped her mojito and thought over the encounter. Ford had been right. She disliked surprises, but this was one that could be great for Quench. Plus, helping out Ryder's best friend would look good on her godmother résumé.

Of course, it also meant she'd be spending a lot of time with Ford. If she did this right, he'd need a complete rework from top to bottom. But it would be worth it.

A trickle of excitement raced through her. This was a challenge. Even though she didn't think Patricia would make Ford happy long term, he needed to see it for himself. And maybe she was wrong. Maybe this woman would truly fall in love with him, and they'd both live happily ever after.

Surprising things happened all the time. Chiara and Ryder had had a rough journey, but they were deliriously happy now. Even Malia and

Palmer had managed to make things work when they'd believed they wanted different things.

Tessa briefly wondered how she'd like to be surprised. With a serious relationship? A sexy affair? A new motivation and passion for her job?

She didn't know. Not yet. But right now, she wanted one thing: to relax and watch the hot cowboys on her screen.

She pressed the play button, dug into her popcorn, and kept her focus on the show.

Chapter Eight

"You did what?" Ryder stopped and stared in shock.

They were walking into the Dream On Youth Center for a special Sunday breakfast. The once-sparse grounds now bloomed with life. A new basketball court, playground, and garden center drew kids of all ages, and lessons were offered in sports and horticulture. Ford had mocked the latter idea at first, figuring no kid wanted to learn how to grow food, but it was one of their most popular programs. He'd grown up eating Pop-Tarts for breakfast and washing them down with packaged juices. It was nice to see a smarter generation more focused on their health.

Ford faced his friend and tried not to get defensive. "Why are you so surprised? You know how I feel about Patricia. Tessa's an expert and can help. All I had to do is give her some notes for her article. And I agreed to do a few podcast episodes."

Ryder tilted his head and shook it back and forth. "Dude, what were you thinking? First up, changing yourself for this woman makes no sense. If she falls for you, are you going to tell her the truth about what you did?"

Ford glared. "I don't know yet! I'll deal with it once we're madly in love, and then I'm sure she'll be flattered. I need some support, man."

He resumed walking, and Ryder followed. "You know I always have your back, but this is a stretch, even for you. I can't believe Tessa agreed to this."

"She'd be great at hostage negotiation."

"You two fight all the time. How are you going to trust her to pick apart your life and . . . remake you?"

Ford waved his hand in the air and pushed through the double doors. "It'll be worth it. I'm tired of chasing other women when my heart is always with Patricia. I want to commit to this process and see if it works."

They entered the main gymnasium, which had been restored to its former glory. It boasted shiny new floors, bright blue paint, rebuilt walls, and a roof that no longer leaked. The closets were stocked with games and sports equipment. The usual sparse crowd of teens from last year had grown to a vibrant group of kids representing all ages. Parents and friends accompanied the youths, everyone waiting in the buffet lines for a hot breakfast and some social time.

Ford and Ryder paused, looking around, then shared a glance. They both had a soft spot for the youth center—a place where kids could be safe and have a good time. They'd lost a few along the way to drugs or depression or heartbreak, but they focused on who was here right now. The grant from the Quench Foundation had also bestowed a counselor for mental health, and now the kids in trouble had a dedicated person to help them through rough times.

"Your wife did good," Ford said with a grin. The foundation had been Chiara's brainchild, and she had given its first official grant to the youth center.

"They all did. That's one powerful group of women." Ryder cut him a side look. "Just be careful with Tessa. She's a fierce one, and I don't want you killing each other."

"I can handle her."

Ryder snorted.

A young man walked over, his shoulder-length hair tied back in a neat band, long legs clad in jeans and old sneakers.

"Hey, Derek! What's up, man?" Ford greeted him, bumping elbows with the kid.

Ryder gave him a hug, slapping him on the back. "Helping out or here for second breakfast?"

The kid gave a crooked grin, and Ford felt his heart lighten. "Both. My mom came with me, too. She's sitting with Maria and Pru."

"How's school?"

Derek's blue eyes were clear and peaceful. "Pretty good. Classes are hard this year, but my boss is cool. Really flexible on my schedule so I'm able to balance things."

Ford's heart squeezed with emotion. Last year, Derek had almost been lost to his addiction again, ending up in rehab. It had destroyed Ryder especially, who was close to the young man and blamed himself for not doing more. But now, Derek had been clean for ten months, working steadily and creating a life for himself. Seeing him now with renewed hope stirred Ford. All these kids were important to him, and volunteering on weekends gave him a sense of belonging and purpose. It was something he admired in others, too. Ford bet Patricia did some things for her community. Her heart seemed to be so open to others.

They chatted a bit more, and Ford made the rounds. He ate eggs and hash browns, joked with the kids and other staff, and settled at the table next to Maria and Pru. The two teens were close but completely different. Pru wore her usual denim jacket and sneakers, peering over her glasses as she assessed the world with her genius mathematical mind. Her parents were always pushing her toward a medical profession, but she was stubborn and dedicated to finding her own path. Some of their fights were legendary, and she sought solace at the youth center.

Maria was petite, with curly dark hair exploding around her head and eyes that had seen too much. She hadn't spoken for two years after being placed with her foster parents, but when she'd been given a canvas to paint, she bloomed. Ford figured she'd be a famous artist one day—her work was disturbing, with bold, dark slashes of color and a moodiness that hinted at her past. She was interning with Quench under Tessa's tutelage, studying photography there and being shown the ins and outs of the art department.

They made small talk as Ford drank his coffee and caught up. "Are you still liking it over at Quench?" he asked curiously.

Maria's face lit up. "Yeah. Magda is the bomb. She's teaching me all about how to catch the hidden emotion in a photograph. And Tessa is so nice. Do you know she hooked me up on one of their big campaigns for their organic beauty spotlight and made sure I was involved with every step?"

"Organic beauty?" he repeated, frowning. "No offense, Maria, but that doesn't sound like you."

Pru laughed. "Right? I told her the same thing, but the stuff she's learning is sick. She'll be able to get a job anywhere after this, plus work on her personal art."

Maria nodded. "It's a way to finance my dreams. At least, that's what Tessa told me. Makes sense."

He drew back in surprise. The girl had really taken to Tessa. He might not get along with her, but the woman had more heart than he'd originally thought. He figured she was only interested in the way she looked and how perfect everything was around her. Seems she was a bit deeper than that.

Good. Because he needed to trust her on some level in order to let her have full access to his life.

After crashing her home spa night, he'd spent the evening writing down every detail about Patricia and sent it over. They were supposed to meet in the upcoming week to begin the process, but when he asked what was next, she refused to tell him. She may not have liked surprises, but she seemed to like springing them on others.

Ryder tapped his shoulder. "Finished? Derek has a group for basketball. You in?"

"I'm in."

Pru and Maria also jumped up. "We're in," they said together.

"Nice. But be easy on the guys, okay?" Ford warned. "Last time you almost gave Manny a black eye with your shoulder jerk."

Pru gave a bit of an evil laugh, and Maria looked smug.

He shook his head and headed outside, ignoring Manny's whine when he saw the girls were also playing. Ford made a mental note to bring that type of energy to the podcasts he did for Quench. Women's basketball was exploding in popularity, and he figured it'd be a great topic to start with. His mind spun with ideas as he grabbed the ball and passed to Ryder, splitting up the teams.

He might be in Tessa's hands, but she was also in his. He intended to give the woman a deep dive into sports, whether she liked it or not.

The thought gave him a burst of energy as he brought his A game to the court.

~

"You did what?"

Tessa ignored her friends' matching guppy expressions and focused on her blueberry pancakes. Mike only used wild blueberries with a touch of fresh whipped cream, elevating him to breakfast God status. If she wasn't getting sex, she'd sure as hell give herself carbs.

Both inspired the same feelings, anyway.

As she often did after getting shocking news, Malia had gone mute, so Chiara spoke. "I don't understand. You don't like Ford. Why would you be giving him a full makeover?"

Tessa forked one more mouthful before answering. "Because he begged me. He's more serious about Patricia than I believed. Thinks he's in love with her."

Chiara groaned. "How could he love her? He doesn't even know her!"

Malia rallied and came back to life. "This is the strangest agreement ever. Did you get to check this woman out when you were at the radio station?"

"No, she wasn't there. But it's a great opportunity. Besides giving us a makeover column from the male point of view, he agreed to do a few podcasts, which will set Quench up for the big reveal of our new sports column."

"I can't believe it," Chiara murmured. "Ford doesn't seem the type to want to change who he is for someone else."

"Love makes us do funny things," Malia said. Her braids swung as she shook her head. "Look at what hoops Palmer jumped through in order to win me over."

Tessa cracked up. "Girl, you wanted him just as bad! You were just too scared to admit it."

Malia stuck out her tongue. "Wait till you get tangled up with a guy. I'm going to torture you."

Tessa practically beamed with pride. "You can try, but we all know I'm immune to boy drama. They come and go like the seasons—to be enjoyed in the moment, then to be bid goodbye when time is up."

"That's awful," Chiara announced. "You just haven't met the man who's right for you. God help all of us when you do."

"Whatevs. In the meantime, I'll help Ford, I'll get a juicy makeover exclusive, and he'll help Quench. Triple crown winner."

"You're terrible," Malia said with a sigh.

"Who's terrible?" Mike asked, appearing at the table.

Chiara pointed across the booth. "Tessa. She's doing a makeover on Ford so he can win the woman of his dreams."

Mike widened his eyes. "No kidding. Didn't think Ford was the type to want to do any of that stuff. You're not gonna make him look weird, are you?"

Tessa laughed. "Of course not. Just let me work my magic. Speaking of which, Emma mentioned she'd drop by today. Has she been here?"

Mike's expression changed in a snap. He stared at the door, a tiny frown of worry creasing his brow. "Not yet."

"Have you talked to her lately?" Chiara asked gently.

The older man scratched his head. "Yeah. We've been talking more regularly. I . . . called her last night."

Tessa tried not to screech with delight. "Good for you! What'd you say?"

Her friends all held their breath. Mike shifted his feet. "I, um, told her there was a Scrabble tournament at the Barnes & Noble and said she should enter."

"And?" Chiara prodded.

"That's it. I didn't want her to miss it."

Tessa groaned. "Mike, enough. It's great you're having these amazing phone calls on a regular basis, but it's been months. You need to step it up."

"You think Arthur is ready to make his big move?" he asked worriedly. "That guy's a real player."

Malia clamped her lips together in an obvious effort not to laugh. Arthur was Emma's dear friend, who was sweet, sophisticated, and definitely not a player. "I think they're just good friends," she said.

"But it could be more if you don't make your move," Tessa added. She didn't think Arthur was interested in Emma romantically, but if Mike waited too long, he could miss his chance. "It's time."

"I know. I just felt I needed to move slow after the way I treated her. I want her to trust me."

Tessa's heart softened. In his fear he wasn't good enough for her, he'd pushed Emma away with a bit of cruelty. It took a heartfelt confession from Emma to make Mike realize he'd been pushing her away because he was afraid of his own feelings, but by then, Emma had decided to move on. For the past few months, he'd been trying to apologize and show her he was ready to take a leap with her.

The bell tinkled, and on cue, Emma came in with Arthur. The couple stopped to say hello, and Tessa studied them. Emma seemed to be comfortable and easy in Arthur's presence. The moment she turned to Mike, though, tension crackled through her body, and her eyes shuttered behind her stylish glasses.

Yeah, Emma still had a crush.

The energy between them hummed—the type of energy Tessa had sensed the moment the two of them had been in the same room together. Mike had originally reacted with cool disdain, but it was the connection Tessa always concentrated on. Words were quite different from actions. She was an expert in reading body language and subtle signs. Mike had fallen for Emma just as hard. But he didn't know how to express it yet.

"Michael. How are you?" Emma asked with a smile.

Tessa noticed he'd stopped correcting his name to Mike and seemed pleased she addressed him. "I'm good. I have a new shipment of wild blueberries for your pancakes. Tessa's having them now."

"They're amazing," she affirmed.

Arthur tilted his head. His fedora gave him a stately air along with his sharp suit and red carnation in his lapel. His smile was kind as he directed his attention to Mike. "I think I'll go the traditional route with eggs over easy and a side of bacon," he said cheerfully. Arthur and Emma took a seat in the neighboring booth.

Mike grimaced, but Tessa saw how he was trying hard to be nice.

She chatted with her friends, catching up on gossip and news on the baby and wedding front, keeping an ear trained on the booth behind them. Tessa listened as Mike kept stopping by their table, complimenting Emma on her new green dress. Her thank-you sounded genuinely surprised.

Malia leaned in. "Stop eavesdropping," she whispered. "He'll never ask her out. He's too terrified."

"He will. He just needs to get up his courage."

"Emma will be celebrating her centennial by the time they go to dinner," Chiara whispered back, her lips tugging in a smile.

Mike came out with Emma's tea and set a cup of coffee next to Arthur. "Did you sign up for that Scrabble tournament I told you about?" Mike asked, his voice forcibly casual.

"I did, thank you. Arthur signed up, too."

A few beats of silence. Tessa winced.

"I didn't know you played Scrabble, Art," Mike said gruffly.

"I didn't, but Emma got me hooked. I'm more of a poker player, but I must admit, there's a certain charm in creating words that fit together. Have you tried that new game Wordle?"

"Oh, it's wonderful!" Emma said. "I'm addicted. Michael, you would love it."

"Maybe you can teach it to me sometime."

"Of course, I'd be happy to."

Tension simmered in the air. Tessa held her breath, casually twisting around to watch the scene unfold. Mike shifted back and forth on his heels, trying not to glare at Arthur, his face twisted up as if he was about to do something horrible.

Oh God. She hoped he didn't say anything he'd regret later.

"Emma, do you want to go out with me to dinner this Thursday night?"

Silence fell. The busy click-clack of dishes and murmuring chatter stopped. Tessa couldn't look. It was too big of a move, yet her heart sang at Mike's bravery.

Seconds stretched. Tension tightened. It seemed like forever until Emma decided to answer. "Yes. I think that sounds lovely."

Tessa's breath whooshed out. Chiara and Malia reached over to squeeze hands, barely able to contain their glee. He'd done it! Mike asked her out, and finally they could move on to a real courtship.

"That's great." Mike turned his head and pointed at them. "Girls, let's go to the steakhouse. Seven p.m. My treat for all of you."

Tessa's jaw dropped.

So did Emma's.

Arthur looked as if he was about to laugh, but he was too much of a gentleman.

Mike directed his next statement to the other man. "Sorry, Art, this is just for the ladies. Hope you understand."

Arthur's lip twitched. "Absolutely. It sounds delightful. I have a card game Thursday, anyway."

Mike stuck out his chest like a proud peacock and strutted back into the kitchen.

Tessa dropped her forehead into her hands. "I can't do this. I'm too tired."

"You're the Cupid in this screwed-up mess," Malia hissed. "I don't want to go to dinner with them Thursday night! I want to have sex with Palmer!"

Chiara groaned. "I can't believe we have to make polite conversation while playing chaperone to a grown man. This is ridiculous. Emma's going to kill him, then us."

"Why are you mad at me?" Tessa asked. "I didn't do anything."

"Forget it. I'm going home." Chiara stood up, grabbed her purse, waved goodbye to Emma and Arthur, and stomped out.

Malia glared at her. "This whole matchmaking thing is backfiring. Maybe it's a warning for you this thing with Ford could be a giant mistake. Maybe you should just back out. Let him do the work on his own."

"I promised him, Mal. Look, I'll talk to Mike and tell him it's best if he goes out alone with Emma, okay? I'll fix it."

"Fine. I'll talk to you later." She disappeared and left Tessa alone in the booth with too many pancakes. She cranked her head around to catch Emma's gaze. "Emma, let me talk to Mike. He just got nervous."

"Tessa Harper, you will do no such thing," Emma said with a snap to her voice. Her lips pursed in disapproval. "Michael will take all of us to dinner and that's that. I don't want you forcing him to do something he's not comfortable with."

Arthur patted Emma's shoulder. "You'll all have a good time."

Tessa gave up. She was becoming exhausted with all this matchmaking.

Maybe it was best she surrender to Thursday night and live to fight another day.

Chapter Nine

Tessa met Ford at the Japanese restaurant he'd planned to take Patricia to on their first date. She winced when she saw most of the seating was at the counter sushi bar and the few tables they did boast were rickety, cheap wood that would be uncomfortable after fifteen minutes. Colorful fake lanterns riddled the walls along with some very questionable decor, including a few giant framed portraits of what looked like fish. Fish about to be served on a plate.

Not an ounce of romance in sight.

Tessa grabbed a wet wipe and quickly sanitized the table while Ford rolled his eyes. "Really? I love this place—their sushi is the best. Patricia adores sushi."

"Not questioning the food, just the atmosphere. How did you think to seduce Patricia in this place? It screams buddy date."

The look of astonishment on his craggy features told Tessa she was in trouble. He really had no clue. "It's fun, casual, and offers little pressure. You think I should have tried to take her to some cozy Italian place with Sinatra in the background and candles everywhere? That would have freaked her out."

"Yes, that should be the plan, freaked out or not. At least it would force her to look at you as a man and not a friend."

He snapped his mouth shut after that remark. She almost felt sorry for him.

"Why are we here anyway?" he grumbled, sipping his water.

"To begin your journey. Plus, you're buying me dinner. I don't feel like cooking tonight."

Ford shook his head. "Should've known." The waitress stopped by and took their order of various rolls, miso soup, and sake. "Did you look over the notes I sent you?" he asked once she left.

"Yes. I have a tentative plan sketched out, but we have to follow certain steps. You may not like what I tell you, but remember your promise. You need to trust me."

He held up his hands. "I will. Stop with all the dramatic suspense. Tell me what you learned."

She shot him a disapproving look but began to talk. "Patricia likes a certain type of man. Unfortunately, right now, you're not it. But we'll get you there." Tessa didn't need her notes; they were imprinted in her memory after studying them for a while. "She's turned on by a very masculine man who's a bit cool around the edges. Basically, she loves the chase—that's what gives her satisfaction. The harder she needs to chase, the bigger reward it is for her."

"I don't think—"

She cut him off with a hard wave. "Just listen. I did some social media stalking. Her pattern is easy to spot. Successful, clean-cut, nicely dressed executive type is her kryptonite. He grabs her attention, keeps her on the line, reels her in, then throws her back in the water. She's heartbroken but not ready to move on yet to Mr. Nice Guy, so she seeks out the same type over and over."

"I can break the pattern."

His emphatic vow touched her. "You probably can, but first you need to be Mr. Hot Asshole. Then you can be nice to her."

"This is fucked up."

"Love is fucked up, dude. Are you still with me?"

He nodded, a bit more forlornly. Their sake and soup were dropped on the table. She kept speaking. "Okay, she likes to be wined and dined.

Did you see her IG? Fancy places with just a masculine hand in the shot. It's obvious she's trying to hide *who* she's with, which makes me think he may have been either a cheater or just recently broke up with someone to date Patricia."

"That is not her. She wouldn't be with a cheater."

"Ford, she may. Listen, this is just recon so we can get her to you, okay? It's a good thing she just broke up with someone, because there's a space there you need to step into. Immediately."

"Awesome. How do I ask her out?"

She snorted. "You're not listening. You don't ask her out. You need to stick another woman under her nose. A woman you're really into. A hot woman who seems to be with you just for the sex."

Ford started to say something, then stopped. His eyes widened as he tried to process what she was saying. "I'm gonna be man candy?"

Tessa laughed. "Kind of. Look, right now it's obvious you're into her, and maybe she's mad at herself for not wanting to date you—knowing you're a good guy—so you need to be the bad boy. We need to clean up your appearance and change your wardrobe. You need to stop treating her like a friend and more like a hot woman who you'd like to bang but can't because you're suddenly hooked up. There's nothing more attractive than someone who's with someone else."

"That's awful."

"Well, it's life."

He slurped his soup and seemed to ponder. Tessa knew she was giving him a lot of info he didn't like, so she waited him out.

"How am I supposed to pull this off?" he finally asked. "There's no other woman in my life, and I'm certainly not going to fake-date some poor female and lie."

"No, that would be too mean. I'll have to do it."

His spoon clattered into the bowl, causing a small splash. "You're gonna what?"

"Shush. I'll pretend to be your current lover. It won't take much—just a few random encounters showing you're a hot commodity. That will grab Patricia's attention and get her looking. With your new appearance and cool persona, I'm sure she'll start seeing you in a different light."

"This is insane," he murmured. "Have you done this with any of your other readers?"

"No, and normally I'd highly advise against it. I believe by changing on the inside to someone you love, you automatically attract the things you want in the universe. Being untrue to yourself isn't the way to find your soul mate."

"Then why the hell are you doing it with me?"

She glowered at his tone. "Because you're stubborn and have convinced yourself all's fair in love and war. I'm being nice and allowing you to use me, because I don't see any other way at this point. You're too far gone."

He scratched his head. "You make no sense. You never did."

"Well, neither do you," Tessa said. "I told you before, I'm not continuing down this path if you're going to insult or badger me along the way."

"Fine! I'm in, whatever you think. You'll pose as my hot sex partner. Awesome."

She spit out half a laugh. "Good. I'll plan to come in during one of your tapings when you're sure she'll be there. We'll put on a show and knock her a bit off course. Your sudden appearance change will go nicely with the story that I bought you all these new clothes so it won't look like you're doing anything different specifically for her."

"This is complicated."

The sushi rolls were dropped off. Tessa took her time swirling the perfect amount of wasabi with soy sauce, then delicately dipped the piece with her chopsticks. The flavor was perfect. The fish was fresh, the rice firm, and she gave Ford points for at least being able to spot excellent sushi. "You'll need to follow my lead when we're together. Also, we'll need to get physical. You're not afraid to touch a woman, right?"

He choked on his sushi. Tessa handed him a napkin and he swiped at his watery eyes. "Are you kidding me? Of course, I'm not afraid—I've had sex before!"

She rolled her eyes. "I know that, idiot. I just want to be sure you're comfortable with PDA. It's the only way to make a quick, lasting impression. You can't pull away if I have to stick my tongue in your mouth."

"This is not happening," he muttered.

She caught the flush on his cheeks and softened. Ford was kind of cute when he was embarrassed. Not that she liked the idea of kissing him. She certainly didn't like whoring herself out for his benefit, but she'd gone over all the scenarios and this was the best one. He needed someone he could trust, and she could put up with a few sloppy kisses. She'd done it before with other men who didn't turn her on. Most of them were nice guys, too. Guys she really wanted to like and settle down with because they'd be great husbands, but she was never interested.

The idea she could be a little like Patricia made her gut coil tight. *Not a good thought to pursue right now.* Besides, she didn't get caught up in ridiculous chases for men who weren't good for her. Silly to even question herself.

Tessa took a sip of the hot sake, which burned going down her throat. Ford did the same and seemed to settle down. "Fine. We'll kiss and grope each other. Not that I think Patricia will care. Don't get me wrong—we'll go with your plan, but I don't think you know her like you think."

She wished at that moment Ford was right, but they'd soon find out. "Good, then we agree. I don't want to send you a script, because it needs to be natural. So go with the flow. The story is I pursued you after

I came to the show last week and we began dating. She doesn't know anything about me, right?"

He shook his head. "Just that you're an owner of Quench. I told her Ryder's wife works there, too, and she knows he's my best friend."

"We can get around the question if she asks why we never dated before this. Let me know when she's there this week and I'll come in."

"Got it."

Tessa nodded, finishing up her sushi, and thought of the best way to approach her next problem. She always took the delicate approach when it came to someone's appearance, but something told her with Ford, it was best to be straight up. "We need to change your look."

"Yeah, I figured a trim, maybe some new jeans? I think my shoes are good, though."

"I'm thinking bigger."

Ford cocked his head. "How big?"

She tried not to look pointedly at his shaggy hair and the beard that hid the lower half of his face. "Massive overhaul. I work with Dionne over at Hair Magic—she's wonderful and takes good care of my readers."

"Aren't they women? Maybe I should go to one of those hip barbers."

Tessa shook her head. "No, we go to Dionne. She'll know what to do with you."

"I'm trying not to be scared."

Her grin was all teeth. "It's overdue. Everyone needs to transform their look now and then. Hey, how many concert T-shirts do you have?"

He literally threw out his chest with pride. "About a dozen. Cool, huh? I frequent this vintage heavy metal store where I do most of my shopping. Not the fancy stuff. I save that for T.J. Maxx. Designer, you know?"

She tried not to wince, but it was hard. "Sure, love saving some bucks, but we're going to upgrade a bit more. I also need to see your apartment."

"Why?"

"Patricia will eventually come over if your plan works. It has to emit the same cool vibe your new look does. Everything needs to match."

He scratched his head. "This is a lot of work."

"Second-guessing? We can pull the plug—it's not too late." Tessa held her breath and hoped he'd agree. She was confident in her abilities, but a strange foreboding gripped her, a warning that told her this time things wouldn't work out the way they normally did. She practically scented fate hovering over them, ready to jump in at the slightest misstep.

Chills ran down her spine. Something was wrong.

Abort. Abort the mission, her mind screamed.

"Ford, maybe we should rethink—"

"No, it's going to work. I'm tired of not getting what I want." Suddenly, his gaze veered and those hazel eyes pierced hers, stunning with intensity. "I've spent most of my life chasing love, and the moment I saw Patricia, I knew. I just didn't know how to convince her. This is my damn love story, and I'm going all the way."

Her breath slowly leaked out of her lungs. Maybe she was wrong. Maybe it would go as planned, and they'd end up happy. She forced a smile. "Then we do it." She patted the napkin to her lips. "When do you think you can schedule the podcasts for Quench?"

Now, his smile seemed a bit smug. "About that. I think you'll need to go through some training first. Women's basketball has been huge in the headlines, and I think it's a good jumping-off point. On-target for your audience, and plenty of topics to discuss. I reached out to one of the players who's been on my show before. She said she'd be happy to be a guest for Quench."

"That's great! We're starting to round up our interview candidates for the new column. There's a lot of qualified sportswriters who have the audience and slant we'd like, but the podcast is more organic."

"Exactly." He pointed at her. "Which is why you need to start learning a bit about sports. You can come over to my place on Friday and we'll combine tasks. You can give my apartment a look over, and I'll introduce you to the joys of women's basketball. There's a game on at seven."

She shook her head so hard she felt her curls bounce. "Hell no. I'm not going to be in charge of this division anyway. I was only authorized to get things set up."

"Another reason to know what you're talking about. Do you want to embarrass yourself in front of your staff? Throw up your hands and say you don't know things because you never took time to do a bit of research? I'm surprised at you. As an owner, I figured you'd want to know a bit about every department your company offers."

Ah, crap. He had her like a cat with its prey, shaking her with his teeth. Quench was her pride and joy, and his insult hit like a sucker punch. Tessa clenched her jaw. "I planned to read a few articles. Listen to your show. I'm not going in blind."

"You need to see an entire game and get an idea of why it matters to so many people."

"That makes no sense. People love camping, but if we did an article on it, I wouldn't need to set up my own damn tent."

"This isn't an article; it's a brand-new division, and you need to respect your readers."

Oh, she hated that he might be right. She silently cursed her friends for getting her involved with this mess. She hated sports more than anything, yet she'd been chosen to spearhead this awful operation.

Tessa narrowed her gaze. "Fine. You can give me a short summary, but I'll know if you're trying to torture me on purpose."

The waitress came around and dropped the bill on the table. Ford grabbed it and flashed her a grin. "Pleasure doing business with you."

She gave a snort. "We'll have to see about that." She ignored his rumbling laugh and swore to come out of the encounter with her dignity.

The insistent beep of her phone interrupted them. She glanced at her text and held back a sigh.

Got a new recruit. Need help. Come quick.

Uncle Bartholomew. She never knew when the calls or texts would come, but she was always ready. Since her mother's brother moved here a few months ago from the West Coast, she'd been the only immediate family in the area to help. She'd remembered his eccentric ways, but lately she figured her parents were laughing their asses off all the way from safety in Florida. He was the black sheep in the family for a reason.

Sheep dog, to be more precise.

But Tessa swore she'd take care of him, and a promise was a promise, like blood was blood. She quickly typed back Be there in thirty.

"Hot date?" She looked up, and Ford motioned toward her phone. "Forgot to ask if you're dating someone specific. Wouldn't want to step on his toes while your tongue is down my throat."

"Cute. Nah, it's . . ." She broke off, used to taking care of her own stuff. Separating her personal life from men was automatic. It'd be easier to let Ford think it was some guy she was seeing. "Nothing serious. But yeah, I gotta go."

"Sure. See ya this weekend. I'll have snacks."

She shuddered at the idea of the stuff he ate but managed to nod politely. "Sounds good. Bye."

Tessa left him, slipped into her car, and drove back to Nyack. Her uncle's house was off the beaten path, with a generous amount of acreage consisting of bumpy green hills threaded with weeds and sticks that would be hell for any landscape company.

She pulled up the curving driveway and parked in front of the simple colonial. The porch was a wraparound but a bit saggy and worn. A line of throw rugs was drying outside over the rail. The door sported stained glass, but the lower part had deep scratches marred in the wood.

Reaching in her back seat, Tessa carefully slipped out of her beloved Louboutins and replaced them with simple Skechers sneakers. She'd learned to dress appropriately before going in. Even though Uncle Bart kept the place clean, you never knew what you'd encounter. His companions had a different view on what constituted a safe space.

Marching up to the front door, she gave a hard knock, then let herself in.

And greeted chaos.

The crowd of dogs came from everywhere. Some bounded down the stairs, others barreled from the kitchen, and a few streamed from other rooms into one yipping, wriggling fur pile around her feet.

Tessa shushed them, reaching out to pet them with both hands and calm their hysterics.

Her uncle appeared in the doorway of the living room, holding a small inkblot that looked more like a rat than a dog. Wild hair sprouted from its head and body. "Hi, sweetheart. Glad you're here. Dom said he couldn't come over, Vin is at the hospital getting his blood level sorted out, and I don't trust anyone else to help. Want a glass of wine?"

She held back a sigh and walked gingerly forward until she was a few inches away from her uncle. The dogs swarmed around her with each step, clinging to her legs and feet. "I told you no more dogs, Uncle Bart. There's not a lot of room left. Do you want someone to call you a hoarder?"

She should've been more careful with her words. Her uncle's dark eyes filled with hurt. "Hoarders neglect animals. And I couldn't say no, Tessa. He was abandoned, and the vet said he's blind. He'll die out there alone. I'm not a monster. I refuse to let an animal die on my watch. His name's Petey."

Oh God. She looked closer at the inkblot and noticed his eyes were scarred over. Unbelievably, the dog wasn't whimpering or shaking, just calmly allowing her uncle to hold him close. Her heart crumbled to pieces, and she half closed her eyes. "Okay. I didn't know. Of course you have to take him. How can I help?"

Uncle Bart's presence was as commanding and intimidating as his voice. The first time Malia and Chiara met him, they thought he'd sprung right out of the movie *Goodfellas*. He was pure Italian, with a stocky muscled build, short neck, and penetrating onyx eyes. He wore a gold chain, a pinkie ring, and jeans with a button-down short-sleeved shirt in olive green. A tat of a pit bull scrolled across his right forearm. His hair was salt and pepper and gelled back from his broad forehead. He'd worked in construction for years, but her father had said some shady stuff had gone down, and Uncle Bart decided to move to New York for a fresh start.

Tessa didn't want to know what that was. Sometimes, ignorance was bliss.

"I need to walk him through the house so he knows where things are. He needs to feel safe. Can you take care of the others and feed them? Everything's in the barn."

"Sure. Where'd you find Petey?"

"The supermarket parking lot. There's a patch of woods in the back, and he'd gotten trapped in the brush. Judging by his condition, he'd been out there awhile." Anger burned in her uncle's eyes, and his hands shook slightly. He'd dedicated his retirement to helping out abused dogs, and each of their rescue stories was personal. Tessa wouldn't want to be caught by her uncle if she ever abused a dog. She couldn't imagine the things he would do to even the score.

She shuddered.

"I'll take care of it—I know the drill by now. Come on, everyone. It's dinnertime."

Barks rose to her ears, and the cloud of fur followed her out the door to the converted barn that now served as an outbuilding just for the dogs. It really was a human-size doghouse. Uncle Bart had done all the work, crafting it in bright red with a sloping roof, tons of windows, and sealed doors to keep the temperature inside consistent.

She opened the double doors and went to the small kitchen, where the refrigerator was stocked with endless fresh dog meals and the pantry was stuffed with various types of kibble. Bags of treats lined the counters. Drawers were filled with bowls in all sizes and colors. She lined them all up alphabetically and began to disperse the food. It had taken a few times before her memory took hold, but now she knew who got what. Axle, the white terrier mix with the missing paw, danced around on his other three legs, while the spotted pit bull sat calmly, waiting for his dinner. The Chihuahua broke into song, her howls expressing excitement for food. Mimi—the sassy Pomeranian mix—guarded her usual spot with her teeth bared, but everyone knew she was all bark and no bite.

"Want some music?" she asked the group.

Dug, the mutt with a limp and torn-up ear, gave a short bark.

"You got it. I think this will put you in a good mood."

She told Alexa to play "Happy" by Pharrell Williams and finished the chores while bopping her head and hips to the upbeat music.

Some of the dogs roared in tune.

She served the meals and cleaned up their play area so Uncle Bart didn't have to bother. There were stuffed toys, squeakers, ropes, and bones to amuse them, and each had a high, comfy dog pillow to sleep on and an individual blanket. Obstacle courses kept them active, and a small television was mounted on the wall that played Animal Planet twenty-four hours a day. The place was more like a hotel for dogs rather than a home.

She'd never been a huge dog person—her parents never had pets—but after falling hard for Chiara's rescue, Dex, and now being around all these furry goofballs, she was starting to think of getting a canine companion.

As long as her designer shoes were safe. And the velvet couch.

Tessa headed back to the main house and joined her uncle. He was on his hands and knees, guiding Petey around the living room, giving him directions in a soft, firm voice.

"Shouldn't he get to know the layout of the barn rather than the house?" she asked. "Unless you're letting him stay full-time with you?"

Her uncle's fat fingers patted the dog with gentleness when Petey ran into the edge of the couch. "No, but I always bring them inside, and there's more obstacles in here. The barn will be easier."

"Did you eat yet?"

He shook his head.

"Let me make you something quick. The dogs are all taken care of."

"Thank you, sweetheart. Have I told you lately your mother doesn't deserve you? She was really mean to me when she was younger. Even blackmailed me once when she caught me skipping school. I don't know how she got so lucky."

Tessa laughed. Her mom was always fighting with Uncle Bartholomew, but she knew it was all in love. "Is pasta good?"

"Pasta's perfect."

She headed into the well-stocked kitchen and got to work. Her uncle liked to cook and oftentimes served Italian feasts to his tight-knit friend group, who he'd brought over from California after he closed his business. Tessa had met them a few times, and each of them owned a crew of their own rescue dogs. They said Uncle Bart had given them a whole new outlook on rescue animals and called him "the dogfella," dubbed from a popular book about a gangster who began rescuing dogs. Tessa had read it a few weeks ago and had been charmed, even though the gangster had killed many people. At least he was trying to do good now.

Tessa found some veggies in the refrigerator and whipped up a simple primavera. She poured two glasses of red wine for them, heated up some Italian bread, added fresh Parmesan, and called Uncle Bart in. He slid into the pinewood chair and placed Petey down. The dog quickly sat at his feet, nose twitching, but remained quiet.

"He's a good dog," she said. Her chest squeezed. "I hate the idea of anyone hurting him."

"Me, too. But he doesn't have to worry about that anymore."

Tessa took a seat next to her uncle. "I cleaned up the barn. Do you need me to do anything else?"

"No, thank you." He made a grunt of appreciation as he ate the pasta. "Tell me about you. Are you dating anyone?"

She smiled and sipped her wine. "No."

His brow arched. "What about that guy you were meeting at the wine bar—Alan? Was he the artist who paints naked women for a living?"

Tessa sighed. "He creates art based on the female body, which I don't have a problem with." She forked up a bite of pasta. "But you don't have to worry about that one. He stood me up. It was humiliating."

Uncle Bart made a noise under his breath. "Forget him. You need to get married to a man who appreciates you. Have babies. Life is too short to be alone."

"You never got married or had kids, and you're happy."

He shook his head mournfully. "I wasn't good enough for any woman to settle down with. I like things a certain way. You are different. What are you waiting for, sweetheart?"

She didn't know. Mr. Right? Did she believe in him? "I guess I'm waiting for a guy who I want more than my single life. I don't like to compromise, Uncle Bartholomew. I think I'm a bit like you—I'm stubborn."

"That breaks my heart, little one. You are depriving someone of your love. You need to be more flexible in your standards. Allow for some faults. But start dating men who can offer you a solid future, not an unstable artist."

"Maybe." She drummed her fingers on the table. "Right now, I'm helping out a friend. He's in love with a woman he doesn't really know, and I'm transforming him to win her over."

Her uncle nodded. "A worthy project. Unrequited love is heartbreaking."

Her lips twitched. "You're a hopeless romantic. I believe it's just wanting what you can't have."

Uncle Bartholomew added a bit more Parmesan, staring thoughtfully at his plate. "Love is usually right in front of us. We just don't like to look too hard."

She tilted her head and studied her uncle. There was an emotion to his words that hinted at a great love, but she knew he wouldn't share easily. He liked to give advice and wax poetic about life but kept his past tightly locked up. Maybe as they grew closer, he'd share more.

A shadow crossed his face, then disappeared. He took a sip of wine and seemed to clear his mind. "I'm having a birthday party for Mimi in two weeks. I'd like you to come."

She blinked. "Mimi, your dog?"

He frowned. "Of course. She's turning five years old the same day Bruno does. I'm hosting a co-birthday celebration."

"Who's Bruno?"

"Dom's pit bull. You met him at the dog park last time, remember?"

The image of a muscled, great beast of a dog who was as timid as a mouse hit her memory. Mimi had terrorized him. Bruno was afraid of everything, but instead of attacking, he covered his paws with his head. "He doesn't like Mimi. Do they really want to celebrate together?" she asked, wondering why she was trying to rationalize an invite to a dog party.

"Mimi loves him or she'd leave him alone. It's good for Bruno. I'll have cake. Bring a date."

"I'll see."

He dropped the subject.

They talked about her parents and Quench, then she helped him clean up. "Bye, Uncle Bartholomew. Bye, Petey." She gave both of them a kiss and left.

Driving back home, Tessa thought about her uncle's words. Maybe he was right. She'd gotten lazy with her dating apps and fallen into complacency. She'd met Alan through her fashion editor but didn't have the heart to tell her he was an asshole who'd stood her up. It had been months since she'd had sex. Time to get back into the single world and freshen up her bio and photos. Or there was that cute guy she'd met at Whole Foods. He was the manager and was always chatting her up, trying to show off the new produce. No ring. Maybe she'd ask him out.

She was getting tired of standing still while everyone else seemed to be moving forward in their love lives. The idea of being left behind or the only single one at the table never bothered her before. But lately, things were changing. It'd be nice to be part of that exclusive group. To lean on someone who really understood her.

Tessa thought about it for a long time as night descended and she drove.

Chapter Ten

Dionne tightened the cape around Ford's neck. He looked in the mirror, his gaze meeting Tessa's, and suddenly he wasn't sure of the whole thing anymore.

He cleared his throat. "Hey, maybe we can just do a tiny trim? I'm not sure I'm into this whole new look thing after all."

Dionne clucked her tongue and squeezed his shoulder. She was an intimidating woman, almost as tall as him, with a badass Afro, gorgeous lashes, and a red-lipped mouth that smiled easy. Under her apron she wore a bright yellow dress with matching heels, as if she were heading to a party rather than a beauty salon. "It's okay, hon. The only time I had a client leave my chair unhappy was the Mohawk incident. I have new clippers now."

"I want to get up."

Tessa winked at Dionne, and they both burst into laughter.

Sweat prickled his skin. Were they going to do something bad to him? It was like *The Witches of Eastwick* and he was helpless. The flash of silver scissors whipped through the air, and his gut clenched.

"Everyone is nervous when their comfort level is threatened. It's normal. You need to trust me, remember?" Tessa reminded him.

Dionne was putting some gel stuff in her hands and began working it through his damp hair. It smelled like strawberries. Surely, he should've gone to a barber. "I trust you. Kind of. But, see, I like my beard. It's pretty hot right now to have the scruff factor. I don't want to look like a sixteen-year-old kid again."

"I need to know what I'm working with under there, hon," Dionne said, poking at the subject of his fear. A tiny frown creased her brow. Her long, tapered fingers probed his jawline. "I think we struck gold."

Tessa leaned in, excited. "I was hoping, but you're never sure. God, what a waste!"

"Yes, but we'll take care of it now."

Ford cleared his throat as both women peered closely at his mouth. "Do I have a safe word?"

Dionne grinned and tugged playfully at his beard. "He's adorable."

Tessa shrugged. "I'm sure some think so."

His pride burned at the dismissal, but then fear returned when Tessa began walking away. "Do it, Dionne. Don't hold back—go with your instincts."

The excitement in Dionne's dark eyes made him twitch in the chair. "No, Dionne, I think slow and steady wins the race, right?"

She laughed a bit evilly and covered his face with a hot, steaming towel. "Just lay back and enjoy, hon. It won't hurt a bit."

Ford whimpered.

Behind closed eyes, his brain spun endlessly, creating awful images that made his heart burst from his chest. How would he get Patricia's attention if he looked stupid? He'd been cursed with babyish features, and the moment his facial hair began to grow, he'd owned that shit and went full out. He looked like a man now. Losing too much hair would expose him and he'd be the subject of women's jokes.

The scissors clinked. His head lightened. He tried to hold back a moan as the towel was moved to cover only his eyes, and the clippers whirred like Leatherface with his chainsaw. Ford fisted his hands and wondered if he should yell for help. Was it too late? Could he save himself? Did Tessa hate him enough to get her ultimate revenge?

His beard was tugged, pulled, and buzzed. Lotion was rubbed into his skin. He caught a flash of light, but then the towel was moved lower, exposing his brows, and Dionne began more horror work. Time warped. He counted his breaths. He prayed.

"Tessa, look at this. Do you believe it?"

Ford heard a sharp intake of breath. "Oh, wow. I wasn't expecting this."

"What?" he strangled out. "Oh God, what did you do? What did you do to me?"

Someone patted his shoulder. He figured it was Dionne. "You gotta breathe, hon. No panic attacks in my chair—it's bad for business."

"What a waste," Tessa whispered again. "All those years gone."

"Yes, but we fixed it now. He'll have a brand-new life."

Ford couldn't take it anymore. "I need to see! Let me up!"

Tessa blew out a breath, seemingly with annoyance. "Geez, you're so impatient. Can he see, Dionne?"

"Sure, why not? I just have to do a little tweaking, but the main stuff is done."

The towel was removed. The chair swiveled and rose up. He blinked as he looked at himself in the mirror, trying to compute the first blurry image of his new look.

Holy shit.

Dionne slipped a mirror in his hand so he could examine his face up close. His brain froze, and he stared for a long time in silence.

He was different. His hair seemed thicker, with a bit of a wave, and was brushed away from his forehead. The beard was completely gone. He hadn't had so much of his face naked since he was a teen, but after a quick panic, he realized his features weren't what he remembered from the past. They were sharper. His jawline was angular. His cheekbones a bit sculpted. His mouth looked full, his lips more defined. His nose seemed thinner and not as bulbous without all that hair sprouting around it. Even better? His eyes had always been his best feature, and now they popped. He moved his head back and forth, catching the different angles, and realized in a stunning light bulb moment that the guy in the mirror was almost handsome.

"What the hell?" he muttered, trying to understand what had happened to him.

"Look at you!" Dionne practically squealed. "That awful beard was hiding a jaw that could cut glass. Do you know what other men would pay for that?"

Tessa stood behind him, catching his gaze in the mirror. "I told you," she said simply. "You gotta trust me. This is the look Patricia wants."

She was right. In a way, Ford finally felt grown up. The idea he'd had of himself from the past was wrong. His new appearance seemed fresher. It would give him more confidence and . . . did he even admit it?

Sex appeal.

"Do you like it?" Tessa asked.

The women waited for his verbal approval. It took a while for him to regain his words. "Yeah. I fucking love it."

Dionne did a little dance with her scissors, and Tessa's slow grin lit up her face.

Ford grinned back, caught up in the mischievous gleam in her baby-blue eyes, the lure of her full lips stained cocoa brown, matching the gleaming corkscrew curls that framed her glowing cheeks. It was as if she was lit from within, and Ford could easily see the reason men would chase her. To be the focus of all that attention; to know you were the one who made her radiant in that perfect moment—it would be a heady rush. He wondered what type of power a man needed to make her burn. Make her want. Make her soften and surrender.

The thought startled him into sitting up in the chair, shaking his head a bit to discard the image he had no right to think about. *Hell, that was strange.* Probably some weird leftover excitement of getting one step closer to Patricia, his testosterone jumping in and hijacking his gratitude into sexual tension.

The moment passed, and relief cut through him. She was back to being just Tessa.

Dionne high-fived her, then him, and he sat back while she finished him up. The whole time he kept staring at himself in the mirror.

"It's amazing what we do to ourselves," Tessa said quietly. Ford caught her scent—a mingle of sandalwood and orchards, mysterious and exotic. "Who we think we are when we're young. Who we allow society to tell us we are. It's screwed up."

Dionne was in the zone, scraping a blade over the edge of his hairline.

He met Tessa's gaze, surprised to see such raw emotion glittering back at him. He answered on instinct. "I never thought I was attractive," he admitted. "I had a baby face. Got made fun of a lot."

She nodded. Somehow, Ford knew she understood. Had seen the recesses of what he'd covered up and not only understood his past but allowed it to finally breathe. Fully accepting him in a way he'd never let another woman see. "No one gets to tell you who you are, Ford. Not the world, or your listeners, or your friends. Not me. Not even Patricia."

His breath caught, and a surging need swept through him like a tsunami, catching him in its force.

"Not anymore," Tessa said. Then she walked away, leaving him in the chair with Dionne. Leaving him changed but no way to understand how or why.

Instead, he concentrated on Patricia. This was his first step to gaining her heart. He needed to keep his focus razor sharp, because everything Tessa offered was to reach that one goal.

Back in control, Dionne finished up, then whipped the cape off with a flourish. "There you go, hon. Be careful with those women you're about to unleash yourself on."

Ford chuckled, paid the bill, and left a fat tip. His body felt lighter, as if no longer weighed down by excess hair. They walked out, and the warm rays of sun on his face made him smile.

"I'm glad you're happy," Tessa said, falling into stride beside him. "You look great."

"Thanks. You were right. Dionne was worth it."

"I only work with the best." She glanced at her watch and picked up her pace. "Speaking of which, our next stop is the men's shop. Time to get you out of those concert T-shirts and into some real clothes."

"Concert tees are real clothes. They make a statement."

"Yes, they do. Which is why Patricia needs to see a different one."

He shut up after that, even though he was a bit surly about having to get rid of his favorite items in his wardrobe. They defined who he was and made him stand out. Dressing like other men wouldn't get him noticed.

Tessa distracted him with a question. "Why don't you wear sports gear? Radio station stuff. Baseball teams. I don't even remember you wearing ball caps."

"I do sometimes, but I'm a big metal head. Those bands made my youth worth it."

"Angry teen finds comfort in *Shout at the Devil*?"

He winced. "It wasn't about devil worship! Plus, that was from the eighties. I grew up two decades later."

"Yet, you wear a lot of eighties stuff. How come?"

Ford half shrugged. "A lot of kids I knew got into that retro stuff, watching the movies and listening to the bands that still toured. It felt free and badass. Maybe there wasn't as much interesting rebellion stuff when I came of age."

He liked her laugh. It was genuine and had that husky timbre that reminded him of those femme fatale actresses from black-and-white movies. Tessa would've been perfect dressed in a sleek gown with a cigarette dangling from her red lips. "We had the Wall Street meltdown and climate change. Isn't that enough?"

"Guess not."

They maneuvered down Main Street, weaving in and out of crowds. He looked longingly at the coffee shop, but she kept her pace brisk, focusing on the path ahead.

Curiosity stirred. "What about you? How'd you rebel?"

"Probably sex."

He stumbled and barely caught himself. She never broke stride, so he hurried to catch up. "Wait—sex? What do you mean?"

Her smile was smug. "I had a pretty happy childhood. Met Chiara and Malia in high school, and we became tight. I hated smoking, wasn't into drugs. But I had a thing for boys."

"What teen girl doesn't?"

"Exactly. I loved the rush of feeling wanted—it gave me a sense of power and confidence. Until I figured out sex shouldn't be a trade-off for anything, especially feeling confident."

"Wise words."

"Took a while to get there," Tessa said. "We all need to make mistakes when we're young—that's how we figure crap out. I still enjoy the thrill of a new relationship, but I don't need the hit anymore. I choose it. Makes a difference, even if you can still get hurt."

Ford was surprised she was opening up to him. He realized Tessa had a way of being deeply involved in a conversation without giving much away about herself. She was a great listener, loved to banter, but rarely shared inner stuff. "Is that why you never got married? Because you don't want to get hurt?" He figured that was most of the planet's way of avoiding long-term relationships.

She gave a disdaining snort. "I'm not afraid of hurt. Not that fragile, dude." They stopped at a polished window featuring men's clothes. "We're here."

He wanted to know more, but she marched into the store and greeted the man behind the counter with genuine warmth. The older man came around, air-kissed both her cheeks, and clapped his hands together. *Does everyone Tessa works with bring this level of enthusiasm to her makeovers?* He had to admit the people she picked were warm and genuine as the gentleman's gaze tracked over his body and judged.

"Ford, this is Roberto. He's the owner and has an intuitive talent for figuring out a man's personal style."

Roberto waved his hand in the air in dismissal. He was bald and wore black-rimmed glasses, black pants, a black silk shirt with red edging, and gleaming black shoes. "I've been in this business since I was twelve and began dressing my four brothers. It's not instinct, just practice." His grin was wide and infectious. "Ford, it's good to meet you. I'm looking forward to fitting you with some new clothes today."

"Thanks." Ford tried not to panic, but the store seemed packed with a bunch of clothes he'd never wear. Sure, Roberto looked great as the man in black, but it wasn't Ford's thing at all. Uneasiness swirled. "Um, I think one outfit will be plenty. Just to give me a taste of something different."

Tessa shot him an amused look. "He's freaking out, Roberto. Afraid we're going to rip away his essence, which consists of concert tees."

"I love vintage concert shirts!" Roberto yelled, taking Ford off guard. "I'm not here to change who you are—just polish out some rough edges. How does that sound?"

Tessa crossed her arms in front of her chest. "Gonna trust me? Or are you about to have another panic attack?"

Ford glared. "I didn't panic. Go ahead. Dazzle me."

The challenge sparked a gleam in her blue eyes. "I intend to."

Her soft whisper caused a slight thrill to course down his spine. The woman was a witch—pissing him off in one instant and fascinating him in the next. Hanging with her felt like getting whiplash.

Spinning on her heel, she disappeared into the racks. Roberto grabbed a tape measure and took his measurements.

Ford noticed the store was empty of customers, which wasn't a good sign. "Not busy today, huh?" he asked casually.

"Oh, we closed just for you," Roberto said deftly, pencil scratching on a pad. "Tessa is my best customer."

He frowned. Something didn't add up. "Wait, I thought she'd never done a makeover for men before."

"Oh, is this a makeover? Fun! She just told me she had a special client and to treat him like family."

Gratitude shot through him. He would've hated doing this in a crowded store or with an audience. "But you said she's your best client. She buys a lot of men's clothes?"

"Of course. She comes in once a month and picks out dozens of outfits. You know the Dress for Success program where they fit women with professional clothes for work?"

"Yeah."

"Well, Tessa does that for men. Chiara's husband, Ryder, mentioned once that one of his high school students had a job interview but had no nice clothes. Tessa came to me, and we began a program so we can serve the men in our community who don't have access to professional attire. I discount the clothes, she buys them, and then she works with a volunteer who distributes to various organizations. It's a great thing, and Tessa came up with the whole idea."

"Huh. That's really cool."

Tessa came down the aisle with a bunch of clothes tucked over her arm. "Roberto, I'm putting these in the dressing room. They caught my eye, so it's only an initial impression. Let me know what you think."

"Of course. I've got his sizes." Roberto clapped his hands again. "This is the fun part. Ready to try on some new clothes?"

Ford's gaze settled on Tessa, who still buzzed around the store, focused on her mission. He wondered how many other things the woman was secretly involved in. "Sure. Let's roll."

He headed through the wooden doors and began to strip.

~

"What do you think?" Tessa asked, taking in the black pants and red shirt combo he'd just come out in.

"Truth?"

"Always."

Ford's grin didn't reach his eyes. "I'd rather stick hot pokers on my body than look at myself in the mirror."

Her lips trembled with the need to smile, but she held tight. "That's not very nice. I told you, Roberto wanted to try something edgy to make sure he wasn't missing anything."

Ford looked around quickly, making sure Roberto wasn't in earshot. He lowered his voice to an angry hiss. "I've been here for over an hour, and I hate everything. I know you think the guy's got a gift, but obviously not with me. Can we just go? My hair will be enough of a change for Patricia."

"No, we can't go, and no, it won't. She'll notice the hair, but we need a jolting reaction. She needs to be able to look at you in a new way for the first time, and that takes more work."

"Great, then I'll wear fringe and cowboy boots. Anything's better than this."

Tessa bit her lip. "Real funny. Take it off; I think Roberto has a new plan."

He muttered something under his breath and stomped back into the dressing room. Ford was definitely picky. Even Roberto was getting stumped, trying different styles of shirts and pants, mixing with jackets, but nothing seemed to spark the right tone.

Roberto came over, tapping his finger against his lip. "I feel like I'm missing something but can't figure it out. Has he always looked like this? Dressed like this?"

"Concert tees and old jeans. We just cut his hair, though. He'd been sporting a full beard and long hair most of his life."

Roberto's light brown eyes lit up. "That's it! I've been missing his hair! So his short hair and clean face is new?"

"Yeah. But what difference does that make?" Tessa asked.

"Everything. You'll see. Just because his hair is short now doesn't mean he's that man inside. Inside, he still sees himself with the long hair and beard."

She looked confused. "I have no idea what you just said."

Roberto puffed out with pride. "I do. Don't worry, I understand now. Be right back."

Tessa sat in the chair and waited. Ford's bare feet peeked from the dressing room. He was talking to himself, probably trying to plan a getaway. Men had no patience for shopping. It was a big reason she liked working with females, most of whom could easily spend eight hours in one store.

Roberto returned with a stack of clothes and tapped on the door. "Try these on. I have a plan now."

"You know, Roberto, I totally forgot I have a dentist appointment at three. I better get going—I forgot to tell Tessa about it."

"Last outfit, Ford. I promise," Roberto said.

"Yeah. Sure. Last one."

Tessa shook her head at the dentist excuse. The man was a terrible liar.

When the door finally swung open, she glanced up quickly, then froze.

Yes. This was who he was.

The outfit was simple. Black textured jeans with a slight sheen to them. The white T-shirt had a black scrolled design on it. The jacket was in various textures like patchwork, but swirled in subtle neutral colors—just a pop of contrast to the simple shirt and pants. Together, it was like an upgrade but still essentially Ford.

"Now, this I like," Ford said, looking in the mirror. "Cool jacket."

Tessa took in the lean fit. She knew Ford preferred baggier clothes, but now she could see the muscles of his arms, pecs, and thighs. Despite his junk food diet, the man had a natural leanness and a nice, tight ass. She got the impression he'd gotten used to hiding his body. Now, he was no longer hiding from anyone. Like his face, his body was suddenly free.

Emotion worked in her throat as she caught the look of almost wonder in his expression. Somehow, this man had deliberately hidden himself behind an appearance contrived to draw no attention. She'd seen it many times before with her clients, but it never failed to thrill her once a person saw themselves in the mirror, stripped of their old limitations.

Roberto sighed with relief. "I was worried for a few, but now we figured it out. Ford, can you buy your concert T-shirts in white or do they just come in black?"

"No, they're available in white. I just figured black is cooler."

Roberto shook his head. "Go buy any concert tees you like, just always in white. With your coloring, black shirts wash you out. Light on top, dark on bottom is what you should shop for from now on. I want to show you some other dark-wash jeans and dressier pants that will fit. Oh, and this denim jacket and a leather one I have in the back will be perfect. Wait here!"

He hurried off and Tessa stood up, approaching Ford to get a closer look at his outfit. Their shoulders brushed. She caught the faint scent of his skin, a pleasant mix of soap and lemon. At least she didn't have to pry him away from any overpowering cologne. She always enjoyed a man's natural scent.

"You look good," she said.

He turned and their gazes met. Humor lit his hazel eyes, and it took her a few seconds to pull back. Funny, now that his beard was gone, the light swirl of brown and light green was almost hypnotizing. "I feel good. I can wear this."

"Sure we can't throw in the bright green shirt? At least for Saint Patty's Day?"

He chuckled. "Hell no. It took longer than expected, but Roberto nailed it." A slight frown creased his brow. "Is it enough of a new look for Patricia to notice?"

"Yes. Never underestimate the power of a tweak."

"So that's it? I'm good to go?"

Tessa smiled slow. "Nope. We have to go over the plan. Your behavior is the most important thing. It isn't going to work if you look like this but still go chasing after her like a starved puppy."

Ford winced. "I hate that analogy."

"Sorry, I won't use it in my column."

His eyes widened as if he'd just remembered something. "Shit, I forgot about that. I haven't seen you taking notes today. Do I have to answer any questions?"

"It's all in my head. Besides, I don't write my column like that. It's not a daily diary of our steps. More of a culmination of the journey. Makes it more organic and interesting."

"I guess I'm just a statistic now. One more Frankenstein's monster for your column."

Tessa stiffened.

He was about to laugh but must have noticed and bumped her shoulder gently. "I'm only joking."

"I don't think of you like that, Ford. You need to know even though I teased you, I always thought you were handsome. You were fine exactly the way you were. I wouldn't have asked you to change a thing."

His shocked expression had her turning quickly, not wanting to see it. She'd already said too much. She was doing all of this for him so he could get his dream woman, but Tessa didn't believe in changing anything just to please someone else. In the end, wouldn't you always wonder why they never loved you before?

But this wasn't her journey—it was his. She'd just make sure to do his story justice.

"Brilliant, Roberto," she said as he returned and she caught sight of the espresso-bean leather jacket he was carrying. It was well worn, soft, and rugged. "That would go amazing with those jeans and some khaki canvas shoes."

"Already on it," he sang, moving toward Ford.

She browsed shoes, picking out a nice pair of dressy sneakers, the canvas ones, and black loafers. At the last minute, she also threw in some black leather boots.

"Are you going to pick out my underwear, too?"

Tessa rolled her eyes. "If you want me to. Here, try these on. They're your size."

Dressed in his original outfit, he toed off his sneakers. "I don't know about those boots."

She gave him a sharklike grin. "Trust me. You'll love them. So will Patricia."

He tugged on the new shoes and shook his head. "You're really into this trust factor. Is that your hot spot?"

She approved the canvas shoes and handed him the boots. "Hot spot? What does that mean?"

"You know, the make-or-break thing in a relationship. You need your partner to trust you. That's how you show love."

She paused, regarding him in surprise. "Pretty deep for you. I think trust is important to any healthy relationship—whether it be friends, family, or a lover."

"Trust is a good one."

Curiosity hit. "What's yours?"

He walked around in the boots, pondering. "Kindness."

She blinked. "Huh?"

"I like women who are really nice. Who show up for people who need them, help others out. I think it's an important trait for a wife and mother. Hey, I actually like these boots. Good pick."

His words hit a spot inside her that she didn't know existed. She'd never thought about a make-or-break trait before. Hearing Ford's forced her to look at him a bit differently. She figured he'd have said sense of humor or coolness, meaning a woman who could flow and lay back and not challenge him too much. It was the rare man who'd call out kindness as the most important trait in a woman.

Was trust really the critical trait she wanted in a man?

She needed to think about it.

Ford paid for the clothes, chatting and thanking Roberto for the help, and then they were back on Main Street. They stared at one another, blinking in the sunshine as cars crawled past and pedestrians walked around them. He shuffled his feet, arms laden with bags. "Well, I'm not sure what to say except thank you."

"Welcome. You look amazing. Patricia's going to be knocked out."

A grin tugged at his lips. She noticed the full curve of the lower and the defined upper. They looked soft, too, as if he used ChapStick daily. "Hope so. You're still coming to my house for the basketball game this Friday, right?"

A groan escaped. "Yes. A deal is a deal. I'll also do a quick stop in your studio tomorrow morning. You're sure she'll be there?"

"I'm sure."

"Good. I'll bring you breakfast, hang on you a bit, and make a deliberate statement."

"I like bacon, egg, and cheese on a roll."

Tessa rolled her eyes. "Fine. We'll work on specific actions at your place, but for now, she needs to get used to the idea you're taken. Remember, if you see her tomorrow, ignore her. She'll mention your appearance, and you need to tell her your girlfriend bought you some new clothes. That's it. Make any excuse, but do not have a conversation."

He tried to scratch his head, but the bags stopped him. "It's going to be hard."

"You have to—"

"Trust you." Ford laughed. "Yeah, I do. See you tomorrow morning." He turned and headed back to his car.

She watched him for a few seconds, wondering why there were so many weird emotions jumping around in her belly.

She was hungry. That was the only explanation.

Tessa walked toward Mike's to get a sandwich.

Chapter Eleven

"Hi, Ford." The low, sultry voice sounded from behind him.

He stopped in front of the coffee maker, where he'd been indulging in a second cup before his show. Fighting the urge to drag his palms down his pants like a teen, he turned around slowly, a smile pinned into place. "Hi, Patricia. How are you?"

She looked amazing. A powder-blue dress skimmed her body like a whisper of a kiss, her hair a silky curtain that brushed her cheek. Her gaze was filled with a bold curiosity he'd never seen before. She took in his new outfit—the leather jacket, jeans, simple T-shirt, and boots—with open appraisal and admiration. "Good. I didn't get a chance to talk with you yesterday. Love the new look."

"Thanks." It took all his willpower not to check on how she felt or whether she tried to go back to her ex. He reminded himself to play the role only to snag her attention. Then he'd go back to his true self. "My girlfriend picked it out."

Her eyes widened with surprise before her gaze moved slower, taking in his clean-shaven face, shorter hair, and relaxed posture. This time, he didn't jump to involve her in dialogue and let the silence lengthen naturally.

"Girlfriend? Oh, wow, that's great," Patricia said. "I know when we had drinks you mentioned it was hard to find someone with the same goals as you."

Ford nodded, keeping his gaze locked on hers. "Yeah. Sometimes life surprises you when you're not looking, right?"

A curious expression flickered over her graceful features. "Right. Well, I'm happy for you."

"Thanks. She's stopping by for a few moments. I hope you'll get to meet her."

"I'd love to."

The lead sales representative came in, crowding Ford out of the kitchen as he took up space with his pressed power suit and large mouth. The guy ignored him and focused on Patricia, complimenting her on her outfit, asking about her sales figures, and peppering the room with gossip. Usually, Patricia spent some time with Jay before their big sales meeting, but Ford noticed she didn't seem as interested today.

Was she looking at him? Or was it just his hopeful imagination?

Ford grabbed his coffee and headed into his studio without a glance back. Once he stepped over the threshold, his shoulders dropped with his breath. That was harder than he thought. He hated being distant, especially to Patricia, and was dying to know what she was doing this weekend. But Tessa had been clear, and things hadn't been working his way. He had nothing to lose by trying something different.

Isaac tapped on the door and came in. "I still can't get used to seeing you like this." He waved his hands up and down. "You're all cleaned up and shit."

Ford laughed. "Figured a change would be good."

"Hell yes. You all prepped? Let's go right into the looming baseball strike and deGrom's crappy elbow before the new assistant coach jumps on. Nice score on him, by the way. None of the other stations have been able to grab him yet."

"I work hard on those connections and only call when I really want a favor. I think hearing directly from the assistant coach will spur some heavy convo on all the changes for spring training."

Isaac held up his hand and gave him a high five. "Niiice. Now I think . . ." He trailed off and his mouth gaped open, gaze focused behind Ford.

"Dude, you okay?" Ford asked.

"Morning, baby. I brought you breakfast." Tessa's voice purred from behind, sounding as sexy as Patricia's. But where Patricia's was smooth and silky, Tessa's held a drawl that hinted at naughty secrets. She would've been great on the radio—a voice that transfixed men in a desperate need to hear more.

But when Ford took in her appearance, he realized exactly why Isaac was still mute.

Damn, she'd brought it hard. Her skirt was a minuscule fabric of black silk. The tuxedo-like jacket almost hit the hem, giving the impression she was wearing little beneath. The V in the jacket cut low, and a gold drop chain was squeezed into her cleavage. She'd pinned her hair up, and all those curls around her face and nape gave off a just rolled out of bed vibe. Sky-high stilettos gave her a boost of height and showed off her muscled legs. Vibrant energy sizzled from her petite figure, matching the fiery blue spark in her eyes.

He'd seen Tessa like this before. Once, at a party when she'd brought a date and was obviously dazzling him. Another time, at some banquet he'd been forced to attend, when she wore a white designer dress that made every male in the room seek her out at the bar. Of course, he'd spilled something on it and received her wrath for a long, long time.

She was probably still mad at him for that move.

Tessa had never brought this powerhouse of female sexiness for *him*. It was a bit unsettling, but he had to quickly don his role because Isaac was staring and Tessa was waiting and he didn't want to waste this precious opportunity.

He put on his big man boxers and strolled over with a warm grin. "You made it. And you look incredible, as usual."

She preened like a good girlfriend, then handed him a brown bag. "Just how you like it. Are you getting prepped for the show?"

Isaac cleared his throat.

"Yes, this is my producer, Isaac. This is my girlfriend, Tessa."

"You were the one who visited before," Isaac said. "I didn't know you were both dating."

Tessa strolled around the small studio, hips swinging in time to the click of her heels. "He played hard to get with me. I finally had to ask him out myself. What does a producer do, Isaac?"

"Oh, we make sure all the sound and tech stuff works. Screen guests for our DJs. Kind of like Oz—I'm behind the curtain."

"Sounds interesting." She hit him up with apologetic eyes. "I'm so sorry—do you think I can get a bottled water? I'm parched."

"Come with me into the kitchen and I'll grab one. I want you to meet the rest of my coworkers," Ford said, sidestepping Isaac's automatic response to go running. "I'll be back in time."

"You always are. Nice to see you again, Tessa." Isaac shot him a look of respect, then shuffled off to his own space.

"Is she here?" Tessa asked in a low voice.

"Yeah, I talked to her briefly. She wants to meet you."

Her smile flashed a set of white teeth. "I bet she does. You were distant?"

"Yes. Didn't ask her any questions. She liked my new look."

"Take the jacket off."

He hesitated but slowly pulled it off and threw it across the chair. Tessa got in close, fiddling with his sleeves, mussing up his hair a bit, and cupping the back of his neck, exposed from his new haircut. Her touch took him off guard, and he stiffened.

Blue eyes darkened. "Don't pull away. Remember, you want me all over you."

"Sorry. I forgot I get to maul you with your full permission."

She laughed and he relaxed. "Let's go. Follow my lead." Tessa clasped his hand firmly in hers and tugged him out the door.

The kitchen was empty, but a group of voices echoed from a side room. Ford automatically grabbed her a bottle of water, trying not to get nervous. He was glancing casually toward the hallway when Tessa took a step in, backing him up against the refrigerator door, her face close to his. Ford opened his mouth to protest, then quickly shut it at her warning glare.

Her arms slid up around his shoulders, and she pressed her mouth to his ear. "I hear her, she's coming. Bite my neck."

"What? I'm not sure—"

"Bite me, dammit!"

He lowered his mouth to the satiny skin of her throat, right where the collar line met shoulder. Then he sank his teeth into the firm flesh.

She made a little moan that had him stiffen in a whole other way, shocking in its intensity. Her scent rose to his nostrils, and he had the fleeting impulse to do it again, just to savor her reaction.

"Oh, I'm sorry! Didn't mean to interrupt!"

Patricia's voice came from a blurry distance, but Tessa quickly pulled away, twisting her head around. "Oops, no, I'm sorry! Didn't mean to make out in the kitchen, but I couldn't help myself." Tessa winked and eased away a precious inch.

Ford dragged in a breath and faced Patricia, who was staring openly at the woman tucked in his arms. He felt like he'd been dropped into a bad rom-com. "Um, hi, Patricia. This is my girlfriend, Tessa. Patricia is a sales representative at KTUZ."

The women shook hands. "I love that you're at a sports radio station," Tessa confided. "We need more female reps."

"Yeah, it can get a little high with the testosterone here," Patricia joked. "Wow, it's so nice to meet you. I love your work at Quench—I'm totally obsessed with your website. I've taken a few courses that I found really helpful for women in business."

"Thanks so much—I'm glad they were helpful." Tessa's hand rested on Ford's chest. He assumed she felt his heartbeat exploding under her touch.

"This is so weird," Patricia said. "I just set up a meeting with your marketing team to pitch spots on KTUZ. Ford mentioned he has an in there with Chiara."

He stiffened, falling into a brief panic about how to explain Tessa's sudden girlfriend status when he'd never mentioned her. But Tessa was quick, her fingers stroking his chest with obvious sexual intent. "Isn't that an amazing coincidence? When our team began to consider bringing sports to Quench, I was initially against it. Then I came to study Ford in his element, and he completely changed my mind." A sly grin curved Tessa's features. "About a lot of things. I admit, I've always crushed on him, but it was so hard to snag his attention. Finally, I just asked him out!"

Patricia smiled. "That's so cute."

"Isn't it? And now he's one of the driving forces behind bringing sports to our readers. His ideas are amazing!"

Patricia pulled back in surprise. "Really? Wow, Ford, I had no idea you were so in touch with Quench's readership. What a great pitch."

"He has vision but doesn't flaunt it," Tessa said. "I recognized it immediately. His proposal and business plan blew the team away. He's also a force in the boardroom when negotiating." A giggle escaped, which was so beneath her, Ford had to remind himself they were play-acting. "And other places."

I will not blush. I will not blush.

Patricia gave a forced laugh, her gaze narrowing in on him.

He kept his smile and stared down at Tessa, as if he couldn't take his eyes off her. "You're embarrassing her," he chided gently, trying to strike the right tone of intimacy.

"Oops, sorry again! Well, I can't stay. I just wanted to drop off your breakfast before getting back to work. Don't forget we have reservations at Jades. Six tonight."

"You were able to get in?" Patricia asked. "I can't even get close—the wait list is insane."

"Ford knows how to get around stuff like that. I swear, he's taken me to these places I thought were dives, and they turned out to be hidden treasures." Tessa reached up, entangled her arms around him like an octopus, and made an intimate noise. "I'll miss you, baby. Have a good show."

After pressing a full kiss on his lips, she strutted out the door.

Silence fell. Ford knew what he did next was key. He touched his fingers gently to his lips, then grinned, turning toward Patricia. "She keeps me on my toes," he drawled. "Glad you two got to meet."

"Me, too." Patricia stepped closer. "I can't believe you're dating her. She's a really big deal. Besides being gorgeous, she runs a multimedia company and is superrich."

"Yes, Tessa is very talented." He bit his tongue to keep from reminding Patricia she was also talented. He had a feeling her confidence wavered beneath the surface. Probably another reason she dated assholes regularly.

Patricia nibbled on her lower lip. "You know, Ford, this seems really quick. Not that I'm judging—God knows, I've jumped into my fair share of relationships—but I worry about you. I don't want you to get hurt."

He tried not to reveal the sense of satisfaction he felt from her words. She didn't like seeing Tessa with him. She just didn't know it yet. "Appreciate that. You're a good friend, but right now, I'm just going with the flow." He glanced at his watch. "Better go. Have a great weekend, Patricia."

"Yeah. You, too."

He turned to head back when Jay's mocking voice boomed through the air. "Hey, Maddox, where'd you find the hottie?" The man had one ankle crossed over the other, leaning against the counter like he'd overheard the exchange by coincidence. But it was obvious he couldn't understand why Ford was suddenly the target of so much feminine attention.

Ford regarded the man with a touch of disdain, but he knew the game. Men always were looking to trade up—from jobs, to possessions, to women. Ford didn't approve and never liked living his life that way, but Jay had no shame in flaunting his success at the poor bastards underneath him. As the leader of the sales crew, he liked to show off his money, custom suits, and fat client roster.

A short silence fell upon the kitchen. Two guys from the sales team peeked curiously through the door. Patricia was waiting for his answer, head gracefully tilted to the side.

Ford grinned. "She found me, Denton." He nodded slightly to Patricia. "See you both later."

He strode out without looking back and was seated two minutes before going live.

Energy rushed through his body. Suddenly, it all seemed possible. All he had to do was stay the course and do what Tessa told him.

Easy peasy.

~

Tessa swung into the restaurant parking lot and cut the engine of her practical backup car, a Chevy Equinox in royal blue. "I see Mike's car. He's here already."

A snort came from the back seat. "Mike was probably at the table half an hour ago, afraid he'd hit a traffic snarl from five miles away. He's a wreck," Malia said.

Chiara sighed. "I still think we should have told him we all have the flu so it would just be him and Emma."

A voice snapped them all to attention, and in an instant, Tessa was taken back to high school English class when they'd been giggling and not paying attention. "Girls, that's enough. This is simply a nice dinner invitation, not a date. I think it's sweet. No pushing tonight," Emma said.

Suitably chastised, they climbed out of the car and checked in. Mike was waiting and had claimed a cozy corner booth. The steakhouse was dimly lit, well reviewed, and boasted a rustic, intimate atmosphere guests loved. Tessa couldn't wait to order the filet mignon with the gorgonzola fries. If she was going to be dragged into a group dating experience, she was going to eat well, and she'd skipped lunch today due to her schedule. She was famished.

Mike flew to his feet, stumbling from the booth. "Emma! Hi, how are you? Glad you could make it. You look good."

Emma nodded graciously. "Thank you, Michael. You look very handsome."

"You think?" He tugged at the collar of his stiff blue shirt matched with navy-blue pants. His blue jacket was dated and reminded Tessa of a retired military member in his dress blues. "Had this in a closet for a while. Don't get out too much. But look, we match!"

Tessa tried not to smile at how the tables had turned. Once, Emma had been tongue-tied, but now Mike couldn't seem to create a full sentence around her.

They each gave him a hug and made sure to squeeze into one side, leaving Mike next to Emma.

"I ordered wine for us," he said, shifting in his seat. The stiff material of his pants seemed to scratch at the wood and raise a strange sound. "But they have tea, if you don't want wine. They even have iced tea. I heard it was good."

Tessa shot a suffering look to her friends. This was going to be a long night.

"I like a glass of wine with dinner," Emma said, sliding off her wraparound shawl. She was wearing a simple blue dress a shade deeper than Mike's suit, paired with low-heeled boots. Her usual hat had been left off, showing Tessa she'd taken some care with her look tonight. In fact, her cheeks were pinkish, which meant she'd used blush. That was a big sign.

"Red okay? They have white. And rosé. And champagne. And—"

"This is great!" Chiara said loudly, grabbing the bottle. "We may need another one."

Emma gave them a sharp glance, but Chiara was already pouring generous amounts.

Tessa tried not to laugh. They'd just gotten here and already it felt awkward. It reminded her of the awkwardness of that Scrabble game over a year ago, when she'd sprung Emma's presence on Mike unannounced and he responded by behaving like a bully. But they'd come a long way, and she really wanted Mike to step up and take the leap.

Without his wing women.

Mike smiled a bit madly at all of them, as if trying hard to keep his energy up. "How was your day? What did you do?" he asked Emma.

"Oh, it was nice. I'm doing a bit of tutoring for this lovely boy down the street. He's dyslexic and having trouble with his English class, so we meet twice a week to work together."

Mike shook his head. "That's so nice of you. Helping the community is important. You are a very good person."

Emma blinked in surprise. "Thank you. You do the same. Feeding the community and giving people a safe place to congregate is a worthy calling."

Mike seemed shocked at her compliment. Tessa almost sighed in longing. Maybe this time they'd see how good they were together. Mike's loneliness after losing his wife and Emma's ability to give and share was the perfect match. *Maybe . . .*

"How's Arthur? He seems good. Fit for his age, huh?"

Maybe not.

"He's fine." Emma stared down at her menu, obviously not wanting to talk about her friend now. "I think I'm going to get the petite filet. With garlic mashed potatoes."

"Oh, that sounds good," Malia said. "I'll do the same, but I want the gorgonzola fries. They're sick. I was so busy today, I didn't get to eat. My stomach hurts."

Mike glared. "That's not healthy at all. You need your energy."

Chiara sighed. "We had some fires to put out today and barely got out of the office on time."

"I could've delivered to you! There's no excuse for not eating. I'm going to yell at both of your partners."

Tessa snorted. "As if the men in their lives have any control of them."

"Yeah!" Malia said. "No one controls me. Especially not Palmer."

The waiter came by to take their order and quickly dropped off bread. Chiara got to it first, but then there was a tussle with Malia in the middle. Tessa had a mean competitive streak, though, so she yanked it away to get the heel.

"Girls," Emma hissed. "What are you doing?"

They froze, realizing they'd gone into a primal state.

Mike muttered under his breath and raised his hand for the waiter, ordering another basket. "Reminds me of when they'd come over after school. They'd hole up in Rory's room and had nonstop appetites. I had to sneak vegetables on their pizza and convince them sweet potato fries were the best."

The memories hit. Tessa shared a glance with her friends as they remembered Rory. God, they'd been so close. Had built an empire together. She caught the slight sheen in Mike's eyes and automatically reached across the table.

But Emma got there first.

Her hand gently clasped Mike's. "Rory was extraordinary and changed the world," she said softly. "Yes, she was taken too soon, but she burned bright while she was here. And you, Michael, had everything to do with it. You never tried to change her, or stifle her. You gave her the funds to start a new business when most parents would have tried to talk her into a respectable, safe job."

Mike looked at Emma, and the moment was almost sacred, as if they were recognizing each other for the first time.

Tessa's throat tightened.

Malia sneezed. "Sorry!" she squeaked, covering her mouth.

Chiara shook her head.

Tessa raised her glass. "To Rory," she said.

Everyone followed, lifting their glasses high. "To Rory," they all chanted.

Some of Mike's nervousness began to fade, and they fell into some easy chatter as the food was served. Tessa ate her steak with gusto, sharing her fries, and pleasant warmth buzzed through her. Mike peppered Emma with questions about her career in teaching, and she blossomed under the attention. Okay, they'd been wrong. The dinner had worked out, and now Mike would feel brave enough to ask Emma out alone. She'd thought their presence would mess it up, but maybe he just needed to gain a bit more confidence.

They pushed their plates away, and Mike beamed at all of them. "That was delicious. I'm so happy you came, Emma. I'm glad we got past all of my bad behavior and you gave me a chance to get to know you."

Emma smiled so sweetly Tessa's heart sang. "I'm glad, too."

"Maybe we can do this more often. The girls love to go to the movies—especially those superhero ones. Do you like Spider-Man?"

"Um, well, I don't know too many people who don't like Spider-Man."

Mike laughed. "Good. Why don't we go next weekend? Girls, you can bring the guys if they want to join us. We can do a Sunday matinee, and I'll close the diner a bit early."

Oh, hell no. She refused to be Mike's comfort blankie for the next few months. It had taken him over a year to be nice to Emma. What if it took another year before he went out with her alone? Her second dad would kidnap her social life and drag them all over town, just because he panicked when he was alone with Emma.

Nope. Not on her watch.

The looks on the faces of Emma and her friends were identical.

Tessa forced a casual grin. "Mike, why don't you order a bunch of desserts. I'm going to hit the bathroom. Girls, come join me? Take your purses; I need some makeup recovery."

Mike shook his head. "See, just like high school. They have to do everything together. You got it—any requests?"

Chiara spoke up. "Have Emma pick."

"Will do."

Tessa got up from the booth and walked down the hallway. Instead of taking a right to the bathroom, she led her friends to the front door.

"What are you doing?" Malia asked in confusion.

Tessa stabbed her finger in the air toward the booth they'd vacated. "I'm giving that man the kick in the pants he needs to step up to the plate! We are leaving them alone for dessert, and he'll be forced to drive Emma home."

Chiara sucked in her breath. "Do you think that's a good idea?"

"I think it's a great idea. Come on, let's go before he sends Emma to find us in the ladies' room."

They rushed out, got in the car, and sped away like they'd robbed a bank. A mile out, Chiara and Malia began to giggle. Chiara gulped for breath. "This feels so wrong."

"Mike's going to kill us!" Malia said, still laughing. "We need to text them both so they don't worry."

"I'll do it," Chiara said. She whipped out her phone and sent two separate texts. "I said Tessa had a work emergency and needed us, so we had to go to Quench. I also instructed him to drive Emma home."

"He's so bad, he'd probably order her an Uber," Tessa said.

"Nope. He doesn't know how to do that, remember?" Malia said.

That brought more giggles. "He may do okay once he realizes he has no backup. Emma's obviously still into him. I bet he can pull it off and ask her to the movie alone," Chiara said.

Tessa sighed. "Hope so. We'll find out soon. They're both going to be mad at us."

"Ah, a text came in!" Chiara read it and bit her lip. "Emma said she's going to kill us and that lying is against the Ten Commandments."

"She always hits hard," Malia said, obviously concerned about her soul. "I hate lying."

"It's for their own good," Tessa said firmly. "Do you really want to see *Spider-Man* with him Sunday?"

Malia shook her head. "No. There's a million other things I'd rather do."

"Exactly. You can thank me now."

They dissolved into laughter again while Tessa brought them home.

It was up to Mike now. They'd done everything to get those two together. Tessa sensed once the barriers crashed down, Emma and Mike would realize they're soul mates. God knows, they deserved happiness and second chances.

She had to believe they realized it, too.

Chapter Twelve

Ford opened the door and studied Tessa in slight shock.

The woman stood before him, her petite, curvy body clad in every type of sportswear possible. A Mets jersey in vivid blue and orange engulfed her frame. Socks were pulled up to the shins of her denim leggings, revealing the Knicks logo. Her wild curls had been stuffed into a bun, and a New York Rangers hat was tilted low on her head. There were twin streaks of black under each eye, as if she were a football player ready to go out and tackle someone.

Of course, she'd paired it all with glittery pink shadow and matching lipstick.

He took in the pure ridiculousness of her outfit with the mismatched sports swag and knew she had no clue which sport was what. Ford burst into laughter, not able to keep it in even though she raised a brow and glared prettily. "What's so funny? Are we watching a game or what?"

"I'm watching a game. You look like you should be listed on eBay for a ragamuffin confused about what sports team she likes."

"Hardy har har. Do you know how expensive this crap was? Thank God for Amazon or I would've never been prepared." She gave a haughty sniff and came in, a small cooler tucked under her arm. "I brought beer."

"I have some."

"Not Blue Moon LightSky with hints of tangerine. I need to watch my calories."

"Not on sports day." Ford flashed her a grin and closed the door behind her. "I got some snacks that will blow you away. That's half the fun of watching a game—what's the matter?"

Her blue eyes had widened as she took in his apartment. His gaze swept over it. He made sure he'd cleaned today, so maybe she was impressed? "You like my place?"

Tessa swiveled her head around and blinked. "Ford, is this the way it's usually kept?"

He decided to lie. It was never this clean. "Yeah, why?"

A groan rose to her lips. "This place is a nightmare! Patricia would run in the opposite direction if she ever came in here. What were you thinking?"

He looked around, trying to see what she saw. He'd been in his apartment for a while and gotten comfy and complacent. It may not have had any fancy furnishings or girly things, but he was the only one who lived there. "What's wrong with it?"

She dropped the cooler and began stamping around like a mini tyrant. "Where do I start? The furniture is saggy and mismatched. Have you ever had it cleaned? Or the carpets?"

Ford scratched his head. "No, I vacuum when there's crumbs, so I figured that's good."

"It's not good. Not at all. And what is this junk?" She pointed to the three large shelves with various sports memorabilia. Trophies, certificates, bobbleheads, and funny items were crushed together.

"Knickknacks." He'd heard that word used before. "Like you have in your place."

Tessa's eyes bugged out. "I have expensive crystals and modern sculptures. This is stuff you'd find in the worst flea market ever." She paced around the small place, jabbing her finger at various things.

"There's no color in here—everything's brown. It's like I'm drowning in mud."

"Brown is neutral."

"To contrast with other colors! And I'm glad you read, but stacking your books in neat piles is weird. Where's your bookcase?"

"Oh, it broke and I never replaced it."

"The walls are filled with baseball posters. Are you twelve?"

Now she was hitting below the belt. He drew himself up to full height and glared. "Those are expensive vintage swag items. I mean, look closer. It's Tom Seaver, Dwight Gooden, and Darryl Strawberry."

"Who cares? Put them in the basement; don't use them as your main decor."

"I don't have a basement."

They stood in crackling silence, irritation popping through the air. Tessa dragged in a breath and looked like she was grabbing for patience. "Listen, I'm sorry. I don't mean to rag on your place. I know you love these things and figure it doesn't matter. But when a woman comes into a man's place, she parallels the rooms to the man. So if it looks sloppy, you look sloppy. If it looks cheap, you look cheap. It needs to show you're thinking of what it would be like to make a home with someone you love. That you're a . . . grown-up."

Oh, he did not like her. She was ruining sports day—his all-time favorite day of the week—and he had to be nice because she was helping with Patricia.

Giving himself a minute, he trudged into his kitchen and grabbed a beer. "So you want me to pretend to be someone else for the benefit of society's expectations?" he asked with a bit of hostility.

"No. You're pretending because you think Patricia is the love of your life," she said simply.

And just like that, he folded. Looked around again, trying to see his apartment through Tessa's eyes. It was a basic layout—a living room, dining room (which he used as an office), kitchen, and bedroom. Yes, there was little color and a musty smell, and the carpet was a bit stained. Yes, the walls were covered in posters, and his stuff was piled up in corners and on the table because it was easier to find. His kitchen was small and had been furnished by yard sales. His toaster only had two slots that worked, and his refrigerator was yellow instead of stainless steel.

And he had absolutely no throw pillows. He knew how women liked them.

Some of his resentment leaked away. "Yeah, I guess I see what you're saying."

Her face cleared and she walked toward him. "Ford, I get it. You've been single awhile and fell into a habit of just thinking of yourself. But Patricia will demand more. I'm assuming you make a good salary?"

He practically sputtered. "I make a lot of money."

She gave a half smile. "Figured. So you can upgrade without it hurting your budget. You don't need a million-dollar place, but some new furniture and easy fixes will brighten things up. New carpet, a bookcase, a few candles. And, of course, some throw pillows."

He tried not to laugh. At least he knew a few things about women.

"Can I see the bedroom?" she asked.

"Maybe that's not a good idea," he said slowly. He'd made the bed and cleaned but had an idea she'd hold a strong opinion.

"I don't care if your dirty clothes are on the floor," she said jokingly. "I just want to see what we can do to quickly spruce it up."

He brought his arm up and pointed. She disappeared for a while, and when she came back, the look on her face said it all. Guess she wasn't a fan of the king-size bed with no headboard, vintage Mr. Met lamps he'd scored in an auction, and wall-size print of the '86 World Series team photo, which cost him a pretty penny. The fur rug was white, though. That must bring a splash of color.

"Yeah, we need to do an overhaul."

"Fine. Can we hit Marshalls and just get some fluffy stuff?"

She narrowed her gaze in warning. "No, it's much bigger than that. Do you want me to help with this, too?"

Oh, he hated saying yes. Wondered if anyone else could do it for him, but who the hell did he know with taste? Chiara? She had her hands full with Ronnie and married life and Quench. At least Tessa was single and already knew what he needed the upgrades for.

His tongue stuck to his mouth, but he forced the words out. "Yes." He paused. "Please."

Her smile was almost evil, but he would've done the same to her. "No problem. I'll help you renovate your apartment so you can have sex with Patricia."

Ford almost covered his face, but he'd learned not to show fear with this woman. "Hardy har har," he mimicked. "Can we watch some basketball now? I feel like I've been crushed by a semitruck."

"Sure. First, tell me how it went with Patricia after I left yesterday."

He filled her in, proud he'd been able to play his role and create a bit of mystery. "I definitely feel as if she's looking at me in a different way. She's really into you—thinks you're some type of celebrity. Who would've thought another woman interested in me would create such a reaction?"

"A very *hot* woman," Tessa corrected, her curls escaping from her cap. "Women can be extremely competitive with each other, even though we hate it. She's wondering what she's missing out on now."

"What's our next move?" he asked, handing her a beer from her cooler and putting the rest in his refrigerator.

She popped the tab. "You keep up the pressure. Be flirty, then pull back and drop my name, like you're reminding yourself you're hooked up. That will intrigue her more. Is there anything coming up at work? Some type of social event where you can get more time with her?"

"Jay is having a gathering. He's a bit of an asshole but throws nice parties. Everyone's invited, but I decided to skip it."

"Will Patricia be there?"

"Not sure. Sometimes she goes. It depends on her plans."

"Okay, mention you were thinking of going. See what she says. If you can arrange it so you'll both be there and hang out, it will be perfect. You need to tell me when, though, so I can clear my schedule."

He cocked his head. "Why? Are you coming with me?"

Tessa blew out an impatient breath. "Of course—I'm your girlfriend, remember?"

"Right. Sorry, I keep forgetting."

"Work parties are the number one places where people hook up."

Excitement stirred in his stomach. He had such hope. If they both went to Jay's party and he was able to grab quality time with Patricia, maybe she'd finally realize what she was missing out on. "I can handle that. Crap, the game started." He turned, his focus lasering in. He turned on the eighty-five-inch television that was his pride and joy and pumped up the volume. "Get comfy. You're in for a treat. What's the matter?"

She wrinkled her nose at the saggy couch. "Is there a blanket I can put down first?"

"You're such a Disney princess."

"And you're no prince."

He laughed but tossed her an afghan, which she smoothly laid out before placing her ass carefully on the couch. He shook his head but swore not to let her irritate him. "Remember, I'm doing this as a favor. I'd be happier watching the game on my own. It's a big one."

"Yeah, yeah, I know. Basketball. Okay, what team are we rooting for? Which one is New York?"

He tried not to lose his enthusiasm, but this was not going to be a fun day. Ford hoped he could look at it as being a good teacher and keep his positivity. "New York isn't playing. This is the NCAA women's basketball tournament—specifically the Final Four. They are the best of the best college teams who have competed all year for a chance to win the national championship. We're down to four teams."

"Simple enough. I've seen the World Series before, so I get the concept. Am I wearing any of the teams?"

He bit his tongue. "No, the Knicks are a men's professional basketball team."

"Right, I knew that."

"This game is between Stanford and the University of Connecticut. Both are great teams."

"I want the one with the wolves on their uniform."

He grabbed for patience. "That's UConn. They're also called the Huskies. Stanford is the cardinal."

"Cool. I like huskies better than cardinals, so UConn is my team. They have the best uniforms."

His teeth ground together. "You don't pick teams because of their uniforms or mascots. You look at the players, the teamwork, the plays. Don't bring that type of disrespect to Quench or you'll get a lot of angry readers."

Tessa pulled a face. "Geez, fine, settle down. I'm here to learn, not get yelled at."

Ford shot her a look. "Okay, so I'll go over some of their top players. Personally, I happen to be rooting for the Huskies, too. Paige Bueckers is on the team and is one of my faves. She's a beast and the national player of the year. Plus, she's only a sophomore."

Tessa nodded. "That's so young for such responsibility."

"College basketball is a completely different thing from the WNBA. But you can trace the greats from college ball, like Sue Bird. She's announcing the game with Diana Taurasi. They're both women's basketball legends. Bird was still playing at forty-one years old!"

"That doesn't sound too old."

He grinned. "That's ancient in the sports world."

"Well, good for Dove. It's about time we compete with the likes of Tom Brady."

"It's *Bird.* Sue Bird. But at least you know Tom Brady, so I'm not gonna get mad."

She stuck out her tongue. He pretended not to notice.

"Let me give you some quick, basic info." He warmed up to his topic, and soon he was sharing specific accomplishments from both teams. He detailed the breakdown of how they got to the finals and who played who. He kept waiting for the sarcasm or her eyes to glaze over, but she surprised him by listening attentively and asking questions when she didn't understand something.

By the time the game was a quarter in, he was psyched. He brought in the tray of snacks he prepped. Then he grabbed the cookie sheet out of the oven, turned it off, and piled the apps into a bowl. Ford plopped down another beer for her. "Help yourself. I made a variety since I wasn't sure what you liked."

He thought he'd done good until he saw Tessa's face.

Ah, crap.

"Are you actually going to eat this stuff?" she asked in shock, blinking at the beautiful tray he'd worked on. "What are those?"

"Corn dogs. Don't tell me you've never had one."

"Thank God my answer is no. I can't imagine what it does to your insides. Do you know soda can actually burn off acid on a car battery? Chiara did an article about it for Quench."

Ford decided not to tell her about the liter of Coca-Cola in the refrigerator. "Well, have something else, then. There're Cheez Doodles. Crackers with Cheez Whiz and pimentos—I had that once down south, and it's damn good. Jalapeño potato chips. But if you wanna go healthy on me, just eat the almonds. They should be tame enough."

She shuddered, which made him roll his eyes. "How do you stay in shape with this type of diet?" she asked. "I'd be three hundred pounds."

He looked self-consciously down at his stomach. He'd always been blessed with a metabolism that allowed him to maintain a decent weight while eating what he wanted. He hit the gym three times per week to stay on top of it, but he didn't have abs of amazement or chiseled pecs. "I don't love working out, but I play basketball, tennis, and swim. Should I get a trainer?" he asked worriedly. "Maybe lift some weights? Patricia would probably expect a cut dude, right?"

Ford steeled himself for a stinging remark, but Tessa's gaze swept over him without judgment. "No, you look great. Women don't expect perfect bodies but prefer a healthy version. It's good you work out, though. With that diet, you'd drop of a heart attack if you didn't."

He relaxed, knowing she told the brutal truth. It was nice she thought his body was good. "Do you feel pressured about your body image?" he asked curiously. He assumed she was obsessed with her appearance and did some intense routine at 5:00 a.m. daily.

She snorted. "I doubt there's a woman out there who doesn't. But I've made peace with myself a while ago. I watch my calories but also indulge when I want. My boobs and butt are big, which I used to hate, but now I like them. Who am I to question what God gifted me? You get what you get and you don't—"

"Get upset." He grinned. "I'm glad, T. Glad you don't obsess over things you can't change when men don't care. Hell, all we want is a naked woman. We don't care about the size, shape, or color—just the lack of clothes."

Her laugh was deep, loud, and a tiny bit rude. He loved it, relishing the sound pumping the room with life, but then the commercial ended and he made himself refocus on the screen.

Ford kept up a steady stream of narration so Tessa could get a solid feel for how the game was played. He yelled as an incredible defensive play broke out, the teams battling back and forth for the ball. "This game is critical. If the Huskies win, they advance to the national championship against South Carolina. They'd been fighting injuries all year, so they've come a long way."

"Oh my God, what type of almonds are these?" Tessa gulped out.

He barely glanced at her, gaze on the screen. "Wasabi."

"I'm going to kill you!" She got up, coming back with a glassful of water. "I had no idea you were addicted to all things spice."

"Some like it hot. Ah—you see that? What a play by Bueckers!"

"How did she grab the ball so fast? I barely saw it!" Tessa frowned and sat down, sipping her water.

"I know. Now watch as the Stanford offense tries to get it back. There—that's Cameron Brink in action. Her moves are sick even though she gets a lot of fouls. And—there's a foul!"

"Wow, she's so pretty." She rolled her eyes at his warning look. "Sorry, didn't mean it as an insult. Oh, she made the shot—yay for her."

He tried not to be amused but was anyway.

The game rolled on, the teams staying tight with the score 39–37 at the end of the third quarter, UConn with the advantage. Tessa tapped her foot madly, on her third beer. "I can't believe Cameron got those last two points right before the end. They need to watch out for her. Why isn't she being covered better?"

His lip twitched. "They're doing their best. Here—we have a bit of a break. Let me explain what each position does and I think you'll understand better." Once again, she listened intently, and Ford got excited at her animation. Something weird was happening here, but he didn't want to ask too many questions in case he ruined the mojo.

Bueckers got injured in the fourth quarter, limping around, but after a heated exchange with the coach, she was still playing. The clock counted down and each player went harder, faster, stronger, channeling all that energy into bringing the best of herself to win.

"She's hurt! She can't do this!" Tessa shouted at the TV. "Get that other girl to take her place!"

"Paige is stubborn. She wants this title."

"I can't look," Tessa moaned. "What if she gets seriously hurt?"

Then Bueckers turned and completed a pass to her teammate.

"Go!" Ford shouted. The ball danced around, shot in the air, and swooshed through the net.

"Yes!" All of a sudden, Cheez Doodles flew up in the air as Tessa jumped and threw her hand up. Seemed she *did* like Cheez Doodles after all.

Ford jerked back, then looked at his female companion, who he always believed was a bit of a prissy pain in the ass. Tessa was into the game as if she'd been a basketball fan from youth. Ford grinned big and proud, taking in the signs of strain on her features, her body poised for the next play and the way she didn't notice what she was snacking on.

This was a version of Tessa he hadn't known existed.

After some incredible plays, UConn finally claimed victory. Tessa jumped up and down. "These women are badass!"

"Told ya." He looked at the food tossed over his carpet. "You managed to impress me, T. Had no idea inside of you, hiding deep behind all that glamour, was a true sports fan."

She gave a half shrug, tugging back her dignity. "This was different. You explained it well, and I was able to follow the game. When is the championship?"

"Sunday. Wanna watch it together?"

She stuck her nose in the air as if considering. "Only if you want to. I can bring over some links to home furnishings and accents for your place. No need to be running back and forth to furniture stores any longer. You can buy it all online."

"Sounds like a plan."

"Good. I better get going. Get some real food."

"I saw you eat the Cheez Doodles."

She shot him a withering look. "You wish. I'd never ingest those; my lungs would turn orange."

Ford reached out and turned her hands up, revealing the orange dust clinging to her fingertips. "Then what's this?"

Refusing to surrender, Tessa gave a haughty sniff. "Residue from moving the bag away."

He laughed, shaking his head. "I'll let you know about Jay's party."

"Sounds good." Tessa grabbed her coat and sashayed out the door without a glance back, leaving him with a wrecked living room and a sense of satisfaction.

Ford hated to admit it. He'd had . . . fun.

He was sure it was a fluke, but for now, he was just going to enjoy it.

Chapter Thirteen

Tessa opened the door after the third round of knocking and gave Ford a warning glare. "Hold your roll. I heard you the first time."

He shook his head, irritation carved in his features. "We're late. The party started half an hour ago."

A laugh escaped her lips as she turned to grab her hot-pink Kate Spade beach bag. "Don't tell me you're one of those who gets to an event on time?"

He muttered something under his breath and transferred the bag from her grasp to his. "There's a time given for a reason. I actually respect it."

"Here's a free tip: never arrive at a social gathering until thirty minutes after the party starts. It avoids a whole lot of awkwardness and ramps up the expectation of your appearance."

"Sure, the expectation of rudeness for discounting the start time."

Tessa closed the door behind her, flipping her oversize Prada sunglasses to the top of her head. "You're hopeless. Let me look at you. Oh, I love those jeans, they're perfect. You look great."

"You think?" He looked down at himself, like he was still getting used to his new look. The dark-wash jeans went perfectly with the white Megadeth shirt, clinging a bit tighter to his shoulders than the usual baggy size he'd preferred. The sneakers were stonewashed gray and looked vintage. He'd gelled his hair back, the natural wave thick and giving him a bit of a mussed look. His jaw was a thing of beauty, cut sharp to show off the curve of his lips, finally left bare from the facial hair. He blinked in the light of the sun, and those hazel eyes shone with the gorgeous hues of green and brown.

"Yeah, I do," she said. "Patricia will notice, too."

She got a kick out of the tiny bit of red that spotted his cheekbones and wondered how often Ford heard nice things about himself. Not enough, she bet.

So many people were lacking confidence in their appearance, it made her sad. Because underneath? Everyone was exactly the same—imperfect and worried what the world thought of them. Tessa craved to show more people the real truth and tried to do that with her makeovers. Maybe this experiment with Ford would finally convince her the work she'd been doing had made a big difference—that it was worthy of her goals. Maybe he and Patricia would fall in love and get married and have babies and owe it all to her. Lately, she was beginning to question too many of her past actions, and she didn't like it.

Tessa shook off her thoughts and refocused. "Speaking of Patricia, let's quickly go over the rules."

"I know what I'm doing."

"No, you don't. We need to be clear about how you act at this party. Is she bringing a date?"

He scratched his head. "I don't know—she didn't mention anyone."

"Guaranteed she won't walk in there alone, so there will definitely be a guy. When we first seek her out, we'll be together, but the greeting will set up the whole day."

"What greeting? Don't I just say hello?"

"God, no! A buddy says hello. You need an approach to set yourself apart from the rest. You'll give her the hot half-hello hug."

Ford narrowed his gaze. "No fucking way. I am not doing anything that's named like a bad sandwich special on Valentine's Day."

Tessa marched forward and jabbed a finger at him. "Yes, you are. You promised to listen to me, remember?"

He blew out a breath like a pissed-off dragon. "Fine. This is so stupid—but go ahead. What do I do?"

She squinted with irritation at his dismissal of her tutoring but figured she'd give him one free pass. "First, you nod at her date with ease, like he doesn't bother you. Then you walk over to her and do the move. Watch me. Just have a relaxed stance and pretend you're Patricia. I'll be you."

"I hate my life right now."

"Just shut up and watch." She imbibed male vibes and asshole coolness and strode over, a half-smug smile on her lips, as if she ruled the world and everyone should know it. When Tessa reached him, she leaned in, squeezing his shoulder oh so lightly, sneaking in a stroke that was half a caress. Her lips stopped inches from his ear. "Hey," she whispered in a low, sultry voice. Her breast brushed his chest, and then she gracefully pulled back, giving them space.

Ford blinked. "That's it?"

She grinned. "Yep. How did that feel?"

A frown creased his brow. "I hate to admit it, but that was a tiny bit hot."

"See? Told you! Now you do it. Remember—you move in with confidence, and you get out quick."

He seemed a bit more accepting as he shook out his body and strode toward her. Tessa got ready to critique his first effort, trying to pay attention to his actions. He closed the distance, and within moments, her senses were hit all at once—the clean scent of man and soap and lemon; the delicious squeeze of her shoulder under his grip; the hot burst of air tickling her ear as he whispered "Hey" in his gravelly, sexy voice. The entire thing lasted seconds, but her whole body seemed to rev up, then still. Her skin prickled with awareness.

WTH?

Tessa took an awkward step back, trying to calm her suddenly rioting hormones that had burst from nowhere.

"Was that okay?" he asked, his gaze leveling her with intensity under his hooded lids.

She swallowed. "Um, yeah. You got it. Perfect."

"Cool. Can we go now?"

The intimate moment cracked and burst, and things went back to normal. *Thank God.*

Ford opened up the passenger door of his black Chrysler 300, but she caught him gazing at her Spider convertible with a bit of hunger. With a mischievous wink, she held out her car keys. "How bad do you want to drive it?"

He laughed. "You're such a tease. Who'd want to drive a yellow car? It's girly."

She dangled the keys from her hooked finger. "You. I see the desire in your eyes. Do you know I hit one hundred miles per hour and my baby just purred for more?"

"Such a show-off," he muttered, shifting his feet.

"Ask for it, Ford."

He rolled his eyes and grabbed the keys from her hand, ignoring her giggles. "Stop acting like a child and get in the car."

She did. He put the beer he brought and her bag on the floor, then started the engine. He drove to Jay's house with a competence that surprised her, obviously enjoying the speed and smooth, tight ride as the wind tugged their hair and the sun showered them with heated rays. She tilted her head back and just gave herself up to the ride. It was only half an hour, but her favorite part was the way Ford didn't feel the need to shout words, or find a great radio station, or chatter about the scenery. He sank into the natural silence, fell into the rhythm of the tires gobbling up the road, and let their surroundings take over.

She liked that about him. Too many men only wanted to make conversation because they needed to hear themselves speak.

They took a right and followed the curving road up a large hill, parking in a spacious lot offset from the main house. They got out of the car, and Ford grabbed the case of beer and bag from the back. "Hey."

"What?" She waited for him to ask last-minute advice on how to handle Patricia.

Instead, he grinned and his eyes squinted a bit as the sun turned his hair a rich golden brown. "You look good, too."

Surprise hooked her on the chin. She automatically looked down at her outfit like he had, then smiled. She'd gone BBQ chic with cute denim shorts rolled at the cuff and with tears at the pockets, a paisley blue-and-white tank, and baby-blue sneakers with a stacked rubber heel that emphasized the length of her legs. Her hair had been pinned on top of her head, and the wind tugged a few wayward curls to lay around her neck. Oversize silver hoops and a braided Brighton bracelet were the only jewelry. She always dressed in a way that made her feel good, but his compliment made her tummy clench pleasantly. "Thanks."

Tessa walked toward the house with Ford, taking in the luxurious surroundings. Damn, she was impressed. It seemed Jay knew how to throw a party, and she considered herself an expert. She noticed Ford's face pull a bit tight as they entered, reminding her this Jay guy was not his favorite.

The house was a magnificent three-level timber masterpiece in the mountains. Resembling a luxurious log cabin, it had multiple decks offering views, a pool and hot tub, and an outdoor bar. The weather was tricky in early April, but they'd gotten lucky with a balmy seventy degrees, practically spring after such a terrible winter.

With a practiced eye, she made note of where different cliques gathered and squeezed Ford's arm. "Are you nervous?" she asked, tilting her head.

He turned and looked at her with a strange expression, those hazel eyes glinting in the sunlight with a bolt of intensity, but when she blinked, it was already gone. "No. I know the plan and can handle it."

"Great. Let's go."

They made their way inside, which was just as opulent as the outside. The open concept allowed groups of people to gather, and a full-size granite bar was built in against the back wall. Music beat from hidden speakers, and the deck doors were flung open, allowing the breeze to drift in. The kitchen was huge, with two ovens and a circle-top counter with leather stools. Servers walked around with trays of appetizers. A couple in bathing suits flew past them, laughing as they made their way to the hot tub. The furnishings and other details continued the same rustic feel, with carved log railings, timber-beam ceilings, and rich, deep colors.

"What does this guy do again?" she whispered as they pushed their way to the bar.

Ford greeted people along the way. "Advertising sales. But his parents own a banking empire. He's always been a sports addict and wanted to make it on his own in radio. Didn't have the personality or voice, so he switched to sales."

"Does Patricia do as well?"

He snorted. "Hell no. Her numbers are high and she hustles hard for her accounts, but Jay is kind of the god of the sales department. Like I said—"

"He's an asshole," she finished.

"Jay!" Ford greeted loudly as the topic of their conversation headed over. "Good to see you, man. As usual, awesome party."

"Thanks, glad you could finally make it." His eyes bugged out as they settled on Tessa. She wanted to squirm under his slimy gaze but held still, leaning hard against Ford. His thick dark hair held a stylish wave, and his features were classically handsome but had no character. Jay reminded her of those cartoon-drawn princes in Disney flicks—handsome at first glance, but if you looked longer, you got bored out of your mind. "And . . . who's this gorgeous creature? I didn't get a formal introduction when you visited the station."

Tessa almost threw up in her mouth.

"This is my girlfriend, Tessa," Ford said.

"It's nice to meet you, gorgeous. Feel free to get comfortable. I hope you brought your bathing suit for the hot tub." His leer was unbelievable. "Or not."

She laughed with him but only for Ford's sake. "Thanks. Depends on my man."

Jay looked at Ford with an assessing expression. "Of course. Let me know if you need anything. Some of the crew are on the deck."

Ford thanked him, and Jay moved on, the shiny peacock in the room.

Tessa met Ford's gaze. "You're right."

"Told ya. What are you drinking?"

She had a white wine and he took a beer, then they went outside. Lofty trees surrounded the property, and the woods behind seemed to sprawl for miles. Giggles and chatter filled the air, mixing with the sound of birdcalls. The scent of pine drifted to her nostrils. "Spotted her at three o'clock," Tessa murmured. "Looks like she brought a date."

Ford swore under his breath. "She's moving on already. I knew it was going to be too late. There's no way she doesn't have a group of men just waiting to pounce."

"Calm down, Debbie Downer. If she's who I think, this guy is just a friend to accompany her. I told you—she'd never come alone to a party. Stick to the plan."

He dragged in a lungful of air and seemed to settle. "Okay."

"Follow me," she said.

They headed straight to Patricia and her companion. The woman was dressed in tapered linen capris, a cute white lace top, and leopard ballerina flats. Her gorgeous hair was tied back in a loose ponytail that exposed the graceful features of her face. Subtle makeup emphasized the plump curve of her lips, angular cheekbones, and gray-violet eyes. Tessa understood why Ford had fallen so hard. Patricia had that fresh girl-next-door look that made men mad to protect her. Not that she knew the woman very well, but her gut had been correct about how Ford should play it so far based on Patricia's previous actions.

Tessa pasted on a wide smile, hanging on Ford like her life depended on it. Excitement pumped up her voice. "Patricia! It's so good to see you again!"

"Tessa, how nice you were able to come." Her smile was genuinely warm, but her gaze slid over Ford's body, lingering a bit too long. "I'm so happy you're both here. How's everything going?"

Without missing a beat, Ford nodded at her companion and strode over with economical, graceful motions. He leaned in and went for it.

Tessa smiled at Patricia's companion, trying to give them their moment, studying the interaction from her peripheral vision. She caught Patricia's body press a bit against his chest; savored the surprised gleam in her lovely eyes as she stared at Ford a bit longer than usual, her teeth biting into her lower lip as if catching herself imagining him in a different way.

Perfect.

Patricia cleared her throat. "Oh, sorry—this is Erik," she said, turning to the man beside her. "Erik, this is Ford, who I work with, and his girlfriend, Tessa."

The good-looking man was dressed a bit formally for a party but reminded her of Henry Cavill, which was always a good thing. Tight cerulean-blue pants, no socks, and a fancy button-down shirt pegged him as comfortable at these types of functions. Definitely wasn't a salesman. More the investor type—he liked designer since even his watch sported a label.

"Nice to meet you," Ford said.

The men shook hands, and Tessa eased Patricia aside so they could fall into light chatter. The whole time, Tessa took in the energy between her and Erik and how many side looks she gave Ford.

Tessa went on a bit, describing some of the amazing dates she and Ford had been on, dropping hints that she couldn't get enough of him. She fell into the role of clingy girlfriend and gathered information. "So tell me what it's been like working for sales," she prodded. "I bet you meet tons of hot men!"

Patricia laughed. "Yes, I do, sometimes. Unfortunately, I've had a run of bad luck. Seems I like to fall for a certain type that ends up breaking my heart."

Tessa gave a sympathetic look. "I can totally relate. I was terrified Ford was just a player, but I'm finally realizing there's a man I can trust underneath. I just hope he feels the same."

"Oh, I'm sure he does. He seems very into you." Patricia leaned in, curiosity sparking in her eyes. "I haven't seen Ford bring many women to these parties, or date much. I guess he keeps his personal life private."

Tessa dropped her voice. "He's more mysterious than he lets on. I love that he comes off with this nice-guy persona, like your best buddy, but underneath?" She gave a shiver. "He's so sexy and deep and . . . dominant. It's like having all the best qualities wrapped into one." Tessa slapped her hand over her mouth to contain her giggles. "Oh God, I'm sorry I said that. TMI!"

Patricia smiled, glancing casually over as Ford talked sports with Erik. "No, it's perfectly fine. I just never would have thought."

On that note, Tessa tugged on Ford's hand, leading him away, making sure to press her breasts into his arm and look up adoringly. When they turned the corner, she eased away. "I planted the seed, and you did the hot half-hello hug perfectly. She was into it. Now, let's mingle a bit and make it look like you have no need to track her down again."

He winced. "Is that not good?"

"No. Did you do that at previous parties?"

"Yep. I'd follow her around most of the time, trying to get her to notice me." He shook his head. "I guess I was pathetic."

"Stop. Don't say that about yourself," she said sharply. "When we love someone, or think we do, any behavior becomes acceptable. There's nothing wrong with showing a woman you care. Not all of us like games."

"Patricia's not like that. I'm telling you, she just got a bit lost from these guys messing with her head."

Tessa bit her tongue. She was done trying to warn Ford about Patricia. She was only here to help, and then it was up to him to move forward. "I'll make sure I disappear later on, and you run into her when she's not with Erik. See if she wants to chat in private."

"You really think she will?"

Tessa squeezed his arm, enjoying the muscles that flexed underneath. "I really do. Can we have some fun? Eat and drink and be merry? Might as well enjoy Asshole's digs for our own nefarious purposes."

He laughed and pulled her to him in a casual hug. "Yes. I think we both could use some relaxation time, especially after the basketball finals. That was high stress. You broke my eardrums during that last quarter."

She frowned, getting mad all over again. "I can't believe UConn lost when they were so close. Not that South Carolina didn't deserve it. Holy hell, Aliyah Boston took my breath away. And when I heard that story about last year, I guess it was fitting they won."

She'd gone back to Ford's apartment to watch the last game, and he'd told her the amazing story about Boston losing last year's championship over a missed shot just seconds before the buzzer. Tessa wondered what that would be like—feeling you let your entire team down, even though it could have been any player, and any moment. She'd decided she wanted to talk about that during the podcast, the pressure female athletes face not only competing with men's divisions but dealing with their own standards when women too many times dealt with impostor syndrome.

"At least this time you threw pretzels. They were easier to clean up."

"Did not."

He laughed, and they walked toward a group of Ford's coworkers. He introduced her, and they fell into a lively conversation. Before long, an hour had passed and Tessa realized she was having a great time. Ford's work family was fun, loud, and easy to get along with. She also watched how Ford was able to get people to laugh easily and open up. He had a jovial warmth, from his tone to his demeanor, that everyone seemed to want to be around.

Finally, Tessa spotted Patricia walking away from the house alone, down the path into the woods. "There's your opportunity. Go after her, but make sure she doesn't know it."

With a thumbs-up, Ford turned on his heel and left. Tessa watched him disappear and wondered why there was a tiny flare of regret poking at her. Probably because she didn't want to see him hurt. She'd gotten to know him better, and the past two weeks hadn't been as bad as she'd imagined. In a way, she'd been having fun.

Tessa put the thought out of her mind and grabbed her phone, taking a few minutes to check in with Uncle Bart and Petey.

~

Ford took the right path that wound past the garage so he wouldn't pass anyone. The sound of gurgling water lured him from the distance, and he calculated he'd meet Patricia by the lake, betting she'd stop by the carved timber benches Jay had specially made.

He walked with his head up, stance confident even though his gut clenched with nerves. So much depended on this supposed random meetup, but Tessa had convinced him if he intrigued Patricia enough, this could be a new beginning.

His nostrils flared when he spotted her standing in front of a small clearing, staring at the lake as if it held all the answers. Her slender arms were crossed in front of her chest, face tilted slightly up, shiny hair pulled back from her face, a patrician profile so beautiful she seemed almost unreal.

Ford's heart jumped. A twig crunched under his feet as he approached. "Nature walk?" he asked, an easy smile on his face.

She turned, and the look on her face stopped his breath. It was different from the other times. Pleasure lit her eyes, an eagerness she'd never shown before in his presence. "Ford. I didn't hear you." A soft laugh escaped her plump lips. "Just taking a break. Crowds sometimes give me anxiety."

He cut off his instinct to comfort her by sharing his own stories of anxiety to make her feel better. Instead, he kept his distance and slowly nodded. "Never knew that about you. Guess most of us wear masks."

"Not you." She shifted her feet, her gaze intent. "You always seem open. Not afraid to share who you are with people. It's one of the things I like most about you."

He refused to shrug or explain, no matter how badly he wanted to. Ford kept to his part and hoped Tessa wasn't wrong. "There's a lot you don't know about me, Patricia." He locked his gaze on hers and refused to look away. Tapping into all the pent-up sexual energy he'd banked for two years, he let it go and felt the air practically charge. "We never got that chance. But maybe that's for the best."

She blinked, then moved, closing the distance. "You think? Because of Tessa, right? You two seem very close."

"She's an amazing woman," he said. Patricia waited for more, but he didn't explain further.

"She is. It's hard not to admire her."

Falling deeper into his part, he arched his brow and dropped his voice. "I'm glad you approve." He deliberately raked his gaze up and down her body, taking his time. "And I'm glad Erik was able to help you get over your heartbreak. You need a man who knows what he wants."

Her tongue wet her lips, and her eyes darkened. *Yep, she definitely likes a man who takes charge.* How'd he never catch that before? Tessa was a genius.

"Erik is just a friend," Patricia said slowly.

"Like us?" His lip lifted, as if amused by her confession.

Her laugh tinkled like wind chimes, and a pretty blush stained her cheeks. "Yeah, like us. Funny, though—we've known each other for years, but you're different lately."

"Different how?"

She took the opportunity to stand inches away. He scented her floral perfume. Studied the pout of her lips. She peeked at him from under thick lashes in a flirty gesture. "Your clothes. Your hair. Even your attitude. You seem more sure of yourself."

He reached out and took hold of her ponytail, tugging it gently and sliding his fingers down the silky strands. Her pupils dilated and she stared back, obviously fascinated. Hell, he'd seen his share of erotic movies. He'd heard about *Fifty Shades*. He could be exactly who she wanted. "I'm the same guy, just not hiding myself any longer. Tessa likes it."

"So do I." Her eyes widened, and she gave a self-conscious laugh. "I mean, I'm glad you're not pretending anymore."

Patricia waited for him to say something, but he'd learned silence was more powerful with her, so he didn't speak. Slowly, he let her hair drop from his grip.

"I do miss spending time with you, though," she finally said. "Maybe we can grab a drink after work again? I mean, if that's okay with Tessa."

Ford took his time. He noticed the pulse in her neck pounding, sensing her arousal. How had he never learned the art of sexual tension? He'd been doing this all wrong. "Maybe."

He wondered if he'd gone too far. If Patricia would back off from his halfhearted answer, but unbelievably, she got even closer. "Good. Thursday? That's your light day, right?"

Ford tried not to reveal the surge of satisfaction that hit him like a wave. He nodded. "I'll see what I can do."

"Great! I'm out of the office the first part of the week, but check in on Wednesday?"

He wanted to reach out and touch her cheek. Lower his head and finally kiss her. Drink in her feminine scent and allow his heart to burst. Give her everything she'd ever deserved.

Instead, he tossed what he hoped was an intimate smile and refused to answer her question. "I better get back to Tessa."

Patricia took a step back, her expression slightly guilty. But there was a fervor in her eyes he'd never spotted before, a confirmation she was excited by their conversation. Excited by him. "Of course. Erik's probably looking for me, too."

They turned and walked back together amid a charged silence.

He'd done it.

Thursday couldn't come fast enough.

Chapter Fourteen

Tessa walked out of the conference room, where she'd held a successful meeting with her internship mentees. Maria was blooming under Magda's photography tutelage; Yeo seemed to be thriving in the lifestyle department, with her TikTok numbers rocketing from her new makeup tutorials on how to wear hot trends; and Kelsey finally had some help with Scott, a whiz at editing and organization. Now Tessa was ready to meet a few more applicants clamoring to get in on the action for other departments.

Mentors were the key, and matching up interns with staff members seemed to be another gift of hers. It took a bit more time, but the outcome was worth it. There were many successful people working at Quench, but not all were good with teaching and training. Hell, most had no patience, which was critical in not undermining the confidence of the young talent. Too many believed Gen Z members were a bunch of entitled, demanding whiners, but Tessa knew they were passionate, driven, and hard workers when they cared about a cause.

Tessa always tried to imagine herself in the roles of others, and though she was no saint, she knew deep within she was blessed with her life. She'd constructed it within her own guidelines, values, and dreams. Too many never got that opportunity. The internship program inspired her to match more restless seekers to jobs that meant something, and she intended to keep expanding it.

She got to her office and dropped in her chair when her phone buzzed. Tessa didn't hesitate to pick it up. "What's up?"

"You need to come over." Ford's gravelly voice was like a sexy whisper in her ears. Damn, the man had a fine timbre.

She clicked on her computer and snorted. "It's the middle of the workday. Not all of us have cushy hours, dude."

"I've been up since four a.m., so don't start with me. There are boxes here, Tessa. Too many boxes, and I have no idea what to do with them."

"Read the labels. You can figure it out."

His sigh was pure suffering. "It's all written in code, and I can't even get to my kitchen. I don't know where to put anything! You said you'd come and help."

"I will. Over the weekend."

"No! Patricia may come over soon."

Annoyance flickered, which annoyed Tessa even more. Why did she care Ford was counting down the minutes till his big date? She should be happy her ingenious plan had worked. "You can't cheat on me so soon. It's too icky."

She pictured him scratching his head and thinking over her statement. "Yeah, but I want to be ready just in case. Plus, the Mets game is on. It will be good research—you need to watch a full baseball game."

"Wait—you're watching sports in the middle of the afternoon, sprawled on the couch with a beer, calling it research?"

"Yep. What's the matter? Can't leave work in the middle of lipstick testing? Cappuccino-colored versus latte—which one will change your life?"

She shook her head, but amusement threaded her voice. "Ha ha. I like basketball. Isn't that enough?"

"No. Baseball is part of being American. Like hot dogs. You need to know the game well enough to talk intelligently to your readers who may call in with a question. Our first podcast is next week. You don't want to embarrass yourself."

She practically spit over the phone. "That's your department, remember? I doubt watching a ball get whacked by a bat will raise my intelligence score."

"Don't knock it till you try it."

She could argue with him all day, but he was almost as stubborn as her. She glanced at her inbox and calendar. "I'll swing by for a quarter, but that's it."

"An inning. God, this hurts me more than it hurts you."

"Ford?"

"What?"

"Hot dogs may be American, but they give you bad gas." Tessa caught the tail end of his laugh and hung up.

She couldn't help smiling a bit as she grabbed her tote and laptop. It probably was a good idea to get his place decorated quickly, then go over the plan for Thursday. She'd begun writing notes on the makeover article, but it wasn't flowing like normal. Of course, she'd never made over a guy before. She was sure by the time their journey was over she'd find the perfect words, and hopefully the post would go big.

"Headed out?" Malia asked in the hallway. Her smart purple Vera Wang suit and sky-high heels practically screamed kick-ass business meeting.

"Yeah. I didn't know you were here today."

Malia grinned and patted her braids. "Closed the deal with the bank, who is now a proud sponsor of the foundation."

Tessa gasped. "Babe, that's fantastic! They are loaded!"

Malia laughed. "Hell yes. Wanna grab a quick coffee?"

"Can't now—I have to meet Ford. I'll text you, though."

"Ford? What—Tessa?"

Tessa blew her a kiss and quickly headed out, not having the time or inclination to get grilled by her bestie. She'd been seeing a lot of Ford, which of course was due to the makeover and training to get Patricia to fall in love with him, but her friends had been getting a bit suspicious.

They'd stared at her like she'd been brainwashed when she got into a lively discussion about Sue Bird and how she was the oldest player in the WNBA.

It didn't take her long to get to Ford's place. At least the outside wasn't bad, and hopefully with the new decor, it would be enough to satisfy Patricia.

He opened the door with a grumpy expression, and she studied the stacks of boxes littered throughout the rooms. The television was blasting as some sports reporter droned on in monotone.

"You didn't even open the boxes yet?" she asked, arching a brow as she stepped carefully through the maze.

"I was waiting for you."

"I don't open stuff, dude." She flashed her lemon-colored nails. "I just got a spring manicure."

Ford shot her a glare, which she ignored, and he disappeared, possibly to get a box cutter or scissors. She took the opportunity to grab the remote and lower the volume. He raced back in the room with a wild look in his eyes. "It got quiet—what'd I miss?"

"Are you serious? It's not the World Series—didn't they just have Opening Day last week?"

"Yeah, but these past few games for the Mets have been the best in years. With the payroll expanding, our new pitcher, and a few smart trades, we decided . . . are you listening?"

"Sure," she lied, wandering around trying to see where the Pier 1 pillow box would be. She couldn't wait to see if the colors would pop like she imagined. "You're excited."

"All the fans are."

"Are we the blue uniforms?"

"No, we're the black. The Mets are playing the Marlins."

"I always thought the Mets were blue and orange. I know people who wear the baseball hats—when did they change their colors?"

Ford's voice cranked with hostility. "Are we discussing colors again? Teams have multiple uniforms. Mets have six. They wear up to three different ones for home games, two for away, and one for batting practice. Not that it matters."

"I'm impressed. Clothes make the man and the player," she announced. Ah, she was sure she'd found the pillows. "Here, open this one first."

Thankfully, a commercial came on, so he ripped the carton open and exposed four gorgeous, fluffy, vibrant throw pillows. The bold burnt-orange and yellow swirls seemed to ignite some energy in the room.

Ford frowned as he held them in front of his chest. "They look different from the picture. Don't you think they're really . . . bright?"

Tessa crisscrossed to another box and pointed with triumph. "There are the slipcovers. You'll love them—my friend was able to rush the order."

He obediently opened the second box and removed a swath of fabric in oatmeal shot with threads of silver.

"Oh, they're going to look amazing." She beamed. "Let's put it on."

Ford gave her a hard stare. "After the game. We can't concentrate on renovation and baseball at the same time."

"I can. I'm a multitasking queen."

"Well, I'm not. Let's sit and enjoy my comfy sofa before we stiffen it all up."

"I relish your appreciation for me trying to help you."

"Sit."

She muttered under her breath but took her usual spot on his sofa. If they ever needed another training session, Tessa would insist they go to her place. "Fine. Tell me what's happening in simple terms that won't bore me to tears."

Ford jabbed his index finger at the oversize screen. "We're rooting for the Mets. We're at bat right now, and the score is still zero to zero.

The players get to bat until they get three outs, then they switch to the field."

"If they don't hit the ball three times, it's a strikeout, right?"

He scratched his head. "Well, sometimes. If they fully swing and miss three pitches, then it's a strikeout. But if they don't swing and the pitch is out of the strike zone, the umpire can call it a ball. If they get four balls, it's a walk and they get to go to first base."

"They need to be careful about deciding to swing, then."

"Exactly."

He explained a few more basic rules that had her nodding. "Kelsey and her girlfriend are big into softball, so I got dragged to a few games. I assume they're the same rules?"

"Close enough."

"Can I grab a Spindrift, too, or will I miss something major?"

She almost laughed at the way he studied her with suspicion to see if she was making fun of his precious game. He grunted, and she made herself at home, sitting gingerly at the end of the awful couch.

She got through the first quarter—or inning—while he explained the endless rules of the game with a patience she appreciated. "See, the pitcher and catcher have a unique relationship. If they connect, it's like magic. There's a respect in that partnership."

"How come you're wearing your baseball cap backwards?"

"Because it's the way I get the team to win."

She blinked. "If you turned it forward, they'd lose?"

"Yes."

She wanted to laugh but knew this was serious for him. "What if they lose when it's backwards? Do you then turn it forward?"

The grouchiness was back, but his face had an adorable type of pout now that his mouth and jaw were exposed. "No, it's always like this. Oh, look at that hit! Holy crap, what a catch! Did you see that, Tessa?" He practically shimmered with excitement and energy. "That's our shortstop, who was able to snag it and get the out. If he hadn't, there would have been a runner on base."

"That was kind of cool," Tessa admitted. "Can we open another box at the next commercial?"

"No. Let me tell you about the different types of pitches. Everything changed this year because there was a big scandal of stealing signs from the catcher. They used to make hand signals to the pitcher between their legs so the pitcher knew what type of ball to pitch."

"They switch balls?"

He glared. "No! I don't mean different balls—I mean curveball, breaking ball, fastball, that kind of stuff."

"Sorry, you weren't clear."

He ripped off his hat and used both hands to scratch his head. The strands stood up in a messy tangle that could be considered sexy. Patricia would definitely think so. Of course, only after this apartment looked less like a fraternity and more like it was owned by a grown-ass man.

Ford was talking endlessly, caught up in the glory and love of the game, his hands moving fast, face animated with passion. Even though it wasn't her thing, she liked that he cared so deeply about something. Maybe that was what she was missing in a man. She'd go on date after date, seeking to connect on a deeper spiritual level. She wasn't looking for someone to be exactly like her, but she'd begun to respect men who believed in something. Ryder was dedicated to his students and the youth group. Palmer's wedding company and family filled him with a purpose that drove him daily. Chiara and Malia both became part of that same devotion.

But the men Tessa met weren't like that. Instead, they were lukewarm about their jobs unless the focus was money. Too cynical to believe they could change the world. Trapped in a routine like they wanted to check off boxes for each level of their life without asking why.

But Ford did. His life was full of purpose, from his job, to his friends, to his love of sports. And he wanted to include Patricia in all of it, with no holding back. It was rare to find.

"Tessa? Are you getting all of this?"

She blinked and the fog cleared. "Yes. I think the guy on first base is going to steal."

He replaced his hat, turned back to the screen, and frowned. "No, he wouldn't take that risk with two outs. There might be a hit-and-run play on, though, which could explain his big lead off the bag."

She gave a delicate shrug and examined her nail. Dammit, one was already chipped. "He doesn't want to wait. He wanted to steal the last time he was on first and looked frustrated he didn't get a chance."

Ford gave her a patronizing look. "Well, he's not going to steal, but I think you're really starting to understand the game better. Most would never have even—oh my God, he's stealing!"

"Told you."

Tessa watched the man on-screen haul his cute, tight ass toward second base like a bullet shot from a gun. She barely flinched when he slid hard past the bag, his fingers still touching as the second baseman tagged him and began yelling at the guy in black that he got him. The coach/umpire person made a hand signal, and Ford sprang to his feet yelling, "Safe!"

Tessa glanced at the tied score. "If they get this run, do we win?"

Ford shook his head. "This is the top of the ninth inning, and we're not at Citi Field, so that means the Marlins get one last shot to beat us. But first we have to get our guy across home plate."

"We will. That guy is hungry."

She was calm as her prediction came true. They scored a run, and the other team couldn't make it up, giving the Mets the win.

Finally. Now they could decorate.

Tessa tried not to smile at Ford's celebration and kept serious. "Are you a sulker if your team loses?"

His grin came easy. “Nah. I like to yell a bit, blow off steam, but then it’s done. I don’t hold grudges or play many what-if games. I think life is more pleasant when you live it as if it’s all a gift. You just get to decide what you want to do with it.”

“Even the bad stuff?” she asked curiously.

His grin gentled and his gaze probed hers slowly. “Especially the bad stuff.”

She nibbled her lip. “Did you have a lot of it?”

“No. I was lucky. A little bullying when I was young, but nothing I couldn’t handle. Another thing sports helped me with. Gave me confidence in myself. It’s hard to find your worth when you’re young. That’s why I think that internship program you’re doing at Quench is so important.”

His words surprised her, along with his truth. Odd how they’d become more comfortable talking openly with each other over these past few weeks. “Well, I’m just glad you’re not one of those awful sore losers who ruin an entire night over one lost game.”

“Nope. But you are.”

She gasped. “Am not.”

He burst into laughter. “You went on for half an hour after UConn lost last week, pulling apart all the things that weren’t fair.”

Tessa gave a haughty sniff. “You’re such a liar. I took your lesson and watched my first baseball game. Can we get to the fun part of this little trip now?”

“Let’s go. I’ll open the rest.”

The next hour, treasure after treasure emerged and Tessa put him to work. They put the covers on the couch, hung paintings, put together a bookcase, and swapped in new trendy dining stools for the kitchen. Dish towels were replaced, and a large tapestry rug was rolled out to cover up some of the worst stains in the living room.

“The floor guy can rip up the carpet at the end of the month, so you can just tell Patricia you’re restoring the wood. But this is a great transition feature, and I got it for a deal.”

Ford groaned as he tugged and pulled the giant rug around to get it straight. "Why are you putting out more pillows? She's gonna think I have a problem."

Tessa rolled her eyes and studied her handiwork. "Trust me, it looks great. Now, let's get all those posters off the wall so she doesn't think you're a teenage boy."

"No! Those came from my dad, when we'd stalk flea markets looking for rare player cards and posters. They have meaning when I look at them. I know they look juvenile, but I can't—"

"Will you calm down? I sensed they were important to you, so I won't take them away. I just need to make them presentable." She slit open another package with a letter opener and took out a stack of frames in various sizes of beautiful grained wood. "We're going to put them all in frames and do a collage. I already printed out the template for the wall over there."

He dropped the edge of the rug and came over. After studying the contents, he got a funny look on his face when he stared at her. "You never planned to get rid of them, did you?"

"No one should get to tell you what to love, Ford. The right person would never even ask."

He gave a jolt, then ripped his gaze away. He didn't speak for a while, and she gave him the space, not sure what was going on. Finally, he nodded. "Thank you, Tessa. That meant more than you know."

Her heart pounded a bit hard in her chest, but she ignored it and focused on her task.

Finally, they were done. The place looked updated and reflected more of a successful man who made a home rather than a room at a dorm. The clutter either organized or gone. The couch and chair looked inviting yet stylish. Accents of color evened out any remaining mud brown, and the walls held some classic photos of historic sports moments in sleek black and white, matching perfectly with the other frames.

"Halfway there. Once the floors are done and we gut the bedroom, you'll be good to go." Suddenly, it hit her that in her zeal to get everything done, she hadn't stopped to check in. "Do you like it? We can change anything you want. You're the one who needs to live here, so I tried to keep your personality and flavor, just streamline it a bit. Especially for Patricia."

"I love it."

Pleasure speared through her. "Oh, good. Sometimes I get carried away."

"You're really good at this," Ford said softly. "All of it. And though at first I thought I'd never get through the game without strangling you, you managed to surprise me."

Tessa waved her hand in the air in dismissal. "It was nothing. Everyone has a gift. Giving people a little tune-up and getting others to love them just happens to be mine."

A tiny frown creased his brow. The deep golden brown of his eyes seemed almost hypnotizing. "Actually, I meant baseball. I didn't think you were paying attention, but you soaked in most of what I said the very first time."

"I have a good memory."

"Funny, me too. It's actually photographic."

"That's right. You told me the night we babysat Veronica." She pondered the comment for a moment. "Mine's not photographic, but I have this talent with people. It's like I sense things about them that others don't. I know what they're going to do, or what they really want. But I rarely tell anyone about it. People think I'm too pretty to be that smart."

Tessa meant it as a joke, but he took her seriously, nodding. "I bet too many do. I think I did."

Her voice died in her throat. She stared at him, unsure of the sudden crackling in the air, the surge of intimacy between them. "You did?"

"Yeah. I'm sorry for that. I think I was an asshole."

Tessa managed to rally. "You were."

Still, he didn't laugh or try to lighten the mood. He leaned in a few inches, and she caught the clean masculine scent of him, soap and spice and skin. "I'll never underestimate you again."

The breath seemed to leak from her lungs. Recognition flowed between them, and in that one instant, she felt completely connected to this man who seemed to truly get her in a way she'd never experienced before. It was heady and powerful.

And it completely freaked her out.

She jumped back, and a maniacal laugh escaped her lips. "Good to know. I gotta get back to the office."

"This late? Wanna get something to eat?"

She stumbled for the door. "No! I'm good, tons of work to do."

"Okay, I'll call you before I meet Patricia. Just to go over stuff one more time."

She stuck her thumb up in the air like an idiot and grinned. "Awesome! See ya!"

Tessa ran to her car, unlocked it, and shuddered. Whatever had happened in there may have been strange, but it was over and there was no need to revisit it. Sometimes, working with someone on such a vulnerable level opened up doors. It meant nothing.

Nothing at all.

Because he was in love with Patricia.

And she would never fit into Ford Maddox's life.

Chapter Fifteen

"Hey, dudes, how've you been?" Ford fist-bumped his friends Ryder and Palmer, motioning to the empty stools he'd saved.

Murphy's was his favorite watering hole, known for their burgers, beer, and mega televisions that broadcast all the good games. The crowd was loud, a bit rude, but good-natured. It didn't hurt that Murphy was a huge fan of his show and always catered to him and his boys.

"Good. Haven't seen you in a while other than the youth center. Glad you called," Ryder said with a grin, giving the bartender a wave as his Sam Adams was slapped in front of him. His ride-or-die was dressed in casual jeans and a T-shirt and seemed to radiate a sense of calm happiness Ford appreciated. Since marrying Chiara and having Ronnie, Ryder was different but better. It was nice seeing his longtime friend settle happily into domestic bliss.

"You saved my ass from playing referee at a rehearsal," Palmer said, grabbing his Guinness with a grunt.

Ford cocked his head. "You own the company. Figured you were too much of a big shot to attend rehearsals."

Palmer snorted, but it came out elegant. The man seemed to emanate class and grace, still dressed in his sharp designer suit, red tie, and real wing-tipped shoes. "I'm usually safe, but the groom has a high possibility of being our next president. I have Emeril in charge, but I may have to head out if I get an SOS."

Ford laughed. "Only you, man. Make sure you extract a favor before the end of the night. In writing."

"Only if the event goes off without a hitch."

They all laughed and drank.

Ryder turned to Ford with curiosity. "You look great."

"Yeah, nice jacket," Palmer said.

Ford looked down at his Def Leppard T-shirt and ragged denim jacket he'd just picked up the other day. "Thanks." He was starting to get to know his style now and was more comfortable picking out clothes. "Tessa got me started on a new look after I got rid of the beard. Patricia seems to like it."

Ryder's brow shot up. "Fill us in on the Patricia thing. Did you start to date?"

He thought of last night and couldn't help the smile that tugged at his lips. The evening had gone flawlessly. He'd kept it to one drink and turned her down when she hinted at going to dinner. It was getting a bit easier to keep the delicate balance of showing he was interested but keeping her challenged. They'd flirted, and Ford got the impression she'd be open to a bit more. Of course, he held back, as Patricia believed he was still with Tessa, but soon the whole ruse would be done and he could finally be committed to the woman he loved. "Kind of. I'm taking it slow."

Ford filled the guys in on his plan, noting their shared glance and drawn faces. When he was finished, there was a strange silence broken only by the shouts and chatter of the bar.

"What's wrong?" he asked. "I figured you'd be happy for me."

"We are," Ryder said, holding his hand up. "But I've seen you do this stuff before, man. Get all focused on a woman you think is the one, get treated like shit, and show up for more. Are you sure Patricia isn't just a game player?"

Ford shook his head vehemently. "No, not this one. She's a sweetheart. She's looking for a guy to really settle down with, but I have to get her there."

Palmer cleared his throat. "Get her where, Ford? Out of the friend zone?"

"Exactly! Tessa's been pretending to be my girlfriend, so that allowed Patricia to see me in a different light. I'm almost there. I'm planning to ask her out soon."

"Tessa?" Ryder asked.

"No! Patricia!"

Ryder jabbed him playfully on the shoulder. "Better clean up your frat room, dude."

"Oh, Tessa helped me redecorate the whole thing. You gotta see it now. It's real nice."

Another strange shared look. Ford slammed his beer down and faced his friends. "Okay, I'm getting weirded out. Why do you keep looking at each other like you know something I don't?"

Palmer opened his mouth, then shut it. He seemed to punt the responsibility to Ryder, who took up the lead. "You've been spending a lot of time with Tessa lately."

"Yeah. I told you, she's doing this whole makeover thing on me and writing it up for Quench, so we have to hang together a lot."

Palmer leaned in. "You seem to be enjoying her company. You used to hardly be able to stand her."

"You could barely babysit Veronica together," Ryder pointed out. "Now, you see her on a near-daily basis."

Ford laughed and relaxed. "Is that what you're worried about? No way, there's nothing going on with me and Tessa. I'm in love with Patricia, and Tessa's writing me up for her column. Plus, I'm helping get the Quench sports podcast running. We're using each other."

Ryder coughed. "In how many ways?"

Ford stared at his friends in shock. "We're not sleeping together! I told you it's not like that."

"Malia said Tessa was over at your house just this week watching the Mets game," Palmer said. "Tessa doesn't like sports."

Ford grabbed for patience. "For the podcast. I forced her to do some research. All right, enough of this. You're both on the wrong path and starting to freak me out. There is absolutely nothing happening with me and Tessa. We're completely different. Sure, we respect each other more, but there's no physical chemistry." The lie burned on his tongue, but he said it anyway.

Any living, breathing guy would have a physical connection with Tessa. The woman was a ball of passionate fire, and it was hard not to imagine her bringing all that life force to the bedroom. But he had to stop the gossip in its tracks or he'd be dealing with this shit every time they had a drink together.

His friends were worse gossips than the women.

Ryder held up both his hands. "Okay, if you say so. We just wanted you to set the record straight."

"And I did. Can we move on now? How's your sex life, Palmer?"

Palmer laughed. "Great. And that's all the details you're getting on that."

"Ditto," Ryder said.

Ford grunted. "You're both getting boring now that you're settled."

"As will you once you and Patricia make it formal. You gonna cook for her on your first date?" Ryder asked.

"Nah. Tessa said she'd set up reservations at a fancy steak pub for me."

"Riiiight," Palmer said, obviously trying hard not to laugh. "When are you doing the Quench podcast? Did you pick your subject?"

"Well, she got hooked on women's college basketball."

"Who got hooked on women's college basketball?" Ryder asked in confusion.

"Tessa. Anyway, I figured we'd tackle professional female athletes for the podcast. Discuss the options available off-season. Too many of them don't get paid enough and need to supplement their income with games outside the country."

"Who're you doing the podcast with?" Palmer asked.

"Tessa."

Another shared look.

Ford glared. "She's one of the owners, so it makes sense she's involved. I gave her a pool of candidates to take over after I leave."

"How many episodes are you doing?" Ryder asked.

"Just three. Then they'll be off and running, and we won't be seeing each other anymore."

"Riiight," Ryder said, draining his beer.

"Thanks for the fun night, guys. I should've had my root canal scheduled instead."

They laughed and finally changed the subject. Ford spent the next hour catching up with his friends, had another beer, and headed home by 10:00 p.m.

A pleasant buzz filled his body, which had nothing to do with alcohol. If things went well with his upcoming "breakup," he'd ask Patricia out for next Saturday night. He needed to make sure Tessa was on the same page about how to handle the next few days. Ford couldn't be known as a cheater. She would know exactly what he should say.

He chuckled at the way Ryder and Palmer had ridden him about Tessa. Sure, he'd been spending a lot of time with her when they'd been natural enemies for years, but it was weird his friends would even think there was a possibility of a romantic relationship between them. They were too different. They'd drive each other mad with frustration if they were involved. Ford could admit Tessa was a lot cooler than he'd originally thought, though. Not as stuck up, and her sharp mind was able to follow sports in a way he rarely saw in a person.

Still. The idea of them together was laughable.

He knew he'd better call her, though. Just for a bit of last-minute training before he saw Patricia again.

~

"I have a date tomorrow night."

Malia and Chiara gave a nice little scream, which made Tessa feel good. God knows, it was about time. Her single status never bothered her, but even she admitted it had been a bit too long since she had some decent male company. Ford excluded, of course.

"Who's the guy?" Malia demanded.

Chiara waved at Mike. "Wait, hold up. I want to give you my full concentration, and I need a glass of wine."

Mike stopped at their table. "How are you girls doing? Refills? Cravings? At least for you two."

He shot Tessa a pained look, and she blew out a breath. "Mike! You can't still be mad at me for ditching you at the steakhouse. I did it for your own good."

He shook his head and wiped his hands on his apron. "That's what I used to say to Rory when I made her stop dating that punk on the motorcycle. She didn't agree with me then, and I don't agree with you now."

Tessa gave him the puppy dog eyes that he was never able to resist. "But you did amazing—you have a real date! Alone! Tomorrow, right?"

"You can come if you want and make it up to me."

They all laughed. "No, you'll do fine. Emma called me and said she's excited."

Mike squinted with suspicion. "For real? Or are you trying to butter me up?"

"No, for real." Tessa smiled. "She likes you, Mike. Just be yourself and have fun."

"Fine."

"Where are you taking her?" Chiara asked.

Mike blinked. "Here."

Tessa's heart sank. *Oh no.* "What do you mean 'here'?"

He threw out his hand. "I'm meeting her here at the diner. I won't cook, though. It will be like I'm officially off for the night—Joe said he'd handle things for me."

"Oh, hell no," Tessa announced, banging her hand on the table. "You will not be here on a date at your workplace, where you can jump up at any ridiculous distraction." Grabbing her phone, she tapped out a number. "Hold on."

Her friends were meekly quiet, probably sensing she'd gone into fixer mode and needed to concentrate.

"Miranda? I need you to squeeze in a reservation for two, tomorrow at six p.m. I know. I'm sorry—yes. Something cozy. You will? I owe you big time, thank you." She clicked off and gave Mike a proud look. "You're going to Mia Casa—my friend will take good care of you."

Malia shook her head. "Dayum, they're booked up for months. Emma will love it."

Mike looked like he'd swallowed a sharp object. "A fancy Italian place where pasta is fifty bucks a plate? Why can't we eat here? Joe'll make her whatever she wants! We'll be comfortable and not stuck around strangers."

Tessa's heart squeezed, but she made sure she kept her voice firm. "No, Mike. You will take Emma out on a real fancy date to a restaurant you don't own. Alone. And you will be fine."

Mike gave her a stubborn glare, but she stared him down and finally he huffed. "Fine. When I mess this up, it will be your fault."

"I shall take full responsibility," Tessa said.

Chiara sighed. "Now I really need that chardonnay."

"Coming right up. But not for Tessa." He stalked off, obviously irritated, and Tessa tried not to laugh.

Malia burst into giggles. "I feel so bad, but at the same time, he's so cute. He really has a crush."

"Finally. It just took me almost two years to get them together!"

Chiara waved her hand. "Okay, back to your dating yumminess. Tell us."

Tessa took a bite of her veggie burger. They waited patiently while she chewed. "Tinder."

Malia groaned. "God, no! Tinder was like my nemesis—I never met one decent guy on that app."

"Well, it's been okay for me, but I hadn't met anyone that really interested me in a while. It's the strangest thing—the last two dates I had set up ended in disaster. The artist ghosted me outright, and the second guy canceled a few hours beforehand." She wrinkled her nose. "I hate being ghosted. It made me begin to doubt myself—my instincts are usually spot-on, even over social media."

"That is weird," Malia said. "I mean, I got ghosted regularly, but you never had my luck."

"Hopefully, this one will show. He works as a pastry chef at Le Doucet Bakery, so he's got a job he's passionate about. He's very cute, and we messaged each other the past few days doing some witty banter, so he's got a brain. I have a good feeling about this one."

Chiara tapped her lips. "Chefs are a bit temperamental," she said slowly. "And they work late nights and every weekend."

"Yes, but he does pastries, so his hours don't suck."

Malia lit up. "Good point! Okay, show us his pic and bio."

Mike dropped off the chardonnays, and Tessa passed her phone around. Excitement flickered. It seemed like everyone was falling in love except her, but a little good old-fashioned lust would put her in a more positive mood.

"Approved?" she asked.

"Yes. Just make sure you text us before you go. I saw the documentary *The Tinder Swindler*, and it was scary," Malia said with a shudder.

Tessa snorted. "As if I'd give some man my money."

"We all fall prey to wanting to believe the people we love. Speaking of which, how's it going with Ford?" Chiara asked, eyes glinting with shameful curiosity. "Sebastian said Ford told him you were watching a Mets game together and redid his apartment. Seems like you guys are hanging out a lot."

Malia cranked her head around. "Hmm, you two couldn't even be in the same room together, and now you're getting cozy on his couch?"

"Don't even start." Tessa plucked the glass of wine from Chiara's side of the table and stole a sip. "It's for my makeover column. The man's in love with Patricia—I'm only helping him get her."

"And the podcast? You two are doing that together, also?"

Her gaze narrowed. "Yes, because you made me! He's only doing a few episodes, and then I think we should hire Aston from LWW Enterprises. She's savvy, has a kick-ass résumé, and knows all the hot topics when it comes to women and sports. Plus, Ford highly recommended her."

Malia nodded. "I really liked her, and she passed both interviews with outstanding scores."

"Good," Tessa said. "In the meantime, Ford will hook up with Patricia, and we'll stop seeing each other."

The words felt strange coming from her lips. She was getting used to his constant texts that turned into jokes and casual banter. Being around him was becoming more comfortable, like he'd become a friend. But she'd have to smother any type of friendship with him once he started dating Patricia. They could never tell her they'd posed as boyfriend and girlfriend, and Tessa couldn't hang out with him at all after they became official.

No big deal.

"Are you still pretending to be his girlfriend?" Chiara asked.

"For a little while longer." She pondered her burger, caught off guard by the sudden emotions at the thought of Ford getting hurt by Patricia. "I just hope she's worth it."

"You think she'll hurt him?" Malia asked. "Did you warn him? You have the most amazing instincts when it comes to people."

Tessa forced a shrug. "Nothing I can do. You love who you love, I guess."

"Or you don't realize who's been right in front of you all along," Chiara quipped.

Tessa's friends stared at her strangely, so she propped her elbows up on the table and gave it back to them. "Say it, dudes. What's the problem?"

Malia cleared her throat. "Do you like Ford?"

She blinked. Then began laughing. "Oh my God! Do you think I'm falling for Ford?" She shook her head, and curls bounced across her cheeks. "We're pretending to be a couple. Catching a few sports games at his apartment and taking him shopping for new clothes isn't dating. You're just desperate, aren't you?"

"For what?" Chiara asked.

"For me to be hooked up like you two! I'm the last single one here at the table, and I think you're worried."

Malia tossed her a gentle look that made her want to scream. "As long as you're happy, we don't care. You've just been a bit . . . off lately. And then you started hanging with Ford, and you have a new pep in your step, so it wasn't a far-off leap to take that he was the one making you happy."

"It's a leap, all right. Right off a cliff." Tessa let out a breath. "Look, I'm happy because the internship is expanding, and I'm doing something different. I'm happy because my best friends are happy, and I like helping people find their happiness. Ford is just my latest victim. Can we drop the subject now? This is no *My Fair Lady* or . . ."

"*She's All That*?" Malia jumped in helpfully.

"I was going to say *The Devil Wears Prada*," Chiara said. "The fashion in that movie kills me."

"Why aren't there more men makeover movies?" Tessa asked. "That's kind of messed up."

"Oh, *Can't Buy Me Love* is one!" Malia practically squealed. "Oldie but goodie."

Tessa snapped her fingers. "*Crazy, Stupid, Love* is another. I love how Ryan Gosling's character makes over Steve Carell. But there's not half as many as female ones. Why are women usually the ones forced to change? Makes me so mad."

"Maybe we can take Ford's story and sell it to a producer," Chiara suggested.

They shared a look and burst into laughter.

Mike appeared by the table and stared at them with suspicion. "Did you girls drink too much? You're awfully giggly. I can give you a ride home."

"We're fine, Mike. Just loud," Malia said.

A reluctant grin flashed. "You girls used to wake me up in the middle of the night all the time. Screeching at scary movies and laughing hysterically at those silly comedies." His blue eyes lit up with the memory. "I miss it sometimes."

At that moment, all Tessa could think of was Rory. Tears burned her eyes, but it was Mike's face that almost made her fall apart.

Tessa got out of the booth and gave Mike a hug. "Me, too. Don't be mad at me anymore, okay? Just promise to go out and have fun with Emma. Give yourself a chance."

He hugged her back. "Okay."

In that moment, hope made everything perfect.

Chapter Sixteen

"Hey."

Tessa blinked and stared at the man framed in her doorway. Ford held a case of beer in one hand—the light, fruity one she loved—and a bag that emanated some amazing smells of garlic and spices. "What are you doing here? It's Saturday."

He gave a big grin and pushed past her without waiting for an invite. "Yeah, I know. The Mets are playing the Phillies—one of our rivals—and you didn't answer your phone. You gotta start picking up."

She stomped behind him in aggravation. She'd just completed a deep conditioning of her hair, which was now shoved into two short pigtails. Her outfit consisted of ragged jeans that were extra big and comfy, Skechers pink sandals, and a T-shirt with Mickey and Minnie on it kissing in Paris. At least she wasn't in a green mud mask, but Ford was making a terrible habit of showing up in her castle uninvited. "You have to stop coming over without my permission. If you ever do that to Patricia, you'll be in the doghouse."

"Don't worry, I only do it with you. I brought lunch—you mentioned you hadn't had Indian in a while, so I picked up some stuff I thought you'd like. Where's your remote?"

Tessa got caught between wanting to forage in the bag and giving in to his outrageous demands. "Ford, I mean it. I had a beauty day planned and was going to organize my shoes, and then I have a big date tonight. I have no time for this now."

His grin caught her off guard. "A date, huh? Good for you. I won't stay long—just for a few innings. We can go over the podcast for next week, and I'll be out of your hair. Besides, you don't need a beauty day or more shoes. You look adorable."

Oh, he did not just say that to her. Steam practically radiated from her pores, but he couldn't tell because he was grabbing plates and unpacking the food. "I do not look adorable," she said through gritted teeth. "I'm a grown-ass woman with sex appeal, and you don't get to tell me what I need to do."

Ford rolled his eyes. "Why don't women get it? Men love jeans, a T-shirt, and a ponytail. You're a beautiful woman, Tessa, and all that extra makeup and costumes you wear are fun, but this shows the best of you. This is a woman men want to hang with. Oh, there's the remote."

The shock kept her mute while he clicked on the game, pumped up the volume, and resumed dishing out the food. It was a backhanded compliment, and she wasn't sure if she should yell or thank him. Tessa chose the middle ground. "Another thing you don't know about women. They don't want a man to 'hang with.' They want to rock his world."

"You do." At her bug-eyed stare, he shook his head. "I mean, you do to other men. I'm sure your date tonight will be knocked out. Now, can we sit and eat and watch some baseball?"

She let him win this round because the curry and coconut rice were tempting her. Keeping a haughty silence, she took her plate and sat on the silver beaded wingback chair. Ford pulled over the glass table, popped open a beer, and placed it down.

"Coasters!"

"Fine, fine." He wriggled around and groaned. "This furniture is uncomfortable. How do you chill?"

"I chill fine. Get used to it—I'm sure Patricia's apartment is nice, and you need to have manners."

"I can guarantee Patricia has a big-ass sectional we can laze around on. She's cool."

Tessa snorted but managed to keep her opinion to herself. The Indian food helped, and she dug in with gusto.

"I want you to focus on the pitching today. Our rotation is finally top notch and our best asset to reach the playoffs."

"We're a ton of games away from the playoffs, right? Why are you so invested this early in the season?" she grumbled.

Ford looked horrified, which was also pretty cute. Those hooded hazel eyes went wide, and his chiseled jaw firmed. His hair was a bit mussed and fell over his broad forehead, flirting with those fierce angled brows. The more time she spent with him, the more she realized how attractive he was. But it was his expressions she enjoyed most—the ones he'd hidden for years under all that facial hair.

"Every game is critical," he said slowly. "Especially for a Mets fan."

"But you have to talk about all teams, not just the Mets. Can't you get in trouble for showing favoritism?"

He gave a half shrug. "No, because I love the game, so I'm always fair. I respect the hell out of the Yankees and every team. I just happen to have a soft spot for the Mets."

"Why?"

A quick flash of a sad smile took her by surprise. "My dad. He was a real fan for the underdog. In fact, he was the one who kept me sane while I tried to excel at all the sports I loved. Kept telling me I'd find my place, but it may not be the one I originally planned for. Man plans and—"

"God laughs."

He nodded. "Exactly. We'd spend Sunday afternoons together at the occasional ball game, even though it was expensive as hell and my parents didn't have a ton of money." He seemed caught up in the memories. "He was a good man. A good dad."

"Did he pass?"

"Yeah, five years ago. Too damn young. It's funny—I'm an adult, but when you lose a parent, it's like you become an orphan. There's really no one else in the world who truly gives a shit about you like your parents. Every time I watch a game, I think of him. It makes me happy."

Warmth infused her. He was so open about his emotions, which was a strange combination with his tendency to be rough around the edges. She'd never really met a man like that before. The ones she'd dated seemed to fall into two camps: overly masculine and in control, or pensive, deep creatives who wanted to steep themselves in their feelings. A longing surged, but she didn't know what it was for or where it came from. "I'm close with my parents, too. A total daddy's girl."

"That doesn't surprise me."

She laughed. "They retired and moved away. I miss them. Can't imagine how hard it must've been to lose your dad. I'm still wrecked over Rory and how Mike struggles daily to accept her loss. How we all do."

"Yeah. I think—holy crap! I think that's going over the wall!"

Tessa watched the guy run hard to first base while the stadium held its breath as the ball soared toward the sky. Then it skimmed right over the barrier edge and kept going. "Home run!" she yelled, pumping her fist in the air. "I cannot believe he hit that slider!"

Ford stopped his own fist pumping and stared at her. "What did you say?"

"The slider. It tripped him up last time against the Marlins, but this time he got right under it."

"Are you kidding me?"

Tessa squirmed under his intense scrutiny. "What? Did I mess up? Dude, calm down—I'm doing my best. Don't be a jerk."

"No, you don't get it." He put down his plate and scratched his head, as if trying to search for the words. "How did you know that pitch was a slider?"

She shrugged. "I don't know. You must've told me a million times what each pitch was. What's the big deal?"

He muttered something under his breath, and she couldn't tell if he was pissed or happy. "Trust me, it's a big deal. People just don't recognize a pitch after being told what it is. That comes after a long time of watching baseball."

She rolled her eyes. "Whatevs. I don't know why you're freaking out. Eat your curry."

He tossed her an irritated look and picked up his plate again. "I have three guests lined up for the podcast. The first episode will be an intro to what Quench wants to cover—you can talk about your own experience with sports and how you all came to realize it was important content to bring to your readers."

She ignored the twinge in her belly and tried to sound confident. "Yep, I got that covered."

"Then I have Erin, who's doing me a favor. We'll do a bit of a dive on how professional female athletes are usually underpaid and have a harder time getting work in the off-season."

Tessa nodded. "I'll make sure I research it. This is an important topic, so I want to continue the discussion."

"I'm here just to get you started. Do you know who you're going to hire?"

"Yes, Aston from LWW Enterprises accepted the position. She'll be perfect for the team."

Ford looked pleased. "I'm glad—she was my pick, too. Aston can get a bit fiery, but I think that will be a draw for Quench listeners. Opinionated, passionate people are what make this country great."

"Agreed. Oh, I like that Nemo guy. Look at him go after that ball—he caught it!"

"Nimmo."

"Close enough."

He laughed, and she laughed with him.

Unbelievably, the next few innings flew by as they each had another beer and traded quips. Today's lesson was on how plays were called and the intricate chess moves a manager had to make about defensive positioning, pitcher/batter matchups, and whether to use a pinch hitter or runner. Tessa still thought the game was super slow—not as exciting as basketball—but she respected the array of puzzle pieces and the classic traditions of the game. She was beginning to see why it was considered America's pastime.

At the commercial break, Ford turned to her. "Tessa?"

"Yeah?"

"Do you think next weekend is too soon to sleep with Patricia?"

She almost spit out her beer but managed to keep cool. "Dude, aren't you telling her we just broke up? I thought you'd have a mourning period over me."

"I will! But if she's feeling the vibe, and I am, it may be acceptable."

Tessa put down her beer and tugged on one of her pigtails to keep herself grounded. "Ford, you have to remember this isn't about sex. You're playing a long game here. I'd advise to take it really slow, because the longer you wait, the better you'll know each other. It also gives plenty of time to build up the sexual tension."

He nodded eagerly. "Right. Tension is good."

"It's everything. Think about the deliciousness of leading up to a good kiss. You have to focus on all the senses, especially to turn a woman on." She frowned. "You do know this, right?"

Now he looked offended. "Of course! Forget it. I was just asking. Let's drop it."

But now he'd opened Pandora's box, and she was curious. "You know you can't turn into a sweet puppy dog after a kiss, right? Remember, you wanted this. Patricia thinks you're a guy who's in command. Hard to get. You can't be pouring your heart out to her right away or she'll take a step back."

"I know! I've been with a million women before—I know what I'm doing."

"A million?"

He gave an irritated huff. "A lot."

Tessa nibbled at her lip. "I'm having a bad feeling about this. Patricia wants a certain type. Can you really be that for her? Is this really worth trying to change for?"

He got up from the couch, all bearish and prickly. "Yes, I keep telling you—I love this woman."

"You love a woman you've never kissed? Or been on vacation with? Or even seen her home?"

His gaze narrowed. "Yes."

"Fine. Then let's get this over with." She patted her lips with a napkin, strode to the kitchen, and returned with a mint. "Take this."

He stared at it with confusion but popped it in his mouth.

She grabbed another one and did the same. Tugging down her T-shirt, she squared her shoulders and faced him. "We better practice."

He blinked. "Practice what?"

"Kissing. I'll let you know if you need a bit of tweaking."

She'd never seen his ears burn red before. "Oh, hell no."

"What's the problem? I won't be mean—I'm here to help you."

He jabbed his finger in the air. "I do not need you to help me learn how to kiss. I'm perfectly capable of turning on a woman, okay?"

"Okay, but you're not understanding. Patricia wants a dominant personality. A take-charge type. This is your remade persona, and I'm the perfect person to practice on—we barely tolerate one another, so if you can turn me on, you got this."

"I'm outta here."

He turned, but she grabbed his solid biceps and held on. "Ford, stop. I think this will be perfect for my column! Sexuality is a big part of foreplay and falling in love. This could be a major turning point in your relationship. Do you really want to leave it up to chance?"

Tessa watched him curse under his breath and march back and forth as if he were trapped in a cage. She waited him out, knowing he'd eventually agree.

"Shit. Fine. I'll do it."

She rolled her eyes. "Wow, thanks. I feel so honored. You can at least be a tiny bit grateful."

He glared. "Don't push it. Let's get this humiliation over with."

"Fine. I'm all flushed and swoony already." His jaw clenched, and she tried not to laugh. God, she loved sparring with him. She felt so . . . alive.

"What do you want me to do?"

"Pretend I'm Patricia. We're at your place, and we just had dinner and some wine. We've flirted. There's a connection, but I'm waiting to see what happens next. I'm excited. Maybe a bit nervous. What do you do?"

He gritted his teeth like he was about to do something he dreaded. Shook out his hands as if to loosen himself up. Then swaggered toward her. His hands grabbed her waist, and he pulled her tight against him. Lowered his mouth.

"Wait."

"What?" he spit out.

She sighed. "It's too choppy. Not natural. You need to feel the dominance in your bones. This is a woman who wants you, but you're the one in charge. You're the one who will lead. Your entire approach needs to have grace and confidence."

"This is so stupid."

"It's not. Try again."

He cursed some more but backed up to restart. He narrowed his gaze as if sending all the intensity of his mind and soul into that moment. This time, he moved slower, more deliberate, and his grip gentled as he snagged her around the waist. He cupped her cheeks and stared into her eyes.

Shivers raced down her spine. He must have been channeling Patricia, because it looked like he wanted to devour her. Tessa tried to clear her throat to break the tension, but as his lips moved toward hers, the gleam of tenderness in his eyes shook her to the core.

"Ford?"

"Yeah?" he whispered, an inch from kissing her.

"This is wrong, too."

"I'm going to kill you."

She broke the embrace, wondering why she felt so damn shaky. "I'm sorry, I don't mean to mess with your head, but that was too . . . much."

His arms crossed in front of his chest. Frustration oozed from his pores. "Great. At this moment, I'd rather be at Shea Stadium in '08 when we lost the wild card and all official hope at the postseason."

"Kissing is more important than baseball. Listen, I know it sounds strange, but there was too much emotion there for a first kiss. You need to hold back. Tease her. Patricia isn't the type to want to go all in with you right away—remember, she's all about the chase. Pull her in with a seduction."

"Seduce you. Dominate you. Be graceful and confident. Got it. Let's do this." He stepped away for the third time.

Tessa quickly licked her lips, shook out her body, and waited.

When Ford turned around, he looked different. Focused, but relaxed. A small smile played about his lips, and his gaze held a knowledge that made her want to know what he was so sure about. He stalked her, slow and predator-like, and Tessa's heart began to race.

Yes.

He stopped in front of her. Reached out real slow and stroked one of her pigtails, rubbing the strands together as he let the tension build between them. His hand slid under her chin and tilted her head up. Their gazes locked.

Then he kissed her.

His lips were soft and light over hers, sliding and sipping like the exploration it was, getting to know her taste and texture. Tessa let her head fall back. *Be Patricia,* she mentally chanted. *Be Patricia. Be Patricia.*

The kiss deepened, but he still held back. The intensity and gentleness were gone, replaced by a masculine command that urged her to give in and surrender to the kiss on his terms.

Perfect, she thought. Exactly what the woman would like.

Tessa began to respond, deciding to take it a bit further so Ford felt completely comfortable. He parted her lips and then his tongue touched hers. A groan released from deep inside, and her body took over with a roar. He tasted of spearmint and something unique, a musky, spicy flavor she craved more of. Tessa leaned in, opened her mouth, and he took the invite with one firm thrust.

Ford kissed her with a bold intensity and thoroughness that made her clutch his shoulders to keep from sagging. Her head spun, the kiss went on, and a drugged looseness softened all her muscles until they seemed to meld together. Her breasts pressed against his hard chest, his hands cupped her ass, and her fingers threaded in his hair as she hung on under the explosive sensations rocketing through her and blasting any rationality far, far away.

From a distance, she heard the soft singing of chimes. Ford broke the kiss, his breath ragged, pupils dilated as he stared into her eyes with a slight shock and a desire neither of them could deny.

He staggered backward. She stumbled and pressed herself against the wall.

The silence seethed with undercurrents.

Tessa touched her hand to her swollen lips, still tasting him, still hungry for more. Ford turned away, adjusting his jeans, shaking his head.

The chimes began again.

"It's the timer. To rinse out the conditioner in my hair." Her voice came out choppy.

"I guess that's important." Was his voice strained, or was it her imagination?

She headed toward the table, where she switched the timer off with trembling fingers. She dreaded turning to face him but dragged in a breath and tried to keep her face neutral.

"You have a date to get ready for, right?" Ford asked.

"Yes! Yes, I better get going."

He ducked his head, refusing to look at her. Oh, she hated this awkwardness that had suddenly sprouted between them, but she didn't know what to do about it. How had the kiss been so . . . hot?

Tessa busied herself with gathering up the empty cans while he headed toward the door. "Great game," she called out.

He hesitated at the door, then turned. "Tessa?"

Oh God.

"Yeah?"

"I'm assuming I passed the test?" When she lifted her gaze, she caught the big-ass grin curving his lips, the teasing in the depths of those brown-green eyes.

Slowly, she grinned back, muscles softening in relief. "A solid B-plus."

"Pain in the ass," he muttered, shaking his head. Then he let himself out.

Tessa practically collapsed in relief. They'd gotten through that sticky situation, but she'd never put herself in that position again.

No more test-kissing Ford Maddox.

Chapter Seventeen

"What are you doing?" Ryder asked, brow raised.

"Ballet dancing," Ford grunted, already sweaty. "What do you think I'm doing? Weight training." He pushed the bar up and down, centered midway to his chest like he'd seen the muscle rats do.

His friend came up beside him, face twisted into a half frown. "You hate lifting."

"Yeah, well, I think having cut arms and abs is worth the price."

"You never did before."

Ford finished his set, clinked the bar back in place, and sat up. He reached for a towel to wipe his brow. "I never had Patricia before. Gotta make it worth it."

Ryder shook his head. "That's fucked up. What if she wants you to turn vegetarian and give up Cheetos? Gonna do that, too?"

"If I have to. Why are you acting pissed? Figured you'd be happy I'm in the gym more."

Ryder glared in frustration. "Not like this! I don't know what's going on, but you gotta back off. You stay in shape fine doing what you like. Hell, you play harder than the young guys on the basketball team, and I've seen you on the tennis court. There's no need to suddenly start lifting because you think Patricia will only love you if you have pecs of steel."

"Abs of steel."

"Whatever. Is Tessa putting you up to all this? Because if so, I think I need to talk to her."

Ford grinned and moved on to biceps curls. "Aww, my protector. No, man, Tessa never mentioned this. In fact, she told me I look good exactly the way I am."

"Then why are you suddenly trying to be The Rock?"

He let out a long breath. The truth was hard to say, but Ryder was his best friend, and knew all his secrets anyway. "I don't want to leave any regrets on the table," he finally said. "If a bit more muscle makes a difference in getting her to look at me, I want to commit. This is my person, Ryder."

"And if she falls in love with you and figures out this was just a hoax, what then?"

"I don't know. I just need to get there first."

His friend let out a blistering curse. "I hate seeing you do this, Ford. The woman meant for you should like most things about you as is. Including your damn muscles."

"But she'll love me more if I'm cut."

Ryder cracked out a laugh. "Fine. But I want it noted on the record I think this is bullshit, and you should listen to Tessa."

"Noted."

"You're doing the biceps curls wrong. Let me show you."

Ford spent the next hour in the dreaded weight room while Ryder showed him the quickest way to do a lean and mean circuit. When he was done and showered, his muscles were sore, but he felt good about trying.

He walked out of the gym, scrolling through email on his phone, and found a research article that was perfect for the Quench podcast. He texted Tessa the link and asked if she wanted to discuss.

Her response came quickly. Can't. Going to my uncle's for a birthday party.

Cool—is it a milestone birthday for him?

A pause. Three dots for a long time. Then . . . Actually it's a party for his dog.

He stared at the text. You're kidding, right?

Nope. Feel free to come as my guest. Chew treats are the present of choice.

He laughed then, wondering what a dog party would look like. He'd planned to watch the game, do some prep work for his show, and get takeout. But spending the day with Tessa at a dog party sounded like more fun. Plus, they needed to go over tomorrow's first podcast episode for Quench to make sure it ran smoothly. Not gonna miss out on seeing this. Address? We can discuss podcast.

She texted him the address with a dog emoji next to a poop one.

Lighthearted, Ford began to drive, stopping quickly at the doggie bakery on Main Street for some wrapped treats. It would be good to see Tessa again in this context. Something fun and casual to get them back on track.

Something to help him forget about that kiss.

The image of her swollen lips opening under his made him shift in his seat. He'd been surprised at the heat between them, the way her body seemed to bloom and soften under his touch. Then again, he'd always sensed Tessa was a passionate woman, so he shouldn't have been surprised she could kiss like that.

No, what nagged at him was the way she'd kissed *him*. The way she fit perfectly in his arms, her curvy body pressed against every muscle. The way she plunged her fingers in his hair and hung on. The way she made a low, hungry moan deep in her throat that made him want to do . . . bad things.

Had she kissed her date like that last night?

He couldn't get to sleep last night for a while, wondering if she was okay. He didn't trust the guys out there on those dating apps. Of course, Tessa was fierce and could take care of herself. But she also deserved someone to look out for her. Care about who she was seeing and if the guy was right for her. Malia and Chiara were probably on top of it, but he couldn't help worrying just a bit.

And wondering if they'd slept together.

Ford scratched his head. No sense in thinking about it. Tessa had her life, and he was in love with Patricia. The whole kissing connection thing was a fluke that was best to forget. A fun day at her uncle's would level the field, and they'd probably end up laughing about the whole episode.

He pulled up to the address, noting the beautiful style of the colonial and the fancy red barn next to the property. Tessa greeted him at the door, but before he could say anything, she lifted a finger in warning. "My uncle and his friends are serious. Please, no jokes."

He blinked. "I promise."

"Okay, come on in." She led him straight into the dining room, where the extravaganza was going on full blast.

Ford felt like he had dropped into a scene from *The Godfather*, but instead of the horse's head in a bed, he was surrounded by dogs. Dogs with party hats. Dogs with silly bow ties and glitzy collars studded with gems that looked real. Dogs in actual clothes or bright kerchiefs covered with cake and confetti.

The rooms looked like they'd been decorated by a professional party planner focused on pleasing canines. The three men holding court looked like old-school Italian mobsters. Ford automatically searched for distinctive bumps under their jackets that hinted of guns.

These men scared the shit out of him.

Tessa gestured them over. "Uncle Bart, this is my friend Ford." Then she introduced him to Uncle Bart's sidekicks, Dominick and Vincent.

The three men stood in a line before him, openly checking him out. They all dressed alike—dark pants, short-sleeved button-down shirts, gold bracelets and chains, and pinkie rings. All had salt-and-pepper hair gelled back from their foreheads. Uncle Bart was stocky, of average height, and looked like a retired boxer. Dom was taller, thicker in the waist, and struck Ford as the hired muscle. Vincent seemed like the gentle one. He sported less of a deep tan but had an elegant white mustache, and when he smiled at Tessa, he flashed a gold tooth.

Ford shook their hands. Her uncle's grip was solid, as were the handshakes from the rest of his crew. "Thanks so much for having me. Um, this is for the birthday . . . guest." He handed over a box of wrapped dog treats in bright-colored frosting.

"Thank you! Mimi and Bruno love treats," Uncle Bart said, his face crinkling when he smiled. He studied both of them together. "Is this the friend you mentioned helping out?" he asked Tessa.

Did she actually blush or was that his imagination?

"Yes."

"Good, good. Any friend of Tessa's is part of the family." Uncle Bart flashed a dazzling smile with no gold teeth, but Ford still felt a trickle of unease. He wasn't sure he wanted the distinction of being in this family, and he definitely would never ask for a favor. "You have dogs, Ford?"

He shook his head. "Always wanted one, but my work hours suck."

"What do you do?" Dom asked suspiciously.

"Sports radio at KTUZ."

Vincent lit up. He was currently cuddling a dark, furry dog in his arms that looked like it had no eyes. *WTF?* "I knew you sounded familiar—I listen to you all the time! Great feedback on the Mets. I think it's our year."

Uncle Bart laughed. "Says that every year," he confided.

Dom kept staring as if he was trying to figure Ford out. He tried to grin like he was harmless, but the man just frowned a bit, as if he didn't trust him.

Sweat beaded Ford's brow. "Well, we're always hopeful. I'm also helping Tessa with a podcast at Quench. They're bringing sports to the site."

"About time," Uncle Bart said, patting Tessa on the shoulder. "Women can do anything men can, honey. Even sports!"

Tessa laughed. "I know. I think we better sing 'Happy Birthday.' Bruno's getting stressed."

Dom gave a huff. "I keep telling him to stand up to Mimi or she'll continue to bully him. But he just won't listen."

"Mimi's only messing with him," Uncle Bart said, adjusting his gold pinkie ring. "But Tessa's right—we should start the festivities. Here, give Petey to her to hold."

The bundle of fur was transferred to Tessa, who cuddled the pup close, speaking in soothing tones. The dog seemed to relax and tilt his head toward her voice. Ford's heart twinged at the sight of those scarred eyes. Poor thing must've had a tough life. He was lucky to be safe and warm in a home where someone loved him.

The party room was a sight he'd never forget. Cheery banners of HAPPY BIRTHDAY MIMI AND BRUNO were strung through the rooms. The formal dining room table had been outfitted with actual high chairs where small dogs were strapped in. Bruno the pit bull, who Ford wanted to keep away from, was seated at the head on a padded armchair. A white-and-brown Pomeranian mix, with pointy ears and chin, sat in her high chair beside him. Clearly, this was Mimi. She wore a pink birthday hat that said BIRTHDAY QUEEN. Bruno wore a blue hat that said BIRTHDAY KING.

In between yips and barks and general dog busyness, the Pomeranian would occasionally hiss and bare her teeth at Bruno. Instead of hissing back and kicking her ass, Bruno trembled and hung his head, obviously miserable.

Great. Even in the dog world, women ruled.

Uncle Bart clapped and lit the candles. The cake was a two-layer delight with a picture of cartoon dogs romping across a lawn. The same words from the banner—HAPPY BIRTHDAY MIMI AND BRUNO—was scrawled across it in rainbow glitter. "It's cake time, everyone! Behave."

Ford tamped down his laughter when the furry crew began howling and barking like rabble-rousers from a frat house. Tessa shot him a look as if to warn him this was normal, but she didn't apologize or look embarrassed. It was obvious she loved her uncle and his friends and didn't care if Ford thought they were strange. The no-holds-barred way she loved was rare, and he wondered why he'd never noticed it before.

Ford joined in on the singing and watched Uncle Bart blow out the candles and pat both Bruno and Mimi. Dom, Vincent, and Tessa clapped. The Chihuahua in the tutu managed to wriggle out of her buckle and jumped from her seat, twirling madly around for cake. The terrier gnawed the end of the tablecloth. The dog with a chewed-up ear and black spots couldn't handle the tension and launched himself on the table toward the cake. In seconds, Dom picked him up, gently scolding, and placed the dog back in his seat. Bruno kept one eye on Mimi as Uncle Bart cut the cake and laid two pieces down on the table.

Ford wished he could've videoed the scene, because no one would believe him.

"Want cake?" Tessa asked.

"Is it for humans or dogs?"

She laughed. "Both—safe for dogs and us. Come on, it's bad luck to say no on a birthday."

Tessa put down the blind dog, who trotted immediately to Uncle Bart without bumping into anything. Probably sense of smell.

"Will Bruno and Mimi not get their wish?" Ford teased, taking a plate she handed him.

"Look, I know this is a bit strange, but you were the one who wanted to come."

"No, this is great! I'd be having an awesome time if I didn't think Dom was picking out a gravesite for me somewhere in the woods of Nyack."

She grinned. "He's intense but harmless. It's the first time he's meeting you, so he's making sure you won't hurt me. The three of them worked together in California and moved here together. They're all like family."

"Including the dogs?"

"Especially the dogs."

She took a bite of cake and glanced over. The three men were breaking up potential dog fights over the cake. When they weren't looking, Mimi growled at Bruno, who whimpered and jumped down from his seat in retreat. Mimi happily stretched out and finished his slice.

A sigh escaped Tessa's lips. "Mimi's such a diva. No wonder she's his favorite."

"Bruno should kick her ass."

"I know, but he's a sweetie. Dom found him almost mauled to death after an illegal dog fight. He had two surgeries but really survived because of his heart. He loves Dom and is a bit codependent. Dom takes him everywhere."

"Are they rescues?"

"Yes, all of them."

"How'd they get into saving dogs? They all seem pretty passionate."

"Not sure. I didn't visit my uncle in California but knew he always had a dog. When he got here, he began collecting strays and abused animals, then recruited Dom and Vin. I warned him he can't have any more, but of course he rescued Petey a couple weeks ago."

"Hard to say no to a blind dog," Ford murmured, finishing his cake.

"Exactly."

"I'm surprised he hasn't recruited you to take one of them yet," he said with a grin.

"My place isn't well suited for animals." A mischievous gleam flashed in her bright blue eyes. "But yours is perfect."

"I told you, my schedule sucks."

"Ever heard of doggie day care?"

He shook his head. "I'm not sure if Patricia likes dogs."

An odd expression crossed Tessa's face, but her tone was light. "If she doesn't, that's a warning sign."

"I'm sure she does." His defense sounded lackluster.

She didn't respond, instead taking his empty plate and walking to ditch it in the garbage. Dom eased in and took her place. Ford stiffened and tried to relax. Like the common advice for dogs, he needed to show no fear.

"You make good money, Ford?" the man asked gruffly. His face was a crisscross of hard lines, with a crooked nose that looked like it had been broken many times.

He didn't bother to worry about the question. Just answered. "Pretty good. Been at the station almost a decade."

The man nodded. "That's an honorable job." He paused. "Who's this girl you're chasing? The one Tessa is helping you with?"

"Oh, a woman at work. Patricia."

Ford tried not to be embarrassed at Dom's raking stare, as if judging him for not being man enough to get Patricia himself. He looked longingly at Uncle Bart and Vin, but no one was coming to help him. Tessa had disappeared.

"Why do you want her?"

Oh God, this was bad. An inquisition from a gangster and he had no idea what the right answers were. Ford swallowed hard. "She's, uh, very sweet. And pretty. And seems to be my type. But she sees me only as a friend, so I'm trying to change that."

Dom nodded, so it must've been a good answer. "Hard situation."

"Yes."

"A very bad thing. Still, why chase after someone when you have the perfect girl in front of you?"

Oh no. Ford played dumb. "Who?"

"Tessa. She's a good girl. Single. I like the way you are with each other. You'd be perfect together."

He made sure his voice didn't squeak like a teenage boy. "Tessa's great, but we're just good friends. In fact, she had a date last night with someone else."

Dom's face turned into a thundercloud. "Who?"

"Uh, I don't know."

"Stay here." Dom turned and went to Uncle Bart and Vin. They seemed to have a mini conference, glancing back at Ford like he'd done something wrong.

Tessa still hadn't reappeared, the dogs were becoming rambunctious, and he wondered if it was time to go.

The three men marched over, Petey now held tight in Uncle Bart's arms. "Who was the man she met last night?" he demanded.

Ford threw up his arms. "I don't know—I didn't ask. Is there a problem?"

Vin sighed. "We always do a background check on her dates first. The last two didn't pass muster, so we made a call and had them cancel."

Ford's jaw almost dropped, but he caught it just in time. "How'd you get that info?"

"We have her password and log-in for her dating apps," Dom said. "Match.com. Singles in the City. HudsonValleyLove. Plus, we have a concerned citizen planted at Quench to cover in-person meetups."

"This one must've slipped past," Uncle Bart said with a frown. "It must be Tinder—she hasn't used that one in a while, so I stopped checking it."

Ford tossed a concerned look at Tessa, who was finishing up in the kitchen. "Um, I don't think she's going to like that much when she finds out. She's very independent."

"Well, no one's gonna tell her. Right?" Dom asked pointedly.

Was he turning pale? "Right."

Uncle Bart pounded his back with a grin. "Good man. Tessa is special, and I'm not about to let a guy take advantage of her heart, or her money. Let me log in, make a call, and check him out. In the meantime, ask her about the date so we can get better intel."

"Me?" Ford asked, his voice one octave too high.

Dom glared. "Yeah, of course."

"Just make sure he doesn't work for the government," Vincent added.

Ford stared back at them, dumbfounded.

Uncle Bart disappeared with Petey at the same time Tessa appeared. "Hey," she said brightly. "Coffee's on. What are you talking about?"

Dom and Vincent stared at him.

"Sports," Ford spit out. "Just . . . sports."

"Why am I not surprised?"

Ford cleared his throat. "Um, Tessa, I forgot to ask how your date was last night."

Dom subtly nodded approval.

"Oh, it was good! He seemed nice. Works as a pastry chef, so we had a great dessert."

"How nice. Where'd you meet?" Dom asked, pretending to be casual.

"Tinder. It's never had a good track record for me, but this guy seems interesting."

"I knew it," Vincent muttered.

"What?" she asked.

"Nothing!" Ford practically yelled. Was his laugh a bit manic?

"Let's have coffee and you can tell us a bit more about this new man," Vin said, looping his arm through Tessa's. "I have a bit of sambuca to make it more interesting."

Tessa grinned. "You always do. How was your last doctor appointment? Is your blood sugar okay?"

Vin waved a hand in the air. "I'm old—I don't listen to doctors. They just want to put you on meds and make money."

"You have to be careful. What would the dogs do without you?"

Ford watched Vin reassess. "Maybe I'll cut back on sweets."

Her smile reeked of victory. "And alcohol," she warned. "I heard of a new app that can test your levels without a blood test. Let me look into that, okay?"

Vin patted her cheek. "You're such a good girl."

Over the next half hour, Ford watched how she interacted with the crew—part mother hen, part jokester—and the way they looked at Tessa made his chest tighten. She came off as someone who would never attend a dog party for an elderly uncle, yet here she was acting as if it was the only place she wanted to be. Ford sipped his coffee, hung with some of the pups, and enjoyed the lively conversation of the group.

Finally, they were ready to go. Uncle Bart sidled up and whispered in his ear like a conspirator. "We're gonna have to abort this guy. Chefs are bad news—he's got an ex he owes child support to, and he likes the racehorses. He'll never be trustworthy. I put in a call, so he should disappear."

"Disappear?" The spit got caught in Ford's throat and stopped him from swallowing.

Uncle Bart patted his shoulder. "Don't worry. You'll watch over her, right? I need another good guy who's in her life making sure she doesn't make the wrong decisions."

Ford almost laughed at the request, but besides old-fashioned fear at "disappearing" somebody with one phone call, he respected Uncle Bart's sense of family honor and duty. He missed his dad and that feeling of familial tightness. His mom had remarried and moved away, and though his stepfather was nice, there was no real connection between them. Being asked to take care of Uncle Bart's niece felt like an honor, even though Tessa was the most independent, stubborn woman on the planet.

"I promise to watch out for her," he said solemnly.

Uncle Bart pumped him on the back, and he caught Vin's and Dom's nods from across the room.

Tessa walked with him to her car. "Hope you had a decent time."

"I really did. Thanks for inviting me. It's nice seeing you all so close."

"Uncle Bart is the black sheep in the family, but I always found him the most fun. And Dom and Vin are now part of the circle, so I feel responsible."

"They love you very much."

She looked up, surprise in her eyes. "Well, you always love family. It's your blood."

"Not everyone does, Tessa. But you don't take any relationship for granted. I'm beginning to see that now." The words popped out without thought. He used to think she was full of ego, but now he realized she passed off many worthy compliments as if she didn't believe them. Her jokes were just that—jokes. But when anyone seriously tried to thank her or praise her, she shook it off.

Tessa had more secrets locked up under that shiny surface. He wanted to know what they were.

But he had to concentrate on Patricia. On their first official date. On convincing her they were perfect together.

Her hand paused on the door handle. "Ford?"

"Yeah?"

Her voice held layers of emotion that rattled him. "That kiss last night? It was perfect. There's no way Patricia can think of you as a friend if you kiss her like that."

Then she got in her car and drove away.

Ford squeezed his eyes shut, not knowing what was going on.

Not knowing if he wanted to.

Chapter Eighteen

Tessa pasted on a bright, fake smile while she stared at the small production booth waiting for her. In fifteen minutes, she was going live with Ford to introduce millions of Quench readers to sports in a new, fresh way.

She was going to vomit.

The producer was rattling off a bunch of instructions, and Ford was joking around with Kelsey, who'd been charmed by his humor and easy demeanor. God knows he was in his element and seemed jacked up to start recording.

Her? Not so much.

Her voice squeaked out in a too-high pitch. "Um, I need to hit the ladies' room. Be right back!" She caught Ford's questioning glance, but she waved her hand in the air like she was good and got the hell out of there.

Safe in her second oasis, Tessa planted her palms on the counter and stared into the gilded mirror. The luxurious bathroom was a huge benefit of Quench, offering a full powder room with a dangling beaded chandelier, baskets of free makeup trials, and a fluffy lavender carpet. The mirrors were plentiful and full size, and the lighting was badass and made everyone look great. Endless products were displayed for touch-ups. The air smelled of tropical coconut.

What was wrong with her?

She looked perfect in her red tailored power suit with red heels. Her outfit always made her feel like a confident CEO, and she needed the reassurance because today she was terrified she would fail spectacularly in front of the world.

Tessa groaned and began to pace. She had to get her shit together. Why was she so afraid of a podcast? She felt as if everyone was going to laugh at her. She may have learned a few baseball pitches and become familiar with some teams and their players, but she was not qualified for this. She'd say something stupid, and it would go viral on TikTok.

Makeup mogul pretends to know sports.

At least they couldn't create a meme since it was only her voice, but that could also be used against her. Maybe she could fake a stomach virus and Ford could do it alone. She could cite the favor he owed her.

She was seriously considering it when the door swung open and Ford walked in.

Tessa blinked. "Um, dude, this is the ladies' room."

"Yeah, I heard about it." He whistled, looking around in admiration. "It's nice. Smells like the beach. How come they don't do this stuff for men's rooms?"

"Because they never have lines, and men just want to pee and leave."

"True." He walked closer, his eyes gleaming with a touch of sympathy. "You're freaking out."

She straightened and threw her shoulders back. "Am not! I'm grabbing a breath before I go out there and dazzle you."

His lower lip quirked. "T, you're gonna be great. Why are you worried? I'll be there the whole time guiding you. You've watched the games and read the research. You got this."

Her heart got mushy in her chest, and damned if her eyes didn't sting. He could be so nice! Even her hated initial nickname was said with affection.

Hesitating on keeping up her ruse, she crumbled, knowing her secret would be safe with him. "I don't think I can do it, Ford. I'm not good at this. I hate being spotlighted with things I'm not good at."

He nodded. "Sometimes we have to stretch in order to grow. Quench is ready for growth. Are you?"

"Yes. Just with someone else doing the podcast."

He laughed and walked over, pulling her in for a quick hug. "Guess what I'm going to ask you to do?"

"I'm not giving up the favor you owe me."

"No, you can lord that over me as long as you need. I want you to trust me. Just like I did when I put myself in your hands for the makeover—which was your expertise. This is mine. I got you."

Something deep inside rose to life and uncurled, as if she'd been waiting to hear those words her whole life.

He stepped back, gazing at her with a touch of tenderness, and the connection between them tightened and hummed—a bond that was getting stronger the longer she spent with him. All of her brash confidence had gone quiet, but looking at him right now, Tessa knew in her heart and soul that she trusted Ford Maddox with everything she had.

I got you. The words made goose bumps prickle her skin.

Slowly, she nodded. "Okay."

"Good. Now let's get out there and show everyone there's nothing you can't handle."

Swallowing past the lump in her throat, Tessa shook out her hair, then her hands, and took a lungful of air. "Let's do this."

He walked out. "Hey, can I use this bathroom while I'm here at least?"

"No."

His laugh echoed in her ears as they went into the booth together.

~

"Thanks for listening, everyone. You can catch us next Tuesday for another segment of *Beyond the Stats*. Ford Maddox will be back with us, and special guest Erin Andrews will chat about unequal pay and how some players are fighting back. Ford, you ready for another round with us, or have we scared you off?"

His sexy, deep laugh poured into the microphone. "I think I can handle it. Looking forward to diving into some of these controversies and getting your readers' perspectives."

"Sounds good. Have a great day, Quench listeners. Peace out."

The light flickered off, and Tessa eased out of her headphones. She beamed at Ford, ridiculously proud of their interaction and chemistry on the show. Ford had done exactly what he promised. He'd smoothly controlled the first half, guiding the questions and format, until she became comfortable and bloomed in her own right.

"That was great," she said.

He grinned. "All that whining and you killed it. I knew once you got talking, I wouldn't be able to stop you."

She stuck out her tongue playfully. "Well, you made it easy. I learned so much, and it wasn't boring, which was my main concern."

He gave her an offended look. "If I was boring, I would've been fired years ago."

"Yeah, but you do hard-core sports. Tossing numbers and stats around until I go cross-eyed. I love when you have guests—those are my favorite."

She didn't realize he was staring at her until there were a few beats of dead silence.

Tessa turned. "What?"

"You listen to my show?"

She shrugged and neatened the studio. "I had to make sure you were good before I asked you to do this for Quench. What type of researcher would I be, as you told me multiple times before when you forced me to watch endless baseball games with you?"

A slow grin curved his lips. The tumble in her belly took her by surprise. There was something innately sexy about the way he teased her, like they spoke their own secret language of edgy banter. It was different from any other relationship she'd had, which consisted of either strictly work friends or sex partners.

Ford was a bit . . . confusing. He didn't stay neatly within the barriers.

And that kiss?

She couldn't think about it. Best to pretend the whole thing never occurred.

"I like that you listen to my show."

She gave a humph and stood up. "Don't get too excited. The moment you get dull, I'll let you know."

"I'm sure you will."

He walked her out, and she introduced him to some of the media specialists that made sure their podcasts reached the maximum level of exposure on social media. The team was a bit starstruck over Ford, and they spent some time chatting it up.

Finally, they got back to her office and he collapsed into the chair opposite her desk, stretching out his legs. "What're you doing next?"

Tessa rolled her eyes and motioned toward her computer. "About a million things to run a million-dollar company."

"Thought you were at a billion."

"This upcoming year we'll finally reach it." Pride raced through her at the idea of having the big B in front of the word. "Especially when I publish your column in a few months. That'll break the bank."

He winced. "You may be giving my life too much credit. Speaking of which, do you think it's appropriate to invite Patricia to a baseball game?"

"Nope. Too much work intersection, and it screams buddy date."

"That's what I thought. I'm bummed because Ryder is busy with Chiara, Palmer is busy with Malia, and my other buddies from the station are away at some broadcasting class."

"How come you're not at it?"

"Don't need it—just the producers. Ugh, these are prime-time seats, too."

"Too bad." Her desk had exploded from this morning, but the podcast had put her in a restless mood. "Hey, is it hard to come down after a show? Because I feel a bit buzzed."

"Yep. That's the difference between writing and recording. You gotta pump your energy level way up to meet the demands of the audience, and when it's over, it takes a while to settle. What are you doing Friday night?"

Tessa was already clicking through her endless emails and wondering how much she could ignore. "Hmm, not sure. Was hoping my Tinder date would write back, but I think I'm getting ghosted again. So strange—I thought we had a great time."

"Huh, that's weird."

His voice sounded strangled, so she turned to glance at him. "Why do you look a bit green? You're not getting sick, are you?"

"No. Um, did you try to contact him?"

"Yeah. I thought we had a decent time, and he seemed into me. But when I reached out, I got nothing back. I'm starting to get concerned. This is the third guy in a row who's ghosted me."

Ford began coughing and swiveled in his chair to face the window. "Maybe it's better this way. I mean, you don't want a guy who doesn't see your worth, right?"

"Now you sound like me."

"Come to the game with me."

She laughed. "Hell no. I have a laundry list of items I can do on a Friday night."

"You don't need a face mask, and you just saw Uncle Bart. I know your friends are busy. Come on—I think it's important you experience what it's like to watch a live baseball game. It will be good for your—"

"Audience. Yeah, so you've said." Tessa frowned. "You must know someone else who would love to see the Mets in prime seating, though."

"I do, but not this Friday."

"What if Patricia finds out? We're supposed to be broken up."

He shrugged. "I don't think it would be a big deal. I just won't mention it."

A strange disappointment tightened her chest, but she shook it off. "You're starting to think devious, like me. I hope I don't have to worry."

"Nope. I told you, as soon as I make her realize I'm the one, I can stop these silly games and we can begin our life together."

This time, the squeezing sensation traveled to her gut. "Fine," she said, pissed that she was experiencing these weird feelings around him. She'd just go to the game and remind herself they were disastrous together. "But they better have some healthy food options, because I am not eating a bunch of hot dogs all night and hearing men belch."

"They actually have veggie dogs now. And wine."

"Okay, I'll go."

He sprang up from his chair. "Cool. I'll pick you up at four—we'll hit some traffic, and I don't want to be late. I'll check in with you later?"

"Yep."

He gave her an air high-five, which she properly ignored, and disappeared.

Tessa smothered a sigh and tried to get her mind back on work. Things were beginning to get real. After his date with Patricia Saturday night and their last podcast next week, there would be no reason to hang with Ford anymore. Which was good.

Very good.

She needed to get back to her real life.

~

"Why do I have a mitt?"

Ford gave her that familiar look like he was barely holding on to his patience. They'd gotten into an argument in the car about what hot dogs were really made of, and when she'd showed him the YouTube video confirming the truth, he'd pouted for the rest of the drive, grumbling about how she'd managed to spoil the last American tradition left to enjoy.

He was so dramatic.

"You have a mitt to catch a foul ball," he said.

"Why don't you have one?"

"I can catch it barehanded."

"What am I going to do with a ball? I don't want one."

He ground his teeth, and she couldn't help the grin that threatened. It was so fun when he was riled up.

"Everyone wants a ball!" he insisted. "Look, the odds are low you'll catch one, especially where we're seated. If you manage to, I'll take it. Okay?"

"Maybe we should give it to a kid."

"Fine. Let's get settled."

Citi Field was a pretty cool place. Besides it being huge, the buzz of excitement and chatter in the air from the fans was contagious. The sea of people similarly dressed in jerseys and hats swarmed her vision. They went up huge escalators, passing Mets banners and trophies, and even got free gifts of Mr. Met bobbleheads. When a guy asked to buy hers for twenty bucks, she quickly tried to make the deal, but Ford got all grumpy and dragged her away, warning her to never ever sell a real collectible.

She told him now he had to buy the veggie hot dogs because he lost her money.

Endless concession stands selling ice cream, fries, hot dogs, and alcoholic beverages lined the broad aisles. Team gear was hawked at every corner. Each of the doorways led out to different aisles in the stadium, and Ford took some time to show her around. They even had a gorgeous lounge with regular food and a fancy bar where crowds gathered to watch from afar, but Ford told her the only place to watch a game was where you saw all the action close up.

She would've been fine with her ass on a cushioned barstool and a drink in her hand. But this was his rodeo.

They made their way down the steps to seats between home plate and first base. Kids and adults were crowded up behind the dugout, shouting to the players. A few came out, throwing signed balls, laughing and joking around with the other players, and warming up on the field.

Tessa laid down the towel she brought after dusting off the dirty seat, then wriggled her butt on the hard plastic to settle in. Ford was right on top of her, shoulder tight to hers. There seemed to be little space between the seats. She watched while he greeted a bunch of people scattered around him, making small talk.

She tapped his shoulder. "Where do I put my bag?"

He blinked. "On the floor."

She made a face at the dirty concrete already filled with stains and loose popcorn. "Ew, it's designer. Can I use the seat beside me?"

"No, someone will be sitting there. Who cares what the bottom of your bag looks like? Hey, it's starting. Listen to the lineup."

"You're so bossy."

"Shhh."

They stood up for the national anthem, and then she reluctantly placed her expensive bag down, planning to disinfect it later. The large screen showed everything going on in the field, but she had a great view of the action. "How come it looks so much smaller here than on TV?" she asked.

"Don't know. But it's more exciting to watch the plays in person. We're in the field first since it's the top of the inning."

"Yep, bottom is when we get last licks."

"Exactly."

Tessa sat back on her hard chair and watched the game. She enjoyed Ford's excitement and the roar of the crowd. She liked seeing the players in their positions up close and hearing the thwack of a bat hitting the ball. She liked getting up and doing the wave and shouting the end of fun lines that flashed on the scoreboard. Concession people walked up and down the stairs, barking out their wares, so by the end of the first hour, she'd already given up on being healthy for the day and indulged in popcorn, a beer, and a Philly cheesesteak.

"When will I need the mitt?" she asked, seriously considering a bag of peanuts. When was the last time she had real peanuts from the shell? When she was young, or ever?

"Never. I shouldn't have brought it. It's just a habit I got into after I went to my first game. My dad got me hooked on the tradition, but most of the seats are now blocked off by netting, and the odds here are ridiculously low. You'd have better luck in the outfield."

Oh well. At least she got a bobblehead.

The game flew by pleasantly. The Diamondbacks had runners on first and second, but the Mets shut them down and they were able to hold their two-run lead.

Ford got up to get her a glass of wine, and she stood to stretch. It was a perfect evening, with a gentle, dying sun and warm wind. She adjusted her ball cap and danced a bit to the Pitbull song that played while couples flashed on the big screen and were told to kiss for the Kiss Cam.

Then there was a new couple on the screen. The guy was decked out in his Mets gear and began to kneel on the dirty concrete floor in front of the woman, who had a cute blonde ponytail and cheerleader-type face.

Was he going to . . .

A ring box came out. The Kiss Cam flashed WILL YOU MARRY ME? The woman flew out of her seat, crying and laughing, jumping into his arms as the camera panned in tight to their matching joyous expressions.

SHE SAID YES!!!! pounded out in neon on the screen, and the stadium clapped and yelled while the couple shared a passionate kiss.

Tessa watched them play out their romance in front of thousands of strangers and felt a deep ache inside her gut. What must that feel like to have a man love you enough to risk a proposal in front of an entire stadium full of people? That man was *all in*. He was committed to love and didn't care if the whole world knew how much he loved his woman.

It was passionate and romantic and wild, and Tessa wondered if she'd ever experience anything like that.

Blinking against a sudden sting in her eyes, she tried to push the feeling back down where it belonged, but it still lodged there in discomfort. She was being stupid. She'd hate being the focus of all that attention. That type of proposal was not like her at all. She was more the quiet, fancy dinner while wearing a killer designer dress type. She was champagne and proper speeches surrounded by candlelight.

Not loud, messy declarations amid hot dogs and beer.

"Got you a lemonade instead of wine—I saw you eyeing them before."

She jumped at the sound of his voice, then swallowed back the last of her emotions. A smile curved her lips. "Thanks."

"Welcome." He pointed to the field. "Look, they're shooting out T-shirts for the seventh-inning stretch."

Her eyes widened, and sure enough, there were people catching blurs of white fabric as they were launched into the stands. "I want one!" she said, jumping up and down. "Let's catch one!"

He started to laugh. "You have a closetful of designer clothes and you want a Mets T-shirt from a launcher?"

She sniffed. "Yes. It's cool."

"Okay, they're coming over here next."

As they got closer, Tessa began to yell and jump up and down with the crowd. Caught up in the fervor, the blonde woman on the field seemed to spot her and, with a shout, began to maneuver the gun so it would point straight toward them. With a pop, the shirt whizzed in the air, and Tessa stumbled across Ford, throwing her arms out as her fingers closed around fabric.

And then it was gone.

She blinked, looking around, and saw a man behind them fist-bump the air and yell, "Yeah, baby, that's how you do it!" He was dressed in a Mets jersey, with his cap backward and his blond hair flopping in his face.

She nudged Ford. "He took my shirt!"

She waited for him to reach over and take it back, but Ford gave her a look. "He got it first, T. That stuff happens at stadiums; you can't get mad."

"No, I swear I had it in my hands and he yanked it away. He wasn't even in our section! He's supposed to be over there, but he came by us to get a shirt!"

Ford began to laugh. "You are so competitive."

"It's not competition. It's fairness."

He tugged on one of her loose curls. "Love and baseball are never truly fair."

"Bullshit."

"I'll buy you a shirt, okay? They have much nicer ones—even jerseys. My treat. Hey, where are you going?"

On impulse, Tessa stalked across the aisle to the next section over, where the guy was mugging for cameras, as if his shirt catch was his claim to fame. "Hey, you grabbed that shirt right out of my hand. I'd like it back, please."

The guy cocked his head and grinned. "Sorry, I got it first."

"No, I had it in my hand and you ripped it away. That wasn't very nice."

Now he looked uncomfortable, his cheeks a bit red as he looked to both of his sides for support. "I caught it fair and square, sweetheart. I'm sure you'll catch one next time."

Sweetheart? Was he patronizing her?

Irritation scratched at her nerves. She lifted her chin and regarded him like a bug under a microscope, sensing there was now a decent crowd staring at them. "No, it wasn't fair and square. You came into my section and stole it from me for a moment of glory. This is my first baseball game, and I'd like a souvenir."

He stood up, T-shirt in his hand, and glared back at her. "You got a bobblehead."

Some of his buddies tittered.

"Give her the shirt, man," one guy with a nice beer belly muttered. "The inning started."

Suddenly, a shadow loomed and Ford pressed against her shoulder. "Problem?" he asked, giving T-Shirt Guy a level glare.

Tessa jerked her head. "Just trying to get my shirt back."

The guy threw out his arms. "She's nuts, man. Maybe you should go buy her a jersey or something. Keep her in line." He finished the joke with a nod, looking for support from around him.

No one laughed. Beer Gut Guy shook his head and muttered something. His other buddies looked away and let him take the fall.

Tessa opened her mouth to give it to him good, but Ford beat her to it. He blocked her body in a protective stance and leaned over. "She's not out of line—you came to our section and ripped the shirt out of my girlfriend's hands. Why don't you do the right thing and give it back?"

The guy squeaked, then looked confused. He blinked once. Twice. "Wait a minute. I know you. You're Ford Maddox from KTUZ! Holy shit—it is you! I listen to your show every morning." Then suddenly, the guy was pumping Ford's hand and apologizing. "I'm sorry, man. I get a bit obsessed when it comes to the Mets."

Ford relaxed and backed off. "I get it. It happens to the best of us."

"Here, take the shirt. Can we get a selfie?"

"Sure."

Ford took a pic with the guy, who was suddenly all smiles and apologies.

Ford nodded. "Take care, man."

"You, too!"

They made their way back to their seats, Tessa's arm tucked firmly into Ford's grip. "Well, that worked out well, didn't it?" she said brightly, gazing up at his face.

"Tessa?"

"Yeah?"

"I need you to be very quiet for a while, okay? I'm mad, but I refuse to give off negative energy from that little stunt you just pulled."

She gasped. "Stunt? I brought justice to Citi Field!"

"You initiated an argument with a stranger over a five-dollar shirt you'll never wear. You're so damn stubborn, you refuse to lose at any competition."

"I'm going to wear the shirt."

Ford was grinding his teeth again.

She patted his cheek and gave him a break. "Okay, I'll be quiet."

Tessa finished her lemonade as the Mets won with their two-run lead safely protected. She walked out of the stadium with her new shirt clutched in her hand, beginning to like baseball a lot more than she ever imagined.

She kept thinking about the way Ford had used the term *girlfriend*. It seemed so natural in the heat of the moment. She wondered whether he noticed but didn't want to ask him.

Ford remained quiet.

Tessa was sure he'd come around by the time they got home.

Chapter Nineteen

Ford wanted to strangle her.

He seethed as he negotiated the crowded roads home, half listening to Tessa's happy chatter about the game, the players, the food, and the overall experience. And her T-shirt. That stupid T-shirt.

Why didn't she act like normal women? First, she worried about where to put her designer purse, and the next moment she's launching herself across the stands and arguing with some stranger, who could've been drunk or violent. Her quicksilver behavior changes kept him alert and engaged, but she was too much of a wild card to ever reach normalcy.

Of course, he couldn't express any of this to her, because she had no clue she had done anything wrong. She only wanted to win.

The real question was beginning to seriously bother him: Why did he admire her so much?

Why was he both mad and a tiny bit proud that she stood up to that guy and fought for a stupid shirt? That she was able to spot a damn slider and enjoy a game when she was a complete baseball novice? That she owned every part of herself with a confidence that was deeply annoying and seriously sexy?

Maybe he wasn't normal, either.

He should be thinking of his date with Patricia right now. He'd invited Tessa to the game because he thought it would be fun for him and a learning experience for her. But once again, she'd captivated him—made things fun and interesting, and yes, completely unpredictable. Women like that weren't his type.

Right?

He pulled up to her house, and she turned to him. "Thanks for the sparkling conversation and the fun time. Let's do it again, okay?" Her brows crashed together in a frown. "Yeah, *not.*"

A laugh almost escaped, but he distracted himself by getting out of the car to follow her in. "I need to use the bathroom before I head home."

"There's a particularly wonderful bush right over there."

"Ha ha. Look, I'm sorry I lost my temper a bit, but there are a lot of unpredictable people out there, and it's not worth fighting one over a throwaway souvenir."

She seemed to soften a bit, unlocking the front door and ushering him in. "Okay, I see your point. I wasn't really thinking of that. I liked that you defended me, though. What a kick he found out you were famous!"

"Yeah, just the kind of fan I always dreamed of meeting."

She laughed, and he headed straight to the bathroom to take care of business. When he returned, he paused in the living room and studied her. Her ponytail had loosened, and curls exploded from under her hat and around her face. The once-neat jersey now held a bunch of wrinkles, and remnants of peanut shells stuck to the material. Her skin was flushed, and her makeup had slid off from the evening humidity. In that moment, she was completely approachable and sexier than in a dress and heels.

And in that wild moment, Ford wanted to kiss her.

"Why do you look weird?" Her questions usually had a sharp edge, but this one had come out a bit breathy, like she was catching his energy and not sure what to do.

"Don't know. I'm getting strange feelings."

He waited for her to laugh and make a joke. Roll her eyes and escort him to the door.

She didn't.

Tessa crossed the room to him and slowly handed him a bottle of water. "For the trip back," she said.

"Thanks."

Their gazes locked. The air ratcheted with a sweet sexual tension that seemed to tighten around them, drawing them close. Ford couldn't stop thinking about that kissing lesson and the way she'd let go in his arms. He'd give anything to experience that one more time.

"Are you thinking about the kiss?" she asked.

He tried to hide his muscle twitch. God, he should've known Tessa wasn't afraid of anything, least of all confronting the truth, even when it was messy. She'd be a loyal, feisty companion to the man she fell for.

Once, Ford thought she'd be a complete nightmare to be in a relationship with. Not anymore. Not as he unearthed all the layers of this complicated woman and found himself wanting more.

Ford cleared his throat. Somehow, they'd drifted close enough that only a few precious inches separated their bodies. "I am. I shouldn't be."

"Because you love Patricia. Because the only reason we ever got together was to make her love you back."

He fell into her deep blue eyes, large and round and gleaming with emotion that tore at his heart. "Yes."

She nodded, accepting, which made it worse. "You better go, then."

He tried, but it was like his feet were stuck to the floor. Her scent surrounded him, driving him mad, that hint of sandalwood and orchards, as contradictory as she was. "I will."

Ford wasn't sure who moved first, but suddenly, she was in his arms and he was kissing her, his fingers buried in her hair, knocking the cap to the ground. The kiss wasn't proper or polite. It wasn't demanding or teasing. It was primal want and hunger, rough and awkward and as real as he'd ever kissed a woman before.

He steeped himself in her taste and texture and smell, his lips moving over hers, pulling a sexy little moan from her throat. Instinctually, he slid his hands around her back, then lower, lifting her up so he could kiss her even deeper. His tongue tangled with hers and she demanded more, so he tilted his head, reslanted his lips over hers, and gave it to her.

The kiss went on until his head spun and his dick ached and his head was completely full of Tessa. Her body clung to his, her arms wrapped around his shoulders, and in that moment, he didn't care about anything but getting her naked and in bed and claiming her for himself.

Just as quick as the kiss began, Tessa broke it off. She panted raggedly, staring at him with shock and arousal. Her lips were wet and slightly swollen.

Reality was like a wave of icy water, rolling through him and yanking him back to sanity. What had he done? What had they done? When had this gotten so completely out of control?

"Tessa, I—"

"This never happened." She straightened up, her expression locked and removed of all emotion. "We just got carried away in a weak moment. We need to move on. Okay?"

She was giving him an out. A way to pretend it was a one-off, something they agreed would never happen again. Ford knew he should be grateful to her, but an ache throbbed in his gut that confused him. Almost like he wanted her to fight for him, like she did for that T-shirt.

But she wouldn't do that. Because he was meant for Patricia.

Refusing to allow himself to grieve something he didn't know, Ford nodded. "Okay."

"This never happened," she reiterated.

Her gaze forced him to repeat the words even as each one tore like a paper cut. "This never happened."

She smiled, but it was strained. "Good. I hope your date goes well tomorrow. Make sure you text me."

"I will. Thanks."

Ford left. With each mile he drove away, the sense of loss deepened, until he cranked up some metal music so he could stop thinking.

~

Tessa spent all day Saturday trying not to think about the second kiss.

By the time she got to Emma's place, she was jumpy and on edge, like a junkie needing a fix to calm down. She glanced at the time and figured Ford would be at the restaurant right now with Patricia. Hopefully it would go well, and she could cut off this strange relationship that was beginning to seriously mess with her head.

"Tessa!" Emma gave her a warm hug, inviting her in.

Emma's house was a sweet Cape Cod, with a small porch, two bedrooms, and a kitchen nook that was furnished in bright colors and spotlessly clean. Every time Tessa walked into the home, she got a sense of coziness and care, just like Emma. The real Emma—not the awkward, stuffy woman she'd first shown to the world, but the one with a big heart looking for companionship and love. It had taken a while to get Emma comfortable being who she really was, represented in not only her appearance but lifestyle, and Tessa saw her blooming this past year in a way that gave her joy.

"I made some snacks for us, and I have the wine you like. I was looking forward to catching up. I feel like you've been busy."

Tessa laughed and settled in one of the sturdy kitchen chairs with lemon-yellow cushions. Green and flowering plants filled the empty spaces, all beautifully cared for and giving off a lovely fragrance. "I think you're the one who's been busy," she teased. "These last two weeks you've had an event almost every night."

Emma blushed a bit but was smiling. "I know, I'm not sure how it happened. There was a Scrabble tournament, and then I went with Arthur to his grandson's birthday party. Then my friend Anabelle called to meet at the library for a fundraiser, and Mike took me to dinner."

"I'm the most interested in that last one," Tessa said. Hope filled her, but she tried to keep cool.

"It was good."

Tessa narrowed her gaze, studying the woman's face. And there it was. The gleam of excitement in the gray eyes behind those trendy glasses; the softening of her features as if caught in a rosy glow. "Oh, it was more than good. Tell me everything."

The girly laugh that escaped Emma's lips made her spirits soar. "At first, I thought he was going to cook for me at the diner—but then he kept driving and surprised me with a really nice Italian restaurant. And pricey, too! I couldn't believe it!"

Tessa tried to clamp her lips shut to keep from cracking up. Thank goodness Mike had listened to her about not having their date at the diner. "That says a lot for Mike. He watches his pennies."

"Yes, and I admire that. He told me to get anything I wanted and even insisted on dessert. The food was delicious. I had seafood risotto."

"Yum. How was the conversation?"

"At first, he seemed very nervous. But we both loosened up with some wine, and I had a wonderful time. He's very funny. And sweet. And the way he talks about you girls! Oh, he loves you all so much."

Tessa grinned, her heart light. "I'm so happy, Emma. You've waited a long time to be treated the way you should."

"He even apologized again and said he never dated anyone besides his wife. And I noticed now when he gets off kilter, he says the silliest things. Do you know he said he didn't think he could possibly be good enough for me?"

Tessa shook her head. "He really admitted that?" Mike never shared his true feelings. He was the crusty type of guy who liked to hide any messy stuff.

"He did. I told him it was ridiculous, and we had a deep conversation about our pasts and what we think of ourselves. He opened up to me. I never wanted the night to end."

Tessa took a sip of wine, a bit giddy for her friend. "How did you end the night? Kissing?"

"Oh, no! We're not ready for that yet. But . . ." She trailed off, cheeks a bit red.

"Tell me!"

"He walked me to the door. And . . . he held my hand."

"Aww!"

"It was lovely. He asked me out again. They're having a book signing for this author I like, and he asked if he could accompany me. I said yes."

"You look so happy," Tessa said.

"I am. I'm just enjoying the moment and getting to know him. We're in no rush."

"That's great! Don't skip over any of the good parts. The getting to know you and the butterflies and the anticipation. The feeling of discovering all those new tidbits of information and putting them together like a puzzle. It's what makes dating so special."

"Speaking of which, how was your date last week?" Emma asked. "Did you see him again last night?"

Tessa hesitated. She'd always been frank with Emma, but this thing with Ford didn't make sense. How could she tell her what was happening when she didn't even know herself? "No, for some reason he hasn't answered my text. I guess I had a better time than he did."

Emma gasped. "Impossible! How dare he ignore you? He'd be lucky to gain an hour of your time."

She laughed. Even Emma's tirade was lovely and polite. "Agreed. I guess I'm back to the drawing board." Tessa took another sip of wine and nibbled at some cheese.

Emma leaned a bit closer, studying her from over the rim of her glasses. "Why do I think you're not telling me something else?"

Damn teacher's intuition. It was like her mother—always knowing there was more to the story. "Oh, nothing. I went to a baseball game with Ford last night. He had no one to go with, so he decided why not torture me?"

"Hmm. Ford, huh? That's interesting."

Tessa arched a brow. "No, it's not. His big date with Patricia is tonight. If I did my job correctly, they'll be madly in love within two weeks and I can stop these ridiculous sports lessons."

"I heard your podcast. It was very funny and lively. In fact, I realized I'd never heard you like that before."

"Like what?"

Emma seemed to pick her words carefully. "Dynamic. You and Ford bantered like you've known each other for ages. There was chemistry."

Tessa stiffened at the term. Lord, she had to get Emma off this topic or she'd slip up. She had to stop thinking about that kiss. That awful, disturbing, wonderful kiss that had come from nowhere.

"Of course there was—we're in passionate dislike." Tessa forced a laugh. "Did you hear from Chiara that Veronica climbed her first cabinet? She wanted more Cheerios and decided to get them for herself."

"No! Did she get a video?"

They fell into chatter about the other girls, and Tessa kept the rest of the evening light and carefree. No more talk about Ford.

Tessa glanced at her watch. He and Patricia should be eating dessert by now. If he was playing it right, he'd be relaxed in his chair, flirting lightly, telling Patricia that it didn't work out with Tessa. She'd told him specifically not to sleep with her but knew he might not listen. If

Patricia went back to his place, and they had their first kiss, it could turn into something more.

He may have sex with her tonight.

She may fall in love with him tonight.

That was a good thing. A very good thing.

Tessa's stomach twisted, so she had more wine and focused on Emma.

Chapter Twenty

The date was going perfectly.

Ford had his car professionally cleaned and picked Patricia up. The quick peek at her apartment showed a lot of modern, sleek furniture with hard edges and trendy lines. He'd filed away her preferred style as important information, even though it wasn't his favorite.

The restaurant was cozy and intimate. They dined by candlelight, and he ordered a bottle of wine. Ford basked in the happy glow of her face as they spoke about work and her goals at KTUZ. He shared how he got into radio, and she confessed she'd been raised by a single dad who gave her a love for sports because he'd secretly wished for a boy.

She was beautiful. Her black dress was short, exposing long, muscled legs with strappy heels. The bodice clung perfectly to her breasts and accented her hips. Her hair was loose, a silky straight waterfall falling to her shoulders. She listened to him when he spoke, seemingly fascinated by his life, when before, her usual response was a warm smile and pat on the arm, like a friend who was talking a bit too much but you enjoyed their company, just not a lot.

Everything was exactly how he dreamed it would be.

Patricia spooned a tiny bit of her lemon sorbet and sighed. "Dinner was delicious. I'm so impressed you were able to get us in here—I've been dying to try it out."

"Me, too." Tessa had been right about taking her to a special place. Better not to tell Patricia it was her contacts and not his that got them in. "So you told me about your dad, and I know you have a sister upstate you like to visit. Any other family?"

She wrinkled her nose in a charming gesture. "A few cousins, aunts, and uncles. I'm not close with them, though. I think family is great, but I want to live my life on my terms. Some of my relatives can be a bit needy, and I don't have the time to give them what they want. I think complete focus on my life and what makes me happy is key, even though it sounds selfish."

"No, I think it's important to recognize limits." He thought of how Tessa took care of her uncle whenever he called and attended a dog party when she ran a media empire. How she dropped everything when her friends called because her relationships trumped all.

No more thinking of Tessa, he reminded himself.

Patricia flashed him a dazzling smile. He was almost blinded by her straight, white teeth. "I knew you'd understand."

He focused his complete attention on her, admiring the graceful way she dipped her spoon, the tilt of her head, the slant of her patrician nose—all the qualities he'd studied when she wasn't looking, memorizing them in his dreams. Now, she was finally here, for him. It was almost unreal, as if he were watching himself from afar. "Do you want to stay at KTUZ for a while? Or do you have a bigger goal in mind?"

"I'm happy right now. My sales are growing, I love the team I'm on, and I'm good at my job. If I can top out like Jay, I'd be fulfilled."

Ford nodded. "Sounds like me. I found my place, and I'm happy to stay at the station. It's nice to settle in and be comfortable, isn't it?"

"Definitely. All of these women who chase endless goals for more—I don't understand. I want to enjoy my life, enjoy my job. Why keep pushing?"

"Agreed." Patricia was definitely his soul mate. He felt the same way. Tessa was a pusher. She was always growing, changing, looking for the next level in her life or relationships. She'd be an exhausting partner and never ready to happily settle down and coast.

"Tessa must be like that, though." Patricia spoke his exact thoughts, and he pulled back slightly, startled. "I mean, look at what she built at Quench. I'm sure that's what made her so attractive." She paused, glancing down at her sorbet. "I'm not sure I can compete with that, Ford."

The quietness in her voice made him stiffen. He knew it was imperative he handled this in a way that extricated himself from Tessa without making him look like a cheating asshole. Even though he felt like one right now.

Stupid. He was being stupid.

"Tessa came into my life when I needed her," he said honestly. "I'll never regret our time together. But we've gone as far as we can, and we're not seeing each other any longer."

"Why?" Those violet eyes seemed wide and trusting.

His gut clenched, and he assumed it was need and hunger for her because she'd been the picture of that for so damn long. Ford swallowed. "Because of you," he said roughly.

"Really?"

He was about to tell her how he'd dreamed of her for years, then remembered Patricia didn't want that from him. She didn't want eagerness and awkwardness and open emotion. She wanted mystery and seduction from a man who called the shots.

He fell into the role like slipping on his new outfits. "Not that I expected it. After you declined my invite, I began thinking of you as only a friend."

Yes, her pupils dilated. She loved the chase. "Oh, not even one little what-if?" she teased, lowering her lashes in a flirty manner. "Not even one naughty dream?"

Ford gave a slow, deliberate grin. "Maybe. But we were both involved with other people."

"Fate finally stepped in," she said. "It was as if I suddenly realized what I want has been right there all this time."

Yes.

Tessa's face flashed through his mind, but he pushed it quickly away. "I feel the same." He slid his hand across the table and confidently took hers, playing with her fingers. He deepened his voice. "Now the question is, what do we do about it?"

She shivered and licked her lips. "Anything we want."

Ford stared at her mouth. Pale pink, with lush lines that begged for a man to kiss her. The idea of kissing her had haunted him for years. "What do you want, Patricia?"

"More. Why don't you drive me home?"

The invite was clear. He wasn't Superman. He was a man of flesh and blood, and there was no way he was turning her down, even if he was supposed to be playing the long game. "I'll get the check."

He paid the bill and drove them to her apartment. She held his hand as the miles were gobbled up. He needed to get this right. Confident masculinity. Slow and deliberate seduction. Their first time had to be perfect so he could finally pull his walls down and tell her how he'd always felt about her.

He parked. Dropped her hand and came around the car to escort her out. When they got to the front door of her apartment, she reached for the key, and Ford knew he had to change the plan.

He wasn't ready for this yet. The stakes were too high.

But he needed to leave her with an impression—to leave her wanting him. So channeling everything Tessa taught him, he gently reached out, snagged her around the waist, and drew her in.

Her eyes widened in surprise, then darkened with pleasure.

Without a word, Ford angled his head and took her lips without a request or apology. Finally, he kissed Patricia Mann.

She gave a breathy gasp, then slid her arms around his neck. He kissed her the way he'd fantasized, until she melted against him, and her head fell back, and she allowed him access. She tasted of lemon and fruit. Her lips were soft and molded to his. Her willowy body pressed tight with a clear enticement.

Ford took his time with the kiss, firmly in control, noticing his body was half-aroused and his mind was crystal clear. Slowly, he broke apart, pressing tiny kisses to her mouth, easing back. "I have to go."

She clung to him. "No. Stay."

He traced the line of her cheek and gave a mysterious smile. "Not tonight."

Ford wondered if she'd get pissed and dismiss him, but his rejection seemed to turn her on even more. She kissed him, tugging him toward the door, but he confidently stepped back. "You're driving me mad," she whispered, half laughing, obviously enchanted by his dismissal.

"So are you. I'll text you." He walked to the car without a glance back, sensing it was the right move.

When he pulled away, he finally let out his breath, his body releasing all that tension. He'd expected a raging hard-on, but it was as if his mind was too engaged with the game to focus on arousal.

Tessa would be proud of him.

He wondered what she was doing tonight. Uncle Bart and his friends had definitely cut off her last Tinder date, and though Ford felt a bit guilty for keeping quiet about their methods, he was also glad she wasn't seeing anyone right now. Which was fucked up, but he was being honest.

He didn't want her kissing anyone else. Not after the way she'd kissed him.

Ford kept driving and ended up at her place. He cut the engine and stared at the darkened house. Her car was in the driveway. A light glowed from the window. Could she be home on a Saturday night? What was he doing here?

He needed to go home.

Instead, Ford got out of the car and rang the bell. He waited a while before she opened it. Tessa's curls spilled wildly around her face. Her pajamas looked soft, in a pale pink with stitched hearts. Fluffy pink slippers covered her feet.

She gave him a haughty glare. "Are you ever going to stop showing up on my doorstep without an invitation?"

His entire body hummed with something that felt a lot like joy. "Not if you don't answer your phone."

"You texted me?"

"No, I knew you wouldn't answer." He paused, shifting his weight. "Are you watching the Mets game?"

"Like I have nothing better to do on a Saturday night," she said with a snarl. "That's ridiculous."

"What's the score?"

"We're down by three. We're toast."

"Not this year. We can come back."

He didn't ask. She just moved aside and he stepped past her, and then they were sitting on the couch, watching the Mets game.

"Escobar's on fire tonight, but our pitching is shaky. We had to go to the bullpen early."

"We still have a chance."

"Want a beer?"

"Yeah, I'll get it." He grabbed one and automatically refilled her wineglass. The scent of coconut and lavender filled the air. Probably a bubble bath. Or that body cream she smothered all over herself to keep her skin protected. He took another sniff and felt his head spin pleasantly.

"How was your date?"

He handed her the wine. Met her gaze head-on. And felt his heart pound in a dangerous, unsteady rhythm. "Good. I told her we officially broke up."

She hid her face, so he couldn't spot her expression. "How'd she take it?"

"She was happy."

A long pause filled the room. "You didn't sleep with her yet?"

He shook his head and took a sip of his beer. "No." He paused. "I didn't want to."

Ford waited for a long discussion on what the hell they were doing. On what the hell he was doing. On what the hell was happening and why he was at her place on a Saturday night after his date with the woman he claimed to love.

Instead, Tessa just nodded. "Cool."

They finished watching the game, yelling their heads off when Escobar cracked a homer over the wall and the Mets ended up winning by one run.

Ford left shortly after that.

He slept deeply and dreamed about Tessa.

~

Mike was singing.

Tessa tried not to gape as she drank her coffee. Malia and Chiara seemed to have the same problem. They'd both dropped their forks and stared at the man in the greasy apron belting out "We've Only Just Begun" in an off-key voice that had most of the diner either laughing or groaning. His body seemed light and airy as he strolled around, refilling coffee and joking with the customers.

"I saw Emma yesterday," Tessa finally said. "Their official date went well. Very, very well."

"I'd say so," Malia murmured. "My Lord, did they—"

"God, no!" Tessa laughed hysterically. "It took them two years to date. Do you really think anything else happened?"

"Sorry, I'm just sex focused right now. All of this wedding planning is putting us in the mood."

Chiara nudged her shoulder playfully. "Sure you're not trying for a baby early?"

Malia laughed, a refreshing change from how devastated she'd been when she'd learned during her fertility journey that she had ovarian cysts, which would make getting pregnant more difficult. "I'm sure it will be a process when we officially try, but at least my eggs are there if we need them. Right now, all I can focus on is the constant family calls grilling me on every wedding detail. And trust me, it's split evenly between my family and Palmer's." Her engagement ring flashed in the light. "I wish we could elope. If our families weren't so big and demanding, we could go to Vegas and get married by Elvis."

Tessa rolled her eyes and returned to her veggie omelet. "You'd regret it. You dreamed of a huge wedding your whole life! Besides, Palmer has a company dedicated to creating your perfect wedding. You have to use it!"

Malia sighed and sipped her tea. "Yeah, but I don't want Palmer getting too involved, because he's a control freak. I want him to enjoy it, too."

Chiara laughed. "He will, as long as he's in charge. Babe, it will be beautiful and perfect, and we're here to make sure you have no worries."

"I know. Thanks—you guys are the best."

Mike appeared at the table with a dazzling grin. "Girls, how are you this morning? Any refills? Oh, I got some nice mango in—how about I bring you a fruit cup?"

Tessa's lip twitched. He was so adorable she wanted to hug him. "Sure. How was your date with Emma?"

He didn't even try to play it cool. "Amazing. We had a great time, and we're going to a book signing this week."

"I'm so happy for you both," Chiara said with a squeal.

"Thanks. How about you? I know we haven't met for Scrabble in a while, but there's a concert I want to invite Emma to next Sunday, so it may be a while longer."

Malia kept a straight face. "That's okay, Mike, we understand. We've got a lot going on, so please don't worry."

"Good. But I haven't forgotten I'm babysitting this week. I can't wait to see my perfect grandbaby."

Chiara laughed. "And we can't wait to have a date night!"

"I'll get you that mango. You'll love it!" He disappeared, and they all grinned.

"You really are a born matchmaker," Malia said to Tessa. "I apologize for giving you crap."

"Apology always accepted."

"Must be nice to always be right about who's meant to be," Chiara teased.

The words struck Tessa right in the chest like a wild pitch. Was it nice to watch a person chase another while knowing in her heart it was wrong? She'd been transforming readers believing she was making a difference in their lives. But what if none of it was real? What if her pursuits up to now truly were smoke and mirrors instead of a lasting change to make someone better?

What if she was a fraud?

All she could think of was Ford. He'd gone straight from his date with Patricia to her house, and they'd never even discussed it. She'd been watching a baseball game because it entertained her and made her feel close to him. When he arrived, her soul seemed to settle and a lighthearted happiness overtook her. She was starting to crave his presence. Somehow their roles had blurred into something more, but she had no idea what, or what to do about it. It had been easier to ignore it and watch the Mets game.

But Ford was going out with Patricia again, and Tessa couldn't be the one sitting at home, full of regrets and doubt, pretending everything was cool.

"Hey, you okay? Your face looks weird," Chiara said, breaking her mental tirade.

Tessa forced a smile, even though her gut said to discuss the whole thing with her best friends. They'd tell her what to do, but first she needed to figure out what these feelings were with Ford. A brief distraction because she was lonely? Or something deeper?

Something that could blow up both of their lives, plus Patricia's.

"Yeah. Fine."

"How was your uncle's dog party?" Malia asked. "I think that's the most adorable thing I've ever heard."

Tessa shook her head. "It was good. He had the place fully decorated with a cake and everything. He's one in a million, along with his crew. Ford got a kick out of them."

Malia and Chiara shared a pointed glance. "Wait—Ford was there?" Chiara asked.

Uh-oh.

"Um, yeah. We were going over the podcast, and he asked to come check it out. It was nothing."

"Nothing," Malia repeated. She crossed her arms in front of her chest and narrowed her gaze. "You're lying, Tessa. You have that muscle tick in your jaw when you're trying really hard to be breezy and casual."

She loosened her jaw and looked offended. "Do not! And I'm not lying—that's exactly what happened."

"No, she means you're lying about what's really going on with you and Ford," Chiara said. "Did he have his date with Patricia yet? Or are you still fake-dating?"

Malia snorted. "Just remember, that's how Palmer and I started out."

Tessa gave a long-suffering sigh and pretended she was exhausted from their fanciful theories. "He's dating Patricia and it's going well. He told her we broke up, so after we finish our final podcast episode, we won't be seeing each other anymore."

Chiara squinted with suspicion. "Then why did you go to the Mets game together Friday night? And why didn't you tell us?"

Crap. Damn Ryder. Why did he have to be such a tattletale? "Because it was research for the final podcast and your husband was busy with you that night. It was nothing."

"Nothing," Malia said. "You like that word, yet it seeps with lies."

The universe suddenly dropped down a gift straight from heaven when Emma and Arthur came into the diner. They stopped by their table to say hello and chat, distracting her friends, and then settled in the booth behind them.

Mike spotted her from behind the counter, and his face lit up.

Until he also caught sight of Arthur. Then it changed into a fierce, unsettling frown.

"Uh-oh," Malia whispered. "Why is he still focused on Arthur? He's just Emma's close friend."

"Because he suddenly caught feelings and is more in tune with his jealousy," Chiara said. "This is not good."

"I can try to call him over here." Tessa raised her voice and waved. "Mike?"

Mike put his hand up and marched toward Emma's table. "One minute," he muttered to them before settling beside Emma and Arthur. "Emma, I'm so glad to see you. You look beautiful."

Tessa spotted the woman's glow between the slats of the booth. "Thank you, Michael. I'll have tea and pancakes."

"Good to see you, Mike," Arthur said in his well-cultured voice. "I'll have the same."

Mike grunted. "Why? You never have what Emma does. Are you trying to impress her?"

Emma gasped.

Tessa closed her eyes. They were back to the nightmare.

"Michael, don't talk to him like that. Arthur is a good friend of mine—what's wrong with you?"

Mike jabbed a finger at the nicely dressed man with the carnation. "My issue is how he follows you everywhere hiding his intentions. I think he's in love with you, Emma, and it's time to face the music. I think it's time he admits the truth!"

Chiara moaned. "Do we stop this madness now?"

Tessa shook her head. "Let it play out—we can't keep trying to save him."

Unbelievably, Arthur seemed calm. His smile was gentle as he reached over and patted Emma's hand, stopping her from exploding at Mike. "I think it's time I do admit the truth," he said. "Not that I was hiding anything, but there shouldn't be a question about where my intentions with Emma lie."

"Finally!" Mike barked. "Go ahead. Admit it."

"I'm gay, Mike."

Silence fell.

Emma glared at Mike, obviously knowing this fact. Tessa tried not to gasp, because she hadn't a clue and usually her radar was on point. It all seemed to fall into place. Emma had been immediately comfortable and open with Arthur because there was never going to be something romantic between them.

"Here we go," Malia said. "I wish I had popcorn."

Mike sputtered, his face turning red. "I . . . I . . . I'm sorry. Ah, man, I'm really sorry. I didn't know." He hung his head, and even Tessa felt bad for him. "I'm an ass."

Emma didn't flinch from the curse. "Yes, at this moment, you are," she agreed. But her voice was soft, and it looked like she'd already forgiven Mike. In fact, it looked like she was a little jazzed at his jealousy.

"It's all right, Mike. I should have let you know sooner when I realized you have deep feelings for Emma. I hope we can be friends."

Mike shot Arthur a grateful look. "Breakfast is on the house," he announced.

"Wonderful. You can bring me a side of bacon, too, if you're buying," Arthur said.

Mike laughed, and the tension eased.

Tessa decided it was the perfect time to do the Batman before her friends realized they'd dropped the topic of her and Ford. "I gotta go. I have an appointment. See you later!"

"We're not done with you yet!" Malia yelled.

She hurried out the door with a grin, grateful for the temporary escape.

Tessa had some figuring out to do.

Chapter Twenty-One

"What's going on with you and Patricia?"

Ford glanced up at Jay, who stood before him with a confused expression. He had noticed the man seemed a bit off since his big party. As the top salesperson on the team, Jay held meetings where he tried to impart his knowledge and share things he did for his big clients in a ruse to look like he was a mentor. Ford knew he was just an egotist. Jay loved having his team admire him.

The past few weeks, Patricia had stopped seeking Jay out for advice, and it was obvious the guy missed her attention. He hated the fact she now spent her free time with Ford.

"Nothing, why?" he asked, turning his attention back to his laptop, where he was researching a possible radio guest.

"You were having lunch together again. You seeing her now?"

The last thing Ford needed was to parade Patricia's interest and spark some asinine competition. He wanted things to run smoothly. In the past week they'd had lunch twice, and they were texting daily. They were beginning to really connect. It was easy to talk to her, and she was stunningly beautiful. They had dinner plans this weekend, and this time, Ford was ready to move forward on a physical level.

He had to make a move. Things were getting too complicated with Tessa.

"We're just hanging out," he replied neutrally.

Jay laughed, but it had a rough edge. "You still with the hottie? Tessa—right?"

He stiffened. "Nope. We stopped seeing each other."

"Man, I don't get it. She was a smoke show. Don't mind if I make a move, do ya?" He winked when Ford gave him a look, his face taking on a frat boy arrogance.

"As a matter of fact, I do. She's with someone else now, so I'd leave her alone."

"Got dumped, huh? No wonder you're with Patricia. I can't blame you. You're practically the last one to sample her. She likes anyone in a power position, so you may have to—"

Ford got up and punched Jay in the face.

The man staggered back, holding his jaw, eyes wide. Ford hadn't hit him hard, deliberately holding back, but he took advantage of his shock. "Don't ever talk about Patricia like that again or you'll end up in HR so fast your head will spin. Got it?"

"What the hell, man! What's wrong with you? It was just a joke."

"I didn't think it was funny, and neither would Patricia. Or Tessa. Keep away from both of them." He grabbed his laptop and left the room, feeling no regret. If he got called out on physical violence, he'd take the hit.

It was worth it.

He'd better text Tessa and let her know about the encounter. He didn't want Jay contacting her to get revenge and try to use her. Not that Tessa would ever go out with the guy, especially with Uncle Bart blocking any assholes. But she should still know.

He'd text Patricia, too, of course. After all, she was his main priority.

~

"I cannot believe you punched him," Tessa said with a laugh. "What did he do?"

"Just stared at me, looking like a guppy. I definitely took him by surprise."

"Who would've thought you had such aggression in you? First the guy at Citi Field, and now Jay. You're like a knight trying to protect a woman's honor."

Ford gave a snort and kicked his legs up on his coffee table. The Mets game was on the television. His laptop sat beside him with a pad and pen to take notes. Ford had gotten back from the Dream On Youth Center, grabbed some takeout, and decided to catch up on some research while watching baseball. He'd automatically called Tessa, who actually picked up, and caught her up on the day's activities. "Trust me—you don't need any man protecting you. I saw you in action when your T-shirt was stolen."

"Yeah, but Patricia will love it. Did you tell her yet?"

"Not yet. We usually talk before bed."

A beat passed. "Romantic. Sounds like things are going well."

"They are. They're going great. You'll be able to officially write your column and share my success by the end of the month."

"That confident, huh?" A short silence buzzed. "I'm happy for you, Ford."

His throat tightened with a mix of emotions he couldn't name. They'd done their final podcast together, and it was a hit. The Quench crew said the listening and download numbers were sky high, and it had brought in a whole new segment of audience. The new host was ready to transition in, and Tessa could go back behind the scenes.

Almost all their bargaining terms were complete. All he had to do was finalize his relationship with Patricia and have Tessa write her column. Then, they'd only need to see each other around Ronnie or their friends. At the occasional party.

She'd probably stop watching baseball with no one to push her, which was a shame because Tessa's grasp of the game and ability to read players fascinated him. Hell, she'd be a great person to interview on his show because of the fresh perspective she gave.

"Thanks. How about you? Did that guy ever text you back?"

"No, he's gone. I met someone at a coffee place yesterday morning. We decided to grab drinks this weekend."

Ford's heartbeat sped up. "Really? Do you know I've never picked up a woman in a coffee shop before? How'd he manage it?"

She laughed, and he savored the sound. It was less feminine than Patricia's—more robust and hearty, like Tessa didn't give a shit who heard it or what anyone else thought—yet she managed to be elegant and a bit haughty at the same time. It was such a strange combination, but to Ford, it all fit into a perfect package.

As a friend.

"We got our orders messed up, which led to a meet-cute and I decided, why not? Maybe fate finally stepped in. I need someone."

He gripped the phone. Half closed his eyes. "Do you? I thought you were happy doing your own thing."

"I'm ready to meet someone now." Her voice grew quiet, reflective. "It's time."

Logically, she was right. On another level, he didn't like the idea of her sharing time with anyone else. "That's great. What's the guy's name?"

"David."

"David what?"

"Why, are you gonna google him?" she teased. "I don't know—he said he works at Meyers Law Firm in Nyack. Divorce lawyer."

"That's not a good sign."

"At this point, I don't care. And neither should you."

He took the hit well because he deserved it. He had no right to any opinion on Tessa's life. It was time to step away. "You're right. Sorry."

A sigh fell into his ear. "It's okay. I think—go, go, catch it, for God's sakes, yes! Yes!"

Ford watched the centerfielder jump up against the wall and take away a homer from the Dodgers catcher. Then with perfect symmetry, he pivoted and threw the ball to second, preventing the runner on first from advancing. "Niiice play!" Ford roared, pumping his fist.

"We're on our way to sweeping another series. This really may be your year, Ford."

"*Our* year," he said automatically, then stopped.

Silence descended. He realized in that moment he thought of them as a team now. He was constantly thinking about her. Seeking out her presence. When they were together, Ford felt a happiness he'd never known before. Like he was . . . complete.

The phone buzzed. He glanced at the text from Patricia.

"I better go," Tessa said. Her voice was cool and composed, as if she knew it was time for him and Patricia to talk. "Good luck on your date. It's obvious you both were fated for each other, after all."

The phone clicked.

A second text buzzed through. Ready to talk? I had such a day!

Ford scratched his head and stared at the screen for a long time. His mind whirled with the possibilities of his choices, but how could he turn his back on finally getting what he dreamed about? Patricia was the one. He'd known this for years. He needed to stay the course and it would all work out.

~

"I've been looking forward to tonight," Patricia said. She stepped aside, and he walked into her apartment.

"So have I." It was the truth. He couldn't count the number of times he imagined himself in her space, sharing it with her, being the man who could touch her. Being the man she wanted to touch.

The rooms reflected who he now knew Patricia to be. She loved modern art and architecture and studied it in her spare time. The jagged lines of furniture competed with glass and startling canvases in whirling, haunting images. Faces hidden in circles; bold brush strokes highlighting a woman weeping; a lightning storm where waves revealed a screaming mouth. There was a darker side to Patricia, something more than what she revealed on the surface with her sweet politeness and warmth.

Normally, he'd be thrilled discovering these hidden layers. He'd learned she'd gotten bit by a dog years ago and no longer trusted animals. She loved high fashion, fancy restaurants, and being included in exclusive groups. She was more comfortable around men than women and didn't have many female friends. She fell hard quickly, loved surprises, and believed in instalove. She could watch a baseball game with him without snide remarks or odd comments, peppering stats like an announcer in the same monotone voice. She never jumped up, threw food, or yelled at a game. She sucked at reading people and appreciated verbal assurances on a regular basis, needing compliments to feel valued.

He'd learned all of this and was about to fulfill his deepest fantasies.

But Ford couldn't stop thinking of Tessa.

He shrugged off his jacket, walking around Patricia's place. "I never would've pegged you for such dark art," he teased. "Always thought you were the Bob Ross type."

She laughed, retrieving two glasses of wine from the kitchen. "I still like happy trees."

He tasted the red and nodded appreciatively at the ripe taste of blackberries and spice. He was impressed by her wine collection, even though he was definitely more of a beer guy.

Patricia stopped next to him, sipping her own wine. Her hair was twisted up, exposing her swanlike neck. Smoky eyes stared through the fringe of her bangs. She wore an eggplant-colored dress in a tight knit that clung to every curve, designed to have any man in her presence question her underwear options. Ford was guessing a thong.

Her hand rubbed up and down his arm. "I like this suit on you. Very sexy."

He'd visited the store Tessa had taken him to and bought a sleek black suit that he paired with a white graphic T-shirt. He felt a bit like the man in black, Johnny Cash, but even he admitted it looked cool in the mirror. "It's not as sexy as that dress," he growled, lifting her hand to his lips.

"I've been thinking about you a lot," she admitted. "It's weird because we've been around each other for over two years, but now I'm having all these feelings. It's almost like all of our interactions built up to this. Like it was fate."

Her words stirred him with unease. His intention had been so genuine, but suddenly, Ford felt guilty. There was no fate. No romance. Their entire relationship was built around a facade that Tessa helped him create, all to convince Patricia he was the one. Now that he neared his goal, doubt assailed him.

Why didn't this feel right? Why wasn't he mad to touch her, kiss her, drag her to bed, and stamp himself all over her body? Why wasn't he dreaming of her at night? Why wasn't he craving her with a raw type of hunger?

He needed to silence the doubts and the questions. Falling into his role, he plucked the wineglass from her hand and set them both on the table. Then, with one easy move, he pulled her to him and kissed her.

Ford took his time, ramping up the sexual tension between them. He caught her moan, nibbled her lips, and finally kissed her deep, the way he'd always dreamed. He let all the emotions he'd been saving up for years unleash.

And saw Tessa's face.

Ford pulled back, panting as he stared at Patricia. She was so beautiful, soft in his arms, the woman who was made for him. But it was impossible to get there until he satisfied this awful, biting, ravenous need for another woman.

"I'm sorry, Patricia. You have no idea how sorry I am. But I can't do this. I have to go."

She bit her trembling lip, violet eyes filled with distress. "Did I do something wrong?"

He hated himself for having her even ask the question. "No. I've been wanting you longer than you think. But I have some loose ends to tie up, and I don't want to be one of those dicks who takes you to bed, then backs off in the morning. Do you understand?"

She nodded, a bit shaky. "Is it Tessa?"

A shudder racked his body. "Yes. I need to talk to her."

"Okay." She turned away, hurt threaded in her voice. "I sensed something was holding you back. I know you're not like those other guys—I know you wouldn't hurt me."

Dear God, he was scum. Lower than an amoeba. He had to get his shit together and tell her the truth. But not tonight. "I would never hurt you on purpose. That's why I have to go."

"Will you call me later?"

"I'll call you tomorrow. I promise."

She wrapped her arms around her body, and the sudden distance between them made him hurt.

Cursing under his breath, Ford grabbed his jacket and left.

It was time to stop running from the truth.

Chapter Twenty-Two

Tessa was in bed, doing some major retail online shopping, when the pounding on the front door started.

WTF?

She got up, not bothering with a robe since she was dressed in shorts and a Quench T-shirt.

Tessa peeked out the window and jerked back. What was Ford doing here, punching her door like a madman, when he was supposed to be on a date with Patricia?

In that moment, all the confusion and heartache and feelings were transcended, converted into something so much better.

Pure feminine fury.

She flung open the door. "What the hell do you think you're doing?" she screeched, refusing to hold back any longer. "Who the hell do you think you are, showing up at this time of night?"

Ford marched in and slammed the door behind him. He was wearing a sharp black suit, obviously new. His hair was gelled back from his forehead. He smelled of rain and soap. His eyes were full of temper and male frustration, which was perfect for her mood, because at this point she wanted to physically and verbally lash out.

"I don't know!" he roared back. "I'm losing my mind, Tessa, and it's your fault!"

Her jaw unhinged. She squeaked out some high-pitched noise as her fury rose to new heights. "Me? You should be with Patricia tonight! The woman you've loved for years and begged me to help you get. You asked for all of this, Ford Maddox, and now you're here playing some serious head games with me. But you picked the wrong person to mess with. Now—get out!"

"No. I need to talk to you." He began to pace, fingers in his hair, obviously as messed up as she was. It made her feel a tiny bit better. "Something happened to me. I've gotten everything I ever wanted. Patricia is falling for me. Tonight, she wanted to have sex with me."

Tessa fell back into a rage. "Then go have sex with her, you idiot! Why are you here?"

"Because I can't stop thinking about you. You're ruining my life!"

She let out a screech and threw the door back open. "You already ruined mine! I think about you at odd times, and when I see you, I get happy. It's . . . awful!"

He shut the door again and closed the distance between them. "I'm not going anywhere until we figure it all out. I need to get rid of this need I have for you all the time. It's driving me mad."

"Good! Because I had a perfectly nice date with a great guy I really liked, and you know what? I was checking the Mets score and wondering what you and Patricia were doing like some ridiculous teenager instead of a grown-ass woman."

"David?" he growled. "Did you kiss him?"

She hadn't, but she was so pissed off, she got up in his face and spit the words out like a king cobra ready to battle. "Hell yes. And it was hot!"

Ford seemed to gaze at her through a mist of fury, which was fine, because she was also seeing red. He blurred a bit as he grasped her shoulders and dragged her to him, and she immediately clung to him because her body was a traitorous stranger she didn't recognize. "I hate that you kissed him," he muttered, hazel eyes wild, hands gentling as he pressed his forehead to hers. "I hate thinking of you with anyone but me."

Her voice broke. "What about Patricia?"

"I left her. Told her I needed to figure things out with you. I'm obsessed with you, Tessa. The only one I can picture in bed with me is you."

She moaned as he dropped a kiss to her cheek, down her jaw, pulling her in tight so she was surrounded by blistering male heat. He rubbed his lips back and forth over hers, allowing her to pull away, giving her the final choice. "I hate you," she whispered, grabbing his face to still him.

"I hate you more."

His mouth crashed over hers, and she was swept away by the roar of emotion exploding deep from within. Tessa wrapped herself tight around him and kissed him back with everything she had, hips grinding against his, already wet and throbbing between her thighs. He never paused, just hitched her up, with his hands cupping her ass to walk toward her bedroom.

"No, here," she demanded.

He cursed and dropped her onto the couch, his fingers tugging off her clothes. She bowed under the rough heat of his hands, the primal demand of his tongue deep in her mouth as she lay naked underneath him. He ravaged her with little finesse as he sucked on her hard nipples, parted her thighs, and thrust two fingers inside with a steady pace that had her sinking her teeth into his shoulder.

He grunted and increased his pace, thumb dragging across her throbbing clit, playing her like his very own instrument.

Her hips arched. "I need—"

"I know, baby. God help me, you're so fucking beautiful."

She practically wept as the tension twisted tight in her abdomen, her body screaming for the climax kept just out of reach. He was rubbing with his palm, and she was right there. He cursed, parting her legs farther . . .

And rolled off the couch.

She tumbled with him, sprawled on top of his chest, and then they were laughing and twisting and taking off his clothes.

"I always hated that couch," he said, kissing her stomach, moving his mouth over the weeping center of her while his fingers continued thrusting deep.

"The carpet's fine. More."

"Say please."

"I don't ask for what I want, Ford. I take." She reared up and cupped him in her hands. His hot, hard length pulsed between her palms, and she guided him to her center, parting her thighs with invitation.

"I knew you were a damn witch. You put a spell on me," he growled.

He quickly pulled a condom from his discarded pants, rolled it on, and paused at her entrance. The tip of him eased a few inches in, and she tightened every muscle in anticipation.

Suddenly, his hands framed her face, those hazel eyes burning through her, taking her apart with the raw, naked emotion fully on display. And, never breaking that intense gaze, Ford pushed all the way in with one hard thrust.

Her head rolled back. She curled her legs around his hips and dug her ankles into his back.

He took her in steady, fast strokes that kept her right at the edge, with a light pressure against her clit, forcing her to pant in frantic breaths. His eyes gripped her as tight as his hands and his thighs and his dick. With one last thrust, he hit her G-spot at the same time he sank his teeth into the delicate curve of her shoulder.

She came hard, screaming his name, shuddering in his arms. Her body broke into little pieces, and she heard his hoarse shout as he followed her over. Then she collapsed.

It took a while for their breaths to even out. They were still wrapped tight around each other, legs entangled, him still inside her, her cheek pressed to his damp chest. The back of her eyes burned, and she wasn't sure why. She only knew she needed him in that moment but didn't know how to voice it.

He scooped her up, cradling her naked body against him as if she were a fragile, precious gift. She was quiet, waiting to see if he'd get dressed and leave; waiting to see if her heart would break apart if he did.

He carried her into the bedroom and lay her down. He disappeared for a moment, and when he returned, he'd removed the condom and put a few more on the bedside table. Ford crawled in beside her, holding her close. His hands in her hair, his breath on her cheek, he whispered her name over and over like a symphony.

"You've ruined me," he finally said, gently kissing her lips. "Now sleep."

She slept with a smile on her face.

Chapter Twenty-Three

Tessa woke up to lazy kisses pressed along the length of her spine.

She curled her toes and arched into the caress like a satisfied cat. They'd reached for each other multiple times throughout the night, catching snippets of sleep in between their voracious love-making. She couldn't get enough of Ford now that he was in her bed. Each time there was something more to discover, deeper pleasures to experience.

Even the silence was beautiful—a blissful, peaceful silence that allowed their bodies to take over. Tessa loved it when her mind was quiet, and with Ford, she was able to drop into the moment with no thought to the next hour.

Until now. The morning after. When everything needed to be faced.

But not yet.

"What time is it?" she murmured, catching her breath when he licked her shoulder, then bit gently.

"Ten."

"Is not."

His low laugh stroked her ears like his fingers began stroking her inner thighs, urging them to part. "It is. Hope you had nowhere to go today."

"Actually, I have to get up right now to get—oh!"

He pressed his mouth to the center of her, his tongue touching all her sensitive, throbbing parts, and she gave up the rest of her sentence and the rest of her morning.

~

"Coffee," she managed to say in a voice hoarse from screaming his name too many times. "I need coffee."

He kissed her thoroughly, pushing her wild curls away from her face. "Be right back."

Tessa smiled into the pillow and waited.

He came in a bit later with a full mug and her phone. "You have a missed call from your uncle," he said, sipping his own brew.

She sat up. "I'll call him back. I just need a quarter of a cup to make sense."

Ford chuckled, his gaze traveling over her naked breasts and shoulders, studying the lines of her face as she drank her coffee.

She kept her attention on her mug, not ready to dive into questions or revelations yet. Finally, she dialed her uncle's number.

"Tessa! I'm sorry to bother you, sweetheart, but I got myself into a pickle. Dom brought me back from the hospital—I sprained my ankle."

"Why didn't you tell me?" she demanded. "I would've gone to the hospital, Uncle Bart. What happened?"

Ford looked concerned.

A pause. "I fell over Petey. It was my fault—I'd let him in the house and wasn't paying attention."

She blew out a breath but knew she couldn't yell at him. "Okay. How bad is it?"

"I have to stay off it for a few days and let it heal. I have crutches, but the damn things are terrible. Dom's here now, but he has to take off. Vin can come later, but I'm worried about the dogs. Do you think you can help?"

"Of course. I'll be right over."

"Thanks, Tessa. You're a good girl."

She hung up and looked at Ford. "Uncle Bart sprained his ankle, and he's going to need some help at the house. I have to take off."

"I'll go with you."

She stared at him with wide eyes. Blinked. "What?"

His smile was slow and easy. "I'm sure you can use help with the dogs, and I like your uncle. I have nothing going on today."

Tessa hesitated. She wanted to ask about Patricia, but something held her back. Was it wrong to live in her bubble for just a while longer? Spend the day with him without the outside world intruding? A short reprieve from reality couldn't harm anyone, right?

"Okay."

"Let's bring him some breakfast—we can stop at the bakery."

Tessa nodded. "Great idea. Thanks."

"I'll jump in the shower. I wanted you to join me, but we'll never get over to your uncle's on time if you do." With a mischievous wink, he disappeared into the bathroom, whistling.

She shook her head, smiling, and finished her coffee.

When they got to Uncle Bart's, he was propped up on the couch with his leg elevated and a soft cast wrapped around his ankle. Petey sat on his lap. Mimi, Dug, and Hamburger the dachshund lay at his feet in a fur pile. Everyone except Petey jumped up to greet them, yipping and then running quickly back to their owner. It was obvious they all sensed something had happened and were keeping watch.

"How are you doing?" Tessa asked with concern.

Uncle Bart waved a hand in the air. "I'm fine—it doesn't even hurt. I'm worried Petey thinks it's his fault, though. He's been depressed."

Tessa pressed her lips together. The furry inkblot did look a little down, barely lifting his head to greet them. "I'll spend some time with him and cheer him up."

"Ford—you came! Good to see you."

"You, too. We brought breakfast in case you didn't have time to eat." He walked over and scooped Petey up from Uncle Bart's lap, cuddling him close. "We'll take care of the dogs today. Maybe Dom and Vin can come over later for dinner? We'll cook."

Tessa arched a brow, but Uncle Bart looked delighted. "They'd love that, thanks. Sorry to crash your Sunday. I'm sure you had plans."

Ford tugged at Tessa's curls and gave her an intimate smile. "Nah, we were bored out of our minds today. You saved both of us."

Uncle Bart shot them a knowing look, pleasure shining from his dark eyes. "Well, well," he murmured.

"Nothing is going on," Tessa announced, not wanting her uncle to get the wrong idea. "Ford and I are just friends. Got it?"

"Of course."

She shook her head. "Eat your egg sandwich. I'll check on the barn."

"Thanks."

She left the two men alone, knowing it was a bad idea, but feeling secretly giddy over their mutual affection and respect. It was nice to have a family member approve of a boyfriend. Not that Ford was her boyfriend. But she'd pretend for a little while.

Just for today.

~

"Grab the rosemary for me, please?" Tessa asked, stirring the chicken with a flat wooden spoon.

Ford's head was spinning from all the delicious smells—he couldn't remember when he'd had such a good meal away from an expensive restaurant.

Dom, Vin, and Uncle Bart were already at the table, drinking a bottle of red wine and arguing over who were the best players on the local football team—which was soccer to Americans. As their voices got louder and louder and their gestures became wilder, he noticed Tessa completely ignored them.

"Should I try to break up the fight?" he asked, handing her a spice bottle with green flakes.

"No, they're fine. Mom's family is super passionate about all kinds of subjects, from musicians to sports. Kind of like you and the Mets. That's basil—rosemary is lighter, with long, thin pieces. There."

He replaced the bottle, watching her season the meat. "I thought you didn't cook."

"I don't." She took a sip of red wine, then slid the roasted potatoes out of the oven. The scent of garlic and herbs filled the air. "But I can if I want to."

"You're an incredible woman, Tessa Harper. I don't think you'll ever stop surprising me."

She shot him a dazzling smile. "Thanks, but most women can do anything they put their mind to. We just choose not to. I'm no different."

He noticed again the way she swatted back a compliment.

The broccoli was transferred to a bowl, where she squeezed fresh lemon and grated pepper over the bright green stalks. "Bring these to the table."

He ignored her for a moment, trapping her against the stove. The men continued their battle in the other room. A crash on the table told him fists were being banged, but he ignored it, focused on the woman before him. "Why do you do that? Refuse to admit you're amazing?"

She blinked. Her skin was flushed from the heat of the kitchen, and her pink lips pursed in surprise. "I don't. I know I'm amazing."

He cupped his hand at the nape of her neck and brought his mouth close to hers. "I hope you do. Because not only have you changed my life, you change everyone you come in contact with. I don't think you're told that enough."

The sudden vulnerability in her gaze ripped through him. He kissed her with a stirring tenderness as his heart seemed to burst from his chest. She was such a fiery dynamo, too many people probably skated past her, believing she didn't need any extra assurances. But she deserved to know how damn special she was. If she were his, he'd let her know every day.

But she wasn't.

Because he was with Patricia.

He stepped back as the thought broke the connection. A flicker of regret flashed in Tessa's sky-blue eyes. Then disappeared.

Her voice was hoarse. "You can take the potatoes over, too."

Ford nodded, delivering the side dishes just as Dom jabbed his finger at Vin and said he was out of his mind. "Gentlemen, I think you're scaring Petey," he said mildly. "Dinner's ready."

The men instantly quieted, turning all that enthusiasm to the food in front of them. Tessa placed the chicken on the table and took her seat.

"Tessa, you are a goddess!" Dom announced, instantly digging in.

"I think Bart needs to get hurt more often," Vin teased. "I forgot what it was like to have a woman cook for me."

Ford laughed at Tessa's eye roll. "Me, too," he said.

"Do you all want to live through dinner?" she asked with saccharine sweetness. "If so, you better get on a better subject."

Uncle Bart winked, forking up a generous portion of chicken. "I think it's wonderful that today the men cook. In my time, we had it too easy. Women run the world now!"

Ford kept quiet at Tessa's look but clenched his jaw to keep from chuckling.

Over dinner they had a lively conversation about current films, the Mets, the tragedy of Italian politics, and of course, dogs. Tessa had kept the majority in the barn, promising to bring them a big dinner.

Petey sat politely on the floor next to Ford, head turned up to catch the scents.

"He likes you," Uncle Bart said, pointing his fork. "You need to get a dog. I'll hook you up with the shelter I volunteer at. Maybe you can convince my niece to take on one, too."

"Why don't you get one together?" Dom suggested. "Split the work!"

Tessa cleared her throat. "We're not a couple," she said. "A dog needs stability."

The men shared a knowing look. Ford figured they'd seen the kiss and come to their own conclusions.

"You and Ford are stable," Uncle Bart said. "Better than that new guy you were trying to make fit. No divorce lawyer is going to give you what you need."

She let out an impatient breath. "David was very nice. His job doesn't stop him from believing in love."

"Well, I don't think he's right for you," Uncle Bart said.

"It was one date! Besides, it's not your business—" She stopped short, staring at him from across the table. "Wait a minute. I never told you about David."

Oh shit.

Ford focused on his plate as a sudden awkward silence fell.

"Uh, yes you did," Uncle Bart said, obviously backtracking. "How are the girls doing? And your godchild—aren't you both co-godparents?"

Tessa slowly put down her fork. "Uncle Bart, how did you know about David? Don't lie to me."

The older man opened his mouth, then shut it. Frowned. "I've been keeping an eye on you. Nothing to worry about."

Vin jumped in. "We were just worried, Tessa. There's a lot of men who want to take advantage of a beautiful woman with money. We're trying to help."

Ford pegged the exact moment she put it all together. He winced, knowing they were all in for it. They'd never get a dinner like this again.

"Wait a minute—you were spying on me? Investigating my dates? Oh my God, that's why the chef never texted me back!"

Dom's face turned hard. "He was scum. Do you know he was married and owed back child support?"

She gasped. "No, I didn't, because I didn't get a chance! He disappeared on me, and now I know why. Were you all in on this? How did you do it?"

Ford admitted to being a coward and kept quiet, letting the other men take the full hit.

Uncle Bart fessed up. "I hacked your social media accounts," he said. "Then I had a PI do a background check to make sure he was worthy before you got too involved."

Ford waited for the explosion, but her gaze had veered dangerously around. He peered up and got caught in those fiery blue eyes.

"Ford?"

"Yeah?"

"Did you tell Uncle Bart about David? Because you and Chiara and Malia were the only ones who knew about him."

Time to face the music head-on. "Yeah, I did. I told him his first name and where he worked, and your uncle did the rest."

Her face was flushed. Her breasts heaved as she gulped in breath. Feminine fury seemed to hold her in its grip, and Ford couldn't help it. His body ramped up and he got turned on. There was nothing more magnificent than Tessa Harper in a full-fledged temper tantrum. She was sexy as hell.

"I cannot believe all of you were engaged in such a horrific, demeaning plan," she snapped out. Her curls bounced as she furiously shook her head. "I began to think something was wrong with me because these men refused to message me back! Is that what you wanted—to have me doubt myself?"

Uncle Bart looked chastised. "No, sweetheart, not at all. I'm sorry—I was just trying to help."

"We all were," Dom said. "We care about you."

"Please forgive us," Vin pleaded.

She stared hard at each of them, then stopped at Ford.

"I'm an asshole," he said.

"Yes, you are."

"I went a bit off the rails thinking about you with this guy. I only wanted Uncle Bart to check him out because it's dangerous out there. But I was wrong, and I swear I won't do it again. Right?" He directed the question to the table, and the men nodded eagerly. Then waited.

"What was wrong with the artist?"

Uncle Bart spoke seriously. "Assault and battery charge on his ex-girlfriend."

Tessa dragged in a lungful of air, held it, then slowly released. She deliberately picked her fork back up and began to eat. "I'll think about forgiving you. I need some time."

"Of course, we understand," Uncle Bart said, looking relieved that he had a chance.

"I'm going to change my passwords, and you are not to spy on me any longer. Understood?"

They nodded again.

Tessa shot Ford a glare, waiting.

"Yes," he said aloud. "But I didn't hack your accounts. I was only the messenger."

"You mean the spy."

He winced. "Yes. The spy."

"You're cleaning up and doing all the dishes."

"Okay."

They ate in silence for a few moments. "So how about those Mets?" Uncle Bart said, clearing his throat.

Ford couldn't help it. He laughed, and soon, even Tessa was grinning.

God, he loved this woman.

The thought skittered through him, then exploded into fragments.

No. He couldn't. He loved Patricia. He was just infatuated with Tessa because she was different and an anomaly and she'd allowed him an opportunity to win the woman of his dreams. He'd transferred the feelings to her, but it was really Patricia he was supposed to be with.

Right?

His gut didn't answer.

Chapter Twenty-Four

They finished dinner, and the men cleaned up.

After coffee and cake, Ford went with Tessa to take care of the dogs. They brought them dinner scraps, and he followed her instructions, amazed at the organized chaos set up in the barn.

After the dogs were fed, they went to the gated space to run and play. Ford threw a tennis ball, and Tessa played tug-of-war with some of the smaller ones. He picked up poop with the scooper, dried their paws with a towel so they wouldn't bring mud into their beds, and settled them in for the night.

When they walked back out, he was exhausted. "Wow, your uncle has a lot of work with the dogs," he said. "I had no idea."

"Yeah, I keep telling him to find a few homes for some, but he's too attached to them. He's passionate about giving animals a safe place to feel love. It's such a worthy cause, I can't get mad."

"What are you going to do this week?"

She stopped, staring up at the half-moon. "I'll come every day and make sure he's got what he needs. I don't mind."

"No, I don't think you do. Even when you're running a media empire."

She shrugged like it was nothing. "Love isn't a burden, Ford. It's a gift."

His chest cracked open. Staring at her under the streaming moonbeams, the wind tugging at her curls, her face tilted up so he could see her open expression, Ford knew something had irrevocably changed between them. Knew he'd have trouble being in the same room with her if she wasn't his. Knew with their tight circle of friends, he was currently screwed, because if he did choose Patricia, he might have to step away from the group to protect his new relationship.

A small sigh escaped her lips. "I know."

"Know what?" he asked softly.

She met his gaze. Her eyes held both pain and resolve. "I know this is a mess we both didn't want."

He took her hand, entangling his fingers with hers. "Let's go home. It's been a long day."

After Uncle Bart had gone to bed, they left. It was quiet on the drive to her place, and when he pulled in the driveway, the tension squeezed between them. Ford planned to stay in the car. Drive to his own house and give himself the space they both needed.

"It's best if you don't come in."

He nodded. "I know."

Ford watched her get out of the car, step inside her house, and close the door. He put the car in reverse, then park.

She opened the front door the moment his foot hit the steps.

"I don't want to leave you. I need you."

She didn't say anything. Just pulled him inside, wrapped her arms around him, and fell into his kiss.

~

Tessa felt the surge of heat between them crackle and burn, and she gasped under the sheer intensity of the raw need between them.

The kiss began gently, an acceptance of what they were in the moment, but as the reality of what they were facing hit her full force, Tessa demanded more, sinking her nails into his shoulders and nipping at his lip roughly.

Ford caught the change in the air, the delicious sexual tension that stretched between them. Right now, she needed to drive all those doubts and fears from her mind. To lose them all in the pleasure of his body and their lovemaking.

He broke the kiss and leaned in. His grit-and-gravel voice rumbled in her ear, causing her to freeze. "I want you to take off all your clothes."

Her body roared to life. Immediately, she grew wet between her thighs, and her nipples poked through her bra, desperate for freedom. He stepped back, breaking contact, and slowly she raised her gaze.

Lust seethed from hazel eyes, which had flamed to a deep gold. He held his body tight, as if afraid to let himself go, and the hunger that carved out the rough lines of his face caused Tessa to follow his command without hesitation.

God, she wanted him to look at her just like that when she was naked. She wanted to be adored and touched and tasted. She wanted to be taken hard, in every way possible, while that sexy voice told her all the bad things he'd do to her.

She wanted all of it.

Her fingers trembled, but she managed to wriggle out of her jeans and shed her top. Tessa paused in her lace bra and pale pink bikini bottoms.

"Everything." A pause. "Please." His voice broke, and it was all she needed to continue.

She stripped bare and stood before him, shoulders back, legs braced apart, confident with her body with all its flaws, knowing who she was without doubt or hesitation.

A curse ripped from his lips. "You're more than I ever imagined. You're . . . perfect."

She couldn't help it. "Then maybe you should do something about it."

His slow grin lit up her insides. "I'm gonna. I'm just taking a breath so I don't embarrass myself."

"That would be a pity."

"Still so much damn sass. I'll need to shut you up after all." He closed the distance, yanked her into his arms, and kissed her.

This kiss was little finesse and all raw need. As he devoured her whole, she hung on and got up on tiptoes so she could have more. He tasted of mint and spice; he smelled of clean cotton and soap. His hands were everywhere, roving over her naked skin, stroking, squeezing, while his tongue dove deep to claim her.

Strong arms lifted her up, and he walked them into the bedroom. The way he gently laid her down contradicted the raw lust emanating from his gaze, and she became a writhing, primitive thing under him, helping to tug off his clothes, mad to feel his skin on hers.

"My shirt's stuck," he breathed out raggedly, half laughing as it got caught around his neck.

Tessa reared up and pulled hard, and then he was on her again, his muscled chest pressed against her breasts, her hard nipples rubbing against his coarse hair. She let out a groan because it felt so damn good to finally let go and fall into his body and all it demanded.

They rolled, and his pants were finally off, and she wanted to touch him, but he put his fingers between her legs and rubbed. Stars burst behind her eyes, and her hips arched for more.

He muttered something dirty, pushed her into the pillows, and began to pleasure her, his gaze fiercely studying her face. "Does that feel good?" he demanded, his thumb strumming her clit. "Or this?" as he plunged three digits deep inside, pumping slow.

"All of it," she gasped.

"Good. This should feel even better." He dragged himself down, kissing her stomach, her damp inner thighs, and then he pushed her legs apart and his tongue was inside her, his lips nibbling and sucking at her clit.

She dug her heels into the mattress, her voice rising to a wail, and came hard. He didn't stop or slow down, and the orgasm rolled into mini convulsions.

She was already limp, so he rolled her onto her stomach and bit her ass, tracing the line of her spine with his tongue. His fingers slipped back inside her to gently rub and tease and bring her right back up, until she was gasping and writhing and pushing herself into the air.

She heard the rip of a wrapper. He grabbed a pillow and shoved it under her hips. Tessa reached up and gripped the spindles on the headboard.

"Look at me," he said.

She had to crane her neck to the side in this position, but it only made her hotter when he kissed her again, slowly pushing in at the same time, inch by slow inch, until he was buried deep.

He stayed there, kissing her, his fingers tightening around her hips. When she pushed back, demanding more, he bit her lower lip, drew back, and plunged in hard.

His name ripped from her lips.

He cried out as he made love to her and fucked her at the same time. Tessa hung on and gave in to the mad, deep strokes inside her, the whisper of his lips on her damp cheek, and the tenderness as he began to stroke her back, her ass, pushing her to the edge.

She came again.

He shouted her name, and somehow, she was falling onto the pillow, limbs trembling. He collapsed on top of her, rolling just enough to the side to take off the pressure yet keeping a bear-tight hold on her body, as if afraid she'd disappear on him.

She caught her breath. His heartbeat slowed. Her fingers entangled with his. He stroked her bare breast.

Tessa closed her eyes.

When she woke up in the morning, he was gone.

Chapter Twenty-Five

Tessa sat in her office and stared at the draft on her computer. She'd been working on the column for a few hours but couldn't seem to dig in. There was a giant writer's block sitting between her thoughts, her vision for the piece, and the reality.

She dropped her face into her hands and gave in to exhaustion.

He'd left without saying goodbye. That told her more than a written note or a guilty morning expression. Their twenty-four-hour hiatus was over. Ford was moving forward with Patricia and couldn't face Tessa to tell her the truth.

She couldn't compete with a dream. She knew from experience loving someone for so long from afar locked away a portion of the heart that couldn't be given to anyone else. Tessa had watched countless makeover readers desperate to gain the prize denied them. It didn't matter if they broke up in the long run.

Tessa wanted to be angry and resentful, but she only felt emptiness. Neither of them had expected the sharp turn of events. They hadn't even liked each other. But somehow, during her effort to make Ford over for Patricia, they'd grown closer, and that damn man had snuck into her heart while she wasn't looking.

Asshole.

She lifted her head and took a breath. He owed her the truth. She couldn't finish this column until Ford looked her in the eye and told her he chose Patricia. Tessa would not allow him to play the role of a coward and sneak away after a passionate night together. She'd had sex before. What had happened last night between them was so much more.

Tessa refused to let him taint it.

She grabbed her phone and sent the text. We need to talk.

In a matter of seconds, three dots appeared. Her heart beat wildly. Are you at the office?

Yes.

I can come to you.

Tessa hesitated, wondering if she wanted such an intimate conversation to take place at Quench. Then again, the staff was bare bones today, and Chiara and Malia weren't coming in. Probably best not to talk alone in her house. The last two times they'd tried to part, they ended up naked.

Okay.

Be there in half hour.

Tessa buried herself in paperwork until the receptionist buzzed her. She rose from the chair, smoothed down her white business suit, and schooled her expression to be calm and controlled.

Ford tapped on her office door and came through.

Her heart squeezed mercilessly with need. God, he looked as tired as she felt. They'd gotten little sleep last night, more focused on other activities. His hair was mussed, and a rough five o'clock shadow hugged his perfect cut jaw. Those hazel eyes gleamed with a mix of raw emotions, none of them good.

He closed the door softly behind him and stared at her. "I'm sorry I left this morning."

The air hummed with awareness. Tessa almost wished for the old days, when his presence would bring only irritation and frustration. Now, there was just a craving to be close, to touch, to hear his voice rumble in her ear. To laugh beside him and engage in their legendary banter that she now loved.

Like him.

She loved him.

The realization crashed through her and punched out her breath. Tessa turned away, needing to grab a moment to steady herself.

She was in love with Ford Maddox.

Laughter warred with ridiculous tears. What a mess. She had finally fallen in love, and he was committed to another woman.

And she had been the one to make it happen.

Oh, fate was a cruel mistress.

"Tessa, when I saw you lying on the pillow, all I wanted to do was reach for you again. But I needed some time to think. I swear I was going to call you today."

She waved a hand, dismissing his excuses. "I know. I'm not mad. I just need to know how you feel about Patricia." She squared her shoulders and pivoted back. "And how you feel about me."

Pain carved out the masculine features of his face. His hooded gaze clung to hers with slight desperation. "I don't know."

Her voice hardened. "Do better."

A curse escaped his lips. He moved a few steps closer, then stopped. "I convinced myself I was in love with Patricia for two years. Over the past few weeks, she's finally opened up. She's looking at me as a potential partner, not a friend. I've gotten everything I've dreamed of, yet I find I'm thinking of you when I'm with her. I'm all fucked up."

Tessa refused to be dragged into some love triangle and fight for a man who'd never be hers. Hell to the no on that one. "I'm not looking for excuses or apologies. I only want to know what you feel. What you want. Because right now, it has nothing to do with me."

"It has everything to do with you." His jaw clenched. "I couldn't make love to Patricia that night. All I wanted was you."

"And now you've had me. Are you able to shake me off finally and move on to the woman you really want?"

Fury emanated from him in waves. "Don't say that about you or us. It's not like that."

"Then how is it?" she asked. "You came to me that night because you couldn't move forward with Patricia until you figured things out with me. Maybe we swerved onto a side road—I know we both weren't looking for this complication. But now that it happened, I have a right to know what you want. Because I'm not playing games with anyone's heart."

He flinched. "I'd never ask you to. I spoke with Patricia today. Told her I was torn because I had still had feelings for you."

"What did she say?"

Ice trickled through her blood when she caught his expression. "She said she'd wait for me. She said she believed we should be together, and that I'd find that out."

The pain felt like a million knives cutting her into pieces, but Tessa made sure she didn't even wince. She hid the agony, tilted her head up, and asked, "What do you want?"

His silence was enough. The only answer she had needed.

Tessa nodded. "It was always about Patricia. I knew that. We both did." Her eyes were dry, but inside, a tsunami of emotion threatened to take her down. "I understand."

"I'm sorry, Tessa."

Her smile was thin and quick. "All's fair in love and baseball. Remember?"

Ford walked toward her, but she backed up, shaking her head. He stopped. "The time we spent together? It was literally the best in my life. You changed me."

Oh, she couldn't do this now. She might die. "I'm glad. Look, I have to get to work. You better go. It's good we sorted things out."

"Tessa—"

"I'm writing the column now, so I'll let you know when it's going to print. You'll need to sign a release form."

"Of course."

She turned away and sat at her desk, staring at the computer. Tessa felt the tension flicking from across the room, the roll of raw emotion that connected them. She heard his breath blow out in a ragged burst.

Then he was gone.

Tessa worked for a while, keeping her brain busy. Then she grabbed her phone.

I need you.

The texts came back immediately.

Chiara: My house tonight? Ryder is out, and Mike has Veronica. Six o'clock.

Malia: I'll be there.

Tessa sent a thumbs-up emoji. Words weren't possible right now.

She'd lost the man she loved. Hell, she hadn't even fought—just gracefully stepped aside like a class-act lady. It was the right thing to do, of course. It didn't matter if she knew Patricia wouldn't make him happy. Ford had to find that out for himself.

The only thing that mattered was it was too late for them.

~

Tessa walked into Chiara's house in her comfy flannel pj's holding a giant bottle of rosé.

Dex leapt over, flagpole tail batting back and forth, and she knelt down to scratch behind his ears. "Hello, baby, I missed you. You're such a good boy." His nose began ramming into her, taking big sniffs, and she laughed and tried to push him away. "Oh, I know, you smell all of Uncle Bart's doggies, don't you. I promise I wasn't unfaithful."

Chiara laughed. "Down, Dex. Give her some breathing room."

Dex pulled back, but his pleading eyes urged Tessa to give him a few more pets. "Is Veronica still following him around all day?" she asked, grinning as the Lab rolled over and thumped his foot in time to her scratches.

"They're the sweetest thing. He lets her lie on him, sit, cuddle—Dex adores her. He sleeps in her room every night now and refuses to come in our bed. He's so protective."

Tessa sighed. "Maybe I should get a dog."

"Oh boy, this is serious. Here's Malia."

Malia came through the door with a box of Krispy Kreme donuts. "It was an emergency," she explained, handing over the sugary temptation.

"Perfect—Tessa brought the wine," Chiara said, heading into the kitchen.

"I'll go with seltzer tonight, I have a big meeting in the morning. Are you all right?" Malia asked, giving Tessa a big hug. "I worried all day, but I knew you wouldn't tell me anything until tonight."

Tessa's emotions were still raw, like a wound trying to heal under a loose Band-Aid. Still, being with her friends soothed a bit of the rawness. "I just want to settle in before I tell you what's happening. Where's Palmer?"

"Out with Ryder. I've been a bit cranky lately, so I needed the break."

Tessa regarded her with concern. "Nothing wrong in paradise, I hope?"

"Oh, no, we're deliriously happy. But I'm living with a man. That means compromising, and I'm not the best at it. I was single for a long time."

Tessa laughed.

Chiara handed her a glass of wine. "Boy, can I relate. It's actually given me a whole new appreciation for Quench. I've been changing some of my writing slants to women with families and how relationships can change and grow. All of them—not just romantic ones."

"It's true," Tessa said. "I watch my uncle Bart, and he's tight with both Dom and Vin, along with every one of his rescues. It doesn't matter what relationship it is. If you love someone, it's worthy and important."

Chiara squeezed her arm. "You see things so beautifully, Tessa."

"I'm sure I read that somewhere."

Malia sighed. "And there she goes again. Batting off a compliment. Sometimes you just need to allow us to love on you, girlfriend. Got it?"

She opened her mouth to defend herself, then shut it. The memory of Ford's words drifted through her mind, basically telling her the same thing. It was strange. She felt confident about many things in her life, but other times, someone else's praise made her uncomfortable. If she didn't truly think she was worthy of a compliment, she refused to accept it. Perhaps it was time to question her actions and make some changes. "Maybe you're right."

Chiara and Malia shared a shocked glance. "Did you really say that?" Chiara asked. "Wow. It's about time."

"You need to picture the compliment as if you were giving it to one of us. Wouldn't it frustrate you if every time you wanted to give us something good, we waved it away like it was nothing?" Malia asked.

She wrinkled her nose. "I never thought of it like that. Ford said something similar to me. I think I understand now."

"Ford?" they chanted together.

And then it happened.

Her lower lip trembled, and she sucked in a breath and took a gulp of wine. "I don't want to talk about it yet."

"Okay!" Malia said in a rush. "Chiara, I noticed you've been a bit off recently, too. Is anything going on?"

"Just stuff. Work and motherhood and trying to juggle things, but I'm happy. So happy." She blinked madly, and suddenly, Chiara put down her untouched wine and mashed her hands against her lips. "I'm a mess. I'm having a breakdown."

"What's the matter, babe?" Tessa asked in concern.

"Tell us," Malia said.

"I think I'm pregnant!" She groaned. "But I don't know. And I think I'm really happy, but I'm also scared and freaking out. I haven't said anything to Sebastian yet."

Dex sensed she was upset and trotted over, pressing his head against her leg in support. Malia gave him a quick pat.

"Okay. Then we do this together. Just like the first time," Tessa said. "Go get a pregnancy test. I know you have a few extra."

Chiara choked out a half laugh. When she'd been pregnant with Veronica, she had taken seven pregnancy tests. Just to be sure.

"Yes, that's a great idea," Malia said.

Chiara agreed and went to pee on a stick. Then she placed it on the sink in her bathroom.

Tessa brought her wine, and they all sat on the floor while Dex plopped himself in the middle, guarding them against danger.

"I'm having déjà vu," Chiara said. "I can't believe we're doing this again."

Two years ago, they'd all gathered to sit on this same bathroom floor when Chiara had called, saying she was in trouble. They'd all agreed to help her raise the baby before her relationship was official with Ryder. They'd had each other's backs their entire lives—like sisters—and Tessa knew in that moment that no matter how bad things got for each of them, together they'd always be able to heal.

They waited the full three minutes. Then Chiara retrieved the stick.

All of them stared at the pink line.

"I'm pregnant," she said. Tears filled her eyes and streamed down her cheeks. "Oh my God, we're having another baby."

"I'm so happy," Malia sobbed.

Tessa stared at her in concern, afraid Chiara's pregnancy had loosened Malia's worry about not being able to get pregnant as easily.

"I'm sorry, Malia!" Chiara choked out. "I know you're going to have your own baby someday. I just know it."

"I know it, too," Malia cried. "Because I'm pregnant, too!"

Tessa gasped. "What?"

"I thought it was from the stress of the wedding that I missed my period, but I was feeling so strange, so I decided to take a test a few days ago just in case. My doctor confirmed it. It's been torture not to tell you guys, but with my fertility issues, I thought I should wait until after the first trimester. I'm only six weeks along, but I can't. I'm going to explode! We're pregnant together!"

They all grasped hands and clung to each other. Dex softly whined and looked at them with doggy concern.

As they wailed with happiness, something broke loose from Tessa's chest and flew free. She began to cry, allowing all her pent-up feelings to release. "I'm in love with Ford!"

Chiara and Malia stopped crying and stared. "I knew it!" Malia burst out.

"Yes. But he loves Patricia—the woman I transformed him for—and it's over!"

Tessa cried and her friends cried, and they all held each other in the circle while Dex just held the space.

And then Tessa told them everything.

Chapter Twenty-Six

Ford stared into his beer as he waited for his friends.

The game was on the big TV, and the crowd at the bar was riotous tonight. His favorite appetizers were on special—loaded potato skins and buffalo wings. It was Friday night, and everyone was laughing and happy.

Except him. Because he'd walked away from Tessa and chosen Patricia.

Palmer and Ryder took the seats beside him, ordered two beers, and waited for him to look up.

When he did, Ryder whistled. "Oh, this is bad. Did Patricia break up with you, man?"

Ford gave a humorless laugh and shook his head. "No. Believe it or not, she's into me."

Palmer narrowed his gaze. "Isn't that good news the woman you've been hot for the past two years is into you? You got what you always wanted, right?"

Ford took a long sip of beer and wiped his mouth. "Exactly. That's the whole problem. I got what I never expected—mainly a demanding, pain-in-the-ass hellcat who made this whole thing happen."

Ryder gasped. "You fell for Tessa?"

Ford nodded miserably.

"I knew it!" Palmer announced. "Those Quench women are potent."

"You gotta back it up, man. Tell us the whole story," Ryder said.

He did. This time, he didn't hold back or give his friends bullshit. When he was done, they had both finished their beers and looked just as confused as he was.

"The real problem is you're in love with both of them," Ryder said. "That's what it sounds like."

Palmer cut in. "Nah, I think he's in love with one of them but doesn't want to admit it because she wasn't part of his plan. I think you really want to love Patricia, but you love Tessa."

"I feel like my head is going to explode. I keep seeing Tessa's face when I left her office."

Ryder seemed to contemplate his words. "Seems to me you made your choice. I'd be honest with Patricia about the whole thing, man. The setup with Tessa, your real feelings, all of it. Come clean, and maybe her response will give you the answer you're really seeking."

Palmer nodded. "Yeah. What he said."

Ford groaned. "You're probably right. I think I need some time with Patricia. Time to get my head back on straight. I never wanted to hurt anyone. I just wanted the woman of my dreams."

"You may have found her," Ryder said. "It just wasn't the one you expected."

The words hit hard. "I'm sure once I focus on Patricia without distraction, I'll know she's the one. And then I'll tell her the truth."

His friends shared a concerned gaze. "And if not?"

"I don't know."

Ryder let out a hard breath. "Well, I'll tell you this, dude. If it does end up being Tessa, you're gonna need to come up with some big-ass grand gesture of an apology."

Ford winced. He thought over the past couple of months spent in Tessa's company and all the surprises he'd discovered. The hidden elements of her heart she rarely showed. How easy it was for her to give her entire self to anyone who needed it. Once, he'd thought she'd expect the entire glass slipper and Disney fairy tale to make an impression. But now, he knew genuine heartfelt truth was the way to her soul.

"We're here for you," Palmer said. "Whoever you decide. Whatever you need."

Ford gave them a tired smile. "Thanks, guys. I appreciate it."

He'd focus all his time and energy on Patricia, building their relationship. It didn't make sense for fate to finally grant his wish, then fill him with doubts.

He'd stay the course.

~

It was late, and everyone had gone home except her.

Tessa stared at the report in front of her. She'd begun to obsess about the readers she helped at Quench and wanted to dig deeper into her growing unease with her role in playing Fairy Godmother. Losing Ford to the woman he said he loved but didn't know seemed to be the catalyst for breaking everything inside her open.

It sucked, because her entire career she'd dedicated herself to changing people for the better. To love themselves. To be confident enough to reach for their dreams. To feel good in their own skin and know they deserve more.

She'd bragged about her perfect statistics in these same people finally getting the attention of the ones they loved. But a call from Autumn had set off a warning bell within, and she'd spent the last few days tracking down as many of her readers as possible, searching for the truth.

Tessa leaned back in her chair, exhausted, going over her conversation with Autumn from earlier in the week. The woman had sounded wonderful on the phone, thanking her again for the help and telling her how much she loved her new job.

"It's so funny how those changes you worked on with me really settled in and made such a difference," Autumn said. "Even funnier? I was always the same person! I could've gotten that promotion or anything else I wanted before; I could just never see it until you made me beautiful."

"You were always beautiful," Tessa had reminded her. "I just tweaked the surface so you could finally see it for yourself."

"I know, and that's what you kept telling me, but I was so focused on my hot marketing director, I couldn't get out of my own way."

"Yes, but that worked out, didn't it?" Tessa asked curiously. "Last time we spoke, you were in a committed relationship with him."

Autumn laughed. "Yes, we were, but it didn't last. He didn't really know me. At least, not the real woman I was underneath the shiny trappings. I convinced myself it would work out, but we broke up last week, and I finally feel free to find the right man for me. I realized I was changing to suit him because I was so desperate to finally achieve my goal: to get him to *see* me. To be accepted by him so I could feel good about myself. What a mess."

Tessa's heart ramped up. "I'm sorry to hear that, but glad you figured it out."

"Me, too. He's already hooked up with a new conquest. Anyway, I just wanted to say again how much you and Quench helped change my life. You were always straight with me and made me feel good about opening up. I'll never forget it."

"That means a lot to me, Autumn. Thanks for calling."

When she'd hung up, Tessa had gone into her files and brought up every single one of her past makeovers. Reread all her notes. And began to contact them individually.

As the days passed and she nursed a broken heart, Tessa figured out 80 percent of her matches who'd been in a committed relationship with the love of their dreams when she wrote their column had broken up. Most admitted that things had gone badly. They'd never felt as if they were truly known, that the changes made to chase love had blown up because it had never been real.

The good part? Most of them felt as if the makeover had helped change their life for the better overall.

But as for the matchups Tessa had been so confident in? Failure.

The truth blew away the foundation of everything she thought she'd been doing. It also caused her to look more deeply within herself and question her own intentions. Was she stuck on outward appearances no matter how she tried to justify she wasn't? Was her need for easy, neat relationships another way she'd blocked herself from trying to find her own person to love?

All those dates over the years flickered by her in one long line of memory. They were always shiny on the outside, but she never allowed herself to be real with any of them. It was easy to keep herself safely tucked away, positive she was open to love but just not finding it.

What if the problem was really her—her inability to share her true self, even though she always insisted she wasn't afraid? It was so much easier to help everyone else with their relationships than focus on her own.

Tessa spent a long time trying to process her whirling thoughts, which always came back to Ford.

Ford—who'd challenged her in so many different ways and saw beneath her polished surface.

Ford—who'd taught her love was messy and raw and didn't play fair.

Ford—who'd walked away while she rationalized and kept her dignity intact.

Tessa groaned and dropped her face into her hands. She was confused. All of a sudden, everything she'd believed was in question.

It was time she figured some stuff out.

Chapter Twenty-Seven

Two days later, Tessa let herself into her uncle's house, smiling at the furry greeting committee that swarmed her feet.

"That you, Tessa?" he called out. The thump of his crutches on the floor made the dogs bark more and run back and forth between them.

"It's me. What did the doctor say?"

"The boot comes off next Friday, so I'm on the mend. Dom's taking me, so don't worry about leaving work."

She gave her uncle a hug, giving him a quick study. He looked well. "I'd rather come anyway. I don't trust you and Dom not to hide things from me anymore."

He shot her a guilty look, but humor twitched at his lip. "I deserved that."

"Yes, and more. But not in front of the children."

Uncle Bart laughed. "Come sit with me a bit before you do your chores."

The television was on full blast, but she didn't say anything. Her uncle was a bit sensitive about losing some of his hearing in his left ear.

She got him settled comfortably, putting his crutches aside, and sat next to him. She scooped Petey up to cuddle on her lap, then allowed the other dogs to jump up on the couch next to her. The furry blanket comforted her and soothed her wounded heart, just like her friends and uncle had.

It had been a long week. After her good cry with her friends, Tessa had focused on the internship program and trying to write the column about Ford. A beauty expo and helping out with the new sports podcast kept her busy enough that she was able to fall asleep.

Unfortunately, she dreamed. Always of Ford. Always of choosing her over Patricia. When she woke up, she had a few precious moments where she believed they were together, and then the truth came crashing in on her, ripping away her happiness. It was like routine torture. But damned if she'd let anyone know about her inner pain. She showed up at work with a smile on her face. No one knew she cared except Chiara and Malia, and they weren't telling.

"How's Ford?" her uncle asked.

She tried not to wince. This was the first time he was truly asking, as if sensing something had settled between them and now he was ready to pry. "We're not together anymore," she said simply. There. This time it didn't hurt as much. After all, they'd never been officially together in the first place. She had nothing really to mourn. "Ford is with Patricia, and we're just friends." Tessa practically choked on the words.

Her uncle focused on the glitch like a predator scenting prey. "Bullshit."

That ripped a laugh from her. "Petey didn't like that."

The inkblot winced, his scarred eyes pointed toward her uncle as if sensing his irritation.

Uncle Bart reached out and patted his head, and the dog settled back in to sleep with a contented sigh. "Sorry. You want to tell me what happened?"

She shrugged, her gaze focused on the television. "It was just a short . . . dalliance. We got caught up in each other and forgot the whole point of spending time together was so he could snag Patricia's attention. Now that he has it, he's with her. I'll be fine."

Her uncle sighed. "It was more than that, sweetheart. I saw it on display, full blast. That boy's in love with you."

Tessa focused on breathing evenly. Her uncle's words seared through the wound and ripped it back open. "No. It was lust."

He snorted. "Not even close. If you think that, you're both lying to yourselves. But who am I? Just an old man with a bunch of dogs and wiseguys for friends."

Curiosity piqued. "Are they wiseguys?"

He gave her a warning glance. "We're not discussing that. We're discussing Ford. I have only one question for you: Why didn't you go after him when you realized you loved him?"

"I don't love him."

Uncle Bart stared at her, disappointed.

Tessa muttered a curse. "Okay, I do. But I'm no weepy, clingy, weak female chasing after some guy who doesn't want me. He'd push Patricia aside if I meant enough to him. He chose her."

"Maybe. Or maybe he was waiting for you to fight a bit. And as for you being weak? No one in the world would ever think that. You tell the truth. You go after what you want. You protect the ones you love at all costs. You're a scrapper. A fighter. Just like your mom." A faint smile curved his lips. "Just like your uncle."

His words disturbed her, changing her idea of how the situation had played out. Annoyed at her sudden doubts, she motioned toward the screen. "What are you watching? I know this show, I think."

"*Grey's Anatomy*."

"Oh yeah. Malia is obsessed with this show. Chiara, too. Are these reruns?"

"Yeah. There's not as many soap operas on anymore, so I like to watch this. Medical dramas are exciting."

She chuckled, watching Patrick Dempsey face the woman he'd had an affair with. She knew some of the big plotlines because her friends talked about it while she rolled her eyes. The main intern doctor—Merry?—had an affair with her boss, who she then found out was married, and it became a messy love triangle.

Uncle Bart hit the volume. "This is one of my favorite episodes. Meredith decided she loves Derek, but he feels guilty because his wife wants him back and he feels he needs to honor his original commitment."

"Why does she want him? He cheated! He was married!"

"Not really. They were on a break. Shush. Listen."

The two were involved in an intense dialogue. Raw emotion flickered from the couple, throwing Tessa off balance. She quickly became caught up in the crossfire as they exchanged words that seemed to tear them both apart.

"Pick me." Meredith stood in front of him, humbled and vulnerable, still dressed in her scrubs. "Choose me. Love me."

Goose bumps broke out over Tessa's skin. She couldn't breathe, couldn't speak, trapped in this nightmare as Derek teared up, obviously madly in love with Meredith. They watched the episode to the end, when Derek decided he had to try again with his wife because he'd loved her first.

Tessa practically spit with fury. "Why would she beg him to love her? She lost her pride and her heart and got nothing out of the exchange. That was awful. I'm so glad I don't watch that show." She went on a bigger rampage, tearing apart the scene, then stopped when she saw her uncle's gentle expression. "What? You agree with me, right?"

"I see something different. I see a woman who's strong enough to fight for who she loves. A woman who will live with no regrets, because what does pride or a broken heart matter if you'll always wonder *what if*? What's wrong about asking for love? Demanding it?" Uncle Bart shrugged. "Seems pretty worthy to me. But again, what do I know? I'm just an old man, alone with his dogs." He flicked the television off. "I didn't sleep well last night, sweetheart. I'm going to take a nap, if that's okay."

"Yes, of course. I'll let the dogs out, clean up, and check back later."

"No need. Dom and Vin are coming, so you're free." He reached out and brushed back her hair with a loving gesture. "You're worthy of so much, Tessa. Make sure you know that, okay?"

She got his crutches, then settled him into his room with Petey.

On her way home, Meredith's words repeated over and over in her mind like a mantra.

Pick me.

Choose me.

Love me.

The words haunted her like a ghost story.

Tessa cranked up the radio loud to drown them out.

~

Patricia was finally coming to his place.

Ford did a final check, making sure everything looked clean and casually masculine. With the updated accents and furnishings, along with the new carpet that had just gotten installed, the space now reflected a confident, single, successful male.

Tessa had done an amazing job.

Her name was like poking at a bruise that hurt like hell, but he kept probing, wondering when it would heal.

Two weeks had passed and they hadn't spoken.

Two weeks of Mets games and not cleaning up thrown snacks.

Two weeks without Uncle Bart, Dom, Vin, or the dogs.

Two weeks without her smart-ass texts or ridiculous designer outfits or late-night chats.

Two weeks without touching her; kissing her; loving her.

Instead, he'd concentrated on building his relationship with Patricia—the woman he'd been obsessed with. And things were good. The chemistry may not have been as strong as it was before Tessa, but it was building. Getting there.

Tonight, he was finally going to take her to bed.

His gut lurched at the thought, but he knew it was nerves. All this planning had led right here. They'd grown closer, and even when he'd been honest about Tessa, she'd waited for him. Hung in. Believed they'd end up together.

Didn't that count?

The knock sounded on the door, and he answered.

"Darling." Patricia greeted him with a kiss. It wasn't his favorite pet name, sounding a bit stuffy, but he liked they were already into the cozy couple language stage.

"You look beautiful," he said, taking in the gorgeous length of her legs revealed by her short denim skirt. Her white tank top had lace around the neckline and matched her sneakers. She'd let her hair down to swing freely against her shoulders—straight and sleek and sexy.

"Thanks. I brought some wine."

More of the expensive red he disliked. "I think I'll stick with beer, but I'll pour you a glass."

She laughed, which still sounded like tinkling wind chimes. "You and that beer. Don't forget it gives you a gut," she said good-naturedly, wandering around his apartment. "Your place is nice, Ford. I like it. Very you. Love the throw pillows."

Ford tried not to wince. "Thank you. It's comfortable. I figured we'd order in. Chinese?"

She wrinkled her nose and ran a finger over his table. Was she looking for dust? No, that would be weird. "Why don't we try that new Mediterranean place that just opened. It's receiving rave reviews. I heard they have delicious lamb."

He had a thing about eating lamb, but he nodded. He needed to make tonight special for her. He'd already lit candles in the bedroom but didn't want to go too far. He was still easing into showing more of his real self, which wasn't as dominant as he'd originally put out.

His fault. He planned on opening up a bit tonight on a deeper scale.

They ordered the lamb. He sipped his beer. They talked about work and the office gossip. Finally, the food came, and even though he wasn't crazy about it, her obvious enjoyment kept him quiet. They finished their plates, cleaned up, then resettled on the couch.

Patricia leaned over and kissed him, her hand rubbing up and down his arm. Her little lace shirt dipped low, revealing the swell of her breasts. He thought about kissing her there, gathering the scent of her skin in his mouth and savoring it. But he didn't and wondered why.

"I'm glad we waited," she said, tilting her head so her hair fell to one side.

"Me, too." Ford automatically reached out and took her in his arms.

She sighed and her lips parted.

He kissed her. She tasted of blackberries. He let himself linger for a while, his body settling in, and realized he'd finally reached the moment he'd dreamed of.

"It's always been you," she whispered against his mouth. "Take me to bed."

Her confession set off warning bells. "Has it?" he asked. His hands stilled, settling on her shoulders. He tried to keep his voice curious rather than curt. "Because I never got the impression you were ever interested in me before."

Her lush lashes blinked. Her red lips pursed in a bit of a pout. "Well, you felt the same way about me," she said with a tiny laugh. "That's what makes this special. We fell for each other at the right time."

"Even though I was with Tessa."

She stiffened. "Why do you have to mention her name? I thought we'd moved on. Decided to be together."

She was right. He had, and he'd told Tessa the same thing. But Ford was beginning to realize a fact that he couldn't ignore anymore. Tessa had told him from the start that by doing the makeover, Patricia would fall in love with a shadow, and it wasn't fair to either of them. He'd played a dangerous game and won—but what was his prize? A woman who didn't really know him?

Did he really love Patricia, or had it been his idea of love, a perfect, shiny trophy he could dream of and pursue? Had he done the same thing to her? Did he even know who Patricia truly was?

She stared back at him, visibly upset, and shame raced through him. He was a liar. To Patricia, to Tessa, but most of all, to himself. And he had to come clean.

"Patricia, I have to tell you something." He took her hands gently. "I'm not the man you think I am."

"What do you mean?"

With a deep breath, he began to speak.

Chapter Twenty-Eight

Tessa glanced at her friends, who were all gathered in their regular booth at Mike's Place. "Do you know what's going on?" she asked. "Why did Mike want us here tonight?"

Her friends looked just as lost. "He called and said to bring you all here for dinner," Chiara said. "When I asked why, he said we'd find out later."

"Weird," Malia said. "Oh, here's Emma."

The older woman walked in wearing tailored black pants and a cute kelly-green silk top. Ever since she'd taught high school English, Emma had been hiding from the world and herself. The confident woman who entered the diner now had changed—her eyes sparkled from behind her tortoiseshell glasses, and she held her head high.

Tessa had wanted to help her lead a happier life and stop hiding, yet the catalyst for the makeover had been getting Mike to notice her. She was ashamed her real goal had been wrapped up in superficial games, but in this case, she knew in her heart it had worked out. Watching them together now, she could honestly say Mike had never acted differently after Emma changed her clothes, or got new glasses, or started being more social. No, this match had come from real emotion and respect for the other. In this one case, Tessa felt good about how it had worked out, because they had each always liked the person within.

"Hello, ladies. Michael called and asked me to join you for dinner."

"You don't know why he gathered us, either? Must be a surprise," Tessa said thoughtfully.

Mike appeared. He greeted Emma with a kiss on her cheek, beaming at her with all the evidence of a man smitten. "Thanks for coming. Sit down—I made a special dinner for you and the girls."

Emma laughed. "But why, Michael? Is something going on?"

He wiped his hands on his apron, seeming nervous. "No. I just wanted to . . . try out a new recipe." He turned to them. "Girls? Wine?"

Tessa spoke first. "We're taking a little break from alcohol for a bit. Can we get seltzer with lemon?"

Chiara and Malia shot her grateful glances. They weren't ready to spill the news of their pregnancies yet.

"You got it. Tea, Emma?"

"I'll have wine."

He nodded with approval and left.

Emma slid into the booth. "It's not crowded tonight."

Tessa looked around. "Yeah. In fact, why is it just us? Did he close or something?"

Chiara tapped her lip. "Oh, he's up to *something*."

Emma sighed and tucked a napkin on her lap. "Well, Michael will let us know the real reason when the time's right. Now, what's new with all of you? Did I miss anything?"

They all shared a glance and began laughing. "Just the usual," Tessa said. She'd catch Emma up privately. Right now, she didn't want to steal any attention away from whatever Mike was up to.

They kept the topics light as he served them chicken cordon bleu that the cook was trying out for the new dinner menu. Fresh rolls with butter, sweet corn, and almond green beans completed the meal. Each time they asked Mike to join them, he shook his head and rushed away. As time ticked by, his energy grew more ragged. The poor man was a complete wreck. Even Emma kept shooting him worried looks as sweat beaded his brow and he popped in and out of the kitchen.

When he was clearing the plates, he spilled the seltzer and began frantically mopping it up with shaky hands.

Finally, Emma couldn't take it any longer. "Michael, what is going on? I know this can't just be about trying out a new menu item. Talk to us."

Hands clenched around a dripping rag, he straightened up and stared at Emma. "Do you know you're an incredible woman?" he finally asked quietly.

She jerked back, eyes wide behind her glasses. "I . . . I didn't used to. But now, you all made me believe it."

Mike's jaw tightened. A stubborn, determined expression carved out his features. "Wait here."

He stomped away, and Tessa patted Emma's hand. The air sparked with anticipation, and she found herself holding her breath, wondering what would happen next.

Mike came out holding a platter. He placed it on the crowded table and stepped back.

Tessa looked at the giant chocolate chip cookie, fresh out of the oven, with crooked lettering that spelled out EMMA, WILL YOU BE MY GIRLFRIEND?

Emma gasped and stared at the cookie.

Mike cleared his throat. "I care about you, Emma. I think you're the most beautiful, sweetest, smartest woman, and you deserve to be happy. *I* want to make you happy. I promise to never be a complete jerk again and will always treat you well. Will you be my girlfriend?"

Emma gave a tiny sob. She looked at the cookie, then him, and then smiled with her entire heart and soul. "Yes, Michael. I would love to be your girlfriend."

She got up and they hugged, and then Tessa and her friends got up and joined them.

Mike's voice came out gruff. "I wanted you girls to be here for this. You were the ones who pushed me. Without you, I'd still be in my house, alone."

Tessa teared up, and Chiara flung her arms around Mike's neck. "We love you," she said with a laugh. "Both of you."

As she watched Emma and Mike hold hands, staring at one another like lovesick teenagers, a knowing crashed through her. Tessa looked at the cookie. Mike had made a grand gesture even after spending most of his life afraid. She'd helped him open up and find love again.

Just like Tessa had found with Ford.

But she'd walked away without a fight.

Pick me. Choose me. Love me.

Suddenly, the realization slammed through her, leaving her breathless. She needed to tell Ford she was in love with him and ask him to give them a chance.

She needed to seize her happy ending instead of waiting patiently for it to be served to her.

Tessa grabbed her purse and practically stumbled forward. "Guys, I'm sorry, I have to go. I have to see Ford."

"Ford? Now?" Mike asked. "I'll tell him about me and Emma later."

Chiara and Malia grinned and pushed her gently toward the door. "Go. Kick some ass. Take what you want," Chiara said.

Malia winked. "It's your turn, babe. Grab your happy ending."

Then Tessa was running out the door, to her car, and toward Ford.

~

When Ford opened the door, her heart sank.

He gazed back at her in shock, hazel eyes swirling with a range of emotions she couldn't read. His hair was mussed. A shadow darkened his jaw. He wore faded jeans and his old black Metallica shirt. His feet were bare.

She shifted her weight, the zeal to come over and claim her man fading quickly under the sting of doubt and the threat of shame. Before she changed her mind, she channeled Mike's bravery—and Meredith's—and took a deep breath. "I need to say something."

His voice was all gravel and grit, sexy and familiar. "Come in."

She did, taking in his apartment, desperately trying not to look for any feminine articles that Patricia might have left behind. It looked the same, though, with all the updates she'd pushed on him. Patricia had probably loved it. The thought soured in her belly, but she had to focus or she'd never get through her speech.

Tessa suddenly realized there was a deep, empty type of silence that she'd never noticed at his place before. She frowned at the TV. "You don't have the Mets game on?"

He shook his head. "Not tonight."

Thrown off balance, she gathered her courage and plunged in. "I think you made a terrible mistake."

Ford cocked his head. "You think?"

"Hell yes, I do. I think you fell in love with this image you had of Patricia and wanted to win her, like some type of trophy. And I don't think it's fair to either of you, because if she's falling for you, it's not the real you! The man who eats Cheez Doodles on the couch and screams at baseball games and doesn't shave. The man who's sweet and mushy and rough and awkward. Not this sleek Christian Grey–type guy who'd cheat on his girlfriend and play head games to make himself mysterious."

Tessa dropped her purse and took a step forward. Her body shook with the need to express everything right here, right now. "I know you wouldn't have fallen for her in the first place if she wasn't a good person. I know she's beautiful and works in sports and seems to walk on water. But she will never let you be your true self. She will never see into your soul and know who you are—who you *really* are—and love you the way I do."

The muscles in his jaw clenched. His entire body stilled, and she noticed his nostrils flared slightly, as if he scented the crackling tension in the air. But she couldn't allow him to speak—not until she was completely done and it was too late to take anything back.

Tessa straightened her shoulders, raised her head, and spoke with her entire heart. "That's right, I love you. And I know it doesn't make sense and that I've spent the past few years disliking you, but sometimes fate fools us all. I'm asking you to give us a fighting chance. For God's sake, Ford, you couldn't have made love to me like that without feeling something—something big and real and scary as hell. We found each other, and it's a gift, and I'm not going to let you walk blithely away just because I wasn't in your master plan."

Another step. She stood only a few inches away from him now. "Ford, I'm asking you to pick me." She gritted her teeth and blinked away her silly tears and took the leap. "Choose me." Her voice broke. "Love me."

Tessa had never gone skydiving, but she felt as if she were poised at the edge of the plane's open door, looking into the vast empty space below her, ready to jump and trust that her damn parachute would open.

She looked deep into Ford's eyes and prayed for a sign. Prayed he wouldn't send her away like Derek and pick Patricia.

And then he moved.

He wrapped his arms around her body and lifted her up, his mouth taking hers in a kiss that took and gave it all back. "I already did," he said roughly, hands tangled in her curls, lips rubbing against hers with an aching tenderness and need that shook through her. "Last night, I told Patricia I was in love with you. I told her the truth about the makeover, what I did, and owned up to all of it. I've been trying to think of a grand gesture big enough to convince you to come back to me, but of course, you beat me to it."

He pressed kisses over her face, breathing her in, and she clung to him, laughing and crying.

"You humble me, Tessa. You challenge me and wreck me and fill me with so much damn happiness, I didn't think it was possible to feel this way. I love you, body and mind and soul, and I'm never letting you go again." His beautiful hazel eyes gleamed with love. "I will always choose you."

She tightened her arms around him, clinging hard as relief weakened her knees. "Thank God. Because that was the most terrifying thing I ever did in my life. I didn't know how it would end."

He kissed her again, deep and long. "There was only one way for this to end, baby. Fate saved the best for last."

"Damn right. Now take me to bed."

He laughed, picked her up, carried her to the bedroom, and kicked the door shut behind him.

~

They lay in the dark, sated. Limbs entangled. Hands clasped. Neither of them seemed able to get close enough. The scent of sweat and sex clung to the sheets.

Tessa's lips lingered on the hard curve of Ford's shoulder. "Was she upset?"

"Yes. But she deserved to know everything."

She paused and craned her neck to look at him. "Did she want to try with you still?"

His smile was gentle. "We talked about what we could be for each other. She was angry and felt cheated, but she's a good person. She ended up being more understanding than I deserved."

She let out a sigh. "I feel guilty since I helped with this whole thing."

"It's not your fault. It was our path to each other, so how can we regret it?" His fingers broke from hers and stroked the curve of her hip.

She shivered as the want began to rise again in gentle demand. "I've been thinking about the column. About what I want to write. What I want to do in the future. I was wrong about my ratio of success in matches. I made a mistake."

"What do you mean?"

She told him about her research and how most of her readers had ended up in broken relationships. "I don't want to write the same column. I need to do something different—bigger than boxing women into believing the real goal is changing for love."

"I think whatever you do will be successful because it will be authentic."

She smiled, caressing his scratchy cheek. "Yeah. You trust me to write what I need to?"

"I trust you with everything."

He rolled over and pinned her to the mattress. His hazel eyes gleamed with a lazy male satisfaction that made her catch her breath. She loved the way he looked at her. "Mike asked Emma to be his official girlfriend. He made a giant cookie."

Ford chuckled but wouldn't be deterred, slowly parting her thighs and nibbling kisses down her stomach. "Mike is a smart guy. He knows chocolate and a big gesture wins over the ladies."

She laughed, then hissed out a breath when he parted her swollen folds and rubbed lightly. "Malia and Chiara are both pregnant."

That gave him pause. He lifted his head. "A lot's happened these past two weeks."

"You left me."

"Never again. You're stuck with me. Anything else before I focus on making you scream my name till you're hoarse?"

Tessa grinned. "I'm done now."

"Good." He lowered his head.

It didn't take long for her to do exactly as he'd predicted.

Epilogue

Tessa raised her hand and waved down the uniformed attendant. "Peanuts, please!"

"Oh, I want popcorn," Malia said, jumping up and down in her seat.

"Me, too," Chiara said, leaning over to address Ryder. "Can you get us popcorn, honey? I haven't seen that come around yet."

Ryder shared a look with Palmer. "Can it wait till the end of the inning?" One look at his wife's face made him sigh and stand. "Come on, Palmer. Anything else while we're up?"

Mike patted Emma's knee. "Do you want anything?"

Emma looked at him with adoration. "No, I think I'm good. I'm stuffed. Who would've thought veggie hot dogs could be so delicious?"

"Told you," Tessa said smugly.

Uncle Bart stood up with Vin and Dom. "I want to grab a new hat at the stand I saw before." Ford had apologized for not getting them tickets to "Bark at the Park Day" at Citi Field, but Tessa personally thought it was good for the men to have a strictly human afternoon of entertainment for once.

Ford tore his gaze away from the field. "Guys, don't be too long. Seventh-inning stretch is coming."

"We'll be right back—the lines aren't bad," Ryder said, squeezing his way out of the aisle with Palmer behind.

Uncle Bart gave a serious nod. "I won't miss it."

Ford handed Tessa the bag of freshly roasted peanuts, and she giggled. "We already had the hot dogs, nachos, ice cream, and pretzel. There's nothing left to conquer."

Malia groaned and patted her belly. "My dressmaker is going to kill me, but I don't care. I never come to baseball games. Isn't food the main reason?"

"Used to be. Now I actually like the baseball." Tessa paused before breaking open a shell as the shortstop smacked a curveball that dropped in the gap in left field. "Go!" she yelled, while Ford added his voice. The runner slid into second and was called safe. She gave Ford a high five and air-fived Mike, who was two seats down and also yelling.

Chiara shook her head. "Who are you?" she teased.

"At least she's still dressing like herself," Malia said with a laugh.

Tessa preened in her Mets jersey, blinged-out denim shorts, and bedazzled high-platform sneakers. Her ball cap was pink and matched her sparkly socks. Ford had groaned when he spotted her that morning, but his grin told her he secretly loved it. She was easy to spot on the big screen, she told him, in case they wanted to make their debut on the Kiss Cam.

The Mets were almost guaranteed to make the playoffs, so they'd decided to all come to a game before the postseason began and tickets got more difficult to snatch. It was a sunny Saturday afternoon, and everyone was in a good mood. Chiara and Malia were blossoming with their pregnancies. Malia's wedding was next month. Emma and Mike were obviously in love.

Everything was perfect.

Tessa sighed with contentment. She'd finally written her column highlighting Ford's transformation, but instead of her usual format, she dug deep into the reasons people end up changing who they are to gain love, or a promotion, or what they see as more than they deserve. It was a raw piece, full of emotion she'd been avoiding after doing the column for so many years, but it ended up going viral.

Tessa had been a guest on *Good Morning America* and spoke about her commitment to focus on being better on the inside rather than the outside. It led to many conversations, some disparaging on social media, but mostly an awareness she hoped could make a small change.

The guys came back and Ford stood up, already prepped for the seventh-inning stretch. He was rocking back and forth on his heels, gaze pinned to the screen, hand thrust in his jeans pocket.

"Baby, we're winning," Tessa teased. "Don't look so nervous. Have another beer."

He shot her a grin, but it looked a bit sickly. Then Palmer, Ryder, and Mike stood up, looking around like they were expecting something. She cranked her head around and noticed Uncle Bart, Dom, and Vin were also standing, staring transfixed at the now empty field.

"What's up with everyone?" she whispered to Chiara.

Her friend shrugged. "Probably just antsy and need to stretch."

The giant screen lit up with Mr. Met bouncing around. The camera panned around the stands, and the Kiss Cam lit up.

"Oh, this is where all the couples kiss. You know, last time Ford took me to a game, I saw a guy propose! Isn't that wild?"

Tessa suddenly realized all her friends were staring at her with open mouths.

Ford looked like he was about to pass out.

Tessa frowned. "What's the matter?"

Confused, Tessa took in Mike's deer in the headlights gaze, and Emma had her hands clasped to her chest like someone had died. Tessa looked around, but nothing seemed amiss.

"Okay, I'm getting worried—tell me what's happening! Are there more free T-shirts?"

The public announcer's voice broke through the stadium, loud and booming. "And now we have a special Kiss Cam moment. Ford Maddox, take it away!"

Tessa blinked. Tried to focus. And then the man she loved was standing before her, holding a ring, dropping to one knee on the dirty concrete in front of everyone while the camera displayed the entire scene to thousands of people.

"Tessa Harper, when you fought so hard for that T-shirt the last time we were at Citi Field, I knew my life would never be the same. I love you. Will you marry me?"

Oh. My. God.

She stared at him and the beautiful emerald-cut ring before her and felt the pressure of thousands of stares, everyone holding their breath, as the world seemed to wait for her answer.

"Yes! Yes, yes, yes!"

The stadium exploded into cheers and claps. Tears blurred Tessa's vision as Ford pushed the ring over her finger, and then they were kissing, and the people she loved were surrounding her with hugs and love.

The Mets players stood outside their dugout, clapping for them.

It was the best moment of her life.

AUTHOR'S NOTE

I had so much fun writing this book!

Thanks to Rob Greenstein, who told me the greatest story about his dad and going to the dog park with his friends, inspiring Uncle Bartholomew and his crew.

Since there was a sports theme in this book, I took some liberties by using real athletes' names, real teams, and real events to create a more authentic story line for Ford. Unfortunately, most of this will be outdated by the time it hits bookshelves, but I made the decision to keep these details in, hoping readers will understand and maybe even look back fondly on those years.

Forgive me if I focused mostly on the New York Mets, as they will always be the team of my heart. I married a Yankees fan, so I understand both sides of the rivalry!

ACKNOWLEDGMENTS

Big thanks go to the amazing Maria Gomez and the Montlake team for their support and help in this publishing journey—you are so valued. To Kristi Yanta for encouraging me every step of the way and making this series one I'm so proud of. To Kevan Lyon, my talented agent, and my team behind the scenes: Nina Grinstead, Mary, Christine, and Kim from Valentine PR. Thanks to my amazing assistant, Mandy Lawler, for all your help along the way and keeping things perfectly organized!

Thanks to all my readers who have followed me through the Twist of Fate series. I can't wait to share what comes next!

ABOUT THE AUTHOR

Photo © 2012 Matt Simpkins

Jennifer Probst is the *New York Times* and *USA Today* bestselling author of eight series, including The Sunshine Sisters, Stay, The Billionaire Builders, Searching For . . . , Marriage to a Billionaire, The Steele Brothers, Sex on the Beach, and Twist of Fate. Like some of her characters, Probst, along with her husband and two sons, calls New York's Hudson Valley home. When she isn't traveling to meet readers, she enjoys reading, watching "shameful reality television," and visiting a local animal shelter. For more information, visit www.jenniferprobst.com.